TOP SHELF STUD

CHICAGO PLAYERS

KATE MEADER

PROLOGUE

Franky

"FIELD TRIP, FRIENDS!"

Kneeling in the grass, I placed the jar on its side and nudged the kale leaf toward the opening.

Dwayne "The Snail" Johnson was chilling under a spinach leaf. A bite-sized chunk was missing—tiny, because *snails*—so one of them had eaten on the ride over to the cookout at the Kershaws. Speedy had retracted most of its body inside its shell; maybe it was digesting its food.

I liked to bring them when we went out, which was weird to observers, but on brand for me. "Your emotional support snails," my sister Cat called them. Of course, being snails, they didn't understand *where* we were going, especially as it was dark inside my backpack. But these tiny, miraculous creatures were exceptionally sensitive. They had four tentacles, two larger ones for detecting light, and two smaller ones for touch and smell. And I called them "friends" instead of "boys" or "guys" because they were hermaphrodites, which meant they all had the ability to reproduce, but for some reason they preferred mating with other snails. Weird, right? What was the point of having the means to go it alone, but you still sought out another of your species to help the process along?

Today, we were at the home of Theo Kershaw, a defenseman with the Chicago Rebels, the hockey franchise my dad retired from a couple of years ago. I had brought my friends because one, it was always nice to have someone interesting to talk to at a party, and two, Theo had a huge backyard, which made for an uncharted landscape for the snails. This spot behind a large oak tree, some distance from the crowd, with its leafy undergrowth and dew-dropped greenery, was perfect. With the distant sounds of music and laughter and the scents of cooking, I felt both safe and pleasantly apart here. Not that anyone ever made me feel unsafe —the Rebels were a very inclusive bunch—but I was constantly aware that I was not like others.

Dwayne "The Snail" Johnson (always known by his full name, thank you very much) was making tracks, sensing a golden opportunity to explore a new habitat. Usually, I kept them in a terrarium in my bedroom, and we made daily excursions to the garden, the one at the back of our house where I lived with my dad, my stepmom, Violet, and my sister, Cat. Today was different.

Today was goodbye.

Tomorrow, I would be heading to Atlanta with Cat to spend a week with our mom, and as I couldn't take the snails with me on the plane and I didn't want to task my dad or Violet with caring for them, I had resolved to release these ones back into the wild. I had briefly considered sneaking them into my backpack for my trip but assumed there might be problems at the airport with the X-ray scanner. Not to mention the ructions their presence would cause with my mother. For most of my childhood, she had despaired of my scientific interests and constantly complained to my dad of the misery I caused her.

It's such a disgusting habit, Bren. You need to talk to her.

At least Caitriona likes music. But Franky? I despair, I do.

The optician said fifteen-year-olds can wear contacts, but she won't do it.

Mom thought my glasses made me look ugly, like one of those girls who would die buried in a book. They would find me, shriveled up, surrounded by disintegrating pages and desiccated snail shells.

Disintegrating and *desiccated* weren't regular guests in Mom's vocabulary, but that's what she meant, so I happily filled in the blanks for her. To be honest, I didn't mind the idea. Books and snails? That sounded awesome.

Speedy was living up to his name, having overtaken Dwayne "The Snail" Johnson on his flight to freedom. I was so involved in my observations that I didn't notice the arrival of company until it was too late.

"Ugh!" I heard behind me.

Feeling my color rising along with the hairs on the back of my neck, I turned to Mikey Callahan, nephew of another retired Rebels player, Ford Callahan. I didn't know him well, but his reaction was, shall we say, unsurprising. Behind him was a boy I didn't recognize and another I did: Jason Isner. At thirteen, Theo's brother—half-brother, to be precise, and I was *always* precise—was tall for his age, even taller than me, and I was two years older. I rarely spoke to him. Partly, because he was a stinky, teenage boy, but mostly because he didn't like me.

There could be any number of reasons why, from the classic undercurrent of tension between jocks and nerds to the fact I wore glasses. They signified physical weakness while he was a healthy, strapping boy, already being talked about in hockey circles as a future prospect for greatness. But the most probable reason for his dislike was my friendship with his brother. Sean was the same age as me and someone with whom I had common interests. He read books, for a start.

Mikey stepped forward, a little too close to the snails.

"Please don't."

"Why? Worried I might"—he lifted his sneakered foot—"stomp on it?"

"Callahan."

That was Jason, controlling the situation with a single word. His voice sounded deeper than the last time I heard him, though I doubted this maturity to his vocal cords corresponded to maturity elsewhere.

He closed the gap between us, subtly displacing Mikey. "What are you doing?"

"Releasing them."

He thought on that for a moment. "Why did you capture them in the first place?"

"So I can study them."

Mikey inclined his head and peered at Dwayne "The Snail" Johnson, who had created a mucin trail over a flat rock near the shrubbery. "It's so fuckin' slimy. Real ugly."

Like you. Unsaid but definitely implied.

I was fairly accepting of this viewpoint, especially when it came to boys. I wasn't pretty or talented on the guitar like Cat. I liked science and Percy Jackson and romance novels and creating habitats for my friends.

Snails and slugs. My best friends.

"Yeah, it is pretty gross," Jason agreed. Mikey laughed at that, as if it was the most original opinion instead of a rehash of what he had already said. Jason met my gaze head-on, his green eyes all challenge, making it clear the snails weren't the only thing that was gross. He and my mother would have so much in common.

The boy I didn't know moved closer to get a better look. "You some kind of nerd?"

Really? How was I supposed to answer a question as stupid as that?

Ignoring him, I stood, pushed my glasses back into place, and moved between the snails and the threat. A quick glance down showed the grass-stained knees of my white jeans and the blue toenail polish that Violet had applied last night while we watched *Little Women*. Timothée Chalamet was the perfect Laurie, despite marrying Amy after being in love with Jo (I had hoped they might deviate from the book, but unfortunately, no). I didn't really understand why the author had to make Jo get married to the German professor at all because she was a writer and, if she couldn't be with Laurie, she would have been better off alone with her books. Violet said that career-oriented spinsterhood would be too modern a take for the time.

But not now. I was pretty sure career-oriented spinsterhood was the life for me, and the reason was the mix of disgust and fascination currently rolling off Jason Isner.

Who was fixated on my chest.

I had started developing late, but my breasts had grown in the last few months. No longer bumps on a log, they filled out my bra and looked far too obvious behind my "Easily Distracted by Snails" T-shirt, the now too-tight one Violet bought for me last year.

My cheeks burned when *he* should be the one embarrassed to be staring at me so obviously.

"Pervert," I said, pushing my glasses back up my nose.

"As if," Mikey responded in his friend's defense, because the idea of Jason Isner showing any romantic interest in someone like me was *incroyable*, as the French would say.

Jason remained silent, just stared at me with those eyes, as hard as emeralds. I kind of agreed with Mikey—*as if*—but I also knew that boys Jason's age were walking hormone factories, barely able to control their impulses and immature sexual feelings. Jason wasn't interested in me as a person, just as a pair of breasts in his immediate sightline.

"Weirdo," he finally said.

"Jock," I snapped back, a rather weaksauce response.

He stepped closer, his breath smelling of fruity Starburst. "Four-eyed loser."

"*Dumb* jock." Heat flushed my neck and cheeks. I wasn't a confrontational person as a rule, but I had to make a stand. For the snails. For myself.

A sneer curled his lips. "Slug Girl."

"Jason!" A new voice entered the arena, one I recognized. Sean, Jason's older brother, was approaching at a clip. "What's going on?"

"Nothing," Jason said lazily, but there was a smirk there, too. He'd issued the final insult, and he knew it would stay in my head forever.

Slug Girl. I shouldn't have minded being identified so closely with the things I loved—even if my research focus had moved to snails lately—yet the way he said it was so dismissive. So hurtful.

Sean turned from his brother to me. "You okay?"

"Of course. Just trying to keep the Neanderthals away from defenseless creatures."

Mikey and Unnamed Boy were already retreating, likely feeling uneasy in an older boy's presence. Jason remained, a young sapling looking to put down roots. That attitude would be useful for a future in professional hockey but would likely piss off any woman he dated. Far too intense.

I glared at him, willing him to leave. Finally, he turned away, but not before I witnessed an eye roll in his brother's direction, one that said, *why are you bothering with this waste of space, dude?*

Once they were out of earshot, Sean checked in again with me. "Seriously, you okay?"

"I'm fine!" My gaze fell to Dwayne "The Snail" Johnson and Speedy, both now approaching the hostas edging the flower beds. The Great Escape, snail style.

I plunked down in the grass, my heart still thundering, determined to watch them to the end. I had come here to say goodbye to my friends, and Jason Isner had ruined it.

Sean took a seat beside me. "So what are we doing?"

"Just sending them onward to new adventures. I'm visiting my mom tomorrow so I can't take them."

"Right." He thought on that. "Looking forward to clothes shopping and makeovers?"

I laughed, and the tightness in my chest eased slightly. Sean and I had become friendly in the last few months, while I helped him with algebra after school.

"Cat will provide good cover. Mom's so excited she has a boyfriend." My sister was dating a rising senior at high school, and my mother couldn't wait to give all the advice in person. "I might be able to hide out and read the latest Sarah Dessen."

"Or you could try to enjoy it. See it as a vacation."

With my narcissistic mother? That time she freaked out in the granola aisle of Whole Foods, the catalyst for us to come and live with my recovering alcoholic dad, was the best thing to ever happen to me. Over the last six years, I'd seen Kendra a few times a year, and it never got easier. I was still her biggest disappointment.

"Not likely. I'll need a vacation when I come back."

Sean's brow crimped.

"What's wrong?"

"It's just—" He shook his head. "My parents are getting a divorce."

"Oh, Sean, I'm so sorry." I reached for his hand, and he let me squeeze it before pulling away.

During our after-school study sessions, we had shared a little, me about my mom, he about his dad. His parents' marriage was in trouble, and having been there myself, I understood what he was going through.

"I guess I'm just hoping I'll still see my dad when it's over." His shrug managed to convey a lifetime of hurt. "He's already met someone."

My mom had met her boyfriend Drew before she and Dad separated, and despite her faults, I didn't blame her for seeking comfort elsewhere. Dad's alcoholism had not made things easy for any of us. But I also knew this: my parents were better off apart.

"Just because I don't want to see my mom doesn't mean you and your dad won't have a relationship."

He huffed. "Just sucks."

It probably sucked for Jason, too. Was I supposed to cut him some slack because his parents were splitting up? With anyone else, I might. But I'd seen how he looked at me, like I was nothing. A bug he'd happily crush beneath his boot.

I didn't want to think about Jason anymore. Sean was the only Isner I cared for, and right now, he needed a friend.

"When I come back from Atlanta, we could go see the new Superman movie."

"You don't even like superhero movies." But I could tell the prospect cheered him.

"The Man of Steel is a ridiculous do-gooder. But I do like Lois Lane and her rule-breaking tendencies. She's got moxie."

"She's got what?"

"She knows what she wants." And she was much more interesting than that underwear-sporting doofus in a cape.

The snails had finally made it to the hostas. Speedy was nestled under a large leaf while Dwayne "The Snail" Johnson was looking for his next meal. They no longer needed me.

"Bye, bye, friends," I whispered. "Have fun storming the flower beds."

Slug Girl won't forget you. And when it came to Jason Isner, neither would she forgive.

Twenty three years later

JULY

CHAPTER ONE

Jason

"WHAT THE HELL are you doing with that box?"

Standing in my new kitchen, Bomb Site Central, I held up two bottles of Sam Adams Summer ale and gestured toward my guest. Theo Kershaw—as in *the* Theo Kershaw, captain of the Chicago Rebels, four-time Cup winner, and a legend in his own time—had just picked up a box, without even bending his knees, and was walking toward the living room.

"It's marked 'bedroom,'" he said as if that was a perfectly acceptable response.

The movers had left it in the wrong room, and now Theo wanted to drag it upstairs because he was a fixer and couldn't leave well enough alone.

"Put it down, dickhead. Come sit in the backyard and drink a beer."

"But it'll only take a sec—"

"T, drop it!"

Chuckling at my outburst, he did as he was told, rubbed his back, and headed my way. The last thing I needed was to be responsible for an injury just as the guy was contemplating a one-year extension with the Rebels. An extension I hoped he would take so we could play together on the same team for the first time in our pro-hockey careers. I hadn't lived in Chicago since college except for a few weeks each summer when I usually helped Theo with the Rebels Youth Hockey Camp. My rookie years were with LA, but the last ten had been with Boston.

Now I was back, feeling like this was where I belonged. Playing with the Chicago Rebels, my hometown team, and potentially with my favorite player.

My brother.

Finding out, when I was twelve, that I was related to Theo Kershaw had been amazing. Even more so was learning that he wanted a relationship with me. My parents divorced when I was thirteen, and Theo was there for me at the worst time of my life. Because it wasn't just the hurt of my parents' split. It was learning who my father really was.

Nick Isner had abandoned Theo's mom with baby T cooking away in the oven and skipped off to college, leaving her and his kid to be raised without his support. Even when Theo showed up at Dad's office at eighteen, with a scholarship to Vermont in hand, not looking for anything other than acknowledgment, Dad didn't want to know. Later, when Theo and I connected, he had tried to cover for Nick and blame his previous bad behavior on our dad's youth.

But I always suspected something was wrong. Knowing how my own father had treated his eldest son had broken my heart. These days I was closer to Theo than I was to my dad. The hockey connection, but more than that. He was my role model in all things, and I was thrilled to finally be living in the same city together as adults.

We headed out to the yard, still relatively pristine because I hadn't had a chance to fuck it up yet. The house was prime real estate on Chicago's North Shore, about ten minutes from Rebels HQ in Riverbrook, twenty miles or so from downtown Chicago. I wasn't quite on the shores of Lake Michigan, but I could see a sliver of gray blue between a couple of the swankier houses on the lakefront, and that was good enough for me.

Theo took a seat in one of the Adirondack chairs, and I took the other, watching for any signs he might have injured himself.

"I'm fine, dude."

I passed him the bottle, and we clinked and sipped. Behind me, a shitload of work awaited, but right now, nothing was pressing and all was good. The summer sky was clear except for a couple of fluffy-as-fuck clouds that made the blue look bluer. Clouds for good.

"That thing safe?" Theo pointed his bottle at the red metal frame several feet away.

"Want to test it?"

"Hell yeah!" He made to get up as I shook my head.

"Your ass wouldn't fit in those seats." Neither would mine. The trials of a hockey player.

Settled back down in the chair, he said, "Probably should yank it before Tilly spots it."

Tilly was Theo's youngest, almost five years old. Rather than remove it, I'd get it assessed for safety because I liked the idea of it sitting there, waiting for a kid to use it. That swing set had spoken to me as my realtor gave me the virtual tour on FaceTime.

"Let me think on it."

Theo gave me a funny look. "You okay?"

"Everly's hooked up with Ryan Coughlan."

"Jesus, that was quick."

Everly was my ex as of two months ago. We'd been together a little over six months, and a while back I had started thinking we should move to the next phase.

We were hanging with my Cougars teammate, Dean Foster, and his wife, Molly, at a cookout. They'd just had a baby, a gorgeous little girl called Jenna, and I was getting a bit broody about it. I loved holding her and feeling that warm little body close to mine, her tiny sighs and gurgles, and her soft, peachy skin against my neck.

"That'll be you next," Dean had said.

Molly laughed and nudged Everly. "You two would have stunning kids."

"Not sure we're going there," Everly said, and quickly transitioned into a request for Molly's artichoke and spinach dip recipe.

Later I'd asked what she meant by it.

"Well, we're not serious, are we? The sex is phenomenal, and we have a great time, but kids? I don't see it."

"At all? Or just with me?"

"Oh, Jason, you're a hoot!"

A hoot. Not that it was the first time I'd heard that or something that put me in a certain box as "unserious." *Dumb jock. Brainless athlete. Too many pucks to the head.* Usually, my four million a year and I were fine with that.

Everly had tried to smooth it over, telling me that she wasn't ready, but there was no shining up that turd. I was thirty-six years old and hankering to start a family. Everly was there, right place, right time, so why not? But she didn't feel the same way. Now she was with Ryan Coughlan, a player with the LA Quake, and rumor had it—if you believed that *Hot Goss* rag—they were as loved up as could be.

I cast a glance at the swing set. Part of me hoped that maybe I still had a shot at a family of my own. Why else would I tell the realtor to offer fifty grand above the asking price? I could just as easily have installed one of those death traps myself anywhere. Yet, as soon as I saw it, I took it as a sign.

Hockey players were superstitious like that.

Theo studied his beer bottle's label, then looked up. "You didn't even tell her you were planning this move back home."

True. "Maybe deep down I sensed it wasn't meant to be."

"Don't worry, you'll have women climbing you like a tree before you know it. You excited to start the season?"

"It's barely the middle of July."

He raised an eyebrow of *your point?*

"Yeah, can't wait," I said with a grin, glad to be off the topic of Everly. Most guys loved the off-season, especially when they had families to spend it with. Don't get me wrong, I enjoyed the break, the time to heal and recharge, but I was a Fall guy. As soon as the weather cooled and the leaves started to change, I was in my element because hockey season was here.

Fifteen years gone, and I had yet to grab the brass ring. But every October, I started afresh with the hockey player's mantra: *Maybe this year.* I was itching to get in there and prove my mettle.

I took another sip. "You any closer to making a decision?"

Everyone wanted to know: would the great Theo Kershaw grace us with one more year? He had hoped to go out on a high last season, but they'd lost the Finals in a heartbreaker in Game 7. He had played one season with his eldest, Hatch, and I suspected he might be ready to call time.

"I hate the idea of missing our shot, J."

"But you're tired."

He expelled a weary sigh. "I am. I haven't told anyone yet, not even Elle, and there's always a chance I'll have a change of heart. But I'm ninety-five percent certain I won't be on the roster next season."

My heart heaved. We had faced off against each other on opposing teams, had even skated together during two All-Star games. Playing on the same side when it counted would have been awesome, but I couldn't begrudge him this decision. He wanted to spend more time with his wife, watch Tilly grow up, and enjoy his grandmother's twilight years (not that Aurora was going anywhere. That dame would outlast us all).

"Would have loved to do this with you, brother. But I'll take all the advice you can give me."

Theo snorted. "Oh yeah? You stopped wanting my advice the minute you hit NCAA."

"Yeah, but now you're an elder statesman. Old as fuck and twice as wise."

Theo sputtered a mouthful of beer. "You little shit."

My grin did its best to paper over the crack in my heart. The years were getting away from us and I wondered if all those things I wanted were still within reach.

Or if I deserved them at all.

CHAPTER TWO

Franky

MY MACBOOK'S computer screen shifted to reveal the smooth-featured face of a baby.

"And hello to my favorite niece."

My sister pulled Emily back from the screen and set her down, probably in a playpen where she could crawl around with her twin brother Henry at their home in Manhattan. The names were a nod to my sister's favorite romance author.

"How did you know?"

"Did you think putting her in a blue onesie was going to fool me?" As if that so-called gender signifier, a relatively recent cultural construct in fact, could fool me about which of my sister's twins were on screen.

"It duped Dan. He picked her up and had an in-depth conversation about boy things before I fessed up."

"Probably good that Emily is receiving the same treatment from her father, even if it is accidental."

Cat laughed. "Don't worry. Between you, Violet, and our uber-successful aunts, my daughter will have no issues recognizing that girls rule the world."

True. Since Cat and I came to live with my dad and the love of his life, Violet, we had become fully immersed in the Chicago Rebels world where the Chase sisters owned the franchise and made the major decisions. The male players were largely pawns on the chessboard controlled by these powerful women. They could hire, fire, trade, or bench them at their whim.

Emily and Henry would grow up in a world with strong female role models, and I hoped to do my part. What else could the eccentric aunt provide?

"Could I say hello to Henry?"

"Of course!"

Cat lifted her son into her lap. "Look, buddy! It's your aunt Franky, the smartest woman you're ever likely to meet."

"I'm sure he'll eventually meet someone smarter."

My sister grinned. "For now, you are the smartest. Henry, did you know your aunt is a world-famous malacologist? What's that, you ask? Oh, she studies snails and slugs for a living. And she writes articles and gives lectures at Lakeshore University in Chicago. And she should be running her own department, but some man came in and stole her job." She kissed the top of her son's head. "Don't be that guy, buddy."

I could feel my face forming a frown, one that my mother would have despaired of because it made me "undateable."

"It might be a little early to project the woes of academia's gender gap on my nephew."

"The earlier the better, I say." She raised her son's hand in a wave, and I committed to memory the sight of his chubby fist and soft, dark curls—a little more reddish in hue than his sister, which is how I could tell the difference—before he left to join Emily off-screen.

Cat turned back to me. "So, has he started yet?"

The "he" was Dr. Marcus Bilson. After a year-long process to find a new chair for the Biology Department at Lakeshore University, the selection committee had decided to hire an outside candidate. Someone with less teaching experience, a Y chromosome, a louder voice, and a sexier specialty: fruit flies. Malacologists, scientists like me who studied mollusks such as snails and slugs, were rather low on the academic specialty rung.

"He has, but we have yet to schedule our first official meeting." However, we had already met unofficially, which I neglected to mention to my sister. Dr. Bilson and I had, as they say, "history." "Don't worry too much about me not getting the job. Department heads end up pushing a lot of paper around. The research suffers, and while it might seem like the next logical step in my career path, this way I can continue contributing to the scholarship."

Or something else. I realized now that being passed over for the department head position might have been a blessing in disguise. I could devote myself to a new enterprise.

Every time I saw my niece and nephew, or ran into any of the numerous Rebels kids, my heart boomed, my hormones went into overdrive, and a little voice inside my head chanted, "Want, want, want." If I couldn't be the "mother" of a department, perhaps I could be the real thing. At thirty-eight years old, I had left it late, but it wouldn't be impossible. Cat was thirty-nine when she had the twins, and medical advances had progressed to the point that women in their forties were birthing children safely.

Like all my projects, this one would require research and a sound methodology. I was a scientist, and I would approach it using a logical and reasoned rationale.

Finding a suitable partner, a man who would want me *and* a child, would be an improbable task, if not impossible. I had considered hooking up with someone at a bar or online for a one-night stand, but the dubious ethics, not to mention my complete lack of game in attracting a mate, made me eliminate that option quickly.

Which left a sperm donor, preferably a man who wanted no part of my or my baby's life. This way, I could control for as many variables as possible. For the last ten months, I had been gathering data on likely candidates and had drawn up a shortlist. I had undergone a physical checkup and investigated hormone treatments to stimulate ovulation. Other than my age, there was no reason why I couldn't get pregnant.

I just needed the male genetic material. Quickly.

"Franky? Hello?"

"What? Oh, sorry."

My sister shook her head. "Dreaming about some slug, I suppose."

For once, no. I wanted to tell her about my plan, but it was too soon. I was also concerned about people judging me for traveling such an untraditional route to making a family.

"What were you saying while my mind was elsewhere?"

Cat gave me an indulgent look. She was well-used to me spacing out during a conversation.

"Just that I talked to Mom yesterday. I think she and Xavier are having problems."

Xavier was my mother's third husband, and the one

who had lasted the longest. Before I could comment, Cat went on. "I know you've set boundaries with her—in fact, she's constantly talking about them as if they're the strangest thing in the world. 'Why would my little girl not want to be in my life?' But I just wanted you to know that she does ask about you."

"Let me guess. She's worried I don't have a husband. Or that I'll never find one. Or that I'll die alone."

Cat grimaced. "All of the above?"

I hadn't gone full non-contact with my mother. We still texted on occasion, checked in at holidays and birthdays, and kept things civil. But after therapy in my late teens and early twenties, I recognized that my mother's narcissism was unlikely to change and that my mental well-being was healthier without her needling criticism.

Cat had a different relationship with her, one that had mellowed with her marriage and the arrival of the twins. My older sister had trod a more conventional path, one my mother saw as valid and worthy. From a vanity standpoint, Mom hated that she was a grandmother, but she also saw it as an opportunity to wield the influence she had lost over us when she gave up custody all those years ago.

"You can tell her that I'm happy with my scholarly pursuits and my mission to become the best aunt ever."

As for my plans to become a mother, I would keep those to myself for now. But I already had an idea for how to obtain the sperm I would need.

Or rather "the who."

CHAPTER THREE

Jason

ONE OF THE nicer things about being back in Chicago was the fact I was never short of a dinner invite. Someone was always cooking, and there was usually a spare seat at the table. With my brother Sean in town, visiting from Boston where he lived—or, according to him, where I'd abandoned him—we found ourselves at the apartment of my niece, Adeline, and her roommate, Rosie, for tacos and margaritas.

Indulging in good food, good company, and strong margaritas—so much so that I limited myself to a couple of sips because I was driving and planned to hit the gym early tomorrow—I regaled the group with gossipy tales about my Boston Cougars teammates while my friend and agent Lauren added colorful "confidential" commentary that had the other guests throwing out wild guesses about who she was talking about.

Meanwhile, there was an undercurrent between my nephew Hatch and another dinner guest, Summer Landry. She had ditched her fiancé, Chicago Rebels player Dash Carter, at the altar a couple of weeks ago, then went AWOL until she showed up a week back. I had recently learned that Hatchling came to her rescue outside the church and squirreled her away to the family's vacation home in Saugatuck. Now they were pretending not to know each other, a complete shit show in the making.

But I didn't have time to deal with that—or enjoy it—because a different kind of hellscape was on the horizon. About halfway through dinner, we were joined by another guest.

Rosie's stepsister, Franky St. James.

We typically crossed paths a couple of times a year, not that we had anything to say to each other after a twenty-plus-year and counting acquaintance. Even the fact she was close to Sean had done little to change our viewpoints. She was still an intolerable know-it-all, and I was still the guy she thought was no better than shit on her shoe.

"Hey, sis!" Rosie jumped up to hug her. "Are you hungry?"

"Starving."

"We were just about to make another pitcher of margaritas," Addy said. "You in?"

"Not for me. I'll just stick with water."

Franky hadn't changed much; everything about her was still calculated to annoy me. Denim blue eyes, typically narrowed in disdain behind her glasses; a chin set stubbornly to emphasize whatever insulting point she had to make; dark hair, usually in some messy bundle on top of her head. That tumbled-out-of-bed rumpus said she had much more important things to be doing than worrying about her appearance. Which I supposed pointed to independence and a fondness of going against the grain.

Or maybe she just didn't give a flying fuck what anyone thought of her.

Today she wore a Lakeshore University sweatshirt—that was where she indoctrinated the youth—over rolled up jeans along with librarian glasses, the bridge wrapped in blue duct tape. The real egghead professor stereotype.

She looked around the table. "I thought Sean was here?"

"He's in the kitchen on a work call," Hatch said. "How was the slug hunt?" Sean had mentioned earlier that Franky was doing some field research nearby and would be stopping here afterwards.

I had never thought her eyes interesting, but how they glittered when her research was mentioned was surprisingly appealing. But then I usually appreciated people who dug their work, even when my comprehension of said work was sub-zero.

"Very productive, though in fact, I was looking for snails. Viviparinae Gray to be exact. They're usually found in colder waters of the north but have started to migrate to the lower parts of the Great Lakes and associated waterways."

"Sounds like a wild time," I said, annoyed at how that sparkle in her eyes had drawn me in.

And here we go. I got the standard Franky St. James sneer before she dismissed me with a look down her nose. Catching Hatch's gaze, I saw his surprise at her reaction, or maybe it was surprise at my own. Why the hell did I care about her stupid snails?

Rosie set a plate down before her with a glass of water.

Franky picked up her taco with slender hands and looked over the group.

"Have I missed the discussion about Summer's sprint from the church?"

Summer avoided looking at Hatch. *Far too obvious, kids.*

"We haven't really discussed it except in surface terms," she said.

"You made the right call. Dash Carter's as spineless as a gastropod." Around her chewing, Franky added, "Slug humor."

Rosie laughed. "Tell us how you really feel."

She sipped from her water glass and, surprise-fucking-surprise, proceeded to weigh in. "I once overheard him telling someone at a Rebels fundraiser that he couldn't make a donation because his mother took care of the family's gift-giving."

"Damning stuff," I said, barely repressing an eye roll.

Franky stared and held my gaze directly. Some weird, fucked-up part of me was thrilled that I had her attention.

"You might think that a meaningless anecdote, but it reflects a negative personality trait that no woman wants in a prospective mate. A man who exhibits that sort of selfishness of spirit is not worth a woman's time. I only wish I'd told you sooner, Summer."

Summer was hiding a smile. "Not sure I would have drawn the same conclusion from that, but there were plenty of other red flags I ignored."

Franky went on. "I imagine he would have provided good genetic material for your children, though. Sometimes that's all you need, especially when we're talking about athletes."

"What does that mean?"

Franky speared me with a look over her glasses, which

had slipped down her nose as she ate. "Only that athletes aren't the most evolved people on the planet."

Oh no she didn't. I couldn't believe she was shoveling this shit in a roomful of athletes and their relatives. Before I could give her a piece of my mind, Hatch jumped in.

"Your dad's an athlete, Franky."

Only one of my favorite players. Legendary center, Bren St. James, had overcome a turbulent personal life and inner demons to win the Cup almost thirty years ago with the Chicago Rebels. That year was a banner one: a Finals win, a team legacy established, and marriages for all the owners to players on the team. I had watched that series over and over as a kid.

Franky considered Hatch's statement. "My dad excepted. And Uncle Remy, who is probably the most evolved man I've ever met. Uncle Vadim is up there, too, though it took him a while. Russians are tough nuts and Aunt Isobel had to work hard to crack him. The rest of them? Idiots."

"Jesus Christ," I muttered.

"I think several of us have a different view of athletes, Franky," Addy said with a smile.

"Well, you already have proof that Lars can produce a healthy child, so you can check that off the list. And I assume he has other positives that prove he's worth your time. After all, you overcame several obstacles to get your happy-ever-after."

Last year, my new Rebels teammate Lars Nyquist had found out he was father to cute-as-a-button Mabel after a one-night stand, and had hired my niece Adeline to be his nanny—which had led to where you'd think it would. Now he stared at Franky and who could blame him? This woman was an acquired taste. After twenty-plus years, I still hadn't acquired it, and I hoped to God I never did.

Rosie was about the only person in the room not offended by her stepsister's absurd opinions. "All those hurdles definitely make it worth the effort, I'd say."

I had plenty to say about that but kept my lips zipped. Most of the people at this table were younger than me and had yet to develop my level of cynicism when it came to relationships. I wouldn't be the one to disabuse them of the hearts-and-flowers romanticism of it all. They'd find out soon enough.

CHAPTER FOUR

Franky

"YOU WANT ME TO DO WHAT?"

I had expected this would go smoother. What I was asking of one of my closest friends was a rather basic request.

Give me this thing you have no need for, something you produce, often involuntarily, and dispose of every day.

Assuming a healthy male with an average sex drive, his sperm was constantly renewing and regular ejaculation helped to prevent prostate cancer. All I was asking was that Sean Isner, my friend of many years, consider his health and donate some of that product instead of flushing it down the shower drain or balling it up in a tissue.

Basic.

But Sean was not greeting my request with logic—given his job as a director of technology for a bank in Boston, I had hoped for better. As he was visiting his Chicago-based family for a couple of days, asking in person had seemed like the appropriate way to handle this. Phone conversations contained too many pauses and the inability to assess body language or facial cues. Texts were no better, though I did like the idea that I could have written something. Planned the wording.

Perhaps I hadn't made it clear enough that I wanted nothing more than his genetic material.

"I would just need a specimen, Sean." Still confused, apparently. "To make a baby."

The mention of "a baby" seemed to wake him up from his stupor, transforming his expression from vacuous blankness to a darker disquiet.

"You want a baby? With me?"

"Not *with* you. That's the point. You would not be obligated beyond the contribution of your sperm. I already have a contract drawn up that would absolve you of any further responsibility. No child support, parental visits, Christmas presents ... I would be raising the offspring myself and wouldn't need a man by my side."

Rather than shine light on the matter, my breakdown of the facts only seemed to confuse him further. Giving him a moment to adjust, I caught my reflection in the bathroom mirror. Messy hair piled high; a Lakeshore U sweatshirt over jeans; fetching blue duct-taped glasses (broken during a recent field trip to the shores of Lake Michigan in search of a different kind of specimen, a *Bithynia tentaculate*, also known as a mud snail). Should I have dressed more formally for the occasion?

Or perhaps I had chosen the wrong venue for this kind of discussion. But Rosie had said Sean was leaving for Boston tomorrow, a day earlier than I'd assumed, so I'd high-tailed it over to her apartment at her dinner invite—tacos, my favorite—and hadn't even had time to change or drop off my specimens at the university lab.

I took a quick look at them now. One of them, a *Viviparus georgianus*, also known as a mystery banded snail, hadn't moved very far. It was still sitting in the corner of my sister's bathtub, contemplating its new surroundings. The other, slightly smaller specimen had attached itself to the shower curtain, leaving a trail of mucin—snail slime—as it inched along, looking for an escape.

Not unlike how Sean looked now.

"Franky," he said, sounding a touch exasperated. Probably because we were discussing something important and my attention was diverted by my work. Story of my life.

"Yes?"

"Why now? And why me?"

I'd already explained it to Rosie and her roommate Summer a few minutes ago in the kitchen. The clock, in common parlance, was ticking. More like booming, a bomb about to explode, where the resulting rubble was a childless future. I had spent the last month making plans and prioritizing my list of candidates.

Sean was at the top of it. He met all my requirements: intelligent, healthy, and unattached. I had a few other criteria, but those were the primary ones. My method was largely scientific, except for one fuzzier variable.

Many of the candidates on my list were hockey players. I knew this world and the people in it, which might seem strange for a woman with my professional interests. Not that I straddled both worlds seamlessly, but my family and friend connections did widen the candidate pool.

After years of studying the hockey player species, I had concluded that they were either hopelessly devoted to one woman (or man) or exceedingly promiscuous. That latter category interested me most, but I was also concerned that they would think I was after their fame or wealth. That I'd be viewed as weird, desperate, or unworthy of a pro-athlete's genetic waste product.

Enter the other category on my list: friends and colleagues. My peers. Sean was smart, well-adjusted, and possessed of exactly the kind of temperament I would like to pass on to my child. I had assumed that temperament would be more open to my request.

"I want a child, Sean. I'm at the stage of my life where I crave a certain fulfillment that I can't get from work or friends or my cats." *Apologies, Beaker and Bunsen, you know I love you.* "I would like to be a mother and my options for the more traditional route—meet someone, date someone, connect with someone—are limited and becoming more so each day."

His expression softened. "It's kind of out there."

Was it? In this day and age, with women carving their own paths and wielding more economic and social power than ever before, was it so unusual? But then women's rights, especially reproductive ones, had done an about-face in the last few years. So-called "traditional values" allied with my least favorite *mis*-prefixed word, *misogyny*, meant that people often looked at more unorthodox journeys to parenthood with a certain slitty-eyed judgment.

Perhaps he needed more information.

"We wouldn't have to engage in sexual intercourse. This would be a purely transactional endeavor with no inti-macy required. I would need to be present, of course—" At his horrified look, I quickly clarified. "In another room. Ready to receive the specimen."

Apparently that level of detail was a bridge too far.

"Franky, I can't do it. I'm sorry."

Disappointment wrenched my gut. I had laid out my case, and this was not the kind of ask that improved with repeating. I had been so sure he would want to help, but evidently, there were limits to our friendship.

"Okay, thanks for listening."

He took a step forward, as if to hug me. We weren't really huggers, and I'd prefer not to start now. Instead, I backed away, my spine slamming into the doorknob, then quickly turned and staggered out. Failed before I had shot out of the blocks.

The hallway was not empty.

Jason Isner stood in a casual lean against the wall, making no secret of his interest in his older brother's personal life. *My* personal life.

Both brothers were tall, dark, and green-eyed, but that was where the similarities ended. Where Sean was kind, empathetic, and warmhearted, Jason was ... pardon my French, a dick. Recently traded to the Chicago Rebels, my dad's old team, he had started popping up in places I usually considered safe from his brand of jockery (definition: mockery from a boorish athlete-type). My local coffee shop, the bar I occasionally frequented with my sister and friends, and now a dinner party.

The years had not brought us closer; if anything, they had entrenched our mutual dislike. But usually I felt on solid, intellectually superior ground around him. Not today. Now he was seeing me at my lowest point.

"Eavesdropping?" I snapped.

"Walls are pretty thin here." He pushed off from one of those supposedly thin walls and moved in closer. Another thing I didn't like about him was how he used his physicality to take up all the room and oxygen. So greedy.

"So you thought you'd listen in on a private conversation?"

"I thought I'd look out for my brother. Or maybe *you* think I'm too stupid to know how to do that."

Still peeved about my earlier comments, then.

"I don't think you're stupid, Jason. But I do think you're emotionally stunted."

He moved closer, bringing all six feet and change to bear as he loomed over my five-foot-five frame. As I wasn't interested in getting a crick in my neck looking up at him, I focused on his throat. Thick, strong, muscled, tanned ... the typical throat of a man who spent far too much time in the gym.

He spoke to the top of my head. "Well, good thing you won't be relying on me to be the best uncle to your kid. As they say, 'Bullet. Dodged.'"

Of course, all he could see was his brother's lucky escape, never mind the pain Sean's rejection had caused me. Tears threatened, but I hadn't cried in close to thirty years and I sure as hell would not be giving Jason Isner the satisfaction of witnessing my breakdown. I needed to get out of here, but I refused to allow him the last word.

"And there you go, proving my point."

And then I crashed through the apartment's front door before he could get another volley off.

CHAPTER FIVE

Jason

THE AUDACITY.

I was still fuming as I pulled out of the parking space just outside Rosie and Addy's apartment in downtown Riverbrook. How in the hell did Franky St. James think asking a guy to donate his sperm was a good idea?

First, friends didn't ask friends for baby batter.

Second, couldn't she have found a boyfriend to do this important task?

Third, failing that, surely there were clinics for this sort of thing.

I had assumed that as a scientist, she'd be all over the test tube, baby-in-a-lab option. A total egghead, this woman usually had her nose buried in a book or a slug lair (or whatever you called a crib for slimy creatures), occasionally looking up to pronounce judgment on vapid, no-brained, muscle-bound lugs who could barely string a sentence together. So sometimes I did have trouble getting words out around her because the rare times we intersected, she insisted on goading me.

But I had no problem using my words when it came to protecting Sean.

My brother was a nice guy—too nice—and despite being two years older than me, I had always had to look out for him. Duty of a jock with the family nerd. Thankfully he'd said no to her absurd request, but Franky was strong-willed. She was probably thinking up ways to make him come around.

That would *not* be happening. A kid with no dad in the picture? Not a chance.

I was still muttering to myself about this crazy situation when I spotted the woman herself. She was walking along the street, in that way people had when they had places to be and people to see, her topknot bouncing, her long stride purposeful and angry. As I drew closer, she stopped, fisted her hips, and looked up to the sky. I doubted she was asking God for guidance. Most scientists didn't believe in a higher power, so maybe she was trying to calculate meaning in the stars. One thing was obvious: she was hurting. She really wanted this, and my brother had let her down.

Don't go feeling sorry for her. Sean had done the right thing.

Rolling the car to a stop, I lowered the window. "You okay?"

Her mouth curled in a sneer, like I was some sleazy curb crawler looking to pick up a pretty girl.

"Why would I not be okay?"

"Because you're standing on the sidewalk, five blocks from your sister's house, after you walked out in a huff. You look annoyed."

"That's your learned conclusion?"

Learned. She never resisted an opportunity to make jabs about my intelligence.

"Just something my dumb jock brain picked up on. You need a ride somewhere?"

"No. My car's back at Rosie's."

So she was walking off her annoyance. I used a rink for that myself, but civilians had to make do with other methods.

"I'll ask again. You okay?"

"I—" She inhaled a short breath. "I will be. This is just a minor setback."

So not going to give up, which meant Sean was still in the line of fire. An outside observer might say this was none of my business, but my brother's welfare mattered to me. Fathering a child that you would never see was not good for anyone in this situation. Ask me how I know.

"What's your plan then?"

"Like it's any of your business." She continued walking.

She was right, except for the Sean aspect. That made it my business.

I drove about a block until I spied a parking spot. By the time she drew even, I was rocking a casual lean against my car.

She stopped before me. "I assume you're being protective of Sean."

Okay, she got it. That was exactly why I was taking time out of my busy evening to speak to her.

"I don't want to see him taken for a ride."

"And you think asking him for a no-strings cupful of sperm is taking advantage?"

No strings. Sure. "What if he agrees, then changes his mind about wanting to see his kid?"

She seemed to be turning that over in her mind. One thing I'd say about Franky St. James: watching her think was fascinating. She lived inside her head, working shit out about science and biology and slugs and snails. Not that I cared for the subject matter, but the thought process she applied to her problems made her interesting while she did it.

"I'm happy to amend the contract that way, if that's what he wants." She moved closer to me, her face animated. Kind of ... pretty. "I had assumed he would be uninterested in any future connection, but it might be good for the child to have a father figure. However, it could be complicated by —" Breaking off, she shook her head.

"Complicated by what?"

"If there was another man in my life after the child was born. But that's unlikely. A slim probability, but even so, we could factor it into our agreement." She jerked out of her reverie. "Did Sean say that was an issue? Did I go too hard on the no-obligation aspect?"

Shit. Here I was giving her hope. "No, he didn't say that. I barely spoke with him about it. He's not interested."

She fisted her hips. "Then why are you even here? I thought you were part of a forward advance to begin negotiations."

"I'm here to warn you off from trying again with him. He's pretty persuadable and once he gets over the initial shock, he might come around."

She folded her arms over the Lakeshore University logo on her sweatshirt. It pushed up her breasts, though I had to imagine what they might look like under all that thicker fabric. For a brief moment, I was taken back to my teen years when this woman's chest fascinated me.

"Oh, really?"

"Yeah, really. You'll start blinding him with logic when really you can't apply facts and figures and scientific method to this. We're talking about a baby."

"Is that what we're talking about?" Said in her droll "you're an idiot" voice. God, she was the worst.

"You can't treat this like a science experiment."

She snorted. "You know *nothing* about it. Neither do you need to worry about your precious brother. I heard him the first time, and I won't be bothering him about it again. I'll just move on to the next candidate."

"You mean you don't even care *who* you get this donation from?"

"Oh, I care greatly. That's why I've created a list of viable candidates with pros and cons. Scientific, but not an experiment, okay? This is real life, a real baby, and I want to give him or her the best possible start in life. That starts with researching likely donors and doing my due diligence."

A list? And Sean was a top contender? Not saying my brother wasn't a good option, but surely Franky could call on any number of academic types. People who viewed the business of having a baby as an intellectual exercise rather than an instinctive one.

Now who's tarring a whole group with the same brush?

"How many other people have you asked?"

"Sean was the first, but now I realize I need a script. Something to keep me on track so I don't get flustered."

Never mind that, though her blunt honesty was refreshing. "Who else is on this list?"

Her mouth ticked up at the corner. Not so humorless after all.

"Wondering if there are any ... hockey players on it?"

I was now.

Franky might be a brainiac, but she also had connections in the hockey world. She knew all the players and their families and could likely produce a list of contenders at the drop of a hat.

If she could get over the fact they were all idiots.

"Are there?"

"Wouldn't you like to know?"

I shrugged, though my shoulder felt stiff. "Don't care, really."

"Well, there are. But if I go that route, I'll need to snag one before he gets scooped up. Lars would have been ideal, but now he's with Adeline ..." She trailed off, musing on missed opportunities. "There are issues with using a pro-athlete's sperm, though. The older ones have often been hit with paternity suits and tend to be more cautious about this kind of thing. The younger ones—well, I have concerns about choosing someone *too* young. The ick factor as well as their underdeveloped brains. *That* would be taking advantage. So the candidates need to be thirty plus, with a healthy history, and of course, willing."

She looked up, appearing somewhat surprised that I was still here. She had gone off into her own world as she outlined her criteria. I suspected her monologue had less to do with providing me with the details and more to do with her need to work it all out in her head. "I'd say I have eight candidates from the hockey world and seven from other areas. Academics and colleagues."

Fifteen saps who had no idea what was coming.

"You already have this list?"

"Of course." Pausing a moment, she studied me. "You're on it."

And here we are. I wondered why she had even stuck around to talk to me. There was no good reason for her to listen to a word I said, but if she wanted something that only a man could provide ...

"Right."

"You don't believe me?"

"Oh, I believe you. You might think hockey players are brainless spunk machines, but if you're not going to go with a sperm bank—why aren't you doing that?"

"The donors lie all the time. I'd rather do my own background checks."

Of course she would. "So hockey players might be as dumb as pucks, but they are generally healthy specimens, which seems to be more important to you. That means someone like me is going to meet all your criteria. Age, relationship status, health."

I was curious about how she might try to persuade me. The idea gave me a thrill, to be honest. Not being her baby daddy but that she would have to ask me. Beg. Maybe on her knees with those blue-gray eyes pleading, her ruby-red lips in a pout, her pink tongue darting out nervously to wet them ... So desperate to be a mom that she would tap a guy she didn't even like to give her the goods.

"Not all."

"Oh yeah? In which category don't I measure up?"

She moved in closer, like she needed to tell me a secret. Her breath was soft against my neck. The scent of her shampoo filled my nostrils, something floral and sexy.

"The asshole one."

"Come again?"

"While having a strong liking for the candidate isn't absolutely necessary, I draw the line at choosing an asshole to be the sperm donor for my child."

And then she walked away, leaving me fumbling for a response.

CHAPTER SIX

Jason Isner has been spotted at Chicago Rebels HQ where insider sources say he is "learning his way around the gym equipment" ahead of training camp, set to begin in just over six weeks. Isner, known in Boston as the Green-Eyed Monster, a nod to his vaunted defense skills, his Kershaw green eyes, and the famous left field wall at Fenway, was brought onto the Rebels roster in a five-year, twenty-million-dollar deal, as the franchise looks to strengthen its defensive bench.

When asked if Isner's surprise addition is being rushed so he can play with his brother, Theo Kershaw, for the first time in their professional careers, Rebels PR claimed this was not a factor. We still have no decision on whether the legendary defenseman will remain with the Rebels or if he'll hang up his skates before the season starts.

- @RebelsInsider

Jason

WHILE MY SEASON with the Chicago Rebels didn't officially start until training camp in a few weeks, I had no intention of showing up on day one out of breath and clutching my side. I would be smooth, sleek, and fit as hell.

Which meant I needed to put the beat down on my cocky nephews. Both of them were forwards—Hatch with Chicago, my new team, Conor about to start his maiden season with Detroit—so they were perfectly placed to suffer while I worked them over on the practice ice at Rebels HQ.

We were taking a break and happily shooting the shit about how my years in Boston somehow left me wanting as a native Chicagoan—no one appreciated my take on how deep dish was overrated—when Conor brought up Franky St. James and her quest for a sperm donor. How he knew was a mystery, but then maybe she was spreading her desperation far and wide, hoping to catch a spoonful.

I was still irked as all get out over how she managed to get the last word the other night. *I draw the line at choosing an asshole to be the sperm donor for my child.* She should be so lucky!

Hatch, my brother Theo's eldest, squinted at Conor, who was refusing to reveal his source like he was Woodward or Bernstein. Annoyed, he turned to me. "Did Sean say anything to you about it?"

"Just that he and Franky are friends and it would make things weird."

Sean was kind of freaked out about it, for which I couldn't blame him. "I told her she was out of her mind," I added.

Hatch tilted his head, scenting blood in the water. "You talked to her about it?"

"I was driving home from dinner at Ro and Addy's and saw her on the sidewalk."

"And?"

"And I stopped to ask her what in the hell she was thinking. If she wants a baby so much, surely there are other options. People who would be crazy enough to have a kid with her."

Conor narrowed his eyes at me. "Isn't that the point? She feels she doesn't have the usual options, so she's resorting to sperm requests from the eligible men of her acquaintance."

I snorted. "Eligible? Right. You know she has a list." Before anyone could ask, I said, "You're not on it, Hatchling. Too young. Neither are you, Connie. Definitely too young."

I assumed so because she specifically said she was looking for donors over the age of thirty and would be avoiding the youngsters because it wasn't already weird enough. To think I was listed, but I was missing the cut because of some technicality pissed me off in ways I couldn't begin to understand.

Hatch was still regarding me oddly. "Are you on it?"

"Apparently, but only as a formality. I don't meet her lofty standards."

"You mean your superior athlete genetic material isn't sufficient?"

Just what I needed, someone else with opinions.

"Some jocks might make the grade. But this one"—I thumbed at myself—"isn't evolved enough. Which is fine because if I had a kid, the entire Rebels roster couldn't keep me away. I'm not like Nick."

Conor shook his head. "It's just sperm, man. People need to be less attached to it."

Hatch pointed at him. "And that's the kind of attitude that's going to get you into trouble. You'd better be wrapping it before you're tapping it, Connie."

They started sniping at each other about birth control and who had the messier sex life. Neither of these kids was in the running with Francesca St. James, but I wondered who was—and why I even cared. Maybe because all this baby talk reminded me of Everly, my ex in Boston.

So I was a touch sensitive about it. Hearing the professor tell me I wasn't qualified for her baby experiment had rubbed me the wrong way. But maybe she was onto something. I tended towards the asshole end of the spectrum in her presence, so of course I wasn't in the running. Not that I wanted to be, but I didn't like being dismissed so readily.

Fuck, I hated all this navel-gazing.

So I was glad when my nephews quit their fraternal bashing and we hit the ice once more.

CHAPTER SEVEN

Franky

I HAD JUST PULLED into a parking spot on Riverbrook's main drag when my phone rang. Sean.

I felt relief more than hope. I had no plan to renew my application, but I did want to talk to him because he was my friend, and my request had blindsided him.

"Hello."

"Hey there. How are you?"

"I'm well. Just on my way to the coffee shop."

"Man, I love those cinnamon rolls."

His nod to that shared memory, the two of us enjoying a pastry as I tutored him in algebra, felt like an opening. Or maybe forgiveness for my ham-fisted approach.

I took a breath. "Sean, I'm—"

"I wanted to say—"

We both chuckled nervously at talking over each other. I spoke again. "I'm sorry."

"That was my line!"

Another joint chuckle, easier this time.

"I shouldn't have cornered you like that at a dinner party. In the bathroom. With the snails as my witness."

"It was certainly a unique setting for your proposal. The whole thing took me by surprise. I had no idea this was something you really wanted."

"It's been building for a while, since Cat had the twins. But I've only really applied myself to the problem this year. Another birthday passed and I started to wonder how I could make it happen. Then who might be a good candidate. You were at the top of my list."

"That's so flattering. I'm sorry I didn't react the way you expected. Or wanted."

"It's okay, I have options. I liked the idea of a friend helping me out, though I'm starting to see that it's a bigger ask than I originally assumed."

He sighed. "It is ... and it isn't. I should tell you why I reacted that way."

"You don't have to explain. But I suppose it would help —as a data point—so I can recalibrate my approach."

He chuckled. "Always with the method. So, yeah, I was shocked, but to be fair, when I thought about it, I realized it wasn't such a terrible idea. Only I've met someone."

"Ah, I see." Sean didn't really share much about his dating life, but I knew he'd seen a woman at his work for a while a couple of years ago and he was sad they hadn't worked out. "Is it Melissa?"

"It is. We've reconnected and it's really promising."

I smiled. "I'm so happy for you. I hope she realizes what a catch she's made."

"Don't know about that. But I do know that helping you out in this way would complicate things."

I agreed. Of course, I didn't expect any donor to never be in a relationship after providing his genetic material, but the timing was crucial. Giving me his sperm while dating someone was probably not going to further Sean's ambitions with the woman of his dreams.

"Understood."

"I would have said something when you asked, but to be honest, I was a bit shell-shocked. By the time I realized I should have explained, you were already gone."

Fleeing the scene of the crime, except Jason Isner was there trying to make a citizen's arrest. As if it was any of his business!

"All reasons for refusal are valid. But I think I understand this one more than any."

"I'm sorry I hurt you. That was never my intention."

"You didn't. It was more a realization that I had handled it all wrong. And then Jason rubbed the salt in and made it clear how absurd he thinks it all is."

"My brother said that?"

"Not in so many words. But I'm well aware of what he thinks of me."

Sean laughed. "You know, you have it all wrong. Jason's the nicest guy, but you tend to poke at him for reasons I can't really fathom. I'm not sure why you've never gotten along."

He once called me a cruel name, and weirdo that I am, I've never forgotten it.

"We're just not on the same wavelength."

"Ooh, jocks bad. Nerds good." He sighed. "Not sure the science is there, Franky."

Maybe not. I knew several smart jocks, but as a rule, I found most of them to be insufferable. Calling Jason an asshole the other night had been so satisfying in the moment. But now? I felt oddly regretful. I was a nice person —I thought—but this man brought out in me a nasty streak a mile wide.

"Well, I don't want to waste a moment talking about your brother. Tell me more about Melissa."

Ten minutes later, we ended the call with promises to check in later. I would be living in Boston for the Winter semester as a guest lecturer at Harvard, so I looked forward to getting to know Melissa better.

Would I be pregnant at that point? I hoped so. If I timed this right and conception occurred quickly, I would be finishing up the semester in Boston a few weeks before my child was born. Of course, I needed to find a donor first.

A text came in from my stepmom, Violet.

> Running late. Order me a matcha latte!

Matcha. *Ugh.*

I headed inside and took my place in line, thinking about my list. I would need to do more research before I approached the next candidate, especially in the region of current relationships. The archives of that rumor-soaked rag, *Hot Goss*, might be useful here. Another column for my spreadsheet.

Behind me, a deep voice interrupted my thoughts. "I hear caffeine is bad for conception."

Of all the coffee shops ...

Because I wasn't a rude person, I turned to face him.

Good God, he was handsome.

The shock almost bowled me over. My dislike of Jason Isner should be the primary emotion here, but apparently my lizard brain had activated, and I could only now view him sexually. A barrel-chested, broad-shouldered, thick-thighed warrior, who would know exactly how to please a woman.

Perhaps that wasn't a bad thing. I certainly didn't want to view him in any other way. Keeping him in his muscle-bound box as a sex object was far safer.

Those eyes, the ones that contributed to his nickname, the Green-Eyed Monster, were doing some sort of sparkling nonsense. Very odd, considering they usually held nothing but contempt for me. Perhaps it was the glimmer that pulled me in, making me notice more details this time. A bump at the bridge of his nose. That scar above his eyebrow, from when he got struck during a particularly brutal play-offs game three years ago. Sensuous lips, the bottom one a little plumper than the top.

I shook myself back to reality, the one where this man was the enemy.

"And what would you know about conception?"

"Just what I read in *Scientific American*."

"You read?"

"*Scientific American*. Yep."

"No, I was commenting on the fact you read. Period."

He did one of those finger gun gestures. "I see what ya did there. Move up."

"Move—?"

He touched my elbow. "Almost time to order, Francesca."

Francesca? No one called me that, except the former head of my department at Lakeshore University and Cade Burnett, one of Rosie's dads. To everyone else I was Dr. St. James or Franky. Discombobulated, I turned back and closed the gap on the person ahead of me.

I was suddenly hyperaware of the blistering energy behind me. I wanted to turn. I wanted to stay stock still. I preferred to ignore him, but I refused to give him the satisfaction of knowing he had made an impact.

I was about to turn back when, thankfully, the person in front of me completed their order.

I stepped up. "Hello, could I please have a Matcha latte, medium, and a Jasmine tea, also medium?"

"I can get this." Jason moved beside me, closer than necessary, his hip touching mine.

"That's quite alright."

"You won't let me buy you a coffee to apologize?"

"I—" The female cashier, who had evidently recognized the great Jason Isner, was clearly wondering why I was not falling to my knees in gratitude. "Apologize for what?"

"Let me pay and I'll tell you."

Sean must have put him up to it. Rosie had also given me the side eye when I shared the broad strokes of our childhood beef. Perhaps she told him. My sister was fond of stirring the pot.

"Okay, that would be acceptable."

"Triple grande Americano," he said. "And two cinnamon rolls."

"Sure. And the name?"

My scoffing laugh went unappreciated by the cashier. Come on!

"Jason," he said with an easy smile as he tapped the payment receiver with his phone. His case was covered in butterfly stickers, which I would have not considered on brand for a hulking brute that stalked the defensive line like he was protecting his genitals.

The cashier handed off his cinnamon rolls, and we stepped aside to wait for the drinks.

"Now, that wasn't so hard, was it?" He leaned against

the back of the espresso bar, as if propping up this heavy piece of machinery with his brutish bulk.

"Triple grande? That's what—four shots of espresso?"

"Uh huh."

"That'll affect your sperm count."

His brow crumpled. "What?"

"Didn't you read that in *Scientific American?*"

"Must have missed that issue." He took out a cinnamon roll and passed the other one in the bag to me. "I know you're a fan."

That gave me the perfect opening. "I just spoke with your brother. We've smoothed things over, and he explained his reasoning for denying my request."

"His new relationship."

"Right. If I'd known, I would never have dreamed of asking." Maybe we weren't as close as I thought.

Jason seemed to read my mind. "Well, he didn't tell me either until last night. I'm guessing it's so new he wanted to nurture it in secret for a while."

Nurture in secret. That's what I would have liked to do with my plan. But now it was out there, common knowledge, and people were going to have opinions. The longer I went *un*pregnant, the more pathetic I looked.

"Continue."

"What's that?"

"This apology of yours."

"What apology?"

I rolled my eyes. "You said—wait, isn't that what you said?"

His eyes did that twinkling thing again, like glittering Christmas lights. *Not attractive. Not. Attractive.*

"Yeah, I said. I stuck my nose in there the other night. Not my circus, so yeah. Sorry."

Worst. Apology. Ever. But about what I would expect.

"Jason?" Two of the drinks appeared on the counter, quickly followed by my tea. I noticed the barista had scrawled a series of numbers on his cup. Her digits, I assumed.

He handed off the Matcha latte to me. "So that's your drink, huh?"

More passive-aggressive digs at my caffeine ingestion. "It's Violet's, actually. I'm drinking Jasmine tea, which is very low in caffeine. Though usually I prefer Earl Grey, which has slightly higher caffeine content."

And now I was rambling. I *never* rambled.

A smile touched his lips. "So I kind of stuck my nose in there, too."

"You did. But it seems that's your thing."

"Meaning?"

I stepped aside to make room for other waiting customers. He followed me, moving closer so our conversation was more private.

"Meaning you've always disliked my friendship with your brother."

"Not true."

"Yes, it is. You once said that you don't know why we're friends."

He opened his mouth. Closed it. Rubbed his chin, which had the barest scrape of stubble and was strangely appealing.

Stubble on a man is always *appealing*. It was a very objective opinion, even when applied to Jason Isner.

"I said that?"

"I overheard you speaking to Sean years ago." Plus, there were all the times he had been directly hateful to me. "It's obviously something that bothered you and has colored your view of me for years. But that's fine. We all hold preconceived notions or carry deep-seated opinions from our pasts."

He didn't appear all that surprised at my forthrightness.

"Guess you're onto something there. I don't recall saying that, though I've thought it. But then Sean's kind of a bookish guy, so maybe I shouldn't have been so surprised that a brainiac like yourself would be friendly with him." He leaned in. "But this goes both ways. On the subject of preconceived notions and deep-seated opinions, you certainly hold a lot about athletes. Kind of fond of the blanket statement there."

"It might seem that way, but I suspect your taking offense is really down to your own insecurity about your intelligence."

"Ah, blame the victim."

I reared back. "Are you a victim?"

"No, I'm not. But it sounds like you're saying my problem with your opinions is *my* fault because I feel insecure instead of *yours* for espousing them in the first place."

Espousing. Where did he learn a word like that?

My shock must have been evident because the oddest thing happened.

The man smiled at me. A genuine and genuinely gorgeous smile that made my pulse jump and my core heat. I was suddenly and unaccountably aroused.

Rhymes with *espoused.*

He inclined his head. "Didn't think I had it in me, did ya?"

I panicked. "Don't know what you mean."

My denial merely emphasized my reaction and let him know that it had affected me. That *he* had affected me.

"Hmm," he murmured. "I think you do." Said so low and, God help me, *sexy*, I took a step back.

I had to. He was just so *present*. My entire body flushed with heat, my sexual awareness of another person never higher. Not even when I was actually having sex with someone.

Worst of all, he knew. And all because he used a word typically not spoken by someone below a twelfth grade reading level. He probably planned it so he could throw it out there as some sort of jibe at *my* jibe about his intelligence.

Applying logic should have been enough to cool me down, but oddly, no.

"You okay?" he asked.

"Perfectly fine."

"You look a little off, like you need to sit down."

"Hey, Franks!"

Violet had just arrived in all her light-up-the-room glory. My stepmom and I were poles apart, yet I felt closer to her than anyone. She was the one person in my life who had never let me down, who accepted me for who I was, who I could rely on for anything.

And I suspected I had hurt her deeply by not telling her my baby plan before I told Rosie. Or Summer. Or Sean.

Or Jason.

Not that I'd told him, but once it was out there, it was impossible to shove the genie back in the bottle.

I hugged Violet while her eyes lit up on seeing my nemesis. "Jason, how are you?"

"Good, Vi." He leaned in and kissed her cheek, which brought him close to brushing his jaw near mine. He smelled incredible. Like sandalwood and amber and bad decisions.

Decisions? There were no decisions, good or bad, to be made around this man.

"So great to see you joining the gang," Violet continued. "If I'd had my way, you would have been on the roster years ago."

Sometimes I forgot that Violet was a part-owner of the Chicago Rebels. She was hands-off, leaving the running to my aunts Harper and Isobel, but she still liked to weigh in on occasion.

"It was a good time for me to leave Boston," he said.

"Oh? Sounds mysterious."

Something passed over his expression, a fleeting ghost of a memory. Boston hadn't been all that good to him, perhaps. He caught my eye, and his gaze shuttered, as if I was unworthy to see that moment.

Strangely, that hurt.

"Pity you won't play with Theo, though," Violet continued. "I just heard he finalized his retirement."

"Yeah, but there's Hatch, so the Rebels will still be a family affair. Just how you like it, boss. Well, I'll let you ladies get on. It was good to see you, Violet." He nodded at me. "Francesca."

Again with my birth name? Where did he get off?

I turned away, so my lizard brain wouldn't have to watch him leave. He was really the most annoying individual.

"There's a table at the back," Violet said.

We grabbed it and took our seats, and after a couple of minutes of family check-ins (my little brother Devon had won a junior hockey game, Dad was perfecting his golf, and Cat had sent more pictures of her little ones), we finally got down to business.

"So—"

"I'm sorry!" I jumped right in because I wasn't very happy with myself. Also, Jason Isner had left me feeling edgy and unmoored.

"About what?"

"I know I should have told you, but to be honest, the opportunity to ask him just presented itself at Rosie's the other night, and I'd been psyching myself up—apparently for nothing—and now everyone knows, and I haven't even talked to you about it."

Vi grasped my hands. "I was going to ask you about the lectureship at Harvard."

"Oh, that. It's practically a done deal. I just need a sign off from the new department head."

She smiled at me grimly. My family were very annoyed at Lakeshore University's selection committee on my behalf.

"We're going to miss you."

"It will only be for a few months. And I hope that during that time I'll be—"

"Pregnant?"

I nodded. "I'm sorry you didn't hear straight from me."

She squeezed my hands again. "Cariño, you don't have to share everything with me. It's fine to confide in your sisters and friends before your mom."

I relaxed a touch. Violet always knew the right thing to say. Since the moment I'd met her and overheard her calling my dad "Nessie," because he was legendary and Scottish like the Loch Ness monster, I was charmed. She'd had tattoos, pink-streaked hair, and a punk-rock aesthetic, and not long after, saved my life owing to an unfortunate allergic reaction to a nut-tinged brownie. The half-Puerto Rican, youngest daughter of maverick Rebels owner Clifford Chase, she had bonded with her sisters later in life. More than anyone I knew, Violet understood what it meant to be on the outside, looking in.

"Do you think I'm crazy to do it this way?"

"Not at all. There are so many paths to parenthood—IVF, surrogacy, single parent, adoption, the old-fashioned way—that no one should dream of judging you for how you go about it. Hell, I carried a baby for my best friends, and your father was all in." Violet had been the surrogate for Cade Burnett and Dante Moretti, Rosie's dads, and was Rosie's biological mom. "I know you've seen Cat with the twins and wondered why not you? If there's no guy in the frame, then who cares how you do this? And it's not as if any child you have would be lacking for family. Look at all the people who love you, Franky. They're going to love your kid, too."

I felt my throat thicken with emotion. I wasn't a sentimental person, but when Violet got like this, I was reminded that maybe I wasn't the logic-bound robot people viewed me as.

"Well, there might not be a kid to love if I can't find the right donor. It's more challenging than I thought."

"Figuring out the right person?"

"That, and asking them in a way that doesn't sound weird." I updated her on how it went with Sean.

"He probably could have led with the 'I'm dating someone' response."

"Maybe. But I didn't really give him a chance to explain. I was too upset, so I blasted out of there. And *he* doesn't make it any better."

"Sean?"

"His brother." At her baffled look, I went on. "Lately Jason Isner seems to be everywhere. With opinions."

"Well, he's a Kershaw, and Rosie is close to them, so

you're probably going to run into him more now that he's in Chicago. Everyone's so excited that he's joining the team. Usually I don't give a flying F about hockey—"

"But it pays the bills."

Violet smirked. "Sure does. But I'm excited that Jason's here. He's going to bring a solidity to the team that will be useful to this group of youngsters."

I supposed he had enough experience that he might be considered a leader-type, someone who could be a good influence. But then there was that cruel streak of his ... Jason Isner was an expert at playing the good ole boy, friend to all. No one suspected his dark side. I had the receipts.

"As long as he keeps out of my business, then he can be as solid as he likes."

"What? Has he said something?"

I waved it off. "He's just protective of Sean. Thinks I'm taking advantage by asking him."

Before we could get into it, I moved the conversation to a discussion of my cousin Giselle's recent engagement. There was always someone more interesting to talk about in the Rebels family.

AUGUST

CHAPTER EIGHT

Jason

ME

Where are you now?

HATCH

Split

ME

Charming

HATCH

No, that's where I am. It's in Croatia. The town is built inside an ancient Roman palace. It's gorgeous.

ME

Meet any nice Croatian girls?

HATCH

I'm not really in the market for that.

POOR KID. About ten days ago, my nephew had flamed out with Summer and now he was finding himself in Europe. But he hadn't forgotten his girl.

HATCH

Summer's doing great with her internship.

ME

You talked to her?

HATCH

No, Addy told me. I'm thrilled for her.

Remarkably mature for a kid barely out of diapers. I could learn a thing or two about acceptance, especially given the latest gossip from my old Boston Cougars teammate Dean Foster. He had messaged me this morning.

Ran into Everly last night with Coughlan.
They're engaged.

That she was halfway to hitched less than three months after our split hadn't surprised me. Dean's follow-up text had, though.

And pregnant.

If I hadn't figured it out before, that clued me in real quick. Not father material.

Was I like my old man? I was so sure I wasn't. How he had treated my brother Theo had disgusted me, while his Act Two with me and Sean had hardened my heart. Maybe even soured me on relationships.

But not the ones with my family. I loved my nephews and nieces, like they were my own, which at this rate might have to suffice. Everly obviously didn't think I was good enough for that kind of life. She saw something lacking in me.

Not so different from Dr. St. James.

Mental headshake. Who cared what that brainiac thought? It wasn't as if I wanted to give her *my* sperm.

The thought tugged at my groin. Not sexy. But maybe a little? Sperm delivery was inevitably connected with sex and orgasms and smooth skin and messy hair ...

Knowing the professor, she wouldn't even want to do it the old-fashioned way. She probably had some sort of meth lab setup in her apartment with test tubes and syringes and specimen cups. Clinical. Cold.

But she didn't seem so clinical or cold when I ran into her last week. If anything, she seemed off her game, all because I bought her a cup of tea and a cinnamon roll and whipped out my big ... vocabulary.

That pretty blush on her cheeks was still on my mind as was the way she stepped away—or practically stumbled—but couldn't stop looking at my mouth. So I might have imagined some of that. Still, I liked the idea I might be able to throw her off that righteous path she had carved out to skip right over me.

"Uncle Jason!"

"Tillington!"

In Theo's backyard, I scooped up my rambunctious niece into my arms. It was kind of weird that my brother was still pumping them out at his elderly age, but he'd sworn Tilly was the last. His little accident was my favorite.

"I can't believe you're finally four years old."

Frowning, she blew out a breath that ruffled a dark curl curtaining her green eyes. "Five!"

"You sure?"

"I'm five. Years. Old. Today's my birthday." A wave

behind her head referenced the gathering of people on site to celebrate this important milestone.

"Cool, cool. So I'm guessing four, I mean, five-year-olds are probably too old for presents, right?"

A vigorous back-and-forth of her head. "No."

"But you must have gotten so many, too many to even be bothered with mine." I gave her a squeeze. "I'll just give it to another little girl. Mabel would probably like it."

"No! She wouldn't!" Tilly usually adored Mabel, my teammate Lars Nyquist's toddler daughter, but apparently there were limits to any bestie friendship.

I placed her down and she stood before me, hands on hips, her expression radiating "don't fuck with me" vibes.

Reaching into my pocket, I pulled out a small mesh bag and handed it to her. Her shamrock-melted eyes lit up as she pulled on the drawstring and withdrew the gift, a friendship bracelet with letter beads.

I squatted down to meet her on her level. "Can you read what's on there?"

She examined it closely, her cute button nose twitching with the effort. "T-I-L—that's my name!"

"Yup. And there's more. J-A-S-O-N, that's me, and a heart. Know what that says?"

"Jason loves Tilly!"

"He sure does. I figured you're getting a million gifts, but maybe you'd like something special for you and me."

She hugged me, and I closed my eyes and smelled her hair. Fuck Everly for making me feel I wasn't good enough for this.

She drew back. "Should be Tilly loves Jason."

"Why can't it be both?" I turned the bracelet around. "It's just a different way of looking at it." I helped her put it on. "But also ..." I pulled out another one from my jeans pocket and put it on my wrist. I'd had fun making them. I didn't even try to palm the task off on my cleaning lady.

"Samesies!" She screeched. "Daddy! Look what Uncle Jason got me."

Taking his eye off the grill for a quick second, Theo said, "Cool. He also put some money in your college fund, though I told him not to bother because everyone's doing that."

"We're saying no to money gifts now?"

Uncaring of the size of her college fund, Tilly ran off to show everyone her bracelet. For a few precious moments, I was the prince of presents.

My brother looked on indulgently, then turned to me. "Now use your uncle-sized influence to bring Hatch home."

"He needs to be a sad boy for a while. We've all been there."

Theo sighed. "But not usually with the woman who jilted a teammate."

"You Kershaws don't make it easy."

My brother snorted. "Like you're not one of us. Plenty of woman trouble in your life, but not a lot of attention to finding the one."

The one. I didn't think about that too often, or at least not since Everly. Not that she was up on that pedestal. Realpolitik was what they called it when world leaders didn't let ideology get in the way of practical decision-making. That was me, when it came to relationships, a practitioner of Real Relationships. The child of divorced parents, who saw love and women with a clear, non-rosy gaze.

While I'd witnessed plenty of successful marriages, my parents' go around the carousel was not inspiring. But then I saw Theo and Elle and their boisterous brood, and something inside me keened with want. My nephews and nieces were the best, and while childless people joked about how great it was to give them back after a babysitting gig, I never did. I loved kids; I just didn't appreciate the hoops I would have had to jump through to get one.

Tilly was running around, showing everyone her bracelet. Most people were nodding absently or ruffling her hair before returning to their conversations, but one person bent down to take a closer look. The professor herself.

Maybe she was checking my spelling.

I hadn't noticed her arrival—no whiff of Sulphur—but now I took a closer look. Rolled up jeans, white tennis shoes, a white shirt that had some transparency to it in the late afternoon August sun. I could just about make out a dark bra strap ...

She looked up, caught my eye, and Lord have mercy, did not sneer.

Ladies and gentlemen, civility has entered the building.

"Well, look who it is," Theo said, as my nephew, Landon, came out with a bag of hot dog rolls. "Sure you don't need sunglasses? Looking a bit squinty there, Vampire Boy."

"Funny, Dad. Hey, J." Landon, Conor's twin, grinned at me. Smart as a whip, he had just graduated from the University of Michigan and was working on a dating app in his parents' basement. Hence, my brother's jibe about his need for eye protection.

"You made your first million yet?"

"It's not about the money. Just trying to help the right people find each other." He winked. "But when I sell it, it'll be worth a lot more than that."

These kids with the confidence levels through the roof. Had I ever been this cocky?

"Damn," Theo murmured.

"What?"

"I need the Kaiser buns. They're Addy's favorite."

Landon made to turn around, but I put a hand on his arm.

"I can get them." That errand would take me past the doc, and maybe I could poke her some more. Verbally.

Because poking her any other way was not on my agenda.

I headed toward the kitchen just as Franky stood and Tilly moved on to her great-grandma, Aurora. The professor saw me approach, but she didn't turn away.

"What's up, Doc?"

Her eyes narrowed, evident suspicion at my friendly tone her instinctive reaction. I couldn't blame her. I had been somewhat of a dick to her about her baby plan, and while I could say she started it with her opinions on the brain size of athletes, I hadn't helped by stoking the fire.

"Just chatting with Tilly about her gift. She loves it."

My social butterfly niece was now showing off to Nyquist's toddler daughter Mabel, currently being cradled by Adeline, who was her mom in all the ways that mattered. These children mothering children.

"Just something fun. Kids these days with their jet skis and cars, sometimes gift-giving needs the personal touch."

"And you made a matching one?" Gently, she gripped my wrist and raised it so she could see better. I couldn't recall us ever being skin to skin before. That sudden charge was shock at her deigning to touch me—nothing else.

"You made this yourself?"

"Surprised I have that kind of dexterity with my digits?"

That's right, Doc. More big words, with a touch of alliteration and innuendo thrown in for good measure.

She raised her cool blue gaze to mine. "Not surprised at your dexterity, just at what you consider to be a good use of your time."

"My family is *always* a good use of my time."

It came out sounding defensive. With this woman, I couldn't seem to go longer than a minute without feeling that burr under my saddle.

"I didn't mean to criticize."

"Sure sounded critical." *Yeah, turn it back on her.* "But hey, you can't help what you think of me, can you?"

"J!" My brother called out. "Buns, dude!"

"Excuse me, I have an errand to run. For my family."

Before she could respond, I left, feeling vaguely irked and supremely dissatisfied. Not sure what I was looking for from that encounter, but I was damn certain I didn't get it.

CHAPTER NINE

Franky

THAT WENT WELL.

I thought it a fairly innocuous observation, but obviously he didn't see it that way. I made him feel prickly, and he undoubtedly had a similar effect on me.

It didn't matter that my ovaries had practically exploded on seeing him hunkered down, talking to Tilly. And then to find out he had made the bracelet for her?

The whole scenario was like adding boiling water to my parched libido. Or perhaps it was the fertility drugs I had started taking to stimulate ovulation. Either way, I was primed to view Jason Isner in a different light.

How odd that it should be this individual who made me feel this way. Any number of the men at this cookout were displaying optimal paternal behaviors, yet I was mysteriously hooked on whatever Jason Isner was selling.

But those were my hormones talking. They didn't

understand the emotional aspect of this. How this man was liable to poke fun at someone like me.

How he had done so already.

Sure, it was years ago when Jason was too young to know better. But I didn't see a lot of evidence of maturity in the intervening years. Rosie thought I was nuts to hold a grudge, and perhaps I was. I couldn't help how I felt. The absurdity of my feelings didn't make them any less valid. (Thanks, Dr. Faison, my therapist until age twenty-three.)

But I had handled our conversation wrong, and I needed to put it right.

He wasn't in the kitchen or the living room. Theo had yelled, "Buns, dude!" Burger buns, I assumed. There was a pantry in the basement, so I headed down there, and sure enough, the errand boy was bent over a large chest.

And speaking of buns ... The position highlighted his ass—his taut, muscular ass—in a way I should not be noticing. Then there were the thick thighs, hairy calves, strong back, trim hips ...

A step on the bottom step yielded a creak.

He looked up, his expression shifting to storm clouds on seeing me. "Yeah?"

"Do you ... need help?"

"Help? From you?"

I hated apologizing. As a child, I used my intellect to win arguments and manipulate the adults around me. As an adult ... I did the same. I rarely felt a need to apologize because I was rarely wrong.

"*Icametosaysorry.*"

"Excuse me?"

"Sorry."

His surprise was quickly replaced by something more

akin to glee. Of course. Leverage had come walking in, wearing glasses and an Irish linen button-down.

Message received. I turned away.

"Hold up there, Doc."

"Would you please not call me that?"

"Why? You're a doctor of something, aren't you, at that fancy university?"

"I am. I have a PhD. But when you say it, I know you don't mean it as an acknowledgment of my intellectual achievements."

He closed the chest and placed a couple of burger bun bags on the lid. "Of course I do. You have a big brain and when I call you 'Doc,' I'm acknowledging that big brain."

"Yes, but in a way that sounds like you're sneering at me."

He growled, and why was that sexy?

"Think we're getting off topic here. I believe you said something that sounded like the quickest damn apology I ever heard. But I'll need to hear it again to be sure."

"You heard correctly. It *was* an apology." I turned away once more.

He coughed significantly. The man was infuriating!

"But what were you apologizing for? So quickly."

I faced him, feeling like a yo-yo. "Our conversation upstairs. You seemed to take offense at my comment about the use of your time in making a gift for Tilly. I didn't mean that how it sounded, or how you took it, and I came to tell you that. I actually think it's lovely that you would hand-make a gift for her."

He shifted on his very valuable feet. A slight flush bloomed on his cheekbones. "It wasn't a big deal."

"Oh, it was. Tilly's going to remember that gift above all others, especially if you wear that bracelet when you visit.

She's a very lucky girl to have so many strong male influences in her life."

"Guess she is. But that's what family does." He moved closer to me. "Have you thought about that?"

"About what?"

"The influences on your future kid's life."

Of course I had. "I have a good support network. Violet and Dad, my sisters, my little brother. I have plenty of friends." *I'm not a complete loser.*

"But the kid won't have a dad. Full-time."

"Lots of kids don't. Or they have dads not worth writing home about. A man in the picture is no guarantee of a good male role model."

"True." He said it gravely, like he had given this some thought. Sean didn't talk much about his father, but I did know that Jason and he weren't close.

"So, going it alone. Pretty brave, really."

I hmphed. "Did you not say I was crazy to do this?"

"I meant the way you're going about it. Asking randos to donate their sperm. That's the crazy part."

I balled my hands into fists. "There's nothing remotely random about my method! The whole point is that I *don't* want a random donation—"

I broke off as his shit-eating grin stretched wider.

"You ass." But there wasn't much heat in it.

"I guess I think that's pretty brave, too."

"Two compliments in less than two minutes. Wonders will never cease."

"I guess not." Still grinning. So handsome.

But temperamentally unsuitable.

"Your turn," he said.

"For what?"

"Give me a compliment."

I rolled my eyes. "Pretty sure I said you gave a memorable gift to your niece. That observation, coupled with an apology for my misspoken words, makes us even."

He scoffed. "Not even a little. You know what I really want? Tell me why I'm persona non grata on that list of yours."

"I should never have discussed that with you."

"But you did. You needed me to know why I wasn't in the running. Or more accurately why I was once in play but then my chance was ripped away."

His chance "ripped away"? As if he would care. Yet there was something about his energy. This really bothered him.

"You were originally on the list because I was being scientific. All men I know of a certain age and health status were included."

"And then ..."

"By process of elimination I weeded people out. As you and I have never gotten along, it made sense to remove you from contention."

He moved toward me. A low-ceilinged basement like this usually felt cramped, but not to this extent. Not to the size of a postage stamp.

"So you brought your emotions into it."

"It's one more variable. Maybe not completely even with other variables, but where all things are equal, that kind of confounding factor is enough to take you out of the running."

"Fair enough. Let's talk about the variable. Or confounding factor, the one that's specific to me. What makes me such a bad prospect?"

Oh, he was taking this *very* personally. Despite having the science on my side, I no longer felt on solid ground. This conversation had revealed a different side to Jason. Any explanation could only come up short.

"For a start, we rarely seem to be able to converse without it devolving into eye rolls and sneering."

He crossed his arms. His studly, thick … *stop it!*

"You do tend to get very facially animated around me," he said.

"I'm not the only one guilty of this. You scowl at me. Often."

"Only because you start it." He held up a hand. "Or maybe I'm predisposed to scowl because I'm bracing myself, waiting for you to unveil your smarty-pants claws and scratch."

That sounded like a concession, which meant I owed him something similar. Quid pro quo, the building blocks of peace.

"And I might start off on the wrong cloven-hoofed foot because I'm expecting you to be mean."

That earned me a lip twitch. I had amused him with my self-deprecatory reference. There was something a touch thrilling about being able to provoke this reaction from him.

"Mean? I haven't a mean bone in my body."

The man couldn't pass more than five minutes without another dollop of innuendo. I moved over it, though my eyes did attempt a slight roll, which he caught like a puck on his blade.

"There she goes."

"You made a dick joke."

"Your mind has to be fairly deep in the gutter to go there, Francesca."

Maybe it was. Maybe I was enjoying this much more than I expected. It felt remarkably like flirting, especially when he said my name like that. It had been so long that I'd forgotten what it felt like. The buzz, the anticipation, the knowledge that sex might be on the table.

Or on that chest behind him.

Damn these fertility drugs, sending my hormones into a tailspin. I needed to shift the dynamic, recall the emotions that had guided me for all these years when it came to Jason Isner and his ilk.

He stood mere inches from me. When had he become so close?

"You think I'm mean?" he asked.

"You have said cruel things to me."

"Such as?"

"It doesn't matter. We've obviously been stuck in warring positions for some time, but even if we're no longer looking at each other the same way, it doesn't mean we've reached a full detente."

"That means a truce, right? Or something close enough?"

I rolled in my lips to hide a smile. How was he so smart all of a sudden?

Maybe it wasn't so sudden. Maybe the intelligence plus muscles in one hot package scares you.

"Tell me one of these cruel things I said, Francesca." His voice was low. A murmur, a plea for understanding.

I was trapped on the bottom step of the staircase. Backing up would look like backing down, yet his closeness was setting off firecrackers in my body.

"You-you called me a name once."

"What did I say?" He didn't even deny it. His ready acceptance of whatever slight he'd delivered in the past threw me.

"It doesn't mat—"

"What was it?"

I snatched a breath. "Slug Girl."

The moment ticked over, my heart with it.

"When did this happen?"

I was abruptly aware of how foolish this all sounded. I was a grown woman, close to forty years old, and I was holding onto this animus for no good reason. I needed to leave. Recalibrate. Go back to my list and assess next steps.

I backed up, but my foot caught on the stair. He grabbed for me and saved my fall, but the move brought me closer to him. My chest to his. My lips to his chin. His hand stayed on my arm, holding me safe.

Making me want.

"You were barely a teen," I said quickly. Desperately. "Thirteen, maybe? It was here, actually. Well, Theo's backyard. I was in the garden and you came along with Mikey Callahan and some other boy."

"And I called you 'Slug Girl'?"

"We were facing off—"

"Like hockey?"

I shook my head. "I might have started it. You were staring at my chest, and I called you a pervert."

"Ah." He smiled, not taking offense at all. "Sounds about right."

"It was clear you and your friends thought my interests, my research interests, were gross. And after some unimaginative name-calling, you got the final word. I know it's silly to hold onto that—"

He shook his head, rubbed my arm. "No, it's not. We all hold onto shit from our childhood."

"It was so long ago." Over twenty years. "It's absurd to hold a grudge, especially for all these years."

"Yeah, but it stuck in your head. It's okay, Doc. If anything, it makes you human."

Arching an eyebrow, I peered up to meet his gaze head-on. My position on the second-to-last step placed us almost at eye level. No neck pain necessary.

"You doubted I was human?"

"I doubted you knew how to bring a human impulse into this baby-making business. Which was wrong of me because you're obviously very passionate about it."

My breath caught. We were still close, our breaths mingling, our bodies brushing, neither of us willing to back down, as if this level of closeness was no big deal.

When it was everything.

"I really want it."

His green eyes flashed. Such an unusual shade, like spring leaves or *Leucobryum glaucum*, the pincushion moss my snails loved.

"I can see you do," he murmured.

A baby. That's what I was talking about, but this conversation had veered perilously off track.

"The name I called you? Twenty-something years ago."

I swallowed. It sounded ridiculous. "Slug Girl."

"On behalf of my idiot, barely pubescent self, I apologize. I was a little dick, and I was probably jealous that you were close to Sean. It was a rough time for me."

Because of his parents' separation. I had suspected that, but I preferred to ignore it. Not give him any latitude. "It's silly to hold onto it. I should have known better, especially as I was older."

"Yeah, the older woman. I had a bit of a thing for you."

My heart hammered hard. "You did?"

"When I was a kid and just discovering girls. I was twelve or so when we first met and you were—"

"Fourteen."

He laughed, the sound graveled and warm. "Your

glasses were always off kilter." He reached out and infinitesimally adjusted my frames, though the only thing off kilter right now was me. "Just something I remember."

What was happening here? This had to be the longest conversation we had ever had, and we seemed to be airing all the grievances and revealing all our secrets.

It was intoxicating.

"The things that stick with us, huh?" He smiled, producing a dimple in his cheek. My heart fluttered. I had never noticed that before.

Because he has never smiled at you.

"So, Francesca, am I back in your good graces?"

"Uh, you were never there. But I'll probably be less likely to go into full beast mode the next time I see you."

That amused him, and it didn't feel mocking. I could tell the difference now.

"Just tiny beast mode," I said. And that amused me, so much so that a church giggle erupted from my throat. Like I was that silly teen who should have laughed off a stupid insult instead of holding it inside her heart for far too long.

"J! You down there?" That sounded like Conor, Jason's nephew.

Jason's gaze remained locked on mine as he returned the query. "Yeah, I'll be up in a second."

"Dad's having a conniption about the buns, dude."

"On my way."

The interruption broke the spell. I cleared my throat of the lump of emotion lodged there. "I should head back up."

"I'll give you a minute, so no one thinks there's any funny business."

I opened my mouth to say that would be unlikely, then closed it again because (a) it might offend him, and (b) after this exchange, was it so improbable?

Funny business with Jason Isner. The world had gone mad.

"Thanks for thinking of my honor."

I turned to take the stairs and gripped the rail so I would be less likely to trip and fall into his arms like some ditzy damsel. Strange how I had liked it, though. I liked how he touched me. It had obviously been far too long.

I looked over my shoulder, but he had already moved out of sight to retrieve the burger buns and ensure no one suspected we were up to no good at a children's birthday party.

CHAPTER TEN

Franky

"LOOK WHAT I DID, MOMMY!"

I turned to the highchair to find my little girl lining up her Cheerios.

"You're so clever. How many have you got?"

"Four!"

It was five but one of them was hidden under a mandarin segment, so I cut her some slack. At the age of two, she was already so advanced.

"Where's Daddy?"

"Out in the garden, darling."

"With the burgers?"

I chuckled. "You know it. Daddy doesn't do much hunting, but plenty of gathering. And grilling."

At the mention of my child's father, he appeared but I couldn't see his face. That was when I realized I was dreaming, but like many dreams, I could control the narrative. My clever child. Her sparkling curiosity. Her dark hair and ... green eyes.

The rarest eye color, something like two percent of the population had it. The statistical probability of a sperm donor with that shade of moss green eyes was ... I would need a calculator to work it out.

Never tell me the odds.

Oh, it was Hans Solo. That made *much* more sense.

"Daddy!" Our little girl held out her arms.

"Hey, punkin! You counting your Cheerios again?" He scooped her up, her dark hair covering his face. I could just make out the strong jaw of ...

Not the man who made the Kessel run in less than twelve parsecs.

I should have been horrified. *Not him. Anyone but him.* But a dimple popped in the hard plane of his cheek and my heart soared.

Or somewhere further south.

He winked one of those glittering green jewels at me. "What's up, Doc?" And then he offered me a carrot as my little girl—*our* little girl—pulled on one of his long rabbit ears.

I awoke with a start on my sofa, sweaty and agitated. Apparently, witnessing Jason Isner play nice with his niece had made an impression. Dreams were such a curious reflection of our subconscious.

Something was buzzing. Loudly. I checked my phone, not the source of the sound. It was 9:07pm and I had been asleep for over an hour since I came home from Tilly's birthday party. The September issue of *Ecology and Evolution* was open on my chest, so I placed it aside and sat up.

My intercom buzzer sounded, and Bunsen gave a hiss. My cat didn't like visitors, and neither did I, especially unannounced ones. My other cat, Beaker, a silly tabby with the personality of my favorite Muppets character, jumped when the buzzer went again and scrambled under the wing-back armchair in the corner.

The buzzer went again, more urgently this time. Whoever it was, was determined to be heard. Placing my phone down, I grabbed my glasses from the coffee table and went to see who was calling at this late hour.

"Hello?" I spoke into the intercom.

"It's Jason."

I must have been still asleep. I could have sworn I heard ... Before I could clarify, he filled in the blank.

"You left your jacket at Theo's."

My jacket? Since when did this man step up to delivery boy?

"Oh, okay." I pressed the entrance button to let him in and instinctively turned to the full-length, gilt-edged mirror near the door.

Then turned away.

I had never cared for this man's opinion, and I wasn't going to start now. On opening the door, I found him standing there with my jean jacket in one meaty paw.

He raised an eyebrow. So expressive, those eyebrows. "Did I wake you?"

"I fell asleep while reading an article about the *Conus gloriamaris* snail." Better to credit my nap rather than his presence for my stunned state.

"Can't say I blame you. You gonna invite me in?"

For God's sake. I stood back to let him by. Instinctively, he hung my jacket on a hook in the hallway and scanned the frame-covered walls, filled with pictures of my family— Cat, Rosie, Vi, Devon, and my dad in assorted combina-tions, then more of me with just my sisters.

Bunsen decided to show his face and immediately went on guard, adding a hiss for good measure.

"You have a cat." Said as if that was so expected as to be a cliché. The crazy cat lady, desperate for a child.

"This is Bunsen. He's a bit fussy with strangers."

Jason viewed my cat with suspicion.

"And Beaker is around somewhere. He tends to hide under the furniture when he hears the intercom buzzer. But tabby cats are notoriously scatterbrained, as you probably know, and—" I broke off mid-ramble. Lately I had started sounding unaccountably nervous in this man's presence.

"What does your family think of your plan?" Asked as if seconds instead of hours had passed since our previous conversation.

"They pretend it's not weird, but then they've also learned to accept that I'm not the most orthodox of daughters or sisters."

He went further inside, which meant I was forced to acknowledge he had something to say and was taking his time working up to it. I closed the door.

"Thanks for bringing my jacket over. There was really no need."

"Figured it was a favorite."

"You did?"

He picked up an ornament on my bookshelf, a snail glitter globe my aunt Harper had gifted me—a Cracker Barrel exclusive—and put it down again. "It has that snail pin on it. I've seen you wear it before, so I gathered it was a regular part of the rotation. Got anything to drink?"

"Like alcohol?" It came out prissy.

"Water will do."

Leading the way into the kitchen, I was conscious of how those keen green eyes took in everything about my habitat. I shivered, the memory of my dream making me uneasy.

"You're going to raise a baby here? Kind of small."

"It has a second bedroom I can turn into a nursery. It's an office now, but I can compromise." I handed him a glass of water.

He gulped it down, and as he was a strange entity in my space, I had to make a choice: look away or become unfortunately fascinated by the thick, tanned column of his throat. I'd rather not say which won out.

Once finished, he set the glass down on the kitchen counter.

"So you're willing to compromise on that."

"On an office versus a nursery? I don't see that's all that difficult a choice. If necessary, I'll get a bigger place, but for now I want to focus on the baby. Jason, what's going on?"

His mouth twitched. "Going on?"

"While I appreciate you bringing my jacket over, I'm not sure our relationship, such as it is, warrants this level of familiarity."

He chuckled and rubbed his chin. "Warrants this level of familiarity? Interesting way of putting it. I guess I'm here to plead my case."

"Your case?"

"To be your baby daddy."

CHAPTER ELEVEN

Jason

I DOUBTED anything I could have said would have shocked Franky St. James more.

I probably should have been pretty surprised myself, but coming to this conclusion was a whole lot easier than it should have been. This might be my last chance at having a kid, and hey, lookie here—a woman who *wanted* one. So it wasn't a regular situation, but I wasn't likely to ever *be* in a regular situation.

I knew this much: relationships were not my bag. Maybe I just hadn't met the right person, but in the meantime, I was missing out on fatherhood. I loved my nieces and nephews, but it wasn't the same. I wanted a kid of my own.

I'd seen how Franky was around Tilly and the other kids in the Rebels verse. She was good at meeting them on their level and giving them the attention they deserved. With the hand she'd been dealt, she had clearly decided a man wasn't a hurdle to her goal. As I was talking with her earlier, I realized: I could take a page out of her book. She didn't need a man, I didn't need a woman, at least not for a romantic relationship. We just needed each other, for this very specific task.

She still hadn't said anything.

"Did you hear me?"

"I'm not sure what I heard."

Not only had I shocked her, I had left her speechless. Now most guys would worry about that. Me? I saw it as a good sign. It took a lot to shut the professor up. This woman was never short of an opinion.

I went on. "So I think maybe we got off on the wrong foot—"

"Over twenty years ago."

"Uh huh. But even if we don't get along—"

"Which we don't."

My cock stirred. Was this hot? It might be. But that wasn't why I was here.

"Then it wouldn't make a difference. That asshole business isn't genetic."

"Sure about that?"

Oh-so-fucking-droll. "You tell me. You're the scientist."

"Well, there are personality traits that follow from one generation to another. But research by Piaget indicates that education and nurture can be just as powerful, if not more so."

"There you go. If Pierrot says so—"

"Piaget."

"Then maybe we should pay attention to the science. I was on your list for a reason."

She took a seat on the sofa, or more like sank to it in a daze. My charm was a weapon, that was for sure.

"Because I was determined to take an unbiased view," she mumbled.

"And look at how quickly you introduced bias, bringing a confounding factor into it that had nothing to do with genetics or science or biology, but a bad memory you had from your childhood."

She peered up at me with suspicion. "Sometimes it's hard to take the emotion out of it."

I sat beside her. "But that's exactly what you have to do. At least for the baby-making part of it. Keep all the emotion for your kid."

Her brows drew together. "Why do you want to do this?"

"I'll be honest, I'm not looking to pump and dump. I want to be in the kid's life."

She gasped. "You do?"

This was where I expected to run into problems. It was one thing to make the donation, but what we were talking about was a lifelong commitment. To a kid, but also to each other.

"Sure. Maybe you don't think I have much to offer, but I'm gainfully employed, have a good support network, and am interested in being a father."

She stood, placed her hands on her hips, and paced a few steps. "But the reason I'm doing this is because the usual options are closed to me. I can't imagine it's the same for you."

"What makes you so sure?"

"You're a professional hockey player, which is usually enough to attract any number of women looking to be wifed and knocked up. You're also conventionally attractive."

Conventionally attractive. Had this woman just called me sexy?

"All true, but there's a snag. I don't want to marry anyone. And if I went into a relationship with a woman and got her pregnant, the marriage aspect would be an expectation. One I don't want to fulfill."

She twitched her nose. Damn, that was cute.

No, Isner. There is no cuteness here. This is a business transaction. Nothing more.

"Why don't you want to get married?"

"Doesn't interest me."

"Is it because of your father?"

I wagged a finger. "Don't bother psychoanalyzing me, Doc. Some guys aren't cut out for relationships."

"But you would be available for a relationship with your child?"

"Of course I would! Why the hell do you think I'm offering?"

With my burst of temper, I could feel the tide turning. She was back on top, using her intellect and sharp-eyed insight to cut through my puny arguments like a scythe through dense jungle growth.

"Perhaps you think this is a way to assert your virility. Or get your revenge for all the times I've poked fun at a jock's intelligence."

"You think I'm that petty? That I'm willing to bring a kid into the world for some childish payback ploy? You must really think the worst—"

She was smiling.

"I deserved that, I suppose."

"You're easily riled."

"Gullible, too."

"I doubt that. It's just I've upended your expectation. The last thing you saw coming was a humorous response from, *shudder*, Slug Girl."

What was happening here? It was like our wavelengths had suddenly aligned. My heart lifted with the potential of it all.

"Of course," she continued, "just because I can see the humor in the situation does not mean I think this is a good idea."

Splat! Flat as a discarded balloon after the county fair.

"How about I state my case?"

"It would help if I could see your side of it."

She took a seat, placed her hands in her lap, and waited expectantly.

I think I was supposed to stand, and frankly I needed to move here. I pulled myself upright, backed up a few steps, and faced her like she was the league's Commissioner, and the future of my career was on the line.

"There's no doubt I can provide financially. I have a big family with a lot of people on board who love kids. You've seen the Kershaws—they're as mad about kids as they are about hockey."

She merely stared, unblinking, not a jot of encouragement. Sweat prickled my brow. My neck felt hot. I was a student in her class, one with a C-average, who hadn't submitted his assignment on time.

"I see my brother with his kids, my teammates with theirs, and I want that. I want to feel that pride and love for someone." The pride and love I didn't receive from my own father. I wouldn't lean into that because the doc would probably pull a Freud, but I would use it to fuel my argument behind the scenes. "I have a lot to give a kid, and to be honest, a child should have both parents around, if possible. I'm not saying you're not resourceful enough to do this, but wouldn't you like to have that extra support?"

Kind of fizzled out at the end there, but I wasn't going to beg her to pick me.

"You make some good points."

"I do?" I took a seat beside her. "I mean, yeah, I do."

"I have thought about whether a child should have his father around—my own father has been a strong and encouraging influence in my life—but I've also been worried about ceding control. I like the idea of making all the decisions."

So the doc was a control freak. I got it. I had a little of that in me as well.

Maybe I could hit it from another angle. "Who else is on your list?"

"Why?"

"Just show me."

She reached for her laptop, and the movement tightened her blouse, outlining the curve of her breast. Not that I was especially interested, but I was a man and when presented with curves, I took my shot and used my eyeballs as the good Lord intended. Francesca St. James had a more than decent rack.

She turned back, completely oblivious to my horn dog ways, and opened the laptop. After a few clicks, she had a spreadsheet up. Several lines of text had been crossed out, but I still recognized a couple of names.

"Boden?" The Rebels goalkeeper was in the running?

"I've met Noah a few times. He seems very placid."

You mean dull? I failed to see what that had to do with a sperm donation.

"Kind of a man whore. There's a distinct possibility he'll be creating little brothers and sisters for your kid all over the country."

She frowned. "I hadn't heard that. I have a Google alert on him and there's been very little said."

"He's pretty discreet but y'know, the guys talk." I moved on to another player. "MacFarlane? Guy's a dick. More than me."

"Is that even possible?"

I knew her game now. "Oh, it's possible. Nyquist hit him at a nightclub because he hurt my niece's feelings." The gruff D-man also happened to have Mabel in tow at the time, which made headlines and inspired Halloween costumes across the land.

"Well, I wouldn't rely completely on tabloid gossip to eliminate anyone. However, I had already discussed him with Adeline, and she confirms your story." She struck him through.

Boden remained. I was also on there, but with that damning line through my name and a note, *temperamentally unsuitable*, which I guessed was a scientific way of saying "asshole."

But it might have also meant more. Not suited to relationships, to fatherhood, to a normal life with a normal woman. That's what Everly had implied. Damn all these women who thought they had a bead on me.

I moved down the list, passing over the crossed-out names—Bilson, Jackson, Nyquist—to another name I didn't recognize, but was still in the running.

"This guy, Charles Compton. What's his deal?"

"Charles is someone I went to grad school with. He currently teaches in London, so that makes the process a little more complicated. But he's not dating anyone right now and he is a prime specimen."

Sounded like a tool. "I assume he's a professor of something."

"He lectures in Zoology at the University of London and is in high demand for conferences. His last paper on bivalve mollusks as an invasive species was shortlisted for the best article of the year in *Nature* magazine."

"Which makes him good donor material, I suppose."

She eyed me. "I suspect you think the opposite."

Leaning back, I crossed my ankle over my knee. Her gaze skittered over my bare legs, then she sharply looked away. Interesting.

"You need to be considering a better balance here."

"Of?"

"Genes. Do you want your kid to be so smart they get bullied? Wouldn't it be better to give the kid the best start in life, the best opportunity to be well-adjusted with a good mix of genetics? You're a smart cookie, but how are you on a football field, baseball pitch, or ice rink?"

Her brows angled together. "You're asking if I'm sporty?"

"You need to mix in a sprinkle of physical prowess. Good hand-eye coordination. Stamina. That way, your kid has choices. Whether to become a rocket scientist or a—"

"Hockey player."

"Someone who likes sports, which, right or wrong, guarantees a higher likelihood of acceptance amongst her peers."

She twitched her nose again. "Genetics doesn't work that way. It's not a percentages thing or a recipe to guarantee a certain IQ or physical talent. Still, your point is well-taken."

I couldn't help my grin. The professor agreed with something I said.

"No need to look so smug. I'm still not sure this is a good idea. You have a very mobile life and could be traded to another city at any moment."

"Not likely. Chicago is probably my last team. As much as I hate the idea, I've got maybe five or six more good years in me. I'm not Theo." My brother had played well into his forties, which was practically unheard of. I didn't see that in my future.

"Okay, but my life is potentially mobile as well. I'm actively looking for professional advancement, which might take me to another university. Maybe even another state or country."

I hadn't thought of that, which probably made me a sexist ass. Of course, the professor was ambitious. Her drive had left her in this predicament in the first place, so focused on her career that she was deaf to the biological clock ticking down on her dream.

She held my gaze. "Are you willing to co-parent a child that might not be in the same city as you?"

"By the time there are any major changes in your life, I'll likely have retired, which means my time is my own. I could move to where you are, or the kid could live with me for part of the year here in Chicago. Where your family *and* mine are here as support."

I needed to lay it out there. Geography wouldn't matter, not where my kid was concerned.

"You've given me a lot to think about."

I narrowed my gaze. "You gonna get squirrely now because of your control freak tendencies?"

"I'm not a squirrely kind of person, but you're not the only option, Jason. I need to weigh this against the potential to have full parental rights with another candidate who doesn't want to be involved. I also worry that we might not be compatible co-parents."

For all her concerns, I felt like this was progress. No way did I think she'd go for this right off the bat. The doc was a thinker, so she needed time to square this away. I, on the other hand, was more instinctive. Witness my showing up half-cocked offering my valuable baby batter and more.

"Okay, I'll leave you to think on it." I took out my phone. "When are you ovulating next?"

"Excuse me?"

Now wasn't the time to get prudish about the details. "I'm guessing time is an issue. My schedule is fairly tight with preseason games then the regular season going full blast. Lots of travel, so we'll want to line up our calendars."

She was staring at my phone. With a slender finger, she tipped it up, so the back faced her. "Why are there butterfly stickers on your phone case?"

"Tilly got a hold of it one day and went to town." They made me smile every time I used my phone.

She frowned as if this was unwanted information.

"Francesca?"

She snapped to attention. "You're right about syncing our calendars. However, first let me decide whether to move forward before we discuss how the sausage is made."

Sausage. I couldn't help my grin.

"You're such a child," she muttered, while her cheeks pinked adorably.

"Maybe so. But *those* are the playful instincts you want to pass onto your kid."

CHAPTER TWELVE

Franky

ROSIE WAS twelve years younger than me and, if official labels mattered to you, was my stepsister. Violet had given birth to her as a surrogate for her best friend Cade, a former Rebels player, and Dante, a general manager of the team back in the day. Ever since, our two families had been joined at the hip. Cade and Dante were my bonus dads, and Rosie and I, despite our age difference, were sisters in all the ways that mattered, especially since Cat had moved to New York for college and stayed there after her marriage.

We were sitting on the well-worn sofa in Rosie's apartment, she with a glass of wine and me with sparkling water.

"So he just offered?"

I was still reeling from Jason's proposal. In four simple words, Rosie managed to convey all the skepticism I felt.

"What do you think his game is?"

Rosie shrugged. "Maybe he just wants a kid."

"But ... with me? It's not like we're friends and had some ancient pact to procreate if no one better came along." That kind of thing happened only in romance novels. One of my favorite tropes, actually. "This is all so sudden. I don't think I've spoken to him more than five times in the last ten years."

"Because of your ancient beef."

"I know you think it's foolish. But we nerds carry the scars more deeply."

She touched my arm and gave it a light squeeze. "I know. I don't mean to make light of it. But it's good you guys made peace, isn't it? It's opened things up between you."

It was weird to say she was right. As soon as he apologized, I let it go. At least, the words, if not completely the feelings of being slighted. A twenty-three-year grudge was hard to hold onto in the face of Jason Isner's smile.

In truth, *that* was what I was mostly worried about. That smile of his was dangerous. I needed the friction to keep my armor in place.

"But why do you think he's willing to do it this way? It's not as if he has problems attracting a woman to have his child."

"But there's a difference, isn't there? It sounds like he doesn't want the trouble of a relationship. He wants to continue doing his thing, but he also wants the good feels you get from being a dad. Some people can compartmentalize. A man whore can still be a great parent."

Was that Jason? I'd done some light Internet research when I started my list, and he didn't date more than the average single hockey player. However, all his former girlfriends were invariably attractive, blonde, and significantly younger than my old bones. Some were barely out of college

—if they attended any institutions of higher learning at all. Not a pair of glasses in sight, either.

Rosie was still talking. "Maybe he's the kind of guy who knows a good opportunity when it comes his way. He sees all the research and preparation you've put into this and thinks: hey, this chick has the right idea! No haphazard family planning with her. Organized, too, so no chance she'd screw up Little Janky's violin practice schedule or her playdates with Arabella and Cordelia."

"Little Janky?"

Rosie grinned. "Jason and Franky. Keep up."

I rolled my eyes.

"He knows you'd make a great mom, sis. He's right."

"Thank you."

She took a sip of her wine and carved out a slice of Brie for a cracker, then passed it to me. I popped that baby into my mouth whole.

"Or maybe he just wants to get into your pants."

I spluttered, sending bits of cracker flying everywhere. "What? That's not on the table."

"But does *he* know that?"

"Of course—well, I don't know. We didn't discuss the particulars." *How the sausage is made.* That cheeky grin and adorable dimple were stenciled on my eyeballs. "It would be a very strange way of making a conquest. No, that's not what he's after."

My sister's sly smile grew wider by the second.

"He's a hockey player. I wouldn't be so sure."

I TOOK a seat about ten rows up behind the bench and gave the men on the ice a wave.

"Take your time," I called out. This morning, I was meeting my dad for breakfast, and while we could have connected at the Sunny Side Up Diner, I liked visiting the rink, an old haunt of mine. In days past, I spent a lot of time here as my dad wound down his career. My teenage self was a wee bit obsessed with hockey players. Determined not to be the plain Jane wallflower who was too shy to talk to members of the opposite sex, I strove to be the most unusual of women: a nerd who was popular with boys.

All my crushes were on the single players, of course. Theo Kershaw before he fell for Elle, Cal Foreman, Dex O'Malley, Bast Durand before they found their true loves. I was notorious for hanging around outside the locker room. Unfortunately, I was (a) too young, and (b) the daughter of Rebels legend Bren St. James. As if anyone would dare look my way.

At least, that's what I preferred to think. Not that my glasses and weirdness and propensity to suffer allergic reactions to everything might be off-putting to professional hockey hunks. By the time I reached college, I had learned to stay in my lane. Good boys with high GPAs who at first saw me as the perfect study partner, then competition for the internships and TA positions they felt were their God-given right. No guy wanted a girlfriend who was smarter than him, and while my weakness might be muscle-bound jocks, nothing real could ever come of that.

So I retreated into my work. It never failed to fulfill me until the day my sister's twins were born just over a year ago and I realized I was doomed to be the eccentric aunt unless I did something about it ...

On the ice were four players, the usual configuration for my dad's early morning "practices." Although he had retired over twenty years ago, he still came out a couple of times a week with his old teammates, Remy DuPre and Vadim Petrov. Sometimes Levi Hunt joined them, which meant there was a lot of center action—and ego—on the ice. Today it was easy to spot who was who. Vadim was more fluid and had barely lost a step despite his bum knee. Remy still had the brute force while my dad maintained his superior stick skills, even in his late fifties. But their fourth wasn't Levi. It was a younger player, one with a bit more stride in his glide, and he was playing defense while the three veterans pounded him with everything they had.

Jason Isner was haunting my waking hours as well as my dreams.

Of course I had seen him play against his peers. He was a formidable force on the ice, and the Rebels had paid millions to bring the Green-Eyed Monster to Chicago to fill the void left by his brother's retirement. I still watched hockey, still cheered for my home team, so that thrill I felt watching his power and skill on full display was normal. I enjoyed the game and the people who played it. That was all.

Three on one, Jason seemed unperturbed by the hockey hurricane blowing his way. He deftly defended the goal, and while he had no one to pass to, he still found a way to retrieve the puck and blast it into the opposite net. Over his fifteen-year career, he had developed into an all-rounder, almost as good on offense as he was defense. He even scored points quite regularly, which was unusual in today's game where the skillsets were so siloed.

When they finished, I headed down to the rink wall. Remy greeted me first.

"Francoise, I wish you didn't have to see that." My New Orleans-raised uncle always called me by the French equivalent of my name.

I kissed his cheek. "Why, because the three of you were soundly beaten by one player?"

"The shame," he said ruefully, but there was humor, too. Remy was never one to take himself seriously.

"You are here to feed your father." Vadim was someone who *did* take himself seriously. "This is good. He is wasting away."

"I doubt that," I said as I accepted Vadim's hug. "But I'll make sure he's fortified."

My father was next in line, bearded as if the playoffs were this month, but then he'd always been a fiend for facial hair. He gave me a big hug then set me back. "Thought we were meeting at the diner." His faint Scots burr kissed the words. Even after all these years in North America, he hadn't quite lost it.

"It's been a while since I've seen you play. Pity you couldn't do better."

"Isner plays pretty aggressive for a practice."

Plays pretty aggressive in all areas, though I kept that to myself.

My dad brushed his hand against my cheek. "I need a quick shower then I'll meet you outside the locker room?"

"I'll be waiting."

And then there was one.

Jason had hung back, and I wondered if he didn't want my father to know about our current relationship, such as it was. Or perhaps he wanted to talk to me in private. I suppressed a giddy flutter at the idea he might actually want to see me. (And behind my dad's back, too!) That boy-curious teen was never far beneath the surface.

He leaned on the wall, sucking down water. I ignored that thick column of neck muscle and focused on his thighs. Better, but not much safer.

"What are you doing on the ice with the ancients?"

He chuckled. "The ancients? Do they know you call them that?"

"Actually, I call them the Three Wise Men."

"Cute. I could learn a lot from these oldsters. Didn't expect to see you here."

"It's been a while since I've visited a practice rink. I used to spend my childhood here when I wasn't foraging for snails and slugs. Violet lamented my behavior."

"Oh yeah?"

"I was obsessed with hockey players. Was always sneaking into the locker room to get a peek. Very inappropriate, but I was fourteen and hormonal."

He shuffled a little closer, still behind the wall, and it felt like the flimsiest of barriers.

"Fourteen and hormonal? I can relate."

"Thirty-six and no change?"

His soft laugh felt like a hug. "That tongue of yours is awful sharp, Francesca. Besides, you're one to talk with your hormones the way they are."

He had me there. "I could say that my hormonal fluctuations have a good goal while yours—"

"The judgment. Here it comes."

That made me laugh, the sound too loud against all the ice. "Seriously, though. Why aren't you practicing with your teammates?"

"I will later if any of them show their lazy asses. I was in the gym when I saw those guys heading out. The lure of skating with legends was too much to resist."

My dad and his cohort were legends, to be sure. That golden season when Cat and I came to live with Dad, when he met and wooed Violet, and the Rebels won the Cup, was a glorious time, indeed.

"I get it. It must be disappointing not to play on the same team as Theo, though."

"It is. But we've played against each other plenty, and I've no doubt he'll be joining this veteran crew before long."

I liked his attitude. Strange to say, but I was starting to see Jason Isner in a whole new light. How odd we had come to this point with my childhood nemesis—overstating it, but the residual unease remained—asking me to co-parent with him.

I was sixty percent convinced that Jason made good points about balancing the genetic input and giving my child the best possible chance to be well-adjusted and not a complete nerd. I had learned quickly how to repel the bullies with my smarts, but what if I could give my child another layer of protection?

However, deep down I knew that this was a fallacy. Genetics didn't work that way. Look at me, the product of a mother with no interest in anything intellectual and a father with sporting prowess and a history of alcoholism. Where did I come from? I may as well have been adopted.

I needed to talk to Charles in London. There was still a chance I wouldn't have to tie myself to Jason Isner forever.

"So, I have something for you," he said.

I raised an eyebrow.

That dangerous dimple popped in his cheek. "Not yet, Doc. You'll get the good stuff when the time is right."

I almost dislocated my eyeballs in not rolling them.

He unpocketed his phone, which he really shouldn't take on the ice, but the Three Wise Men had rules about checking because of their ancient bones. Tilly's sweet face popped into my head. *Butterfly stickers and friendship bracelets.*

He passed the phone to me.

On the screen was something like a medical report. My pulse sped up as awareness dawned.

"Is this ... a semen analysis?"

"Figured I'd give you some idea of the quality you're dealing with. See those results?" He pointed generally at the screen. "Top of the range, Doc."

He was correct. These results indicated very healthy numbers for volume, concentration, motility, and morphology. Any sample from this man would be A+.

Aiming for a polite aloofness, anything to calm my heartbeat, I passed back the phone. "Thank you for getting the test done. It will certainly save time, if that's the route I take."

He placed his hands on the wall. "I'm not gonna ask where your head's at, Francesca, though I'm pretty sure I have some idea."

The ego on the man. "Oh, really? How are you so sure?"

He leaned in, his breath close to my cheek. "Because you didn't say no."

He was right. If I'd thought this a terrible idea, I would have dismissed it outright. But I didn't. Now here he was with the full court press and the sperm analysis, practically a love note for a science nerd like me. Not to mention a woman in a hormonal riot fest.

Nimbly, he scaled the rink wall in a foxy-fast nanosecond, though he could have gone through the gate. It was right there!

"You know where to find me." And then he was gone.

CHAPTER THIRTEEN

Jason

DOC

You're full of surprises.

ME

There's also a French pre-K in the city. Not sure I'd like the kid to be able to talk about me in another language though.

DOC

Or be immediately more stylish or cooler than you.

ME

I am the definition of cool! Why hasn't anyone come up with a hockey-focused pre-K?

DOC

How about we let the kids reach appropriate ages before we break their bones, teeth, and spirits? At least seven.

I OPENED THE DOOR, expecting to see Paige with the boys. Instead, I was greeted by my father. My half-brothers, Ezra and Liam, waved at me.

"Hey, guys! Great to see you."

And it was. We did a couple of fist-bumps that morphed into something cool and complicated—Ezra was twelve and had more coordination, but ten-year-old Liam did his best— and they trooped past me into the house. I had wanted to wait until all the boxes were unpacked and the place was boy-friendly before inviting them over. Paige, my dad's current wife, had said she'd drop them off for an afternoon of video games and pizza.

Living in Boston for the last ten years, I didn't get to see them as often as I'd have liked. That would change now, and I hoped to establish closer relationships with them. But it also meant seeing more of Nick, which wasn't ideal.

"Did you want to come in?" I asked him.

"Sure. Paige told me to get the skinny on the new place."

"Is she okay? I thought she'd be bringing them over."

He held up both hands. "Oh, she's fine. Well, she has a migraine, but that's par for the course for her."

My father, ladies and gentlemen. Empathy personified.

The boys had already found the unhealthy snacks I'd laid out for them on the coffee table. I was prepared to buy their affection with treats, if necessary.

"Can we eat these?" Liam asked, looking to his brother for guidance.

"Course we can," Ezra responded. "That's why they're there."

"Yeah, Liam-o, they're for you."

Liam grinned, probably because I'd given him a cool nickname. He was definitely the more bookish of the boys, a little shyer than his big brother.

"So, I've got the new Sonic game and the hockey one, too."

"Are you in the hockey one?" Ezra asked.

"No, but Theo is. It's the legends edition."

"Cool," Liam said, then went for the Doritos.

I looked to my dad, but he had already moved into the kitchen, heading for the backyard. I caught up with him.

About ten years ago, he had started dyeing his hair, looking to stave off the onslaught of age. Approaching his mid-sixties, he was clearly anxious to maintain touching distance with his wife, almost thirty years his junior. He should have been sliding into retirement, but kids and a hot wife cost money. After various stints as a local alderman—

yeah, people voted for him—he had returned to practicing law.

Out on the patio, he turned back to me.

"Would have thought you'd want to buy a place on the water."

"Something about this house appealed to me."

He nodded. "Good place for family gatherings. You ever think about that?"

"Family gatherings?"

"Having a family." He met my gaze levelly. "I've always been surprised you haven't settled down by now, Jason. I see that girl you dated—what's her name, Everly? She's moved on."

"And I'm happy for her. Things usually happen for a reason."

"That's what I've always said. You are where you're meant to be."

Not quite what I was going for. Individual choices were key. Leaving your kids behind as collateral damage was not the acceptable result of some laissez-faire psychobabble that boiled down to "shit happens."

Before I could respond, my father placed a hand on my shoulder. "Now you're back in Chicago, I'm hoping we can see more of you. The boys need their big brother. All their big brothers."

What about their father? Did they need him?

Rage rippled through my veins, but now wasn't the time to lose it. Those were the hurt feelings of a kid, and I was an adult man who should just accept that his father was a dick.

"I'll be here for them. I'm going nowhere."

Two hours later, my brothers had whipped my ass in Hockey All Stars, and we were waiting on the pizza delivery. I was in a bit of a salty-sugar coma myself, but I figured one day wouldn't hurt.

The doorbell rang and Ezra yelled, "pizza!"

"Yep. Go get some plates—ah, hell, forget it. We'll eat straight from the box. But grab a roll of paper towels from the kitchen."

The boys cheered, so I guessed Paige was probably fussier about table manners, which was her prerogative as a mom who had to clean up after her little monsters.

I opened the door and got the second surprise of the day on my doorstep.

Francesca St. James.

She looked exactly the same as always—hair loosely tied back and up, glasses pertly positioned on her nose, that jean jacket with the snail pin—but today it all had a different effect on me. While her stubborn chin and assessing gaze annoyed me before, now I just saw a smart woman on a mission.

And I liked it.

I especially liked that she was here, because—well, it could be good or bad. Maybe she preferred to turn me down in person because she was brought up well and wasn't afraid of speaking bluntly.

"Hey there! I thought you were the pizza."

Behind me, one of the boys cheered at something in the Avengers movie we started watching after the video games. Probably Captain America kicking Hydra ass.

"Oh, you have company," she said. "I can come back or—"

"You could come in. My brothers are here, the younger ones."

"I don't want to disturb your family time. Do you have a second to talk?" She took a step back, and my heart sank.

This didn't sound promising at all. Much easier for her to escape in the sensible Honda Civic parked a few feet away.

I closed the door behind me, leaving it ajar.

"Everything okay?" It had been a week since I saw her at the practice rink. I had reached for my phone a million times to text her, but other than a few reminders that I existed, I'd left her to think on it. She needed calm, placid energy—not really my wheelhouse—rather than me sending her pictures of every hockey-themed onesie I had come across during my casual Internet searches.

She hadn't answered yet. If it was no, surely she'd just put me out of my misery.

"Francesca, have you something to tell me?"

She bit her lip. "Perhaps ... you should look at the contract first."

Holy fuckaroo. "Are you saying ... yes?"

"I ... might be?"

Her eyes rounded behind her glasses, a little fearful, or maybe just asking herself, "what have I done?"

You've made my dream come true, that's what.

Joy slammed through me. I lifted her off the ground and released a yell that let the world know nothing would ever be the same again.

"Jason!"

I placed her on the border wall edging the steps up to my front door.

"You haven't even seen the contract yet!"

"I don't care. That's just the details. We're actually doing this!"

My hands were on her hips, holding her in place on the wall, and because I was close, her thighs naturally parted, like they had no choice when faced with my enthusiasm. I had been in this position before with women, and it had never not led to more interesting positions. Sexual ones.

I really should release her, but I didn't want to. I wanted to stay in this perfect moment when the anticipation of our enterprise had yet to run into cold, hard reality. There was a baby to be made, a life to create, a wave of joy to surf. From here on out, we would be linked together inextricably.

She had moved her hands to my chest, not pushing me away, just pressing slightly, as if to test my muscles. *Test away, baby.*

"What tipped you over? Saw me out on the ice and figured, 'that's the one'?"

"Sure, that was it." She chuckled before morphing into her usual stoic self. Serious business, baby-making. "You really should read the contract before you get too excited."

"Too late. You've found your guy."

No way in hell was Franky St. James skipping out on this deal. I was already all in.

***

"YOU'RE GOING to wear out the floorboards."

I stopped pacing my living room and turned to Lauren. I'd known this woman since we first met at Rebels Youth Hockey Camp almost twenty-five years ago. That was a crazy summer—I had just connected with Theo and Lauren had just met her half-sister, Sadie, for the first time, after their dad was imprisoned for embezzlement. Lo had been a terror to Sadie during a tricky time, but they worked it out. By the end of the summer, we were the best of friends, Sadie had fallen in love with former Rebel Gunnar Bond, and I had fully gelled with my new brother.

Lauren and I both went on to successful careers in pro

hockey. She retired from the Chicago Athenas at the ancient age of twenty-eight and had since become an agent, about to start her own boutique outfit. People said you shouldn't mix business and friendship, but I had never doubted that Lauren had my back when it came to managing my career and advising me both personally and professionally.

Though she wasn't a family law expert, she had one on tap, who had gone over Franky's contract and suggested some changes. I had assumed we could do this between-friends, sign-on-a-cocktail-napkin style, but I had no idea how complicated it could get. Medical care, schooling, the kid's living arrangements, even holidays—all of it had to be negotiated before my sperm met her egg.

As for the mingling of body fluids, and how that would take place, that was a whole other test tube of sperm.

"She should be here by now," I said as Lauren leaned back on my sofa and eyed me critically. "What?"

"I don't understand why you're doing this."

"Franky would make a great mom."

She raised an eyebrow. "Interesting that this is your first line of defense. I never thought she wouldn't, but maybe you're worried that people will see the two of you as co-parents and wonder 'how did *that* happen?'"

"Is that why you think it's weird?"

"No. I think it's weird because you're my age and you've already decided you're not likely to meet someone to fall for in a real sense. You have years to spread your seed and find a woman who'll put up with this." She waved a hand over me.

I mimicked her action. "This?"

"I've never seen the appeal personally, but you're not a

complete troll, Jason. Some women think you're hot—in fact, you're trending in the top ten of HILFs right now."

"HILFs?"

"Hockey Hunks I'd like to, uh, get to know better. The second H is silent."

Those stupid lists. Like they had any reflection on real life.

Lauren narrowed her gaze. "Would this have anything to do with Everly recently announcing her pregnancy with Ryan Coughlan?"

"Good for her."

"Sure." Only Lauren knew how much it had hurt. "She's just one woman. One relationship that didn't pan out."

I took a seat and faced her. "I can't say seeing Everly happy and knocked up with Coughlan didn't throw me. But she's not the first time I've struck out."

"The supermodel?"

Zara was probably out of my league, not that I'd have ever told her.

"Or that influencer chick?"

"She was kind of on the young side." I could admit it now.

"And using you for clout. Have you ever thought that these women you date are just incompatible because of ..." She counted off on her fingers. "Age, intelligence, different time in their lives? You should be using a matchmaking service or swiping right on women who are in the market for marriage and kids! Not fathering a kid with someone you've never liked because you think it's your last shot."

"Matchmaking service? Are you doing that?"

She reddened slightly. "I'm the same age as you, J. The options are even less viable for a woman." Lauren had never seemed all that interested in settling down. Then neither was I. "I'm alpha testing Landon's app," she added.

"So how's it going?"

"We're not talking about *my* sex life."

I sighed. "These women I've dated—I never went in with the intention of long-term until Everly. And now I see she wanted someone younger, with more potential." Coughlan was barely twenty-five, Hatch's age, and I suspected now that they'd been together before we parted. It had all happened so fast.

Everly had wounded me, not going to lie. When someone betrays you like that, it turns a part of you inward. My heart might be ice-compacted when it came to women, but not with others. I had a lot of love to give, only now it would be all for my kid.

"It made me realize that the relationship stuff is too complicated."

"And a kid with a stranger isn't?"

The doorbell chimed and I hopped up like a scalded cat. Why the hell was I nervous? This was Franky St. James, who I had known for years. I was doing *her* a favor.

I moved toward the door and called out over my shoulder. "Maybe you shouldn't be here if you're going to be all Negative Nelly about it."

Lauren cackled. "Oh, you couldn't pay me to leave."

"How about twenty percent instead of ten?" I pulled the door open.

I was determined to be stone-faced and serious. No giving Franky any leeway when I had important things to discuss, such as the minimum age for the kid to get a tattoo.

Unfortunately, she looked *hella* cute in her glasses—duct-tape free today—and flowy peach dress with boots and an oversized sweater, a battered leather satchel over her shoulder. Her hair was pushed back and piled high in a clip, though tendrils fell, softly framing her face. For a second, I could only stare, which meant she was forced to speak first.

"Hello?"

Yep, there was something wrong with me.

"Hey, come in. No lawyer?" I had assumed she would bring someone to have her back.

"I didn't feel a need to—" She broke off as she spied Lauren waving from the couch. "Hey, Lo."

That sounded kind of familiar. Having not lived in Chicago for several years, I wasn't completely up on who knew who or how strong the connections were amongst my friend and family group in my hometown.

"Franks! So good to see you."

Franks? Lauren and the doc hugged, and I realized I was behind the eight ball.

"Didn't realize you guys were pals."

"Of course we are. Game watch and book club buddies." Lauren winked at me, then turned back to Franky. "This combo is kind of blowing my mind, girl."

"You're not alone there," Franky said with a quick glance at me. "So, Lauren's your wing person?"

"Yep. If you'd rather wait until you have someone at your back—"

"No, not at all. I had a lawyer draft it, so the basics are there. Anything else, we can negotiate. And I know Lauren is your friend and agent, but I trust her to help us both." She extracted a sheaf of papers from her leather briefcase. "Shall we start?"

"I DON'T SEE why I shouldn't be paying for the medical care. For the pregnancy *and* for the kid."

Franky folded her arms. "You can put money in the trust and we can draw from that, should we need to. But as the child will be living with me full-time, it makes sense that they're on my health insurance plan."

"Even though mine is probably better."

Franky shot a quick glance at Lauren. "Seems persnickety."

Lauren shrugged. "I agree with Franky. The living arrangements should determine the dependents and thus, the health insurance issues. The trust you both set up for the kid seems like a good way to handle anything that falls outside those parameters. I also agree that Franky's pre-natal care should be covered by her own insurance and not out of pocket for you, Jason."

We had hashed out most of the sticking points: holidays, parental rights, health screening of both parents prior to conception. The financial stuff was important to me, but I also recognized that Franky was independent and financially stable. There was no doubt the kid would be well provided for.

We still hadn't discussed how this conception would occur. The contract specified artificial insemination, so I needed to know exactly what that meant.

"As for the logistics of the donation—can we talk about that?"

Franky sat up a little straighter, and a faint blush crept up her cheeks. "Of course. What did you need to know?"

"Is this happening at a clinic?"

"Well, it could, if you want to do it that way. But ..." She eyed Lauren, who had picked up the contract and was reading it upside down. "I'd rather do it in my apartment. Home insemination."

"But not the natural way?"

"If you mean sexual intercourse, then no. There's no evidence in the literature that penile penetration improves the chances of conception."

Penile penetration? My penile penetrator liked that idea. Or maybe I liked how those big words sounded out of that smart mouth.

"So I come over to your place with my donation—"

"Actually, you would come pre-donation ... as in arrive at my apartment before you've masturbated."

"And I'm out." Lauren stood and grabbed her purse. "I think we have the legal stuff worked out. You guys can discuss the specifics that do not need to be detailed in written form."

I grinned up at my friend. "Thanks for sticking around until it got awkward."

She grinned back and bent to kiss Franky on the cheek. "I can stay if you'd prefer." She added, "no offense," to me.

"None taken." I liked that she was looking out for another woman in case the conversation turned inappropriate. Though I wasn't sure how we could discuss the details without some reference to bodily fluids and jacking off.

"I'll be fine, Lo," Franky said. "Thanks for being there for both of us."

"No problem. I'll see you at Book Club?"

"Yes. Oh, have you read the latest—"

"Sure have. Lips zipped." She shot a furtive glance at me, then back to Franky. "They won't like it."

What did that mean? But Lauren had already scooted out, leaving us alone.

"Who won't like what?"

She offered a saccharine smile. "Nothing you need to worry about. So where were we?"

"Masturbation."

Her cheeks flushed. "Right. Well, a clinic seems rather sterile, and I don't see the need to pay someone to insert the genetic material—"

"My sperm?"

She stood and walked over to the window that overlooked the backyard, and in the distance, Lake Michigan.

"There's a swing set out there."

I rose to stand beside her, careful not to touch because— I didn't know. My fingers itched to do something other than shake hands to seal the deal. Stroke her back, rub her arm, anything to create a connection that superseded the black-and-white of that piece of paper on the coffee table.

We were about to create a life.

"It was here when I bought the place. By the time Super Kid can use that, I'll need to replace the rusted bones."

"We had a playset like that in our yard when we were kids. Our dog Gretzky used to go mad when we were on the swings. I miss that mutt." She turned to me. "I know the idea of masturbating into a cup seems strange. That's why I'm trying to make it feel, uh, cozier, by facilitating the hand-off at my apartment."

Cozier? Like Fall vibes for your jerk off sesh? Before I could make a smart-ass comment, she went on.

"And you would need to wait until you get there because the sample should be used within sixty minutes. What if you get into a car accident on the way over, not the kind where you're hurt, but one where the specimen is damaged or decayed while you're talking to the police or—"

"Okay, okay." I held up a hand. "You've obviously done your research, so we'll do it like that." I'd take her apartment over a clinic any day, and an on-the-spot wank with the professor close by versus a lonely jerk-off in my empty house.

Though why it mattered that she was close by ... well, it mattered for the next step in the process. Her part in all this. It wasn't as if I'd imagined we would do this in a more personal manner. By having sex.

Sex with Francesca St. James.

Had I thought about it in a non-procreative way? Of course I had! I was a hot-blooded male in my prime who thought about sex multiple times a day, sometimes with one partner, sometimes with multiple, but never with myself. What was the point of a healthy imagination if you didn't use it for taboo sexual fantasies? So the doc hadn't entered the rotation until recently, but she was there, and rising to the top because of our current connection.

If she wasn't dating or in a position to find a man to father her kid, maybe sex wasn't of interest to her. She was probably one of those cold, clinical types who thought sex should be quick, two pumps and done, to fulfill a biological function or produce a child.

But I could change her mind ...

"Jason?"

"Yep?"

She blinked and adjusted her glasses. "You're looking at me weird. Were you thinking about sex?"

"I'm always thinking about sex." So much for my poker face. More like poke-*her* face.

"I'm sure you can't help it." She patted my arm condescendingly. "I do have one more thing to discuss. Who else is in the loop."

"Okay. Well, Lauren knows."

"So does Rosie. Anyone else?"

I shook my head. "You'd rather we kept the circle small."

"I would. Sure, everyone knows I asked Sean and probably assumes I'm working my way down a list of candidates. There will be enough pressure as it is in trying to conceive. If too many people are aware of our enterprise, that may create unreasonable expectations all around."

It made sense. The last thing I needed was my family or teammates sticking their noses in.

"And when we hit the jackpot?"

Her lips curved slightly. "So sure of yourself."

"You bet I am. This is going to work."

She inhaled a deep breath. "We would have to wait until the twelve-week mark before any announcements. How good are you at keeping secrets?"

"Terrible. But I won't let you down, Doc."

SEPTEMBER

CHAPTER FOURTEEN

Franky

IT DOESN'T MATTER *what you look like. This is not a date.*

Then why couldn't I stop looking in the mirror?

I appeared worried instead of excited. I might be pregnant within hours—okay, days—so I should be thrilled at the prospect. But the prospect happened to involve Jason Isner.

I had tried with Sean. Charles, too. A few days ago, I called him in London and made my request. He declined, and part of me was oddly relieved. He was nice about it, even regretful, but he said the world was too messed up to bring more children into it. I agreed on the first part but not the second. Children would make it better. How else could we fix the world without imparting values to the next generation?

Meanwhile, my options were shrinking along with the viability of my eggs. Two refusals, my hormones screaming.

I had a genuine, hand-to-God offer to help me conceive a child. I would be a fool not to take it.

Jason had signed the contract with its amendments quite quickly, which meant he recognized the urgency. An old maid, getting older by the second, my chances at conception diminishing with every moment I hesitated. This could be my last shot, though it wouldn't be Jason's. He could impregnate anyone.

So why had he chosen me?

Because I did feel like I was chosen. The geek blessed by the star quarterback with a quick fumble behind the bleachers. Jason had his pick of prospects, while I had my rapidly shrinking candidate list and fading chances of getting pregnant.

I threw open the door.

He looked far too handsome. Hair still damp from a shower. A navy-blue Henley highlighting his chest and arm muscles. Faded, threadbare jeans completing the casual yet irresistible ensemble.

I had made no effort apart from exchanging my bathrobe for a LU sweatshirt over leggings. Because this was not a date.

"Hello. Come in."

He walked by me, and I got the scent of danger. Okay, sandalwood and musk cologne, but danger all the same.

"How are you feeling?" he asked.

"How am *I* feeling?"

"Yeah. You nervous? Weirded out? Regretting your life choices up until now?"

It was nice of him to acknowledge the oddness of the situation. "A little anxious. I want it to work."

"You're ovulating at the moment?"

"Not precisely." I supposed it was too much to expect

he'd understand female biology. "Ovulation typically lasts twenty-four hours, but a woman's fertile window is five to six days prior to that. I've calculated that I have about three days left before ovulation, so four days total. And I should inseminate each day for the best chances."

He didn't even blink. "So I should stop in daily for the next few days?"

"If you're available."

"Training camp starts next week, but until then I'm wide open."

We were doing this. I wasn't sure how we had reached this point so quickly after I had requested Sean's donation. Barely a month had passed, and I was on the cusp of doing something monumental.

"Okay then! Let's get this show on the road."

He smirked. "Yeah. Let's."

I led him to my bedroom, something I had longed to do in my teen years (not Jason, but a boy my age) but never got the chance to until I unceremoniously lost my virginity to Duncan Horovitz during my freshman year at the University of Chicago. I pointed at the side table. "I've made preparations."

"No meth lab?"

"Excuse me?"

"Because we're cooking up a baby." He took a seat on my bed and reached for the specimen cup. "Not sure it'll be big enough."

"The average male ejaculate is between 1.25 and 5 milliliters. That's less than a teaspoon."

"Hmm, it always seems like more."

"It also decreases with age." He frowned, so I rushed on. "But it can be more if you've abstained or have gone a while between ejaculation events."

There was that smirk again. "Love it when you talk dirty, Doc."

"That's not—oh, a joke." I snatched a breath. "When did you last masturbate to completion?"

"How does knowing that help? You need whatever I can provide today."

So he didn't want to share the details, and I didn't want to know them. No disappointment here.

"I've also provided tissues, lotion, and ..." I grabbed my laptop from the dresser. "Access to ethical pornography."

Bafflement lined his brow. "What the hell is ethical pornography?"

"It's pornography where the performers are paid fairly and certain standards are followed in creating it. Consent, mostly. A lot of pornography doesn't adhere to high standards for a workplace."

He snorted. "The low standards are generally the point when it comes to porn. Don't worry, I won't need a video, unless ... is that something you've done?"

"What?"

"The ethical porn. Is it one of those 'upload yourself beating off deals'?"

Was he for real? "You think I would have done that?"

"You're raving about how ethical it is. Figured you might have contributed to make the porn workplace safer."

"Oh, shut up. I'm trying to help you out here." He would have liked to see me masturbate?

He leaned back against one of my many pillows, waving the sample cup like a goblet held by the king. "I prefer my help to be the hands-on kind."

I hoped he wasn't suggesting ... I waited for the Jason Isner smugness indicators, but he remained passive. I placed the laptop back on the dresser. "I don't think that's a good idea. It blurs the lines."

"Wouldn't want to do that," he murmured. "Don't worry, I can manage with my filthy imagination." He cast his gaze around as if looking for inspiration.

I shot a furtive glance to my underwear drawer, not to guide him there, but because now all I could think of was Jason Isner in my bedroom masturbating while I was on the other side of the door. Listening.

That would not be ethical at all.

"I'll play music loudly so you won't have to be concerned about ... restraint." Was he noisy? Quiet? Gruff? Gentle?

I would never know.

"Is there anything you need from me?" I held up a hand. "Be serious."

Another grin, followed by the pop of that dimple. "Think I've got it from here."

I left him to it and immediately turned on the sound system. Quickly I scrolled through my playlist. Should I have asked if he had a preference? Did it matter?

Taylor's *Life of a Showgirl* seemed appropriate here, particularly "Wood." I suspected Jason Isner knew nothing about Taylor's music, but this would be a fun joke that I could enjoy. I hit "play" and turned up the volume, then I retreated to the kitchen, the farthest place from my bedroom. I boiled a kettle for tea, another sound that would muffle any noisy output.

What was he doing in there?

Exactly what you hired him for.

Okay, "hired" was all wrong. After all, Jason would be involved as far as he wanted to be. I was skeptical of his interest in the long-term nature of the enterprise, though.

He would likely get bored after a while, and we would eventually have to come up with a different custodial and financial arrangement. After all, my own mother had determined motherhood wasn't for her when she dumped us with Dad. But it wasn't because of Cat—no, I was to blame. Too weird. Too geeky. Too uninterested in the things she cared about like make-up and pretty dresses. And as a result, she gave up on us.

If any child I conceived with Jason wasn't sporty enough, I couldn't imagine him maintaining his interest. If he hadn't lost it long before then.

I looked down at Bunsen, who was viewing me with bored disinterest.

"It'll just be us, Bunny. Me, you, Beaker, and the baby."

Bunsen hissed, not liking the sound of that. He would come around.

Jason

WELL, this was weird.

I had all the ingredients for a good time: lotion, tissues, and my right hand. But the vibe was the oddest setup I'd ever experienced. This *was* what I signed on for, though I had to wonder why we couldn't just do it the old-fashioned way.

I'd seen how the doc looked at me when she answered the door. That was appreciation in those smoky blues, and that faint blush when I mentioned my love for her dirty talk definitely stirred me in the right direction. So she was far from my usual type, but I could have managed, knowing I would be making a mini-Jason.

I looked around. So this was where it all *didn't* happen.

I'd say this for her, the room had personality. Moving closer, I scanned the shelves. A couple of things that looked like science models, a diorama of a glass room with a red open-topped coupe, a Funko Pop figure in a box—Cameron from *Ferris Bueller's Day Off*. The diorama was Cameron's dad's car, the one they "borrowed" for the eponymous day. There was a small gift card attached to it.

Best day ever, remember? Love you, sis! – Cat

Tons of books, a mix of fiction—mostly romance—and science lined the lower shelves. So, the doc was a romantic at heart. When had she given up on finding true love? So she wasn't my type, but if anything proved the adage that there was someone for everyone, it was having seen plenty of teammates, family, and friends find love over the years. Sure, half of them were divorced, but they'd still trotted as far as the altar. They had still believed. Maybe the doc had been unlucky in that area. Or she was too busy figuring out how snails do it to reckon with the human side of it.

That was her research focus: mating habits of snails. I had checked out her faculty page on the Lakeshore University website. Her bio photo showed her prim and serious, sexy librarian style with those slutty little glasses. If you liked that sort of thing.

This woman was smart, though, and I had to admit enjoying all those big words. *Ejaculate. Masturbation. Ethical pornography.* Damned if I understood how detached she could be about it all. I was about to jerk off into a cup, and she was playing Taylor Fucking Swift.

I had the album like everyone else.

The idea that I could produce no more than a teaspoon

was ludicrous. I'd done my research and the minute we signed that contract, I stopped my spank. I knew how important it was to produce in quantity, though I was fairly confident the slightest drop of my powerful sperm would do the trick. Christ, all it took was one night and a defective condom for Theo to get Elle pregnant. Surely, with this much planning, I could manage the same with Francesca St. James.

It would probably help if I took my jeans off.

I pushed them down my thighs with my underwear, grabbed some lotion, and sniffed. It smelled like jasmine— her scent. I was already halfway to a chubby but knowing this was the stuff she used on her body got me harder. Maybe this wouldn't be so difficult after all.

I stroked once, acknowledging the weirdness. Not my dick, just the situation. Though in fairness, my cock did feel strange in my hand. Like I'd never touched it before, or it belonged to someone else.

Not really the direction I wanted to go in, but damn, this would be easier if I had access to ... ethical porn.

I huffed out a laugh. After all my professions of ease, now I was thinking I might indeed need a helping hand. But I refused to watch porn, no matter how ethical it was. Instead, I imagined what Franky might be doing now. Was she in the living room reading one of her academic journal articles, trying to block out how the sausage was made?

(Sausage. Ha!)

Was she hiding away in the bathroom, worried she might hear something she shouldn't?

Except she should hear it. She should hear the effort that went into producing one half of her kid. Maybe she was closer than I thought. On the other side of the door, listening in a non-ethical way.

My cock jumped, liking that notion. Liking it a lot.

I shot a glance toward the door, covered with a poster of the periodic table of elements. Of course. It wouldn't be so terrible if she was close by, the delicate shell of her ear pressed to the wood, (*naughty, naughty, Taylor*), maybe her hand down her pants.

Oh, my dick liked that big time!

I stroked harder, taking it from root to tip. Pearls of pre-come were leaking from the crown. Did we need that for the baby? Probably not, and neither did I think it feasible to try to save it while I was getting a rhythmic stroke going.

"You there, Francesca?" I whispered. "You listening in on the action?"

No answer. My filthy brain insisted she was, though. Not only that, but she was touching herself, running soft fingers through her wet pussy while she strained her ear for my moans and fuck—that felt *so* good.

My hand moved faster, flying up and down, tugging hard because that was how I liked it.

"Yeah, baby, just like that." The doc was stroking herself, but she had enough coordination to give my dick the love it needed. Surprisingly agile for a nerd. "Use your mouth. Use that sharp tongue to suck me."

And she did. She had wicked skills in that department, but then I'd always assumed she was a Jill of all trades. Probably not a lot that brainiac couldn't do if she put her mind to it.

Intelligence had always turned me on. I didn't get much chance to date brainy women. They'd usually made up their minds about me before we even got to that point.

She had. Dr. Francesca St. James. And as hot as this imaginary situation was, the bottom line was that she only wanted my sperm, not anything else. I was no better than a stable stud, a top shelf Thoroughbred, but a stud all the same. We might be planning a co-parenting setup, but she clearly thought I'd bail when I got bored, like my dad had done with us.

That should have been a dampener on my jerk off, but something about how mad it made me took me through that last stretch. Heightened everything. My balls sizzled and lightning bolted through my body, the supercharged zing of oncoming release mere seconds away.

I grabbed the cup and placed it over the crown of my dick just as it exploded, along with a loud yell from my throat.

After I'd come down, I listened. Sounded like Fleetwood Mac's "The Chain." Had she heard? Or was she a better person than me?

I sat up and checked the cup. Definitely more than a teaspoon, but not as much as I expected. After cleaning myself up with the provided tissues and pulling my jeans back on, I headed to the door. I had thought the poster pinned there was the periodic table, but no. It was the Purriodic Table and the elements were all kittens. You thought one thing, and then it turned out to be something else ...

No dirty-minded professor waiting outside.

I went to the bathroom to wash my hands, then sought out my baby-making partner. She was sitting at the table in the kitchen, her cat on her lap, sipping tea and reading something on her iPad. She didn't look like she'd made a mad dash back from listening in or like she had any particularly fulfilling experience herself.

She looked up, her gaze drawn to the cup in hand.

"Delivery for the doc."

She released a sigh. It was one of relief, and my heart

keened at the sight of her face, racked with such naked need.

I placed the sample on the table. "What's next?"

She stood, sending the black cat in a graceful spring to the floor, though he hissed his disapproval of me and maybe, this entire enterprise.

"I need to inseminate. And it would be best if you left while I did that."

Right. I shouldn't have been surprised, but it felt strange that she was here when I played my part, but I couldn't be when she played hers.

I would respect her boundaries all the same. "Same time tomorrow?"

She nodded. "If that's still okay with you."

"I want to see this through."

She blinked and smiled. "Thank you. You've no idea how much this means to me."

I thought I did, but as I left, I figured my feelings on the matter weren't all that relevant.

CHAPTER FIFTEEN

Franky

ME

How does the moon cut its hair?

DEVON

?

ME

Eclipse it.

DEVON

That's worse than Mom's material.

ME

Vi's dad jokes are how I was raised. It's a family tradition.

She said you needed help with algebra.

DEVON

I'm going to play hockey. Not seeing how math is relevant.

ME

Hate to break it to you, Dev, but math will make you a better player. Ever heard of the rule of reflection?

DEVON

Nope.

ME

Because you need to get through algebra before you can take geometry. An understanding of angles is a hockey player's secret weapon.

DEVON

You can help if you want to.

ME

I *do* want to. Now what did one wall say to the other?

DEVON

Not sure I want to know.

ME

I'll meet you at the corner.

DEVON

Your worst yet.

ME

Oh, is that a challenge? Also, that doubles as math humor. Most likely they met at a right angle.

I CHUCKLED at my silly joke.

"Dr. St. James, have I said something amusing?"

Looking up, I met the department head's gaze. Dr. Bilson—or Dr. Bilious as Violet called him—had interrupted his pontificating on the new faculty requirement to submit weekly activity reports to ensure I was still paying attention in today's faculty meeting. Luckily, I could multitask with the best of them.

"I fail to see how creating a paper trail documenting my work meets department goals. Such busywork infantilizes the faculty who have more pressing uses for their time."

Dr. Bilson looked surprised at this challenge to his authority. "Asking faculty to keep me informed of their productivity contributes to the greater enterprise."

Sure. In Communist Russia.

The meeting continued without further disruption. At its end, I had just reached the door to the department conference room when Dr. Bilson spoke.

"Dr. St. James, do you have a moment?"

So close.

Today was the last day in my ovulation window and I needed to meet Jason at home for the next "delivery." For the last three days, he had come to my apartment and come in a cup while I turned up the music and imagined him on my bed. Or in my bed.

"I have an errand to run, Dr. Bilson, so if you could make it quick?"

His bushy eyebrows met as one, similar to the larvae of a pasture day moth, and I wondered how I had ever found him attractive. Two years ago, during a cocktail reception for up-and-coming faculty leaders at a conference, we got into a spat over his misunderstanding of the comparative mitogenomics of freshwater snails.

You should read St. James et al on this topic, he had said.

He went on to mischaracterize my research and to ask if I understood the concept at hand. His face, when I held up my name badge, was, as they say, priceless.

I had rather enjoyed his grovel and then enjoyed the conversation that focused on how much he respected my research, even though he clearly didn't get it. What could I say? Fruit fly researchers were rather one-track. Three glasses of reception-quality Chardonnay later, and I was ready to end my dry spell. At the time, he was an associate professor in a biology department at a small liberal arts college in Maine. Now he was my boss.

"You know, it's perfectly fine to call me Marcus," he said. "After all, we are old friends."

I offered a thin smile. While we had never discussed our sexual history, he didn't mind being overfamiliar with me, a reminder that we had a connected past that he could weaponize at any moment. "How can I help?"

"I'll need the performance reviews for your teaching assistants by the end of the week."

"Yes, I saw that in the email you sent to all the teaching faculty."

He cleared his throat, a rather annoying habit. Marcus was in his mid-forties, divorced with no children, and I suspected, willing to again "discuss" my research after three glasses of indifferent Chardonnay.

"I spoke with Chairman Phillips at Harvard yesterday. We had some issues to discuss in our roles as academic thought leaders ..."

I wondered if Jason would wear that navy-blue Henley today. It should have clashed with his eyes—blue and green should never be seen, they said—but somehow it all worked to define his pectorals magnificently. The fantasy of this man in a Henley was helping me produce the uterine contractions necessary to ensure his sperm reached my egg.

In other words, an orgasm.

I snapped out of my lewd thoughts to find Marcus staring at me. "Perhaps we should discuss it over lunch?"

"What's that?"

"Your guest lectureship at Harvard. As I was saying, your absence will be quite disruptive—"

"Are you saying you won't sign off on it?" Panic flushed my veins.

He gave me that look, the one women everywhere have suffered since the first time a man realized he had leverage over a better-qualified female colleague.

"Not at all. But sabbaticals and absences need to be approved by the department head."

"The guest lectureship *at Harvard* was approved by your predecessor. You can't pull the rug from under me now."

He chuckled darkly. "I have no intention of doing so, Franky. I would just like to discuss how it will impact the department."

"Over lunch."

"You make it sound so horrifying."

He sat back, satisfied with his progress. Perhaps I was being too harsh on him. Perhaps this was the only way to get ahead. We would make a super couple in academia, big fish in our small pond, though how would he feel about my child-rearing plans?

He doesn't have a dimple in his cheek or a wicked smile or delicious muscles.

Of course he doesn't. He's not Jason Isner and you should be glad of it!

"I think it's important that we observe the correct protocols around approvals for absences, Franky. Obviously, you've been given a lot of latitude here by my predecessor." Another oily smile. "But I plan to keep a closer eye on how the department's resources, including its faculty, are used. Shall we say noon at my office?"

Damn. Perhaps Jason would be okay with rescheduling to this evening.

"Of course. See you then."

CHAPTER SIXTEEN

Jason

TRAINING CAMP STARTED the last week of September, which I was glad of because I needed my mind to be on hockey instead of whether I was a father to be. It had been almost two weeks since I last delivered my genetic material to the doc and I hadn't heard a peep from her, except for her smart-ass comment about the cats having more rights than me.

I was feeling pretty good about the previous ten days of

camp. I was gelling with Nyquist, who had taken over as captain from Theo, and even had some decent practice shifts with MacFarlane. Coach had options for the defensive line, which was basically why I was here. While I highly doubted I could fully fill my brother's skates, I had youth (sort of) and stamina (definitely) on my side.

I picked up my phone from my cubby in the locker room. Still nothing from the doc. I was going to have to go over to her place and suss out the situation.

Twenty minutes later, I hit the intercom button for Franky's building and waited. Waited some more. Just as I was about to leave, a fuzzy voice emerged from the speaker.

"Hello?"

"It's Jason."

The entrance buzzer sounded, and the main door opened. Up the stairs I bounded, and when I reached it, her door was ajar. I pushed it in.

"Doc?"

Sniffles. She was sitting on the sofa with a box of tissues and reddened eyes. Something in me reared up, an urge to hurt what had hurt mine.

"Who did this to you?"

"You did! Or more to the point, you *didn't.* I'm not pregnant!"

Shit. "You're sure?"

"I got my period today."

I took a seat beside her, the rage in my chest at seeing her so upset barely subsiding to a simmer. If we'd been friends, I would have put an arm around her, given her physical comfort, but we weren't. We were in a weird liminal space where the rules were slippery and unknowable.

"We can try again."

"I-I know." She pushed her glasses back up her nose. "I just thought that now it was happening that it would be—"

"Happening?"

"Yes. I assumed the hardest part was finding the candidate. That wasn't hard at all. You just rocked up and offered!"

"You make me sound easy."

She raised an eyebrow. I had amused her.

"You did offer your services rather quickly. Have you ever impregnated someone before?"

I averted her headlight-bright gaze. "No. But there's nothing wrong with my boys."

"So it's my fault?"

"Didn't say that. Doc, you're a scientist. Think it through. Did you really think we were going to succeed the first time out?"

She blew out a breath that ruffled her bangs and set her chin stubbornly. "I wanted it to."

"You know something? I've wanted to win the Cup for my whole career. Fifteen seasons and no joy. Didn't mean I didn't try or that my team was no good. It just didn't happen. But I still think I can do it this year because if I was to give up on that dream, I'd be giving up on life!"

She peered at me. "I can't believe you've never won the whole thing. Though you came close three years ago. McCluskey should have been ejected for that hit he made on you."

That hit ended my playoffs a round early. Who was to say how far we would have gone if I'd stayed in?

"You've been keeping track of my career?"

"Purely from interest in the gruesome details. So much blood." She reached for my eyebrow, her fingertips soft against the scar left by McCluskey's stick. In an all-out melee, I'd lost my helmet, and that wily prick went for the kill. Anyone with eyes could have seen he did it deliberately, but the zebras were skating blind that night.

I was glad my old misfortune had given her something to think about other than her own misery. *Our* misery, because we were a team here, and I wanted this, too. Maybe I liked her warm fingertips on my face as well.

"I think I can win this year."

"The Cup?"

"Among other things."

She dropped her hand. "A baby's not some trophy you can parade around."

I chuckled. "If there's a baby in the picture, you can bet I'll be holding that little warrior aloft before getting him baptized in the hardware!"

That made her laugh and winning *that* seemed like a huge victory. If I could do that, I could make a baby *and* smash the Finals.

"Banking on a boy?"

I shrugged. "I don't mind. As long as they're healthy. Now how about some tea?"

Another scoot of the St. James eyebrow.

"I can make tea, Doc. No need to look so skeptical."

"I'm not. Tea would be lovely."

Franky

DISAPPOINTMENT STILL GNAWED AT ME. Jason

was the last person I had wanted to see and now the only person I could imagine being here with me right now.

There were plenty of people I could call to be my shoulder—Rosie, Cat, Vi, Dad—but somehow it felt right that I share this mini-heartbreak with the man who could potentially fix it. Jason was right: there was no reason why we couldn't try again, yet every day that passed was a day I was less likely to conceive.

I was old in fertility terms. Jason was in his prime. Only two years younger than me, and he was considered the perfect specimen. It didn't seem fair, but life often failed to measure up to equity standards, especially when it came to men and women.

I could hear him puttering about in my kitchen. He didn't know where anything was and not even how to make tea the way I liked it. I could have gone in there and taken over, but I liked the sound of him in the next room. It was similar to when I heard Beaker crashing into something in the bathroom. There was comfort in knowing I wasn't completely alone. As my cats had yet to learn how to make tea, Jason would have to do.

I thought back to my plan to get pregnant, assessing each step in the process to see where I might have gone wrong. Jason was right—not that I'd ever tell him—that a first-time attempt wasn't guaranteed to work. Sure, if I was a teen fooling around with her boyfriend who insisted on "just the tip," I would probably be knocked up by now because that was the way the universe worked. But, even in making all these preparations, taking the fertility drugs, and ensuring the best possible conditions for conception, it still hadn't worked.

Was I missing something? Home insemination was a proven method but had a roughly eighteen percent success rate. That was probably less for someone who was older than thirty-five, geriatric in pregnancy terms. So we were looking at a one-in-six or seven chance of getting pregnant.

Not great odds.

I could improve them with additional insertions of sperm, but it might take another six months, or longer. Would Jason be willing to participate for that long? And how would he feel about being little more than a delivery mechanism for his valuable genetic content?

"Milk? Sugar?" he called out.

"Milk, please. No sugar."

A minute later, he arrived with two cups of tea. I had already put a coaster out for one and now I added another. He placed the cups carefully.

"Thank you."

"No problem."

He took a sip of his own and grimaced slightly, which made me smile. What a trouper. But would he be such a good sport if I tied him up for six months or more?

"I might go the anonymous sperm donor route."

He stared at me over his cup, then placed it back down on the table.

"You're already giving up? Why?"

"Because this might take a long time. And in the meantime, you would be beholden—well, obligated—"

"I know what beholden means."

Of course he did. "To be on call for monthly donations. It's a lot to ask of you, and it'll just get weirder."

He snorted. "Weirder than it already is? Don't think that's possible. Look, I understand if you're having second thoughts about me as your baby's daddy. Maybe now you've gotten to know me a little, I'm not what you had in mind."

"You were never what I had in mind! That's not it. I

think you'd be a fine donor and father, but the burden it places on you is more than I considered. I had hoped it would be one and done, but what if it's five, six, seven months, and still no baby in sight? Are you prepared to roll up here monthly on an indefinite basis, dick in hand, reporting for duty?"

My outburst had clearly shocked him into silence. Then a small smile curved his lips, a smile that turned wider as the seconds passed.

"What's so funny?"

"Dick in hand, reporting for duty. You sure do have a way with words, Doc."

I placed my head in my hands. "I don't want you to worry about being a prop in all of this. Because you want to be involved as a father, it might be psychologically ruinous for your role to be seen as merely biological at this point." I peeked at him through the cage of my fingers.

He narrowed his eyes at me. "I think you're trying to bamboozle me with your vocab there, but I'll try my best to generate a plain language summary. You're worried that this process will take a toll on my mental health."

How rare to meet someone who could take my often torturous way with words and translate it into language the average person could understand. Most men I knew were either so smart that they saw my speech patterns as a challenge or too stupid to even try to parse my meaning. I had to admit I spoke this way sometimes to test someone—and here was Jason Isner blowing away all my preconceptions.

"I am."

He placed a hand on my back, gently moving it around in circles meant to soothe, but which did nothing of the sort. His touch was fire. Damn those fertility drugs for making everything so ... lusty!

"Franky, I never thought this was going to happen the first time out. Sure, it might be tough for us both if we're six months in with nothing to show for it, but I think it'll be tougher for you. Now anything worth doing is worth doing well. And by well, I mean sticking at it until we're both damn sick of each other, or there's a baby in your belly."

I loved when he got riled up, and I'd clearly annoyed him with the notion of letting him off the hook. He hated the idea that I wasn't giving him a chance to make it right. The warrior athlete in him saw success as the only option.

Was it possible I'd chosen the best possible father for my child?

"You make some good points."

"Fuck yeah, I do." He dropped his hand and returned to his tea. "Hey, this stuff isn't half bad. Now how about we coordinate calendars for next month?"

He had talked me off the ledge and thankfully, removed his strong, warm hand from my body. All was right again. Sort of.

I sipped my Earl Grey tea, surprisingly well made and steeped to perfection. "Let's."

OCTOBER

CHAPTER SEVENTEEN

Jason

THE PRESEASON WAS FINALLY WINDING down with our fifth of six games scheduled for Detroit. The league made as much effort as possible to plan these games to minimize travel, so while we'd already played in Boston and Minneapolis, a trip to Detroit was like a walk in the park. Except I was tired from the travel, and maybe a little from the stress of arranging my next DoorDash sperm delivery.

Because I was set to be on the road in the days prior to Franky's next ovulation window, we had decided that she would come visit me in Detroit. This meant we had to sneak around, which to be honest, was kind of hot. Not that I needed this situation to be hot. I could jerk off on demand, but I also liked the idea that we were planning a special meet-up in service to conceiving our kid. A story we could tell the little one later.

Though the doc might not want to share that at all.

Finding her so upset that it hadn't worked the first time had ripped my heart out. I hated to see a woman teary-eyed, and while I'd long tried to ignore the fact Francesca St. James was a woman, this whole situation made it very clear that she was. The emotions, the biology, the fact I was breeding her—that was classic caveman shit right there. And then to hear that she might not want my donation after all? Thank God I managed to talk her down. No way was I letting her weasel out of our deal.

Franky was scheduled to drive up early and check into the team hotel before we got there. That way, we could meet up for the hand-off—heh—after I got there, try again before curfew, and maybe give it one more shot before the game tomorrow.

My biggest concern was the fact I was rooming with my nephew Hatch, so I'd have to slip away and avoid his questions. Luckily, he'd made up with his girl Summer before the preseason, so he was likely to be distracted.

We had just dumped our overnight bags in the hotel room and were slipping out of our suits when Hatch's phone rang. His grin was wide enough to power the Detroit grid and made my own heart sing because cover was rolling my way.

"Hey, Sunshine. So good to hear from you."

I pulled my sweats on and hung my suit. "I'm gonna go for a walk. Maybe an hour?"

Hatch gave me an absent wave. Perfect.

I shot off a text to the doc as I walked out into the corridor.

ME

All checked in. How about you?

DOC

I've run into a problem.

ME

What problem?

DOC

Can you talk?

I nodded at Noah Boden, our goalie, who had just come out of the room next to mine.

"You heading down for a bite to eat?" he asked.

"It's only four o'clock."

NoBo frowned. "So?"

"You go ahead. I've got to make a call." But where to make it? This entire floor was filled with players.

I hovered around the elevator bank until the doors closed on Boden, then I took the other car to ... *where, where?* The spa. All I needed was a quiet spot to talk. I found it in the sauna, which was unattended and really fucking hot.

I called Franky.

"Hello?"

"What's going on?"

"Beaker threw a fit and made me late leaving. Then the car broke down, and I had to call AAA for a battery boost, so I was a couple of hours late. I've yet to check in."

Shit. "Where are you now?"

"In the underground parking lot of the hotel."

The players were going to be swarming the lobby any minute, looking for food and company.

"Stay put. I'll meet you down there."

Five minutes later, I found her and her sensible Honda Civic in the parking lot. She unlocked the door, and I slid into the passenger seat, then took a moment to slide it back so it was less cramped.

"Hey."

She released a breath, and was it my imagination, or was that relief in her expression? I liked that. I wanted to be the guy who saved the day.

"I'm sorry. I know that under the radar is better and I really have no reason to be here that would pass muster—are you sweating?"

"I had to call you from the sauna. Listen, we can figure this out."

"I suppose it's possible most of the players don't know me at all. But if I ran into Hatch ..."

"You won't. You're gonna go in there and check in."

"But—"

"In a disguise."

She blinked. "A disguise?"

"I bought some things from the hotel gift shop." I passed over a small shopping bag.

She pulled out my purchases one by one. Sunglasses, a head scarf with dragonflies on it, a "Home of Motown" ball cap, and a key ring.

She held up that last item. "'*I heart Detroit.*' Not sure I do."

"If you conceive this weekend, you're going to be head over heels for Detroit. I figured that might be our good luck charm."

I hadn't meant to say "our"—or any of it, really. But when I saw the key ring, I thought it might be a good omen, like a rabbit's foot. Minimum, it couldn't hurt.

"I'm a scientist. Good luck charms aren't really in my wheelhouse."

"Well, I'm an athlete and good luck charms are definitely in mine. We're a superstitious lot. I always tie my laces in a certain way, with a triple loop, and I say a little prayer between each tie-off." At her skeptical look, I added, "It works seventy percent of the time."

She turned the key ring over in her hands. "Maybe I need to get superstitious." Her gaze strayed to the sunglasses. "This might draw more attention to me."

"Better to have attention than recognition. Wrap up your hair because that shade is kind of striking."

Now why on earth did I say that? Immediately the energy shifted in the car, the air charged and thick.

She touched her hair tentatively. "It's just dark brown. Nothing special."

I passed over her comment because I sure as hell wasn't going to convince her that there was no such thing as "dark brown, nothing special" about Francesca St. James's hair. It had coppery highlights that reminded me of Fall and pumpkins, though I could have been distracted by the start of hockey season. What did I know?

Using the rearview mirror, she tied the scarf so it covered her hair. Kind of grandma Babushka, but then she added the sunglasses, and it was all French New Wave glamour. We tried it with and without the Motown hat and decided to go without.

Outside the car, she popped the trunk, and I pulled out her roller board.

"How do you feel?"

She chewed on her lip. I couldn't see her eyes behind the sunglasses, but I got an impression of enjoyment.

"It's like we're planning a heist."

"The Great Baby Making Caper. Starring the Muppets. As in us."

That made her giggle. I hadn't heard her laughing

much, but it had a husky quality that hit me right in the balls.

"Thanks for coming to my rescue."

"We're not out of the woods yet, Doc. I'll head up to the lobby, and then you follow and check in. Text me your room number when you have it."

I turned to go. Every cell in my body screamed at me to look over my shoulder, but I wasn't sure I'd like what I saw there. Better to stride forth and not get tangled up in whatever was making my pulse thump wildly.

Because this was one of those hotels where you had to switch elevators at the lobby, I planned to loiter in the gift shop while I waited for Franky's text. But I hadn't reckoned on how disasters happen in multiples.

As soon as the doors opened, I ran into my nephew Conor.

"J-man!" We fist bumped and hugged.

Now, I loved all my niblings, but I had a soft spot for Connie, probably because he reminded me most of my big brother. The kid had inherited Theo's talent as well as his exuberance and no-filter way of looking at things. He was starting his maiden season with Detroit, and he was as excited as a puppy in a pile of leaves.

With a guiding hand on his back, I walked several feet away from the elevator because this was a little close for comfort. "Hey, kid, you jazzed for the game?"

"Jazzed about taking you and H apart, you mean? Oh yeah!"

I had no doubt he would do well, but I wasn't ready to to be mowed down just yet.

"So, not that I'm not thrilled to see you, but why are you here?" He lived in Detroit, so he wasn't staying at the hotel.

"Hatch and I were supposed to be meeting for a bite,

but he's not answering his phone. I sent you a bunch of texts as well."

"Yeah, well—" Out of the corner of my eye, I spotted her exiting the parking elevator and heading to the front desk. She was right—she did stand out but no one would recognize her, I was sure of that.

Conor followed my gaze, so I distracted him with a hand on his elbow. "Let's head into the restaurant and call Hatch to come down. I left him in the room, talking to Summer."

"They're having phone sex, aren't they?"

"Thought I'd give them some privacy."

Conor grinned. "That's considerate."

"I'd do the same for you if you managed to stick to one girl."

"What? I wouldn't get phone sex privacy because I like to play the field?"

"You're an exhibitionist. You don't care." We made it to the restaurant entrance, just off the lobby. I could already see NoBo waving at me from a large table, and a couple of the guys were with him.

"You want it to be just us, or are you ready for a little trash talk?"

The Kershaw smile broke out in full. "I wouldn't mind getting into the heads of a few Rebels." He gestured to the hostess that we were joining their table, then turned to me, his expression curious. "J, are you sweating?"

Bricks. I looked over my shoulder. No sign of the sixties film star or her big-face sunglasses. Looked like we were in the clear.

CHAPTER EIGHTEEN

Franky

MY ENTIRE BODY WAS BUZZING.

I couldn't recall ever being this excited. The disguise, the sneaky ascent up the elevator, keeping my sunglasses on during check-in, which I hoped came off as mysterious rather than rude. The only thing missing was a fake ID, and I was glad the desk clerk didn't say my name aloud when I handed over my driver's license. She probably surmised I wanted privacy.

Most thrilling of all was spotting Jason with Conor in the lobby and watching as he surreptitiously steered him away from me to the restaurant. In the mirror behind reception, I spied them standing at the host podium, chatting away as they waited to be seated. I wanted Jason to look at me, but of course that would have defeated the purpose of going under the radar.

And also, *why*? Because we were partners in this

subterfuge, I supposed. It couldn't have been because the idea of sneaking around was sexy.

Jason had looked *so* good in his gray sweats and Rebels zip-up. I couldn't help noticing how his pants had clung to his strong thigh muscles as he sat in my car. How his sheer bulk ate up all the space and made me feel petite. Not that I felt like some Shrek-like ogre in most men's presence, but I did feel oddly feminine in Jason's.

Most likely it was because of how crazily hormonal I usually was whenever he was around. After all, his role was to appear as I was ovulating, and our relationship was wholly focused on what needed to happen to get me pregnant. It definitely placed us in certain biological lanes. Him the provider of sperm, me the vessel for nurturing a child. A heteronormative viewpoint that was strangely arousing.

I sent him a text with my room number, then immediately regretted it. What if someone saw my name pop up on his screen? He was with his nephew and possibly other teammates now, sharing a meal. It wasn't as if he could leave them—

A knock sounded on the door.

I checked the peephole. Jason stood there, hands in the pockets of his sweats, staring straight at me. I had sent that text two minutes ago.

I opened the door, positively giddy with excitement, and grasped the zipper of his jacket to pull him inside. He kicked the door shut behind him.

"I can't believe—"

"We almost got—"

At talking over each other, we stopped and burst into laughter. I lay my forehead against his chest and absorbed the vibrations of his joy as they melded with my own.

I looked up at his smiling face. "That was a close one."

"Sure was. Wasn't expecting Connie to throw his hat in the ring there. Thought it would be Hatch or NoBo who gave us the most trouble."

"The woman at the desk gave me the weirdest look, and then I got in the elevator with one of the newer guys ... Asher something?"

"Hell no!" He gripped my hips and pulled me in. "He didn't recognize you, did he?"

"No. I've never met him, but I've seen his photo online. He exited on the fourth floor, so I'm guessing you're all on that level."

"Yeah, one floor down. When you sent the message, I made my excuses."

And practically stormed up here. That he had arrived so quickly, no muss, no fuss, no games, was both thrilling and confusing.

"This is pretty exciting," I murmured, my hands on his chest. I moved my fingertips furtively, checking for steeliness. He would barely notice, and I would have more data.

His fingers flexed on my hips. Subtle, but undeniably present.

"I feel like we got away with something," he said.

My breathing was coming in shallow draws, and I had the strongest urge to reach for his mouth and cover it with my own. His gaze dipped to my lips, then back to my eyes. My lips again, and oh God, he was going to kiss me.

I wanted it, possibly more than I had ever wanted anything.

But it would complicate an already complicated situation. I stepped back and exhaled.

I avoided looking at him in case I saw something that made me jump into his arms and claim the kiss I so badly wanted. Instead, I picked up the scarf I had used for my disguise—so pretty with its dragonflies—folded it neatly, and placed it on the nightstand.

"This worked so well!" I sounded slightly hysterical. *Calm down. Remember why you're here.* "How much time do you have?"

"I'm meeting the guys for dinner in the lobby at 6pm. I mean, real dinner—right now they're smashing apps in the hotel restaurant."

"So just over an hour. Not that it takes long." I put my hand over my mouth. "I didn't mean to imply that you're speedy or lack stamina in that area."

He tilted his head. "No? Well, it's different when you're going solo. Or when someone else is waiting on the other side of the door for a delivery."

"I suppose it is." I looked around, abruptly aware of how the room's coziness. "Maybe I should leave so you can ..."

"And go where? We can't risk you being seen."

"The bathroom. I can go in there and put on headphones."

"Or you could just stay."

It was like a bomb had exploded. Did he mean I should be in the same room?

Just in case there was any misunderstanding, he added, "And watch."

CHAPTER NINETEEN

Jason

ASK AND YOU MIGHT RECEIVE.

The glittering excitement in her eyes the moment she pulled me into the room had been a sight to behold. And the way she laughed and vibrated and leaned her forehead on my chest told me more about this woman than I'd ever known before.

At heart, she was a rule breaker.

Who else would try to conceive a child in this way? Who else would choose, or accept, a guy so different from her own mindset? This was a woman who pushed boundaries, in her work, in her life, in her mind. She had enjoyed our caper, and I suspected she might be willing to cross another line and enjoy it a little more.

"You want me to ... watch?"

She didn't sound horrified. More ... curious. That was the scientist talking.

I hoped it was also the woman thinking.

Either way, I took it as encouragement and plowed onward. "Is that something you might be interested in?"

The slender column of her throat bulged on a swallow. Rather than answer my question, she posed one of her own. "Would it help you achieve orgasm?"

I could feel my mouth kicking up at the corners. "Yes, Francesca, it would help. Not that I had problems before, but I think I might produce a bigger output if I had someone else participating."

Sure, let's use the science as our excuse.

"What kind of participation would you expect?"

That's more like it. Ever the investigator.

"Whatever you're comfortable with. You can sit in that armchair and watch. Or put that scarf over your eyes and listen. You can sit on the bed and touch me. You can wrap that dainty hand of yours around my cock and stroke."

With each escalation, color crept into her cheeks, and her breathing became more ragged.

"Or you could stay in the bathroom with your headphones on and imagine what I'm doing. Like last time."

She raised an eyebrow. "You have no idea what I was doing last time."

"Sipping tea and stroking your pussy ... cat."

She gave a silent huff of laughter. Another thing about the professor ... she enjoyed a dirty joke.

"Would you expect me to reciprocate? Have you present when I complete my part?"

"Not unless you want that. I recognize it's a special thing for you, a ritual of sorts, and I don't want to interfere with that. It's not a quid pro quo. I just think it would be hotter if I could jerk off in your presence."

She licked her lips. "Okay. Uh, let me get the supplies from the bathroom."

While she did that, I peeled off my jacket and tee. When she returned with the lotion in one hand and the sample cup in the other, I was already pushing my sweats down.

She ran her eyes over my body. "I saw you in one of those holiday calendars once."

"Yeah, did that a few years ago. I've had a few injuries since." Appendix removal, hip surgery.

"You look better now. More ... rugged." Her voice turned to gravel on that last word. She placed the lotion, tissues, and cup on the side table. "Are you sure you want me here?"

"Francesca, nothing would give me more pleasure." My cock had already started swelling as soon as she laid her hands on my chest, and now I was in "intriguing bulge" territory.

Her gaze dipped to my underwear, the cotton straining with my erection—I mean, how could it not? I was turned on. She had turned me on, and she had to have known the power she had over me.

Another dart of her tongue over her lips. "What do you need me to do?"

"What do you want to do?" I didn't want to put any pressure on her. She could have said no, especially once I started stripping, but she was here. Still. Because she wanted to be.

I was banking on her wanting more than just watching.

"Could I touch you?" she asked.

"You can do anything you want."

"That's quite the offer."

Touch me, Doc. Take those eager hands and stroke me from root to tip.

She placed a hand on my chest—and remained still.

Peered up.

Sighed.

"You feel like a marble statue. Like Michelangelo's David."

"That the one who's naked in some museum in Italy?"

She nodded as her fingertips started to wander, mapping the topography of my chest. "The Uffizi in Florence. It was quite shocking at the time, but even more so during the Grand Tours of the nineteenth century. People were scandalized at the sight of marble genitals."

Now "genitals" is probably the least sexy way to describe a guy's junk, but not when spoken by Franky St. James. She was close enough that my dick strained and touched her hip.

She coasted her hand down the hard planes of my stomach and lingered at the waistband of my boxer briefs.

"You should take these off."

"You do it."

"I wasn't planning to be so involved."

"Yet here we are."

Involved in this encounter and maybe in other ways. We were trying to make a baby, and that was about as involved as you could get, I reckoned.

She kept her eyes on mine as she rolled my underwear down, but not all the way. Just enough to let my dick spring free and make itself known.

I would have forgiven her for dropping her gaze to the rather forceful presence between us, but she kept her eyes on mine. Somehow that was hotter, probably because she was wearing those slutty little librarian glasses.

"Lie down," she said softly.

I did as I was told after kicking off the underwear. Lying back with my arm behind my head, I let her look her fill. She tracked every inch of my body, her appreciation evident. I'd never felt sexier than this moment with this woman looking at me like she wanted to lick me all over.

"Touch yourself." Her voice had taken on a husky tone and Jesus, I was hooked. *More of that, baby.*

I took myself in hand and gave my cock a good, hard stroke. I was already leaking. My balls were as heavy as ten-pound gym weights. This wouldn't take long, but damn, I needed it to last.

With the way Franky was looking at me, I needed to stay in this moment forever.

A quick inhale, and there was no doubt her nipples were peaking behind her blouse. Did she want to touch herself? Touch me? Come closer? Kiss me?

Kissing would be personal, though.

Like this already isn't?

I needed her closer. "Sit beside me, Doc."

She didn't hesitate. Something about her quick acquiescence sent a surge of pleasure through my body. I squeezed the base of my cock, anxious to stem the sensations that threatened to run riot through me.

"You saw my calendar?"

"The whole world saw it." She sounded put out.

"Don't like anyone looking at me?"

"I can't begrudge the orphans or kittens the benefit of your time."

So she didn't like anyone seeing me half-naked, not even on behalf of innocent kittens. This revelation was incredible.

"Now, only you get to see me. Right here. Right now." Another stroke, and pre-come seeped over my fingers.

She licked her lips.

Fuckkkk. I wanted that pretty, smart mouth on me, but that would defeat the object of this exercise, which was to get my sperm inside her sweet, hot pussy. I resolved to make it my mission: one day, I'd fuck her mouth, watch her take me all in, and unload down her throat.

Today it was enough to have her want me and not know what to do with it.

She moved a hand to my thigh and gave a light scrape of her nails over the skin. I could feel her energy vibrating, her need this bright, brilliant thing. Maybe it was the baby fever, but I liked to think it was also me.

"As much as you want, Francesca."

"W-what?"

"Touch me wherever you want." *Or yourself.* I didn't say that aloud, though I had to wonder how wet she was. I knew having an orgasm when she did the insemination was supposed to aid in encouraging my boys to swim their little tails off.

Her hand curved around my thigh, in between. I parted my legs to give her access.

"Could I cup your testes?"

All praise the doc's vocabulary. That shouldn't have been hot, but here the fuck we were.

"Cup away."

She fondled and gave a light squeeze, and Christ, that was so damn good. Her fingers were warm, curious, and when she palmed my balls with a slight roughness, I lifted a couple of inches off the bed.

My hand flew faster along the length of my cock, the

sensations building and building in a way I recognized. "I'm gonna come."

She continued to cup and stroke my heavy balls, her slender fingertips driving me wild.

"Francesca, I'm—baby, get the cup."

"What? Oh, right!"

She grabbed the cup off the table and held it over the crown on my dick just as I came. This orgasm was definitely longer and more powerful than before. Not sure if that meant a higher volume, but it felt like more.

More chances of hitting that egg. *Boom.*

I took the cup from her and scooped up as much as I could. I got the impression she was reluctant to touch my dick—apparently my balls were her line in the sand.

I handed the cup off. "Just gonna clean up."

She nodded as I grabbed my clothes and headed to the bathroom. A quick wash—and the addition of clothes, because not dressing would seem presumptuous—and I headed out to the room.

Franky sat on the bed, her hands on her lap, all prim and back to business.

"You okay?"

"I don't think you realize how grateful I am, Jason."

She sounded so serious, nothing like the tease of before. I took a seat beside her.

"I get it."

"I'm sorry, but I think I need some time alone. For the next step."

I was disappointed, but I couldn't let it show. Maybe she felt that part was personal to her and my contribution wasn't necessary beyond the sperm. I couldn't very well cajole her into letting me watch.

I'd flown too close to the sun.

"Sure, whatever you want. This is your show."

"Thank you."

My cue to leave, which I did as quietly as possible.

CHAPTER TWENTY

Franky

"ARE BEAKER AND BUNSEN OKAY?"

Rosie flipped the phone's camera to frame Bunny lying imperiously on the sofa. I assumed Beaker was lying terrified under it.

"Of course they are. It's like a vacation for them when Momma's out of town. So how are things in Motor City?"

I filled her in on my adventures in sperm delivery—the caper aspect—though I left out the steamier details. That memory certainly helped to fuel the required orgasm as I completed my end of the bargain after Jason left my hotel room.

My sister laughed at our shenanigans. "I still can't believe that you and Jason are now baby-making besties."

"I wouldn't say that," I said glumly. "There's this weird tension between us."

"Oh?"

"I think he wouldn't mind if we had sex."

She cackled. "Of course he wouldn't mind! I wouldn't care for a quick roll in the hay—said no man ever. Has he asked?"

"No, but he—he jerked off in front of me."

"Hello! And you're only telling me now?"

I sighed. "Things were vibing after the sneaky hotel check-in. I think we both enjoyed the subterfuge and there was this energy between us, like buzzing electricity, and while we were thinking of the logistics of giving him space to produce his donation, he asked if I wanted to stay and watch."

"Yeah, he did! And?"

My cheeks heated. "It was very ... sexy."

"And how involved were you?"

"A little, but then I asked him to leave right after." I had wanted him to stay, but we had already crossed too many lines. "It's weird that he wants to be part of this, isn't it?"

Rosie hummed. "The sex part or the baby part?"

"Both?"

"I don't think you realize how amazing you are. Or how attractive! Were your glasses on or off?"

"On."

"There you go! He digs your nerdy persona. As for why he wants to be involved with the baby, I can't really say. I assume you've asked him."

"He doesn't trust relationships, but he wants a chance to be a father."

My sister thought on that for a second. "Sounds like you have that in common."

"What do you mean?"

"Come on, Franks. Kendra did a number on you, and it certainly didn't help that some of the guys you've dated have been unappreciative of your intellect. I'm not sure of Jason's situation, but I've heard he doesn't get along with his dad, so maybe that factors into it somehow?"

Maybe. But I suspected something else with Jason. Something that stopped him from committing.

Not that I wanted him to commit to me. But if he wanted to be part of my baby's life, I needed him to be serious about it.

"I get the impression that he's interested in making the baby the old-fashioned way."

"Bow chicka wow wow! Now we're talking. And you're worried about all the emotions wrapped up in that?"

"Yes? It's sex with the purpose of creating a child. That seems highly emotional to me."

Rosie blew out a breath. "But only if you let it be. It's not like you have a thing for Jason, do you?"

"God no! But he is exceptionally attractive, more than I'm used to." Or deserve. "However, we are not compatible in any way other than, perhaps, sexually. And even then, I can't be sure."

I had a pretty good idea, though.

"What's the worst thing that could happen?"

I fall in love with him and then I have to see him—forever—because he's the father of my child.

"The sex is terrible?"

Rosie chortled. "Better you know now instead of fantasizing about it and thinking you missed out."

She had a point. Though I already knew: the sex would not be terrible.

Jason

. . .

SURROUNDED BY CHICAGO REBELS PLAYERS, Conor stood at the table in Pico's, a Mexican restaurant we had found a couple of blocks from the hotel, and raised a glass.

"Here's to a good game tomorrow, a hard-fought battle where the Motors set the tone for the rest of the season! AKA kick Rebels ass!"

I shared a quick glance with Hatch. "Why is he here again?"

My nephew squinted up at his baby brother. "Because he's a Motors PSYOP. Everyone thinks he's a goof when really, he's a menace."

Forward Cody Jacobs threw a balled-up napkin at Connie. "You're the opposition! Why are we letting you make toasts?"

"Because I'm new to the league and you all think I'm the cutest motherfucker to ever walk this green earth."

Peyton Bell, another of the Rebels forwards, shrugged. "He is kind of cute. Like a mascot."

I pulled Conor down to the seat beside me. "Best not to outstay your welcome."

"I could never." He leaned over to lock eyes with his older brother, seated on my other side. "How's your girl?"

"She's good. Sent me a picture of her desk at the office." Summer was a hockey stats nerd and had recently joined Lauren's new sports talent agency as an analyst. Hatch showed us a photo of a desk in an office, but instead of folders and office equipment, there was a full-on cheese plate.

"Cheese?"

He grinned. "Uh huh. It's our thing."

I slid a glance to Conor. "It's their thing."

"Damn, that's romantic," his brother said. "You gonna jerk off to that cheese plate later?"

Hatch nodded. "I just might. Or maybe one of the racy photos my girl sent me."

"Fun times with your hotel roomie later, Uncle J."

Not if I could help it. The idea that Franky was in the same hotel and no one but me knew was making me a little crazy. My phone pinged and I surreptitiously checked it.

"The doc again? What's going on?" Conor had seen the incoming text from Franky earlier, but as far as he knew I was speaking to the team physician.

"Nah, but I should give him a call."

Thankfully, the meal was at an end, though NoBo was trying to convince everyone to order tres leches cakes all around. I had promised Franky I'd deliver another sample before the night was through—hedging our bets seemed the way to do it—but I wasn't sure how appropriate it was for me to ask her to participate.

Had she hated what happened earlier? She had ushered me out mighty quickly, and while I knew the sample was viable for a short period of time, I couldn't help getting the impression she had been embarrassed about what occurred. As much as I hated the idea, this time, I would retreat to our previous method.

DOC

Are you nearby?

ME

Can come over now.

DOC

Yes, please do.

As I headed back to the hotel, I wondered about couples with fertility problems, the ones that had to time sex to the point where it turned into a chore. I tried to imagine sex with Franky as a chore. Or just sex with Franky, period. Unfortunately, a little too easy to picture.

And there I was getting hard again, when really that was not the energy I needed here. I needed to treat this as the job it was and not let any other factors, well, *factor.*

I had barely raised my hand to knock when the door opened.

Damn, she looked sexy in those leggings and a Lakeshore U sweatshirt with her glasses slightly askew, her hair bundled up and held in place with a clip. The clip was shaped like a snail shell, which tracked, of course.

"Hi," she said brightly. She seemed nervous.

"Hey there."

We stood staring, like drinking each other in was an Olympic sport.

"Could I come in?"

"Oh yes! Of course!"

I closed the door behind me. "I should say sorry."

Her brow crumpled. "Really?"

"What happened earlier. I crossed a line."

"You think so?"

"Don't you?"

"When you left, I felt awful." Her eyes welled.

Damn, I had really screwed up here. I grasped her hand and sat her down on the bed. "Why, Doc?"

"Because—because I panicked. I wanted you to be here for the next part. But I was uncomfortable with what it said about me. About being needy. I don't want you to ever think I'm clingy or desperate for your attention."

If she needed me, she only had to ask. I would be there

for her, no matter what. After all, we would be linked for life because of this baby.

"It's okay to need people."

"Up to a certain point. I think I was worried that the intimacy of it all would be confusing. We're not a couple, at least not in the traditional sense, and I don't want you to feel obligated to hold my hand through this."

"Yet I didn't mind when *your* hand held my balls."

She snorted. "Okay, down to brass tacks."

"Brass balls, more like."

"You certainly have them." Her smile was a little sad. "You're braver than me, Jason. You have desires and wants, and you put it out there. While I have desires and wants, and I put them back in a box."

I understood her reticence. Nerds never had it easy.

"Yet, you put this plan in motion. You turned this need you had for a baby into something actionable. Made it happen with some outside-the-box thinking."

"You think so?"

I smiled. "I do. And it's understandable that what's happening draws us closer together. Gives us all sorts of ideas and pushes the boundaries."

"The boundaries are there for a reason," she murmured, "yet crossing them is quite thrilling."

I inhaled deeply and took my shot. "Are you trying to tell me that you'd like this baby-making business to be more ... sexy?"

"I don't think it could get *less* sexy. Syringes are a bit of a buzzkill."

I was still holding her hand. I traced a finger over her palm, then her wrist. She shivered.

"You'd like to go a more natural route. A sexier route." I leaned in. "You want me inside you when I come?"

I suspected she wanted to remember how her baby was conceived and "turkey baster" was not it.

Her mouth wobbled. "Only if you'd like that."

"Oh, I would. Very much. But I have a special request."

"You do?"

I nodded. "If we do this, we do it my way. Do what I tell you, and I promise you won't regret changing the rules of play."

A tiny gasp that tugged at my groin. The doc liked Bossy Jason.

"As long as everything we do is aimed at making a baby."

"Are you trying to get out of certain sex acts?"

She bit her lip. "I'm just not sure certain sex acts will contribute to the enterprise."

I stood and removed my jacket, then my tee. "Such as?"

Just as before, she couldn't take her eyes off my chest. I rubbed my hand over my pecs to let her know how touchable I was.

"Which sex acts, Francesca?"

"Things like non-penetrative sex. While undoubtedly pleasurable, it would be a distraction from the main goal here."

"So the goal is a baby, and I've been doing some research."

"Oh?" She looked hopeful, or maybe she liked the idea of me doing research.

I pushed down my sweats, my briefs with them. "On orgasms. How more powerful ones can trigger uterine contractions and draw the sperm to the egg."

Her eyes were focused on my cock, which I now took in hand—and stroked.

She pushed her thighs together. Perfect.

"That's not all I found out. Eyes up here, Doc."

She glared at me, but I could see that hint of humor playing on her lips. "Are you saying you don't want me to pay attention to your penis?"

"Not when I'm telling you all about my scientific findings. Take off that sweatshirt."

She peeled it off, revealing a white bra, trimmed in lace. And whaddya know? As suspected, the doc had a gorgeous rack with beautiful swells above the border of the cups.

My thirteen-year-old self high-fived present-day me.

"Carry on," she murmured.

"What's that?" *Those pretty tits ...*

"Your scientific findings."

Right. "So a woman's orgasm changes the pH balance of her pussy—"

"Vagina."

Now it was my turn to suppress a smile. "So it's more receptive to a guy's swimmers. Leggings off. Now."

"To be precise," she said, "the orgasm changes the vaginal pH to more closely match the pH of the sperm sample. This creates a more hospitable environment for the sperm." At the mention of sperm, her eyes fell to my cock, so I moved in a little closer.

"Love it when you talk dirty, Doc. You're overdressed."

"Oh, right!" Pushing off her leggings, she left on white panties. They matched the bra, and I could see the dark shadow of her pubic hair. I liked that she wasn't overly groomed down there.

"So we're agreed, orgasms are good for the baby-making process."

"They're good, but they can be just as easily achieved with (a) missionary for you, and (b) masturbation for me.

Any bonus sexual acts are leaning into the pleasure aspect rather than the procreation."

I curled my hand around her jaw. "If I can create an earthquake inside you, baby, then that's gonna send my swimmers straight to home base. And if you can milk my cock with, first, your tight little fist, then your greedy pussy, then I'm going to shoot so hard your eggs will be screaming for my boys. Now how about you touch my cock and let me show you how good this baby-making business can be?"

CHAPTER TWENTY-ONE

I HAD ALWAYS SUSPECTED Jason Isner was a crude-mouthed asshole jock at his core.

What I had never suspected was how much it would turn me on.

While the science on penetration, sperm volume, and vaginal pH was mixed, the basics were the same: get the sperm into the uterus. And if we could enjoy the process along the way, then what was the harm?

It's only sex.

Tied to my baby-making dream.

I could separate it. I would have to.

Besides, Jason was giving me this gift. Why not make this enjoyable for him? Not only that, give him a more active role to suit his rollicking id and need to play at alpha baby daddy.

He hadn't exactly shoved his dick in my face, but it was

there: flagrant, rampant, begging for my attention. A little like the man to which it belonged.

I touched a finger to the crown, rubbed along the slit— and sucked the salty fluid off my finger.

He groaned. "That's my girl."

I was nothing of the sort, yet that possessive utterance thrilled through my veins. Apparently, I wanted to belong to someone.

The power I felt as I wrapped my hand around him was electrifying. I thought for a moment that maybe I could own him with this small gesture. Retain some control over the situation. Stroking up and down, I relished the feel of the velvet sheath over steel. Part of me wanted to lick and suck, but that was far too removed from the goal.

But touching him felt so good. Watching the pearls of pre-come leaking over my fingers was much more arousing than I expected. My nipples peaked to hard points, my panties turned damp with desire.

His face was creased with an almost savage lust. "You keep that up, I won't last."

And we needed him to last, at least for a little while.

"Lie back, Francesca."

I pulled back the covers and lay down, my head against the pillows. Jason stood over me, drinking me in. I wasn't the dewy, fresh ingenue he was probably used to. I was closer to forty than thirty, with cellulite dimpling my thighs and a less-than-flat stomach.

He didn't seem to mind. If anything, my body appeared to excite him.

From the nightstand, he grabbed the scarf he had bought for me to use in my disguise.

"What's that for?"

"Earlier I mentioned superstitions. Little things we do

as part of our pre-game routine." He wrapped the scarf around my wrist and tied it in a knot. "I usually tie my laces three times." He knotted the scarf again. "For luck."

"I don't believe in that kind of thing."

He tied it again.

"If you don't believe in it, then there's no harm in doing it, right?"

He completed the third knot.

"If it makes you feel better." It was okay to indulge him on this. Just a silly superstition.

He knelt on the bed and moved a hand to my inner thigh. "So soft," he murmured as he coasted that hand down over my underwear. Laying the heel of his palm flat against my vaginal opening, he gave me a dirty rub that had me arching off the bed. My instinct was to close my legs.

"I need full access, Francesca. But if that's not okay …"

"It's okay." More than okay.

He peeled off my panties, then parted my thighs once more, all while watching. Devouring me with his gaze. That heated regard, that intense absorption of my body, made me wetter than I had ever been with a man. And he had barely touched me!

"We really should … get on with it."

"Should we?"

"I don't want to, uh, waste that erection."

He snickered. "Are you implying I can't get hard again? Or stay that way?" As if I had challenged him, he moved between my legs and spread me further apart. With his fingers, he touched, stroked, speared, and claimed me, spreading my wetness around, glancing brushes against my clitoris that drove me wild but never enough to get me close. Which was good. I didn't want to risk climaxing before he buried himself deep.

"You like this?"

"Yes," I barely managed.

"And this?"

I loved that he was checking in. I nodded. Nodded again.

"Tell me."

"Y-yes."

That pleased him. And oddly, *that* pleased me. Decades of feminist striving out the window.

"I want to taste you."

"You-you don't have to. I know most guys don't like it."

"Got a source for that, Professor?"

I swallowed as another lick of sensual flame shivered through me. "Just anecdotally."

His expression flickered then returned to that confident arrogance I was starting to enjoy. "Some asshole you dated?"

"It was a personal preference." *Of his.*

"That left your sweet pussy out in the cold." He moved in close, his breath hot between my thighs. "Do you like this, Francesca?"

"I-I don't know. I've never had anyone perform cunnilingus on me."

I was thirty-eight years old. The admission should have been embarrassing, but this was a night for honesty. If we were successful, there would be no more of these encounters. This might be my last shot at good sex.

"Just tug on my hair if you want me to stop."

"O-okay."

His tongue lapped between my legs, the sensations incredible. My hips shifted, my core craved. It had never felt ... never been so ... never ... *oh.*

I tugged on his hair. He looked up.

"Sorry, I-I don't want you to stop. I just needed to express my ... approval somehow."

"Moan, scream, scratch, tug—whatever works, baby." And then he returned to making me do all those things. Finally, I had to push him away.

"I'm too close. You need to be inside me now."

"So bossy," he murmured, but he moved over me and settled, rubbing his erection—which I need *not* have worried about—over my soaking folds.

"Please," I begged, not caring how I sounded. Desperate, and I worried it wasn't just for a baby.

His chest against mine, the lovely weight of him, the feel of him hard against me—it was all too perfect, and he hadn't even penetrated me yet. I worried I would orgasm the moment he inched inside, and it would be over too quickly.

I suspected he was concerned about this, too. His hand stroked my ass, squeezed and kneaded. His mouth was close to mine, and his eyes held my gaze as he waited.

I ran my thumb along his bottom lip, desperate to ask for the one thing that terrified me most.

Kiss me.

It was such a personal request, so unnecessary to the goal of conception. At the last second, my innate common sense kicked in.

Kissing would not further the mission.

"Please," I whispered.

He stroked inside me with a single deep thrust that made me come at once.

"Fuck," he murmured against my lips as my vaginal walls gripped him fiercely. "You feel ... so ... tight. So ... good."

"You have to—"

"I know, Francesca. I've … got it from here." He rocked into me, rolled out, maintained the rhythm as those hunter green eyes bored into my soul. Filling me completely, he moved inside, finding points of pleasure I never knew existed.

He moved a hand to where we were joined, his fingers parting my sensitive flesh and stroking my clitoris.

"That's it, baby. You're gonna come for me again."

That had never happened. Sometimes it wouldn't even happen once, but apparently Jason Isner knew more about my body than I did. Waves of sensation were starting to build and build and build until I could contain it no longer. I moaned as the release wrung me out and left me limp.

He cupped under my thigh and thrust once, twice, three times, finally unloading a roar of pleasure and a flood of heat and baby dreams inside me.

He stilled, but stayed, as if remaining inside me would create some sort of protective barrier, allowing his boys to reach their goal without hindrance. Scientifically, this was absurd, but unscientifically … I was not opposed.

I loved how he felt. Inside, outside, all around.

He lay his forehead against mine. "I have a good feeling about this."

So do I. But did I mean the baby or something else?

After a moment, I let out the breath I'd been holding. "I-I have to go through my routine."

"Right." He slid out, dare I say, reluctantly? *Ludicrous, Franky. Absolutely ludicrous.* "What do you need?"

"Pillows."

He passed two over and I placed them under my butt, raising my hips. I was just about to put the coverlet over my body when he beat me to it. Either he was extremely sensitive to my needs, or he didn't want to look at me any longer.

"I'll just clean up."

"Okay."

You bet I looked as he headed to the bathroom—that hockey butt was amazing. This whole experience had been amazing, a once in a lifetime opportunity. As I fingered the knots in the scarf on my wrist, I focused on wishing for conception, praying that his puck found the net. I was suddenly tired, worn out from the drive and the stress of arriving late, as well as the anxiety of sex with a hockey god.

Though that had been lovely. A memory to treasure, especially if it resulted in the ultimate gift of all.

CHAPTER TWENTY-TWO

Jason

SHE HAD DOZED off by the time I came out of the bathroom, curled up under the covers, dreaming about being a mom, or maybe dreaming about what had just happened.

Wishful thinking, Isner.

As for me, I was awake and dreaming, because that was probably the hottest sex I'd ever experienced.

Was it the fact we didn't like each other before? Was it the sneaking around? Was it because she wanted this kid so badly that she was prepared to go to any lengths to get it, even hooking up with a guy she didn't respect much? Or maybe it was just super sexy to go raw and know your seed was making a mad dash for the finish line, that biological imperative taking over and making everything so goddamn fucking primal.

I had to say I didn't object to her following my instructions, or how her eyes hazed over with my dirty talk. Honestly, I had loved every minute.

But now that I had fulfilled my function, I needed to go. Only my feet were suddenly clay, a bad trait for a hockey player. If I had skates on, could I glide my way out of here? Or would I be stuck at the bathroom door, staring at the woman who might soon be the mother of my kid?

I moved closer and took a seat on the bed beside her. She stirred, her eyes fluttered open, and she smiled.

That smile was something else. So she was in a vulnerable spot, well-fucked and sexed-out after the good time I'd given her. As she had never shown me anything close to that kind of affection, I had to blame it on the power of my cock.

Dick of a thousand smiles.

I couldn't help myself: I had to touch her again. I pushed a strand of hair behind her ear. She had removed her glasses and placed them on the nightstand.

"I fell asleep?"

"Just for a few minutes. I think you're worn out with the stress of it all." My fingertips liked where they'd landed. They continued to stroke the side of her head, and she leaned into my hand like a sleepy kitten.

"Are you leaving?"

"I thought you might want some time to process what happened."

She blinked slowly. "We said we'd try again tomorrow before you headed off to morning skate."

I nodded, weird hope taking root in my chest. "We did."

"It might be easier if ... you stayed."

"I wouldn't have to worry about getting caught going back and forth."

"No. And while there's no scientific evidence that multiple attempts in a twenty-four-hour period increase the chances of conception, there's also no scientific evidence that says they don't."

I *loved* when she applied the science.

"If I stayed here, we could take another shot or two before the morning."

No correction to my addition of "or two" to that proposal.

The coverlet had slipped, revealing those stellar tits cupped by that sexy bra. Jesus, I was getting turned on again, but I had to give her a chance to recover.

"I'm kind of hungry, though," she said.

"You haven't eaten?" I'd had dinner with the boys, but it seemed like hours ago. "What do you need, Doc? We need to keep your strength up."

"It's probably not great for pre-natal nutrition, but I'd love a hamburger."

"Give the little one a taste of meat, huh?"

She looked prim. "I'm not going to even bother correct all that's wrong with that statement. Any chance you're hungry, too?"

Hell yeah, I was. For more of that sharp mouth and sweet pussy. But for now, I'd make do with room service.

"Let me grab the menu."

WE PUT IN OUR ORDERS—CHEESEBURGER for her, double cheeseburger for me—and then we sat on the bed, side by side. She had covered up with her LU sweatshirt and leggings and insisted I do the same.

I got the impression she liked my body a little too much.

A few minutes later, she got a call. "Sorry, I have to take this."

"Go ahead."

It sounded like her place of work, though it was kind of late. I'd assumed her gig was more nine-to-five. Her manner went from the playfulness of earlier to the gravity I expected she needed to project in her role as a serious academic. I heard snatches—something about a form that needed to be signed, a scheduled video call with someone, an article she was writing. I strained my ear for details, wanting to know more about her. My brother Sean had the goods from years of friendship, and I was playing catch up. All I knew was that she wanted a baby.

She clicked off and gave me a tentative smile. "Work."

"Everything okay?"

"Yes, just some questions about an article I'm co-authoring with a colleague in Edinburgh, and which journal we should submit to. My preference is for an open access publication, which means the department or I am on the hook for submission fees."

"You have to pay to publish?"

"Not always. Most traditional journals will take a submission and, after a rigorous peer-review process, will publish if they think it meets their standards and the needs of their readership. Then researchers, but more often, university libraries pay massive subscription fees for the privilege of reading the article they or their own faculty wrote."

That sounded screwy. I tried to wrap my head around it. "So, you do the research and provide the product, then the journal doesn't pay you a dime but instead makes you or your university pay to read it when it's published?"

"Exactly!" I had evidently hit a nerve. "And often the research is federally funded, so your tax dollars paid for the research and private companies, aka academic publishers, reap the profit so I can say I'm published in a peer-reviewed journal."

"Hmm. I'm guessing the publishers tell you they're providing a valuable service."

"You know it. Which is why they hate open access journals. Those journals make the work available to everyone—no subscriptions required—but someone has to pay to keep the lights on. Lakeshore University funds some open access publishing submissions, but the chair of my department has to sign off on it. He and I have history—"

"What kind of history?"

She rubbed a cloth over her glasses. "We slept together a couple of years ago while he was working at another college."

My pulse spiked. "Now he's your boss."

"Correct."

"Was he on your list?"

"He was. But I wasn't sure he would make a good candidate. He would want to be in a relationship. He didn't like it when I told him we weren't compatible." She caught my eye. "Sexually."

This was more like it. "Earth didn't move, huh?"

"You could say that. It's made things a little awkward since he became my department head. Also, I applied for the same job, so there's a weird dynamic. Having to go cap in hand to ask him to fund the publication of my article is annoying. He's rather pompous about it and annoyingly officious in his new role."

Never good to shit where you eat. "So tell me about your research."

"Oh, that would bore you."

Maybe she assumed I wouldn't understand. "Try me."

She paused a moment, probably thinking of how to explain it to a dummy like me. "My current research is on the mating habits of gastropods, particularly pulmonate land snails and slugs. I'm studying how often self-fertilization occurs."

I already knew mating was involved somewhere, and I had a *ton* of questions. "You mean snail sex?"

"Correct. Many species of gastropod—that's the class name we give to snails and slugs—are hermaphrodites. They have both male and female sexual organs that are simultaneously functional. Basically they can impregnate themselves, if necessary."

"And they do that?"

"Not always. That's what's interesting. Why don't they? Why do they go through mating rituals and seek out the company of others in their species to procreate? We assume it's because there's a biological imperative to keep the genetic line varied and less susceptible to inbreeding. Yet we don't know for sure. If humans didn't need a partner to procreate, and there were no biological risks to self-fertilization, would they dispense with the necessity of the mating ritual?"

"Isn't that what sperm banks are for?"

She shrugged. "But it would have been *so* much easier if I could produce my own sperm."

I chuckled. "One woman shop, no need to even leave the house. But I have to say the way we went about it tonight was a whole lot more fun."

She blushed and hot damn, I liked that. "That's probably why slugs and snails go to the trouble. Fun."

My phone buzzed with a text from Hatch.

Hey, you okay?

ME

Yeah, met a friend. Don't wait up.

HATCH

Very suspicious, but okay.

"One of your teammates?"

"Hatch. I told him I was staying out for the night."

Another blush, and while I wanted to tease, I held off. The vibe between us was too enjoyable, and I didn't want to ruin it.

The food arrived and we settled in to eat as I asked her more questions about her research. Then she dropped this bomb.

"Another reason the mating ritual is dangerous for some species is the risk of apophallation."

"Do I want to know?"

She had a sly smile on her face. "They can become locked together during mating and when wiggling apart won't work, one snail bites the penis off the other."

"Jesus!"

"Sometimes the penis-owner will even bite its own member off."

"Seems a bit over the top."

She assessed her half-eaten burger. "Some guys will do anything to avoid staying the night."

I snorted. Christ, she was funny. How had I not known this?

"What?" she asked, because I was staring at her like a lovesick fool.

"It's just strange that we never knew each other. Like this."

Her smile was like a secret I wanted to unlock. "I suppose it is."

CHAPTER TWENTY-THREE

Franky

THERE HAD BEEN a distinct shift in the energy between us. Sex had a habit of changing the game.

But there was more to it than that. We were talking, and color me shocked that he was interested in my work. He had no problem following along, either, and had even asked intelligent questions.

Not such a dumb jock after all.

It had been a long time since I slept in the same bed as a man—Marcus, actually, two years ago—and I was nervous. I took a shower after dinner while Jason tidied up and called room service to pick up the dirty dishes. Cleaning up would make me feel better, and I imagined the sperm had already made their way to my uterus (probably high fiving each other on the way). There would be another chance during the night.

I shivered at the thought. More sex. More orgasms.

More of that perfect weight on me, his calloused hands kneading my butt, maybe his mouth on my breasts. He hadn't done that yet, and I longed to have him imprint himself on every part of me. I was at risk of becoming attached here. Hopefully I'd be brave enough to metaphorically bite the penis off and send him on his way.

When I came out of the bathroom, the lights were dim except for one nightlight on his side.

He has a side.

He was under the covers, shirtless and grinning. "Cute T."

It was a picture of a snail with the slogan, "Snailed it!"

"My brother Devon got it for me." I slipped under the covers. "Are you looking forward to the new season?"

He knew I was nervous, but he didn't mock. "Yeah, I am. I felt like I'd done all I could in Boston, and to be honest, I wanted to be closer to family."

"Sean said you don't really get along with your dad."

"Oh, he did, did he?"

Oh dear. "Sorry, it's none of my business."

"No, it's fine. Just odd to think of you talking about me to Sean."

"So when you say you want to be closer to family—"

"I mean Theo and his lot. Ezra and Liam. My mom, too. But not Nick."

"How come?"

He leaned back, his arm behind his neck to reveal a surprisingly attractive tuft of underarm hair. I wanted to snuggle in right there.

He noticed me noticing. Another cocky smirk.

"Let's keep the pillow talk to after."

"After what?"

"After you show me what's under that cute T-shirt."

"You know what's under there."

He reached for my chest, turning his hand so his knuckles grazed the tops of my breasts through the cotton.

"Pretty tits, but no bra this time." He lay back, pushed the covers down, and patted his abs. "Over here, Doc."

"What?"

"I want you on top with your gorgeous tits bouncing while you bounce on my cock."

I blew out a breath. "Your mouth."

He leaned in, his lips close to mine. "Think you like my mouth."

I did. I liked its shape, its texture under my thumb, that sensual curve when he found me amusing. But mostly I liked what came out of it: anything from sexual innuendo to soothing words, all wrapped up in that deep-seated confidence in who he was.

"Me in the cowgirl position would be counterproductive to the gravitational forces required to ensure your sperm reaches its goal."

"Damn, those big words you use are hot. And I told you we were doing it my way."

With just a fraction of his warrior strength, he scooped me up and placed me astride his stomach.

"Oof!" I gasped as I settled my sensitive flesh over the heat of his abs.

"No panties."

"It seems foolish to place barriers in the way of this."

His eyes smoked over. He liked that—taking me without protection, the intimacy of skin-on-skin, my core damp, and getting damper.

Pulling at the hem of my tee, he raised an eyebrow. I loved his eyebrows—they told stories, and right now, the story was: *you're in for a helluva good time.* Was it odd to enjoy this?

Making a baby should be a joyful experience. But only if you were in a loving, committed relationship.

I didn't need Jason Isner for anything more than his sperm. I didn't need his gorgeous green eyes or square jaw or arrogant smile. I didn't need the comfort of his body or the assurance he gave me that maybe I wasn't so crazy to start this journey after all.

But this was nice. More than nice.

I peeled off my T-shirt, suddenly conscious of my age. My breasts in cups looked decent, but without, they just ... flopped there.

He cupped the weight of one and gave a squeeze that made me squirm, producing more delicious sensation as my core became wetter. Scooting up, he positioned himself so he could lick a nipple, then take it in his mouth with a lusty suck. He plumped and kneaded as he suckled, creating rivulets of pleasure throughout my veins. Behind my rear, I felt the insistent bob of his cock as it sought my attention. It would get its turn.

But first, I would get mine.

I pulled back, and he was forced to release my breast with a pop and a graveled groan. Leaning over to the nightstand, I picked up the dragonflies scarf I had removed earlier before we ate.

"Superstitious, Doc?"

"Not in the slightest." I wrapped it around his wrist and twisted, then tied it to the corner of the headboard.

"Now, that's unexpected," he said, his voice husky.

"How many times did you say you tie your laces before a game?" I knew but I wanted him to say it.

"Three." I tied two more knots in the scarf. "Still have my other hand free, though."

"This bed is too large for me to tie off your other hand. But I expect you to be honorable and not use it."

His lips twitched. "Honorable? Not sure I've ever been accused of that."

I moved my rear back fractionally until it met his cock, and then I rubbed myself on him. His eyes fluttered closed, then opened.

"See how far you can get," I murmured.

He placed his free arm behind his head. "You're in charge, Francesca."

I wasn't but it was nice of him to say so.

Raising myself up a few inches, I reached behind to grip him, loving the hiss of pleasure he released as I touched him. And when I lined him up and sank down to take him in fully, his free hand formed a fist. He wanted to touch me badly.

So I touched him enough for both of us, all while we stared at each other. Watching this powerful man unable to move—or choosing to suffer under restraints from which he could easily break free—was exhilarating. I coasted my palms over his strong chest muscles as I seated myself deeper and deeper.

"You're gonna need to move soon," he gutted out.

"Worried I might get stuck here?"

I could feel him swelling inside me at the notion.

"No other place I want to be." The words emerged ragged. "But you need to work my cock, baby. Show it some love."

The way he spoke to me ... I was so turned on. So close to coming, and neither of us had touched my clitoris. Just his mouth, his words, the fullness, the secrecy of it—I was completely undone.

I leaned forward, gripping the headboard, placing my breasts within reach of his mouth. He leaned up to take one inside, at the same time thrusting up into me. Pushing deeper.

As I lost myself and a little of my heart, inch by glorious inch.

CHAPTER TWENTY-FOUR

Jason

I AWOKE TO A BUZZING. My phone? I checked to find
a couple of messages from Franky.

> I'm outside.

> Are you awake?

Then another buzzing sound, but this time my
intercom.

My phone said 7:15am, which meant I'd been asleep for
three hours. The season was in full swing with five games
behind us. The last eight days had been a killer road trip—
won two, lost one—and I was looking forward to pizza on
the sofa, catching up on my shows, and icing my knee,
which was playing up after the last game in LA.

But Franky was here.

Was this bad news? If she was pregnant, she would

probably have texted after my last game. Showing up in person seemed like an ominous sign.

I bounded down the stairs and opened the door. She had descended a couple of steps, evidently giving up on rousing my tired ass, but now she turned. In her brown blazer over a cream turtleneck and a green corduroy knee-length skirt with tobacco-colored boots, she was what you would see in Merriam's beside "liberal arts professor, subspecies: New England."

She pushed back her glasses. "You're awake."

"Wasn't that the point of the messages and the loud buzzing?" I stepped outside. "Are you okay?"

Her gaze dipped over my body. Color pinked her cheeks, but it might have been the chill in the air. "It's thirty-five degrees, Jason. You're going to freeze."

So I was in my underwear. She was lucky I was even wearing that. Or maybe unlucky she'd missed out on the main event: a naked Jason Isner.

"Are *we* okay?"

Her lips curved, her smile spreading like golden butter across her face.

"We are."

That big, and getting bigger by the second, grin could mean only one thing.

"Doc, are you ... pregnant?"

"Yes!"

I'd imagined this moment. I had thought that maybe there would be smug satisfaction at having made a woman, *this woman*, pregnant. But that didn't even enter the picture.

Okay, perhaps a little.

Mostly, I felt an overwhelming abundance of joy.

I picked her up and spun her around. "We're havin' a baby!"

She gasped a laugh and thumped my shoulder. "Jason, put me down!"

"Nope."

"You're going to put your back out."

"Not a chance. I'm as limber as they come." I could barely feel the throb in my knee. "Plus, this might be the last chance I can lift you because you're about to get heav-*y*."

That made her laugh, and she was still laughing as I brought her inside and kicked the door shut. I placed her down gently but kept my hands on her hips.

"How are you feeling? When did you find out? Have you seen a doctor? I mean, a real doctor, not a PhD. No offense, but you're not really qualified to birth your own kid here, Doc, so don't even think that's an option."

"Never said I was. To answer your questions, I'm feeling fine. No morning sickness yet. I found out yesterday after I took six different brand pregnancy tests. I've not seen a doctor, but I have an appointment the day after tomorrow. And yes, she's a real doctor, though she might have a PhD as well. Many medical professionals do."

Wow. How had I gone from thinking this woman was an insufferable know-it-all to loving that she had all the answers?

She smiled up at me. "Your boys did well."

"Told you spicing it up was a good option. My swimmers needed the freedom to roam."

"I guess they did. You were right, but don't get used to hearing it."

That night in Detroit, almost three weeks ago, we had used that hotel bed well. Once more after dinner, and twice again overnight because we couldn't keep our hands off each other. We had stayed in touch by text, but nothing beat seeing her in person.

We were going to be parents.

I grinned. "Come into the kitchen and tell me all the details."

"Sorry, I have a class to teach at eight, and then I have a call with a colleague in Philadelphia."

Disappointment checked me. "Okay. You want to come over tonight and celebrate?"

"I have a prior appointment, I'm afraid. I wanted to give you the news in person, but there isn't really anything more to tell."

Hmm. Why did this feel like the kiss off? And more to the point, why was I trying to force her to play at happy families? Sure, I wanted to be involved, but this was her deal. We were not a couple.

"Okay, I should let you get on."

She took a step back, then jumped forward, and gave me a hug.

"Thank you, Jason."

Wrapping her up tight, I shut my eyes and touched my lips to her hair. It had been forever since I'd held her, and knowing the last time was the night we made a baby washed over me like a soft wave of lust mixed with pride and not a little sadness.

Because this also felt like goodbye.

Goodbye to our efforts to conceive. To sneaking around. To the fun times we had in bed—and out of it, if I was being honest.

She pulled back, though her fingers lingered on my chest. "I should let you get back to sleep. You played well this last week."

I had something to play for, that sizzle of anticipation. Now I had even more on the line.

I was going to be a dad.

"Thanks to you, too, Francesca." I kissed her forehead, inhaled her scent, let it buoy me. "We did it."

She nodded, words seeming to fail her. I knew how she felt. Then she stepped outside to get on with her day without me.

CHAPTER TWENTY-FIVE

Jason

EVERY YEAR my brother threw a banger of a Halloween party at his house. As we were scheduled to play a home game on the holiday itself, it meant this year's event had to happen the night before. I loved these parties. Ever since I was twelve, coming here—or to any gathering at Theo's house—cemented my love for his family and the realization that my dad was lacking in all things parental. I suspected my father had been invited tonight, but he usually declined because seeing his ex-wife, my mother, reminded him of his bad behavior. I wouldn't miss him, but it was nice to see my mom. I waved at her. Looked like she was dressed as a witch. Classic.

The first person I ran into was Conor, but not the Conor I knew. He wore a very tight yellow sweater cropped to reveal his abs, along with skinny jeans that looked like they might burst at the seams any second.

Then there was the make-up.

"What's happening here, Connie?"

"Tonight, it's Jinu. K-pop boy band member by day, soul-eating demon by night."

Landon appeared behind him, similarly dressed but with a glossy pink wig.

"This some pop culture thing I know nothing about?"

Landon grinned and flicked his hair dramatically. "I'm Romance. That's the character's name, but he's got an evil streak. Well, they all do because, demons."

"Pity you didn't consult with us beforehand, little bro." Adeline appeared, wearing hot pants and a long, sleek purple wig. She kissed my cheek. "We're the stars of the show, Huntr/X." She pointed at Rosie and Summer over by the mantelpiece, who were similarly dressed in bright wigs but with slight variations on their outfits.

"Which show?"

"K-pop Demon Hunters! We're the demon hunters. These guys are the prey." She flicked a thumb at her brothers.

I had so much to learn.

"You're ... let me guess. Carmy from *The Bear*?" My niece grinned. "Love it, Uncle J."

At least someone recognized me. Looking around, I spotted *Squid Game* players, a couple of Deadpools, Rick and Chelsea from *The White Lotus*, and people in what looked like teddy bear costumes. I later learned they were Labubu, another pop culture sensation of which I was completely unaware. I would be a father soon, and I needed to up my game.

No sign of Francesca. I expected she would be here as she had come last year. I was trying not to get all Daddy Dom, but I needed to talk to her.

I did a walkthrough, stopping to chat with teammates and Theo, dressed as Mark from *Severance*. His Helly was off chatting with her bestie, Jordan Hunt, who had come as Glinda in *Wicked*.

My brother hugged me. "Some great blocks in that last one, J."

"I'm sure you have notes."

"Me? Nah. I'm not going to Monday night QB it. You're doing it your way."

I truly wished we could have played on the same team, but now my hope was to honor his legacy. Out of the corner of my eye, I spotted someone in a schoolgirl uniform with braids, but when I turned, she was gone.

"... and he asked me for tickets, but I said he should talk to you."

"What's that?"

Theo frowned. "Dad. He wanted tickets to the game tomorrow for him and his cronies."

That was why he'd left a couple of messages. There I was thinking he was calling to congratulate me on my play.

"Kind of late."

"That's what I said, so he called Hatch and got some that way." Theo looked like he wanted to say something.

"Go ahead."

"I know he's a jerk, but he's still your father."

I reared back. "You're taking his side?"

"Dude, there are no sides. So he handled it all wrong, but it was years ago. Maybe try to get along to go along. There's Ezra and Liam to think of."

If only they didn't come with the baggage of Dad.

"I'm going to get a drink."

"Sure. Knock up some Italian beef Sammies while you're at it, will ya?"

Right. My costume. I grinned and headed on my way.

I ran into Elle, aka Helly from *Severance*, sporting a red wig and a blue top and pencil skirt.

"Lookin' good, Ellie K."

She chuckled. "So great to see you, Jason. I was talking to Jenny, and she was telling me all about Sean's new girlfriend."

I wasn't really interested in Sean's new girlfriend, except for the fact her existence kept my brother on a short enough leash he never once thought of saying yes to Franky. A great outcome for me. So yeah, hooray for Sean's girl.

"Hey, have you seen Francesca?"

"Franky St. James?" As if there was a different Francesca.

"Yeah, I need a word with her."

"She was here earlier with Tilly. Maybe the back garden? They like looking at the snails after it's rained."

That made me smile, though I had to lose it quickly because Elle gave me a funny look. I headed out back, and there they were, both hunched over the wet path that wound its way through the yard. Speaking in hushed tones, they didn't hear my approach.

"See this shell—that part of it is called a lip. That tells us if its fully grown or not."

"Like tree rings?" Tilly asked quietly. She was so smart. She had a purple wig on with a long braid similar to Adeline's.

"Sort of, but not so precise. Smoother shells usually mean adults and ridges usually mean babies. But remember what I said about touching them?"

"Don't, because I wouldn't like it if someone picked me up without permission."

Franky nodded her approval. "Correct, we don't do that. Plus, they carry diseases."

"Hey there," I murmured.

"Uncle Jason!" Jumping to a stand, Tilly grabbed my thigh and held on. "We found a snail!"

"That's cool. So, not sure we've met before. Who are you again?"

My niece frowned. "It's me. Tilly."

"Oh, I thought you were a ... demon hunter! Fought any bad boys lately?"

She stood back and took a martial arts stance. "I'm Rumi and I'm going to get patterns all over my body!"

"Patterns mean she's half-demon," Franky said.

"Like Rumi." My niece nodded enthusiastically.

"Tilly, we're going to do the apple bobbing!" Elle's voice rang clear through the night.

"Wait for me!" My niece took off, her purple braid swinging behind her.

And speaking of braids ... I'd been right when I sensed this woman's presence earlier. She was dressed as Wednesday Addams with braids, a school uniform, and black lipstick.

"A naughty schoolgirl?" I asked even though I doubted the doc would go sexy on purpose.

"The skirt should be longer, but I had to use Rosie's costume. She went as a too-sexy Wednesday three years ago when the character was last popular."

The skirt was pleated, schoolgirl uniform style, and looked so hot on her. The combination of prim braids with the skirt that showed off her legs—albeit in dark tights and clodhopper shoes—had my dick stirring behind my apron.

"And you're ... a chef?"

"A specific chef. Carmy from *The Bear*. It's a TV show about a restaurant."

"I see. And you know about *K-pop Demon Hunters*?"

"Are you kidding? I am *so* down with what the kids are into. Haven't you heard? I'm gonna be a dad."

"Ah, so the rumor is true."

"Sure is. You're giving snail tours?"

She smiled. "Tilly's interested so I thought I'd show her the ones that like to come out after the rain."

"Show me."

She blinked. "You want to see the snails?"

I want to see them through your eyes. "Educate me, Doc."

"Okay." She hunkered down, which sent her skirt riding up along with my dick. Heh. Still a horny teenage boy at heart. The backyard security light shone on a brown-shelled snail sneaking along the path.

"This is your typical garden snail, *Cornu Aspersum*, which means 'spotted horn.' It's rather plain and ubiquitous but exhibits many of the characteristics we associate with snails."

"Such as?"

"First, the shell, which is protective and has three to four whorls. It also has a foot, hence its classification as part of the genus gastropod, which means 'stomach foot.' They use this appendage to inch forward, leaving behind a mucus trail."

I listened to her speak, loving her enthusiasm about this most commonplace of creatures.

"So this is a hermaphrodite?"

"Most species of snail are. It's an evolutionary adaptation that ensures their continued success. Of course, people think these ones are pests and work to eradicate them because of the damage to plants. But they're mostly harmless in a garden like this." She turned to me and placed a hand on my bare bicep. "You must be cold."

"Not really."

"It's not the first time you've appeared half-naked outside."

Inside, too. And hardly half-naked, but I was wearing short sleeves. Gotta show off the guns, and if it drew certain hands to reach out and touch …

"Guess you have that effect on me, Francesca."

She stood. "Let's get you to some place warm."

I pulled myself upright. "Perfect. I'd like to talk to you in private, too."

She opened her mouth—I assume, to object—so I stepped in and placed a finger on her lips. "I want to hear about the doctor's visit, and I'd like to plan how we're going to manage this with all the family members around."

She grasped my hand and pulled it away. "We probably shouldn't be meeting in the dark like this. I don't think anyone would buy your cover about snail education."

So droll. "Meet me upstairs in Adeline's room, second door on the left."

"If I must." Very Wednesday.

I gave her a moment to head inside, then followed. Unfortunately, I ran into Conor again, who halted my progress.

"Were you talking to Franky just now?"

"Yep, what of it?"

My nephew reared back, as if struck. Such a drama queen. "Uh, pretty sure you two are sworn enemies."

"That would be you and Rosie." Listening to those two in the same room together was enough to give anyone an earache. "I get along just fine with the good doctor."

Conor crossed his arms over his too-tight crop top. "The good doctor? What's going on here?"

"Maybe I needed to get to know her a bit better. Anyone who can spend time showing a kid some backyard wildlife can't be all bad."

My phone buzzed, and I checked it, expecting a message from Franky. This message was from my dad. He had sent photos of the boys: Ezra was a skeleton while Liam wore a Transformers costume. Behind them Nick stood with a vampire outfit while Paige was dressed as a nurse.

I was far too old to let this bother me, but every time he checked in like this, I was reminded of the Halloweens I went without him, the holidays he spent with his new family, and the shit he had pulled at every turn.

One more thing came to mind, with a thumping drum-beat: *I will not be like you.*

CHAPTER TWENTY-SIX

Franky

IT WAS GOING to be hard to stay away from Jason.

Not that I had to stay away from him. After all, we were both adults and any time we spent together could be done in an adult fashion (not *that* kind of adult). Jason had every right to be involved, which was the only reason I had agreed to meet with him in Adeline's childhood bedroom.

Only now, I wasn't so sure. For a start, there was a bed. Expected for a bedroom, but not helpful when I needed to be looking at Jason as the father of my child and nothing else.

Not as sexy.

Not as attractive.

Not as possessed of amazing forearms and even more stellar thighs.

We should meet for coffee—well, coffee for him and tea for me—in a public place or at a doctor's office for my first major appointment. The initial one tomorrow was a confirmation of pregnancy with my GP, but I would have to see a gynecologist in a couple of months for a more complete checkup. Jason could come with me. If he wanted to.

Where was he? I couldn't hang around here for much longer. It looked suspicious.

The door opened, and in he came, but he didn't look too pleased about it.

"What's happened?"

He closed the door behind him and blew out a breath. "Conor."

"Is everything okay?"

"He's suspicious of us. Or why we're talking to each other."

"Okay." Conor was the least of my problems.

Jason took a seat on the bed beside me, still visibly on edge. "And my dad's a jerk."

Ah, that made more sense. "Generally or specifically?"

"Generally. But tonight he sent a picture of his family, so specifically, I guess."

"Can I see?"

He opened his phone and handed it to me.

"They're cute. How well do you know them?"

"Theo knows them better, but now that I'm back in Chicago, I've been hanging out with them more. I would just rather not see my father."

"Must be tough. But the boys are probably so proud to have a famous hockey player for a brother. Well, two. And nephews as well, though it must be odd for them to be uncles to nephews so much older than them." The Kershaw family tree was complicated. "You remember what it was like when you first met Theo."

"I just wanted him to like me."

"Your little brothers want that as well." I rubbed his arm, his strong, unyielding bicep. "How about your dad's wife? Do you get along with her?"

"She made a pass at me once at a Christmas cocktail party."

I took another look at the photo. "Slutty nurse seems eminently suitable."

His shoulders started to shake.

"Jason?"

He turned, his mouth stretched in a grin. "You're funnier than you look, Doc."

"Better than looking funny, I suppose. So, tell me why this bothers you so much?"

"I dunno. I feel like he's shoving his new, improved family in our faces. He fucked over Theo, left my mom on the hook for raising me and Sean, and he's probably planning his exit strategy from this lot."

"If that's the case, then your duty is to your brothers. You know that nothing he does has to affect you."

"Sounds like you're speaking from experience."

I took a breath. "It took me a while to figure it out. My mom married my dad because she thought being the wife of a pro-athlete would be glamorous and her road to fame. She wanted to be a WAG, maybe even launch her own reality show. But she married an alcoholic, and her daughters—one of her daughters—didn't match the image she wanted to project. I wasn't pretty or girly or into make-up. I liked ugly, slimy things like slugs and snails, and I wore glasses and was allergic to everything."

He blinked. "You were? Are you still?"

"I've grown out of most allergies, but I still have an issue with nuts. I carry an EpiPen with me at all times. Two, actually."

"And that's okay during pregnancy?"

I smiled. "Yes, it is."

I could see him filing that information away. Jason Isner was becoming easier to read. "Good. Go on."

"I guess what I'm trying to say is that our parents have an impact, especially when we're younger, but eventually we have to let go of the resentments. I know that's easier said than done, especially when you feel wronged by someone. But your life is good, Jason. You have a great family, an amazing career, a child on the way. The one blot on it is your father. Don't let that dull the shine of the rest."

"Such wisdom."

"It's what Wednesday would tell you. Well, she'd probably recommend some macabre revenge plot first."

He pulled at one of my braids. "You look cute. Sexy, too."

"Jason."

"What? Don't pretend you weren't feeling up my chef's arm in the guise of comforting me."

This guy was unbelievable.

And unfortunately correct.

"So what if I was? I can kill two birds, comfort with a quick feel-up. I'm multi-talented."

"Yeah, you are." He stroked my cheek. "And you're so freakin' hot in your slutty librarian glasses. And that mouth —Christ, the things I want to do to that mouth."

My pulse was unsafely high, myocardial infarction-levels of peril. Slutty librarian glasses? Was that a thing?

"L-like what?"

"Like this."

He didn't hesitate in touching his lips to mine. It was as if he'd been waiting for an invitation. For me to drop that last brick in the wall and let him in.

I had wanted him to kiss me in that Detroit hotel room. Earlier than that, actually, at Tilly's birthday party. I didn't believe in manifesting things, but my body language was clearly reflecting my desires.

His lips tugged at mine, then a slight pause to give me a moment to resist—not a chance of that happening!—before he took control. The kiss was divine, stars bursting, thunder rolling, and then he gave my braid another tug. That should not have been sexy, but his mouth on mine and everything about him was overwhelming and arousing. Plus, we were on a bed, of which he took full advantage.

I should not have agreed to meet him here. But this kiss was so good, as was the weight of him over my body. Then he raised the sensual stakes as his hand wandered under my pleated skirt and foraged a while.

He drew back. "These tights are pissing me off."

"That's the idea." The break in the proceedings came with a cold rush of common sense. I sat up, pushing his hand away. "I'm not making out with you in your niece's bedroom at a Halloween party."

"News flash: you just did. Plus, I'm upset and sex would make me feel better."

Graduated to sex rather quickly, there. "I won't be having sex with you ever again."

The saddest sentence ever uttered.

He snorted. "Got what you wanted, huh?"

"Jason, we're not in a relationship. At least, not that way. Messing about with each other is just confusing."

"So I can have sex with anyone else?"

"Of course." I *despised* that idea with the hatred Tesla held for Edison. But I wasn't prepared to give in here, so it was unfair to ask him to be celibate. "We're not a couple. You can do whatever you want, and so can I."

"So *you're* going to have sex with someone else?"

Feeling miserable at the notion, I still needed to chase this to its logical, feminist conclusion. "If I want to."

He stood and paced for a few seconds before facing me, hands on hips. "But if we want sex, then why not with each other?"

"Because, Jason," I started, feeling like I was explaining to my students that the deadline for the paper was 5pm, not the morning after, "that's what couples do, and we are not a couple. Are you worried that I'll be bothered by you with someone else? I won't."

Liar, liar, braids on fire.

"No?"

"Like I said. Not a couple."

His incredulity was a living thing, showcased in flashing eyes and a mouth that clearly wanted to bite my head off, or dare I hope, kiss me again. Angrily.

"This is bullshit. Was the sex not good?"

"Of course it was. It's like pizza. Even bad pizza is decent."

"What the fuck has pizza got to do with it?"

"Just the analogy with pizza is apt. Even bad sex is decent because you're getting some."

He stared at me, his eyes cold and hard. "I have no idea if you thought it was good or not."

I stood and placed my hands on his chest, not one of my better ideas. But I was committed to my principles now and apparently, touching him would help get my point across.

"It was good, Jason. And it had the desired result. A baby. Now I'm giving you permission to return to normal programming."

Though it made me ill. Better to draw the line now before we became too close.

"So speaks the professor, the woman of logic," he said bitterly, before walking out.

NOVEMBER

CHAPTER TWENTY-SEVEN

Jason

THE LONGHORN BAR in downtown Dallas was hopping, and remarkably friendly toward the Chicago interlopers who had put the beat down on the hometown team.

NoBo brought over a tray of shots. "Courtesy of our friends behind the bar."

Lars Nyquist narrowed his gaze. I liked the gruff defenseman and newly minted Rebels captain. We were often paired on the same line, especially now that the powers that be were looking to create the magic of Theo and Lars. In romantic terms, Nyquist was partnered with my niece Addy, so that made him family.

"Are we sure they're not poisoned?" Nyquist asked. "We did just shut them out in pretty embarrassing fashion."

Boden had already knocked one back.

"Royal taster," I said. "Let's give it thirty seconds."

Our tender frowned while I watched for signs of imminent retching. "Those guys are legit. They're just hockey fans."

"Fair enough." Bell, aka Dingaling, knocked one back. Asher followed like a little lamb.

Hatch returned from calling his girl. "Shots? Nice."

Normally we'd be back to Chicago right after the game, but we had a double header with the Steers, so after a day off, the home team would have a chance to get their revenge. The younglings were in the mood to celebrate.

You know who wasn't? *This guy.* I was still annoyed about Franky giving me permission to date—or fuck—other women. Like I should just carry on as if my world had not been rocked by the events in that Detroit hotel room.

We made a baby and now I was supposed to run around sticking my dick into women *not* carrying my child? Make it make sense.

"Hey ho, hottie at six o'clock." NoBo lifted a shot glass to his lips. "You know something? I think she's got Isner in her sights."

"I very much doubt that." Skeptically, I glanced over my shoulder and locked eyes with a hot blonde in a pink, bejeweled cowboy hat. She lifted her hand in a flirty wave. When I turned back to the guys, they were all grinning.

"Definitely likes 'em older." Gaultier giggled. He got like that after two beers and a bourbon.

"Who you callin' old?"

"Aw, you worried 'cause you found a gray pube down there?" Boden grinned and knocked back another shot. I hoped it was contaminated.

Hatch nudged me. "Maybe you should talk to her. Let off some steam."

I had been acting like a cranky asshole. This morning, I'd snapped at Hatchling because he was taking too long in the hotel room bathroom, and I'd spent two minutes in the sin bin for hooking during tonight's game, which broke my thirty-six-game streak of penalty-free play. We still won, but I couldn't believe I'd let my emotions rule and affect my game.

"Sorry I was a dick earlier," I murmured.

He waved it off. "I'm serious. It might make you feel better."

Doubtful. I wasn't in the mood for shots or puck bunnies, so I headed up to the bar for a beer. While I waited —these bartenders weren't such big Rebels fans after all—I felt a nudge at my elbow. Turning, I got the surprise of my life.

"Nazarov!"

"Isner," my old pal said seriously, before a smile touched his lips and I was wrapped in a huge hug.

Russian-born Alexei Nazarov had played NCAA with me at the University of Michigan before we were drafted and went our separate ways, me to LA, him to Miami. We had run into each other semi-regularly over the years, but it had been a while owing to him being on IR with Seattle for the best part of last season.

"What the hell are you doing in Dallas?"

"I am visiting an old friend, but I caught the game. You played well, considering those bones of yours are aging rapidly."

Still the same old Nazarov. "How's Seattle? You back to fitness?"

"Getting there. And Chicago? You must be glad to be closer to your family."

"Yeah, it's great. I miss Sean—he's still in Boston—but I like being near Mom and Theo's brood. And Lauren, of course. You probably heard that she's my agent now."

"Yes, I knew that." A flicker of something passed over his face before his expression reverted to his usual stoic self. Lauren had gone through the women's program at Michigan at the same time as us, and my recollection was that she and Nazarov had once been friendly.

"You should visit Chicago," I said, testing the waters. "We could all get dinner."

"Perhaps." He looked over to my crew. "They are getting younger."

"Yep. Every rookie these days looks like a pimply-faced adolescent."

"We got old when no one was looking."

Over his shoulder, I spied the cowgirl whispering in the ear of a pal, then batting her eyelashes my way with a come-hither grin. She was exactly my type—cute, curvy, and cheerful. Hatch was right. A night with her would probably rejuvenate me more than the ice bath I sank into after tonight's game.

Nazarov was studying me. "Something is different with you."

"Yeah, Alexei. Wrinkles." But no gray pubes yet. Fucking NoBo.

"That's not it."

Something was building inside me, a geyser bursting to gush.

"I'm going to be a father."

His eyes lit up. "Jason, that is fantastic."

"So I'm keeping it on the downlow. The mom is barely a month in and we're not telling anyone for a while." Now that the pressure valve had released a touch, I could go back to normal.

"I knew you were seeing someone in Boston."

"No, that didn't work out. This is someone else in Chicago."

His expression darkened. "Lauren?"

"No, not Lauren." Though that was interesting. "You don't know her."

His shoulders relaxed, the storm cloud passed, and his lips curved at my cloak-and-dagger efforts.

"It's kind of complicated," I went on. "We're not a couple."

"Ah. The condom broke."

"No, the condom did not break!" I said that a little loud, so I lowered my voice and tried again. "It's planned. We're in this together."

"That is good. Though it sounds like you wish for more."

Nazarov was always good at reading people. It made him a great center and a wily competitor. He waited for me to spit it out.

What could I say? That the most independent baby mama ever born got what she wanted and was moving on with her life? She was probably looking for a real dad for her kid, some smarty-pants professor type like that London dude who got awards for articles about clams.

"She's one of those DIY gals. Doesn't want me to pay for anything or take my input or ... other stuff."

He remained annoyingly silent.

"Shut it."

His barely-there smile reached his eyes. "Have you told her that you would like more from ... whatever it is?"

"It's not like that. But I suppose I'd like us to be a little closer."

Sexually, for a start.

"Well, you have to figure out how to navigate the next

few months without losing your mind. If you and the mother are not meant to be, then you must accept that. Or get over her by getting under a cowgirl. We are in Texas after all."

His phone rang and he checked the screen with a frown. "I should ..."

"Go ahead." This interruption coincided with the bartender finally giving me the time of day. "Sam Adams Winter ale. And another round of shots for the boys."

Someone placed a hand on my back, and I turned, expecting Nazarov or Hatch. The actual was far prettier.

"Hi," she said, kind of breathily. "I'm Farrah."

She looked like a Farrah, and with that tight, white T-shirt, showcasing tear-drop tits and the hot pink cowboy hat, perched jauntily on her head, she also looked like the kind of woman who could take a man's mind off his troubles.

"Jason."

"Oh, I know."

One of the perks of the job. Everyone knew who you were and women were never hard to attract. I had permission from the doc to return to normal programming, right?

"What are you drinking, Farrah?"

CHAPTER TWENTY-EIGHT

Franky

MY SISTER HAD many good attributes: she was a great cook, a loyal friend, and a mixologist par excellence. But her ability to craft a cheese plate was probably her most underrated talent. I sighed at seeing it laid out like a Bake-Off showstopper on her coffee table.

Summer nudged me. "You, too, huh?"

"I love a good cheese board." I would have to stay away from the Brie and feta, but the hard cheeses were fair game.

"Are you sure you don't want a martini, Franky?" Adeline handed off a Cosmo to Summer, who took a seat on the sofa, an iPad in her lap.

"No, I'm fine. I've a slight headache so I'll stick with the water." I was going to have to come up with better excuses during these early weeks of my pregnancy.

Esme Fitzpatrick sipped a dirty martini. A good friend of Rosie and Adeline, she was the daughter of Tara, the

Rebels' hair stylist, and Hale Fitzpatrick, a former general manager. I didn't know her that well, as she was much younger than me and had recently moved back to Chicago after graduating from NYU.

"Franky, those boots are gorgeous. Frye, I'm guessing?"

They were my favorites, a warm brown and well-worn. "Good eye. 'Tis the season and all that."

Lauren came rushing in. "Sorry I'm late, guys. One of my players needed to be talked off the ledge. He thinks he offended a veteran player at a cookout when he told him he didn't like red onion in the man's guac." She shook her head. "That's me. Therapist to the rookies. Ooh, look at that sexy cheese board!"

Once a month we met for Bonking Book Club, a reading group focused on romance. This month, we were reading a super sexy enemies to lovers historical, and I was looking forward to taking my mind off Jason and whether he was having sex with someone in the present.

Rosie came in with a sleeve of crackers because you could never have too many carbs. "Before we get started, could we talk about how amazing Hatch played last night in Dallas? That third period was phenomenal!"

"And your man and Isner in those waning moments?" Lauren spoke to Adeline, referring to her boyfriend Lars, who also had a great game. "I didn't think we'd ever see a better pairing on the D-line than Theo and Nyquist, but those boys are gellin' like Magellan."

There was some chatter about the game, and I offered a few comments, so it didn't look like I was trying to avoid conversation about Jason.

Summer smiled and held up her iPad. "Should we talk about the book? I had no idea these Regency ladies were so forward-thinking."

"Oh, first, we need to get a caption for this." Esme held up her own iPad, but not to an electronic page of text. This was a photo.

Of Jason in a bar with a woman.

My heart clattered wildly, and I wished my glasses would fall off my face and shatter into a million pieces.

She was cute and blonde and pert, and with that pink cowboy hat, likely Texan. This was probably taken at a post-celebration drink after one of the games—they had won both—with Jason partaking of the spoils of victory. In the world of professional hockey, that generally involved the soft, sensual comforts of a woman.

Her head was tilted up, her eyes adoring, her breasts perking. With their mouths close, the pheromones practically wafted from the screen.

"Oh, Uncle Jason!" Adeline grinned. "So nice to see him meeting someone. I think he was bummed after he broke up with Everly."

"Hatch said he's been kind of a bear on the road trips," Summer added. "Hopefully this helped relieve some of the stress."

Lauren shuddered. "He's both a friend and a client, and I really don't want to think of him with Miss Perky Texan Tits, thanks very much."

Cosigned. Thank you, Lo.

Esme gestured with her glass toward me. "Speaking of action, how's the baby plan?" My desperation was still a hot topic in Rebels circles.

"Still working through my list. I want to be sure I make the best decision."

Summer looked at me approvingly. "Iconic."

"That's my sis." Rosie smiled and winked at me.

Adeline opened her mouth to ask a follow-up question, I assumed. Lauren cut her off. "I'm dating someone!"

My baby fever was instantly forgotten as everyone peppered Lauren with questions about her love life. She was rather coy about it but caught my eye, which confirmed that she had fallen on her sword for me. I sent her a look of gratitude. I doubted she knew about my pregnancy, but she did know that Jason and I were trying.

Adeline clapped her hands. "Okay, book club time. And then we can catch up with our other not-so-guilty pleasure."

Summer looked confused. "What's that?"

Lauren gave a sly grin. "Oh, you'll see."

I opened my Kindle e-reader to the highlights of our book club choice and put thoughts of Jason and Miss Perky Texan Tits from my mind.

"SO THE FIVE characteristics of Annelida are a segmented body, also known as ..."

"Metamerism," someone called out.

"Correct. What else?"

"Bilateral symmetry?" another student weighed in. "And a coelom. Not sure if I'm pronouncing that right."

I nodded at Gina Alvarez, one of the more promising students in my class. "Yes, a coelom is a body cavity. Annelida also have what else?"

No one offered to complete the list, so I finished it for them.

"A closed circulatory system and a well-developed nervous system. The average earthworm has incredibly complex internal organs."

I clicked to a slide showing a drawing of an earthworm's coelom. "And how many species of annelid are there?"

"Over twenty thousand," a deep voice called out.

Not one of my students, yet I would recognize that voice anywhere. I peered up to the back of the lecture hall to see a tall, muscular silhouette.

Almost two weeks had gone by since we last spoke at Halloween. He was mad at me, and I understood he needed space. I needed the same, not because I was angry, but because spending time with him would weaken my resolve. I had been doing so well. I certainly did not need him to waltz in here and continue to turn my world upside down.

"Twenty-two thousand, actually," I called out as if it was perfectly normal to have a famous hockey player answer questions about earthworms in my auditorium.

"Sorry, Doc. I forgot how precise you like it."

The entire lecture hall of forty-three students in my Animal Biology II class turned at that excessively familiar tone. The whispers started immediately.

"I think we can end this a couple of minutes early. Don't forget that your papers on your choice of Annelid and its distinct characteristics are due on Friday at 5pm. No exceptions. And of course, it would be lovely if some of you chose the less common of the species. Leeches are very interesting to this professor!"

Jason worked his way down the steps, while the students gawked and nudged each other. Just watching how he commanded the room as he descended had my heart beating wildly.

Like he belonged to me.

But that wasn't true. Could never be. Jason and I might be sexually compatible but that was where the chemistry ended. We had shared something special in that hotel room, an experience that produced a child and that I would treasure forever. But I couldn't let the emotions of that play into how I felt about him. There was too much at stake.

The students were slow walking their way out of the auditorium, partly because class had ended a couple of minutes early, but mostly because of fascination with my visitor. He nodded at a couple of them. One stepped forward as he made eye contact—Bella Corbin, a very pretty blonde.

Not that her prettiness or blondness had anything to do with it. Perhaps I was sensitive because she was similar in appearance to the woman photographed with Jason in that bar in Dallas over a week ago.

"Hi, Mr. Isner, I'm a huge fan."

"Thanks, I appreciate that." Barely looking at her, he carried on until he reached the floor. Bella looked like she was about to swoon as one of her friends elbowed her to make tracks. A couple of students stopped to ask me questions about the essay and how "hard" the submission date was. While I wanted to answer—*"What about 'no exceptions' is so difficult to understand?"*—Jason signed a couple of autographs, even using the inside cover of Smith and McGowan's *Animal Biology* textbook.

Finally, we were alone.

"Didn't know you were such an expert on Annelida," I murmured as I tidied up, anything to occupy my shaking hands.

"Wikipedia is my friend, though I'm sure you don't approve." He leaned against the podium as I shuffled my notes. "Is it true you can cut an earthworm in half and get two living worms?"

"That's a myth. Depending on where the cut is made,

the worm *may* be able to regenerate part of its body. But you won't get two independent, living entities."

"Always learning, Doc."

That was me, the egghead educator.

"Why are you here?" It came out sounding a little brusque.

"We haven't talked in a while. Except for a few texts."

"Which I've answered."

He folded his arms across that expanse of chest that made a great pillow. It shouldn't have. It should have been hard and unyielding, yet my memory of lying there was indescribably fond.

"Single word answers. How are you? *Fine.* Anything I can do for you? *No.* Do you hate my guts? *Probably.*"

I gathered up my papers. "You never asked that last question."

"What would you have said if I did?"

"I don't hate anyone."

"So a multiple word answer."

"I'm not going to apologize for giving you the freedom to date whomever you like."

He looked up at the ceiling, then down again. "That's not what our fight was about, Doc, and you know it."

"You shouldn't have called me that in front of the students. It sounded too familiar."

He stepped forward. "That's what we are to each other. Familiar. Friendly. Fuck buddies, if you'd only accept that we have more chemistry than a Bunsen burner."

"We have to draw a line." Jason should have no problem moving on to the pretty barflies who loved a hockey player. Judging from that photo, he already had. I just wasn't sure why he was so sore about it.

"Sure, we can draw a line. But you're not going to cut me out of this baby's life before it's even started."

"I'm not—"

"Dr. St. James." A new voice cut in, as welcome as a cold toilet seat. Marcus stepped forward, his gaze cutting between Jason and me. "I noticed that your class ended early so I wondered if there was a problem."

"No problem." As if I needed to explain how I conducted my classes. As Marcus showed no sign of leaving, I added, "This is a friend of mine, Jason Isner."

Marcus blinked up at Jason, who had a good eight inches on him. *In all areas*, a baser part of me whispered.

"Nice to meet you. I'm Dr. Bilson. How do you and our Dr. St. James know each other?"

Jason opened his mouth, but I got there first. "Jason plays professional hockey with the Chicago Rebels."

"Old friend of the family," Jason said, and it wasn't my imagination that he moved closer to me. "Well, more than friends."

The last thing I needed was my personal life put on blast. Marcus's eyes narrowed, waiting for someone to explain what Jason meant by that cryptic statement.

"We're about to head to lunch—"

Marcus cut me off. "I was hoping we could discuss your open access funding requests."

"I have that on the agenda for our weekly meeting," I said. "Scheduled for Thursday."

"Right." Still no sign of a departure, so I took the initiative.

"Let's catch up later." I moved toward the door while Jason watched our dynamic with interest. Then he raised an eyebrow and grinned.

"So, lunch?"

CHAPTER TWENTY-NINE

Jason

LUNCH WAS MORE than I had hoped for, which only went to prove that my expectations when it came to Franky St. James were startlingly low.

"I usually eat in my office."

"Good thing I brought supplies." I patted my backpack. "So what's the deal with that guy?"

"That's Dr. Bilson, head of my department."

The guy who got the job she wanted *and* who she slept with a couple of years ago. Also on the list.

I followed her through the hallways of the university, which yielded plenty of funny looks. Of course, people were going to wonder what the beautiful brain was doing with a lug like me. Let 'em.

In her office, a pretty brunette behind a desk looked up. "Oh, Dr. St. James, Dr. Bilson was looking—" She broke off on seeing me. "Hello."

"Hey there."

"Dr. Bilson found me. In class. Where I was supposed to be." She waved behind her. "This is—"

"Jason Isner," the desk girl said. "Hi! I had no idea you ..." She trailed off, looking to the professor for guidance.

"Old friend of the family," I said. "Planning for my post-retirement life. Thinking of going back to school."

"Oh, wow!"

"This is Jolene," Franky said. "She works for the department part-time and is also a very talented malacologist. Jo, I'm taking a quick lunch in my office before the graduate seminar."

"Got it! Do not disturb."

We headed inside her office, which was about what I expected. Books and papers covered every shelf and surface, while the walls held diplomas and framed art of snail shells. All very Franky.

She moved to a small fridge and withdrew a minuscule sandwich.

"That's it?"

"I also have some fruit." She pointed at a solitary apple sitting on her desk.

"Good thing I came prepared." I removed two containers from my backpack, along with a bottle of dressing, cutlery, and napkins.

She blinked. "You brought lunch for me?"

"Yep. I'm not convinced you're taking this nutrition thing seriously, Doc." I had no idea but seeing that sandwich firmed my resolve. "I made a salad, and before you can say 'kale sucks,' be aware that you won't even notice it because the dressing is so damn good."

I set it all out on her desk while she looked on, incredulous.

"You made the salad from scratch?"

"Yep. The dressing, too." I opened the salad bowls and let her gaze at its colorful glory. Leafy greens, grilled chicken, hard-boiled eggs, vine-ripened tomatoes, red onions—all miraculously still in place despite traveling in my backpack. "And not a nut in sight."

"This is awfully kind, Jason."

I wasn't doing it to be kind. I was doing it because I cared about her well-being and the well-being of our kid.

"Now let's eat, and then we can talk."

We sat in surprisingly companionable silence, which was usually hard for me because I was chatty by nature. Something about the doc calmed me, though, even when I was mad as all hell at her. When we were done, I cleaned up, passed her a bottle of water, and told her to hydrate.

"So that guy got your job?"

She dabbed her mouth with a napkin. "It wasn't my job, per se. Dr. Bilson does have quite a lot of leadership experience, and it worked out because now I can devote myself to the baby."

I supposed I should be glad that her career would take a back seat to our child's welfare, but something about her statement niggled. I didn't like the idea that the doc couldn't have it all, especially when we were in this together.

"He was on the list."

"Purely to ensure a bias-free method. Now, why do you think I'm trying to cut you out? And what has it to do with our respective sex lives?"

I had to give it to her. The doc didn't beat around the bush.

"I don't always express myself well. Along with being annoyed I wasn't getting to have sex with a hot woman in my niece's childhood bedroom during a family Halloween party, I was pissed that you were giving me permission to fuck anything that moves. I don't need your permission, but I sure as hell don't like the idea that you think I'm so desperate for it, I can't keep it in my pants for a while."

She opened her mouth. I held up my hand.

"Not finished. Mostly, I was annoyed about my father sending me a picture of his replacement family, which makes me a total dick because who gets annoyed at seeing pictures of little kids in Halloween costumes? Apparently I do. But I'm guessing I don't like pictures of my father because it reminds me of his infidelity and how he screwed over my mom. I was *possibly* projecting some of that onto our situation. I can hardly look like a good dad-to-be if I'm catting around, can I?"

She remained close-lipped.

"That wasn't rhetorical."

"Oh, right. So you feel weird about sleeping with someone while the woman carrying your child waits in the wings? And this brings up memories of your father's bad behavior?"

All she was missing was a couch, the Freud beard, and a German accent.

"It doesn't seem right. I don't want to be ... like him."

"You're very self-aware, do you know that?"

My body flushed at what sounded like a compliment. "Well, I do tend to act out and then figure out I was a big baby later. Does that amount to self-awareness?"

She rolled in her lips.

"What?"

"I think you have a very clear sense of honor, Jason. Your father has repeatedly disappointed you, has broken what you consider to be the code of a parent. Now I've put you in a position where you're worried about looking like a creep. If you sleep with someone and everyone knows you have a so-called 'baby mama' back in Chicago, the optics are concerning."

That was my baby mama, smart as a whip. "In a nutshell."

"I understand your predicament, but I still can't agree to be on deck for your needs because it would make you feel better about where you decide to insert your penis. I'm not here for your convenience."

"Damn, you think it's convenient I want to bang you? I'll tell you right now it is very *inconvenient*."

"I can see that." She picked up what looked like a fake snail on her desk, turned it over, then put it down again.

"I've had chances, you know," I said.

"I'm sure you have." Was that a tremor in her voice?

"Plenty of 'em. Hot blonde in Dallas last week couldn't keep her hands off me."

"Yes, the gossip sites couldn't keep their hands off it, either."

So, she *had* seen that photo. To be honest, it was a good thing there was photographic evidence because the memory of Farrah was kind of fuzzy, not because I'd had too much to drink or the night got away from me. There was only so long a man could be entertained by a pretty pair of tits accompanying dull-as-dirt conversation. I had found myself bored stupid halfway through my first Sam Adams Winter ale, long before Farrah's breathily verbalized offer to "suck you so hard you'll see stars."

Franky raised her gaze to mine. "That must have been very gratifying for you. Still got it."

This woman was impossible! I stood and pointed. "I didn't go for it, even though I could have. I don't need your permission to bang anyone, Doc. We're not a couple."

"Exactly the point I've been making. But I will leave it to you to decide how you want to deal with your epididymal hypertension."

"Oh, please educate me."

"Commonly known as blue balls."

I clutched my chest, all affront. "I think you know exactly how I'll be dealing with it. Playing a little Taylor Swift and imagining you stroking your pus—"

"Jason!" She burst out laughing, and that sound was enough to lift that slab of pressure off my chest.

I retook my seat. "So, you and that Bilson guy?"

"There is no me and 'that Bilson guy.' I know I indicated at Halloween that I might want to sleep with someone. However, I was merely making the point that I could. Dr. Bilson would be the last person on my list."

"And you don't want to with anyone else?"

"It had been a while before ..." She waved her hand between us. "So that should tide me over for the foreseeable future."

"Glad to give you some spank bank material. Or whatever a lady calls it."

"Rosie calls it the rub hub. Or Netflicks." She sounded so serious, so Francesca. I loved when she got that look on her face.

I'd gone into this, offering up my superman genes so my kid would be athletic and strong. Now I was thinking that if our little one didn't have a sporty bone in their body but instead grew up with this woman's intellectual curiosity and interesting way of looking at things, I would be unbelievably blessed.

She met my gaze head-on. "I feel like something else is bothering you."

She was right, but then she so often was.

"It's killing me, not being able to share the news." Mostly, it hurt not to be able to talk about it with her while I was throwing a hissy fit about not getting any. "Eventually we have to tell people, unless you don't want to."

We had verbally discussed the secrecy aspect during the trying phase, but there was nothing in the contract about who we would tell and when it would happen. Sure, it would eventually have to get out because I couldn't be in my kid's life incognito, but the longer we kept it under wraps, the deeper the wound of inadequacy festered.

While my mind ran all the way to the finish line, Franky said, "Jason, of course we will be sharing the news when it's a good time to do that. Maybe after the first ultrasound in early January? I just want to get through the first trimester first."

Of course she would be worried, especially being older. A lot could go wrong in the first three months.

"Sounds good. I want to tell people, but I also like the fact it's our secret."

She smiled. "So do I, and I kind of want to hold onto it a little longer. As soon as it's out there, everyone will have an opinion. They already did when they found out I planned to do this my way."

"You're worried about what people will think? Or that they won't understand why you chose me?"

Frowning, she pushed her glasses back. "What's to understand? You're an incredibly viable candidate. Anyone could see that."

Everly didn't. But what did that matter now? My ex was happy. I was happy. No sex in my immediate future, but at least Franky and I were talking.

The world, previously tilted off its axis, was right again.

"If anything, people will wonder why you chose me," she added. "That's the true oddity here."

I chuckled. "Why wouldn't I want a brainy mom for my kid?"

Her smile froze for a moment. Before I could ask if I'd said the wrong thing, there was a knock on the door and her assistant called out, "Dr. St. James, your graduate student seminar starts in five."

"Thanks, Jo." She turned back to me, her expression smooth again. "Are we good?"

"Yes, Doc. We're good."

CHAPTER THIRTY

Franky

"I'M ABSOLUTELY STUFFED!" Rosie leaned back in her chair and patted her stomach. "Not sure I have room for pie."

"A full stomach should never get in the way of pie," Cade said.

"Amen." Dante stood and started clearing away plates.

As my only contribution to the Thanksgiving meal was two tins of cranberry sauce, I jumped up to intercept.

"I'll take care of the dishes. Finish your wine, relax, take it easy."

"Be thankful?" Vi said with a grin. She picked up her glass. "I won't say no to someone else doing the washing up. Devon, could you help your sister, please?"

My fifteen-year-old brother rolled his eyes but did as he was asked.

I loved our blended family Thanksgiving with Rosie,

her dads, my parents, and brother together for the holiday. Dante and my dad did most of the cooking while Cade and Vi gossiped like they didn't already catch up at least once a week at their regular coffee date. Cat was sometimes with us, but this year she was spending the holiday with her husband's family in Westchester, New York. Earlier, we had all crowded around my laptop and marveled at how big my niece and nephew had grown.

I wondered what they would think of the fact there would be another guest at the table next year. My child. Would Jason stop by for future Thanksgivings? We had outlined sharing holidays in the contract, and if he truly wanted to be involved, he might be here.

Over the last ten days, he had made either daily stops by my office for lunch or had sent over food using Kennedy Durand's Can Do concierge delivery service, a popular option for the Rebels players and staff. Taking care of the baby, though I liked to think he was taking care of me.

Devon was on rinse duty while I Tetris'ed the heck out of the dish placement in the dishwasher.

"So how's it going?" I slid a look at my brother. "Did you do okay on your algebra test?"

"I texted you about it. I got an A-minus."

"Right! You did." I had helped my brother with some tutoring a few weeks ago, and of course he had already texted me to say he did well. Yet, I'd forgotten because my brain was mush. We chatted some more about school, his favorite video game, some weird prank one of his friends played on him. A few minutes later, Rosie walked in and touched Devon on the shoulder.

"What?" he asked.

"I'm tagging you out. It's an improv thing."

Devon screwed up his eyes. "Am I supposed to say something funny?"

"No, you're supposed to take this wonderful opportunity to leave the kitchen because I'm taking over in this 'dishwashing scene.'"

Devon grinned. "Awesome. Later, Franks."

"Later, Dev." I turned to Rosie. "Are you actually going to help, or are you trying to avoid your dads asking about your sex life?"

She shuddered. "They're so progressive it's scary. Cade actually dropped off a family-sized box of condoms the last time he came to visit my place. And Dante allows this nonsense—he's supposed to be the hard ass prude."

Dante was a lot of things, but prude wasn't one of them.

"Vi's not much better," Rosie went on. "I think she and Cade spend their time thinking up ways to embarrass me."

"You're unshockable. Just be glad you can tell them anything."

My sister leaned against the sink, *not* rinsing any dishes. Improvising idleness.

"Is there something you can't tell Bren and Vi?"

I hadn't meant it like that, or maybe I had. "I'm just reminding you of how lucky you are to have such cool dads."

Rosie hummed. "So, what's going on?"

"Going on?"

"You didn't eat much and usually you are all over those mashed potatoes like Bunsen with his cat treats. You're not drinking either. I know you want to prepare your body for when you get around to conceiving, but is there something you're not telling me?"

I was dying to share my news. I couldn't rely on Jason as

my comfort through this. If it was just the two of us keeping this secret, then we would be constantly drawn to each other like magnets to metal. Or my favorite parts to his favorite parts. (Genitals, in case that wasn't clear.)

I guided her into the downstairs bathroom, just off the kitchen.

"I'm pregnant."

Cue Rosie's squeal. "I *knew* something was going on. You've been avoiding me whenever I ask you out."

"I am busy, trying to prep for the next semester in Boston." Information I had not shared with Jason. "Do you still want to sublet while I'm away?"

She grasped my arms. "Yes, I do but stop changing the subject. This is amazing! How far along?"

"About six weeks? I have an OB appointment at the beginning of January, but I've had the pregnancy test with my GP and a general checkup. It's definitely a go."

"And?"

"What?"

Those green eyes she shared with her mom and my aunts glittered. *You know who else has gorgeous green eyes ...*

"It's Jason, right?"

"Correct. He's very happy." Though he only saw me as the brains of the outfit. My contribution was to the kid's intellectual prowess, not much else.

While you saw only muscles when you said yes to him, right?

Not the same thing at all!

"I'm so pleased for you. I'm guessing it's lips zipped until you're into the second trimester?"

"Exactly. Dad and Vi will go nuts. And then there's Kendra."

My mother would have plenty of opinions, especially about the fact I was doing this without a man.

"Sis, I think you're so brave, but you won't be alone." Rosie hugged me close. "You have me and Cat and everyone who loves you. If you need a birthing partner, I'm your girl!"

I hadn't even thought of that. Would Jason want to be there? Probably not. It was kind of messy. But then this whole situation was the dictionary definition of "mess."

DISPIRITEDLY, I looked in my fridge. This was far too much food.

Violet and Dante had noticed I didn't eat much and assumed I would be hungry later, piling me with enough leftovers to last through New Year. Now it was the Friday after Thanksgiving and the thought of all this food going to waste offended me.

I had an idea and called Lauren to run it by her.

"Hi, Lo, it's Franky."

"Oh, hey. Is everything okay?"

"Yes, yes. It's fine. So this is going to seem weird ..."

And it was. But here I was with key and alarm code in hand, about to do a food drive-by for the man who was fathering my child. This afternoon, the Rebels played Minneapolis, so he would be back in a few hours. Wouldn't it be nice to come home to a full fridge of Thanksgiving leftovers?

I made it inside without any trouble. Previously, I had only come as far as the front door, and before that, the living room while we discussed the contract. Both times, I had been too nervous to take in more than the contours of his home. The house had a welcoming openness to it, pleasantly decorated in creams and navies, with a plethora of photos on the walls. Jason with his nieces and nephews, his younger brothers, Theo and Sean and his mom. None of his father, which wasn't surprising.

Sean had told me Jason had bought this place as soon as he signed his contract with the Rebels. It was a lot of house for one person. Professional athletes were used to capacious arrangements, though I considered this more comfortable than luxurious. Less bachelor pad and more family style ease. It reminded me of the house I grew up in, where we lived with Dad after Mom decided—and *decided* was the operative word—to suffer a meltdown in the granola aisle of Whole Foods. Right after, she checked into a spa for a rest, while checking out of motherhood altogether.

I loved that house and, as my family still lived there, often found myself returning to it as much for the comfort of the familiar surroundings as the joy of spending time with my parents and little brother. This home gave off a similar vibe.

I headed to the kitchen and found my lips curving at the sight of the fridge covered in magnets, all the cities he had played in, I supposed, propping up polaroids with his niblings as well as childlike artwork. Snails were the focus, which meant these likely belonged to Tilly. That was so sweet, and I luxuriated in the fantasy that maybe he kept these pictures because they reminded him of me.

Slug Girl.

Opening the fridge, I got a mild shock: it was already filled with Tupperware containers. It looked like he had brought leftovers home from the Kershaws' gathering the day before Thanksgiving. Well, I felt rather foolish. But I was here now. In for a penny.

I wandered around the first floor but didn't dare go

upstairs. It comforted me to get a sense of who he was, of who I had invited into my life. I spied trophies on the shelves, more family photos, a hockey puck that must hold some special meaning. On the coffee table were books.

Baby books.

The standards, of course, such as *What to Expect* and *The Expectant Father*, but also one on co-parenting. Beside that was a book of baby names—as if he had a choice in the matter—and one on child development in the first year. At the bottom of the pile was a basic biology text about the animal kingdom, the kind that was usually assigned to high school students.

Was Jason trying to meet me at my level? Or just learn more about the inner workings of his baby mama's weird mind?

Above the fireplace was a big screen, and while I wasn't really much of a TV person, I was anxious to see how the game was going. As if my boyfriend was playing.

I turned it on, lay out on the sofa, and settled in to cheer for my home team.

<hr>

SOMETIME LATER, I woke to my body cocooned in the warmth and weight of someone else. I should have been freaked out, but I wasn't. I knew instantly it was Jason.

My slight shift woke him up.

"Hey there, Doc," he whispered in my ear.

"Hello. What time is it?"

"Close to ten." I had fallen asleep during the hockey game, so that was at least four hours ago. "I got in about an hour ago. You didn't reset the alarm."

"I hadn't intended to stay. You should have woken me up."

"You looked so peaceful and like you needed the rest. So, do you usually break into random houses and watch hockey?"

I smiled into the decorative sofa cushion. I still hadn't turned around. "Not a break-in, but guilty as charged to watching hockey. You played well."

"So you saw the game? Or did I send you to sleep?"

"I was awake for most of it."

"I liked seeing you here on my sofa."

Don't get used to this. I turned in his arms, the comfort of it overwhelming. "I borrowed a key from Lauren. I wanted to give you some Thanksgiving leftovers, but then I found you were well stocked up."

"I am. But I'll never say no to more." He rubbed a hand soothingly over my stomach. "Does your body feel different?"

"Not really. I've been getting sick in the morning, but I take ginger and feel better. And my clothes still fit."

"How was the holiday with your family?"

"Nice. Rosie and her dads were there, too. We usually share the holiday with them, which I've always loved." Though this time, I felt a little off about it. Seeing everyone so loved up made me feel the lack of a partner for the first time.

So foolish. Here I was growing a child without having to go through the steps of settling down with a man, and I was feeling left out? Perhaps that's why I was here, looking for comfort in all the wrong places.

"It's pretty cool to have all that support."

"It is. I'm very lucky." I needed to appreciate it more instead of wanting things I couldn't have.

He stood from the sofa and winced.

"What's going on? Are you hurt?"

"Just a little sore after the game. I'm going to enjoy the next couple of days off."

I was abruptly aware of what I'd done. Crashed this man's life when all he wanted was some peace and quiet.

"I should leave you to rest."

"I napped on the plane and now I'm hungry. Let's break bread together, Francesca."

I couldn't say no to that.

There was no missing the extra care he took to walk toward the kitchen, and this place was big, so it took a while. I followed, taking note of his gait. He was hurting.

"How about you sit, and I'll heat up some food?"

"You're a guest," he said.

"I'm an intruder. Let the woman feed the victorious warrior, home from battle."

"I know you're being sarcastic, but I kind of like the fantasy that presents, so carry on." He took a seat at the kitchen island.

I removed a few containers, but before I went about reheating anything, I put together an ice pack inside a Ziplock and a Rebels dishtowel (the team had cornered the merch market on everything). Wordlessly, I passed it over and he took it equally silently, save for a grateful nod.

"So, what'll it be?"

"Uh, everything?"

I grinned. "Going whole hog Henry the VIII, huh?"

"The fat king with the zillion wives? Never understood the appeal."

"Women are drawn to guys with power and riches." I started dividing the leftovers onto plates according to required cooking times. "Looks don't always factor into it."

"Might have had something to do with the fact he could execute you and your family if you didn't return his interest."

"Or the fact that every woman thinks she can change a man, even a murdering psychopath."

He gave me a look.

"I don't mean you."

"I'm a lot of things, but murdering psychopath isn't one of them." He paused a moment. "I've changed my opinion of you."

"Well, that's hardly surprising. Your opinion of me was wrong to start with. What I mean is a guy's fundamental nature. If he doesn't want to settle down or stay faithful or change his bottom-line understanding of how relationships work, then no woman is going to be able to overcome that. It would require ... therapy. And the percentage of guys who are willing to do that kind of work is minuscule."

"So what's my fundamental nature?"

I was speaking in general terms. I hadn't expected him to call me out.

"You've already told me that you don't want a long-term relationship or marriage but that you *do* want a child. On the surface, those wants appear to be antithetical to each other. Most men who want children also want the security of a wife or partner to go with that."

"But I don't."

"But maybe you did at one time? Want a wife?"

He thought on that for a moment, a strategy he used when he needed to reframe his thinking—or hide something. "A little woman back on the homestead, cooking up homemade meals, and keeping the house nice?"

"Deflection. The tool of the scared."

"Not deflecting and certainly not scared. I like leaving

my options open when it comes to women but choosing the woman who will be the mother of my kid is a different prospect. She needs to be a certain type—mature, responsible, ready for motherhood."

"Ah. Which is generally not the personality type of the women you like to date. So you had a dilemma—"

"And you presented me with the perfect solution. A woman that will make a rockin' mom and who I trust as a co-parent."

But not the kind of woman he wanted to keep the home fires burning.

"And you don't see yourself with a wife?" Apparently, I *really* wanted to know.

"I'm pretty happy with my life now. The kid will change that because my kids will always come first, but I won't have to spread my bandwidth over multiple competing interests."

He had a lot of people in his life: three families across multiple generations and now a child on the way. Of course he wouldn't have time for anyone else—now. I hadn't missed how he pluralized "kid," either. Ours wouldn't be his last. He might think he had no time for relationships, but he would eventually fall. Men like him always did.

I shifted my attention to the artwork on the fridge. "Tilly did a great job of these shell whorls."

"She's a smart kid. But our kid will be smarter."

I had wondered if her intellect might be "normalized" by the gene pool at my disposal, but I was starting to realize that Jason Isner was one of the smartest people I knew.

"That's not really how it works. But we'll adore her anyway."

"Her? That's what you think?"

I smiled. "Until I hear otherwise, I'm carrying a Valkyrie. A Viking shieldmaiden."

"I know what a Valkyrie is, Doc. I've seen the *Thor* movies."

Of course he had.

CHAPTER THIRTY-ONE

Jason

FINDING the alarm off was disconcerting, though I wasn't too worried because my spare key on the entryway table suggested Theo or Lauren had stopped by.

Finding Goldilocks on my sofa was even better than I could have imagined.

Franky was curled up on my sofa while the TV showed ESPN's Coby Dawson interviewing my old captain on the Cougars after they had lost their game. I picked up the remote and muted it, then took a seat beside Sleeping Beauty. (I was *killing* it with the fairytale references.)

I had gently removed her glasses and grabbed a fleece blanket from a basket by the side of the sofa and draped it over her. Then I snuggled into the ten inches of space she had left on her right side and placed an arm around her waist. My hand moved tentatively over her stomach.

My baby inside my woman.

And with that happy thought, I had fallen asleep.

Now she was cooking for me. Sure, it was leftovers, and anyone could throw mashed potatoes in the microwave, but it was still nice to have someone waiting on me. Of course, I had to be careful about that illusion because that was all it was.

Dr. St. James was not wife material.

Maybe for someone, a nerd like London Clam Guy who probably had a housekeeper on hand because he and his egghead wife would have all this important research to do. A nanny, too, because they certainly wouldn't have time for child-raising. I hadn't thought about that. What was the doc going to do there? That level of detail wasn't laid out in the contract.

We sat down at the kitchen table with our meals. Dante's mashed potatoes were creamier and fluffier than my mom's, but Aurora's yams were still the best of all of the veggies.

"So, how's the childcare going to work?"

Franky looked up sharply.

"Not a trap. Just wondering."

"I was thinking of taking a sabbatical for the first year while I write a book."

"You're writing a book?"

"Yes, on the mating habits of gastropods. I've written a few articles, and while this is an ostensibly esoteric subject, I think it has enough merit for a monograph."

Just when I thought I couldn't be any prouder. "You're going to be tired those first few months."

"I expect that. I may hire part-time childcare, but I'll be doing most of it myself. I want to be sure the child bonds with me and not some stranger."

A little defensive, but I got it. Women were expected

to do it all, and the doc would be hyperaware of the expectations around motherhood, especially the single variety.

"You're not alone in this. The baby's due in early July, so we'll be in the off-season then. That's the first three months covered."

Her eyes went wide. "But we won't be living together."

No, but she could move in here for the summer. The place was certainly big enough—I had bought it with a family in mind. The thought of her here ... didn't terrify me? Probably because I liked the idea of having my baby on site. Franky was just a bonus.

Best not to spook her. "I can pick the princess up from you, let you get your rest and some work done, then drop her off."

She nodded slowly. "Perhaps. I'll be on summer break then anyway."

"Right. Or you could start your book in the fall, enjoy your time with the baby."

She looked thoughtful for a second. "It's going to really change our lives."

"It sure is. But I think we're mature enough to handle it."

There was that sexy curve of her lips.

"Okay, you are. I'll be doing my best to act like I know what I'm doing."

"I saw the baby books."

I wasn't trying to hide them, though I probably shouldn't leave them lying around in case my family or teammates came over.

"Just trying to do my part."

"I appreciate it. Though I'm not sure how much of a say you'll get in the naming."

"Hold up there. If I leave it to you, we'll be naming our kid Escargot or Snaily Cyrus."

She laughed. I loved the husky timbre in it. "What about Shelly? Because—"

"Right, snails have shells. There you go again, Frank-explaining stuff to me. I did graduate magna cum laude."

"What did you major in?"

"I was pre-med. Thought I might have a career in physio or sports training if the hockey thing didn't pan out." *That's right, Doc. I know my biology.* Especially female anatomy.

It sounded like my academic achievements hadn't come up in conversation with Sean. I wondered what she'd think if she knew every insult she threw my way about dumb jocks and brainless athletes had spurred me on. Had made me study harder, determined to prove her wrong. So we were kids, but those childhood slights had stuck. Slug Girl accepted her weird and went on to become a world-famous expert in her field. I worked my ass off on the ice *and* in the classroom because success—in all things—was of paramount importance to me. Not that I took a single iota of credit for the doc being such a big shot, but she definitely had more of an influence on me than I would ever admit aloud.

"And there I was thinking you coasted by on your thick thighs and sparkling smile."

"Didn't hurt. But I knew I wanted to be a hockey player the minute I saw Theo Kershaw play when I was eight years old. Then finding out a few years later that the guy was my brother?" I gave a low whistle. "Mind blowing."

"I bet it was. I love seeing how close you've become. Theo's a wonderful guy."

"He is. And he's built a great life." *Watch out. Might be sounding a little jealous there.* "Is there pie?"

"Of course there is. Stay there and I'll serve it, my lord and master."

She was kidding, but again, I loved the dynamic here. Not that I wouldn't be happy to get my own pie, but eating together and joking about baby names? This was my jam. Or maybe I was just desperate to Frankenstein a family life together because my own was so inadequate.

After pumpkin pie with vanilla ice cream, I took care of the dishes while Franky put the rest of the leftovers away in the fridge.

"I'd better be off," she said.

"Not sure I like the idea of you driving at this hour." Or leaving at all.

Napping with her on the sofa, my arm around her middle, had given me all sorts of ideas.

First, about the tendrils of hair curled along her nape.

The curve of her neck, as graceful as a swan with one tiny little freckle I wanted to lick.

The warmth of her body as she unconsciously pressed against mine.

How I wanted nothing more than to drive into her and hold myself deep before I let go of everything I had inside her.

I followed her to the door, every cell in my body screaming to say something. Anything to make her stay.

She turned, adjusted her glasses, and looked at me. "Are you sleeping with anyone right now?"

I'd had chances, plenty of them. Instead, I'd put myself on a self-imposed sex fast because ... hell, I didn't know why.

Yeah, ya do. Because the puck bunnies couldn't hold up their end of the conversation, dude.

"Nope." No point explaining. She might get the wrong idea.

"I imagine you're tired—"

I cut her off with a kiss. I would never be too tired for this. For her.

She gasped into my mouth and made a hot, needy sound that went straight to my balls. I grasped her ass and ground her body into my cock, the part of my anatomy that had craved this woman for weeks.

She drew back, her plump lips kiss-swollen, her eyes lust-stoked. "Just sex, Jason. I know we have this connection now because of the baby, but I'm not looking for anything more than what we've already agreed upon."

I'd take that for now. Still, I couldn't resist a dig. "So, I have my uses."

She rolled her eyes. "Please don't go all sad sack because you consider yourself objectified. I also happen to like you, which I never in a million years thought I would say. Feel better?"

This woman's mouth would be my end. I fucking loved when she got all spiky and sassy.

"Thank you for acknowledging my male fragility." And then I kissed her again.

After a minute of deep, desperate tonguing, I pulled back. "I need to lock up and set the alarm. You head upstairs. First door on the right."

"Okay," she murmured. "Don't be long."

I could say I raced through the shutting-up-shop routine because sex was in my immediate future, but I also made sure to double-check every window and door before setting the alarm because, for the first time, I had more than a few trophies to protect.

I had *her*.

She was already in my bed, lights low, covers up to her collarbones, when I slipped into the room. A peek of bra strap sent my mind spinning.

I unzipped my jacket and ripped it off, throwing it over the clothes she had folded neatly and placed on top of my dresser. A study in contrasts.

She held up a hand.

"Let me savor it."

That just made me harder. Slowing down was not where I wanted this to go, but if that was her wish, I would suffer.

"How about you strip me?"

She swallowed and pushed back the covers. As she knelt up, my eyes feasted on her curvaceous body in a blue bra and panties. No tights in sight, thank God, but her abdomen was a little more rounded.

I moved closer to the bed and watched avidly as she curled her slender fingers in the waistband of my sweats.

She peered up at me. "Am I going too slow?"

"Thought that was what you wanted."

"I don't want to torture you." A hitch at the corner of her mouth said otherwise.

"I can handle it. Can you handle me?"

She pulled my sweats down, slowly, and proved that she could indeed handle me. I bit back a groan.

"I'm not sure. You're so ... thick."

"Thought you'd have a better word than that."

She stroked hard, thumbing the crown of my cock. "I think 'thick' is the most appropriate word to describe you. Thick cock, thick thighs, thick—"

"Careful, Doc."

"Lips."

That made me laugh. "Thick lips?"

She shrugged. "Not my best work."

I loved her sense of humor, that dry way she had with her. It was understated and sneaky and laced with her intelligence. Such a turn on.

I was beginning to think I was completely fucked here.

My cock was close to her mouth, and I was waiting, wanting, *dying* for her to do something about it. Another stroke, a dart of her tongue over her lips, a close examination like I was one of her specimens.

Then she applied a gentle kiss to the head. Not a suck, not a lick, just the sweet pressure of her lips, and I started leaking like a battered watering can.

"Francesca," I moaned.

Those cool blues flashed. She liked when I called her that. I liked when I called her that. Why weren't we fucking *all* the time?

When she finally took me in her mouth, the answer came to me: if I had this woman in my bed as much as I wanted, I would never leave. No family visits, no hockey games, no finding out who inherited the company in *Succession* (I had just started the last season). This woman and her gorgeous, velvet mouth would be my constant, only obsession.

"I'm not going to last, Francesca," I panted. But she didn't stop, and I didn't stop, and for the first time, I came inside her, not caring that it wouldn't result in new life.

Because it had already resulted in so much more.

CHAPTER THIRTY-TWO

Franky

I WOKE up to the sound of music and the smell of bacon.

I gave a cat stretch and let my mind stray to last night. It was wonderful—or at least, a wonderful release. Maybe I could do this, occasionally sleep with Jason to scratch an itch. Help us both out.

The image of that cute blonde, the one from the *Hot Goss* website, popped into my head. So he claimed he'd had "chances" but he hadn't indulged, whether out of guilt or honor or something else. It shouldn't have mattered, but it did. He had kept himself for me.

After a visit to the bathroom, I went downstairs. Jason was dancing to Bruno Mars while waving a spatula. For a few lovely seconds, I watched as he twitched his hips and shook his ass, the very firm and muscular rear I'd had the pleasure of gripping hard last night.

"Hello."

He whipped around. "Mornin', Doc. You hungry?"

"I am a bit." I moved forward and took a seat at the kitchen counter, which gave me the perfect view of the proceedings. This man cooking and dancing, happy as a clam. Anxious to avoid falling into his thirst trap, I refocused my attention on the backyard and the swing set surrounded by rust-colored leaves. A different kind of trap.

He handed me a cup of tea before returning to the stove. I took a sip. Earl Grey, perfectly steeped, the right amount of milk.

"You have tea in your cupboard?"

"I've got plenty of treats in my cupboard."

"Seriously, you have the tea I like?"

"Not some strategy to lure you into my bed, Francesca."

"No?" Because that would have totally worked if I knew about it.

"Nope. I have other ways of doing that. I just figured you might come to visit on occasion to discuss this joint enterprise of ours, and if that miracle ever occurred, I would like to be able to offer you a cup of your favorite hot beverage. It's not a big deal."

Oh, but it was. I took a sip to calm my frazzled nerves. That kind of sweetness was not on my bingo card, and I wasn't sure how to handle it.

"Thank you. That was very thoughtful."

"Tell that to every girl I've ever dated."

"That was your first mistake. Dating 'girls.'" I finger quoted "girls" because he definitely liked them younger, which can't have been conducive to a fulfilling relationship for a man of Jason's intelligence. I wondered if the women he slept with bored him.

"Just an expression. The women I've dated haven't really appreciated my kind gestures."

"Such as?"

"Well, one girl—woman—liked frogs. She had frog-this and frog-that in her bedroom, so I got her a special visit to the zoo in Boston to see the frogs up close and talk to a frog expert. A whaddyacallit?"

"Herpetologist." Though I suspected he knew exactly whaddyacallit.

"Yeah, that. Turned out she only liked cute little images on T-shirts or stuffed toys. She thought the genuine article was slimy and gross, but it wasn't. That was an interesting date. Me and the herpes guy got on like a house on fire."

I pursed my lips against a smile. *Stop making me fall for you.*

"Then there was the time I took a woman to this fancy restaurant in the North End, which is usually Italian, but she liked French food. Said crème brulee was her favorite, so I had a special one made by the chef—who I knew from this regular poker game—with her name burned into it with the blow torch, and she said I was trying to make her fat. Didn't appreciate it at all."

"Can't win."

"Right!" He shook his head sadly, though I could see the slightest grin teasing his sensuous mouth. He waved between us. "This, though. This is uncomplicated."

"Jason, this is the definition of complicated."

"I mean, from a dating perspective. We've kind of put the cart before the horse, figured out the end game—Super Kid—and now we're working our way back to basics. Mashed potatoes, cups of tea, great sex. Before you know it, you'll have to acknowledge me in public. And there you go, we're a couple."

He grinned, like it was the funniest thing. And while he could see the humor in our unusual situation, I couldn't.

It was bad enough I'd included him in my life—forever —because he wanted to be involved in his kid's life. I got that. I loved that. But I couldn't allow myself to fall for him as a potential partner. That would be disastrous.

Heartbreaking.

That swing set out back would be for his kids, plural, the children he would eventually have with a woman better suited to his big personality. I was too much of a wallflower to attract a buzzing bee like him for longer than a few seconds in the eon of our lives.

"This was a one-off. Don't rely on me for your sexual gratification."

He stirred the eggs once more, turned off the stove, covered the buttered toast, and placed it in front of me.

"Even when you're not around, maybe I'll think of you. Add you to the rotation."

I picked up a fork. "What an honor. Though the heavier I get, the further down the list I'll fall until, plop, I fall off altogether."

He took a seat beside me, and we instinctively clinked our forks like we were toasting breakfast. I chewed on my eggs, which were delicious. He couldn't even mess that up.

"Don't be so quick to self-deselect from the spank bank, Doc."

"Time and circumstance will do that for me. Luckily, you can let your imagination run riot because you won't have to see me for most of the pregnancy."

He frowned. "What does that mean?"

It was not my best moment, but it was time he knew.

"I won't be in Chicago."

"Won't be in Chicago?" Said slowly like the words made no sense.

"I'll be in Boston for the Winter semester. I have a guest lectureship at Harvard."

Dr. Bilious had finally signed off on it after making me explain, in writing, how exactly my absence would benefit Lakeshore. My open access funding requests were still under consideration.

His mouth fell open. "But you're pregnant!"

"Jason," I said in my calmest, soothe-the-beast voice, though I suspected it would come out a touch patronizing. "This has been planned for some time. There's no reason why the pregnancy should interfere with that."

"No reason? How about healthcare?"

"A recent study ranked Boston as having the best medical infrastructure in the world."

His frown deepened. "What does that have to do with having a baby?"

I took another bite of my eggs. However, I'd lost my appetite in the face of Jason's expression of betrayal.

"I'm doing my due diligence now and making sure I have an obstetrician I can trust while I'm there. People travel for work all the time."

"Not the same. You won't know anyone." I saw the moment the light bulb went off. "Except Sean."

"I'm sure I'll be seeing your brother occasionally, and it's great to know someone in a strange city. But I also have colleagues in Boston who can advise on all sorts of things. This will be a five-month appointment."

He was doing the math in his head, his mouth clamped so tight he would need a dentist. "Starting in January? So you'll be traveling back to Chicago close to the due date?"

"About a month before. People have been pregnant before, you know."

"But you haven't been." After an unsuccessful stab at

his fluffy scramble, he pointed an egg-free fork my way. "I don't like this plot twist. At all."

I was rather touched, though I suspected it had more to do with one of his sexual gratification options drying up or concern that I wouldn't look after his precious Super Kid. Well, I was perfectly capable of looking after both of us. This baby business had been *my* idea in the first place.

He remained quiet for a moment, likely planning his next salvo. I braced myself.

"Doc, if you don't want to have sex with me, just say so. Leaving the city is kind of drastic."

"This was planned before I even knew I'd be pregnant—"

"And maybe you should unplan it, because I sure as hell don't think you should be gallivanting around the country when you're about to have a baby."

"Says the man who lives, breathes, and dreams hockey. While gallivanting around the country."

"Don't make this a feminist thing. I'm all for you working until the day Super Kid starts getting antsy about making a break for it. I would just rather you were doing this close to home. To your family and the people who care about you." He pointed. "And being near Sean isn't the same."

I was starting to piss him off. Time for the kill shot.

"You're overreacting."

A dark flush appeared across his cheeks, his fury peaking. "I am not."

"My plans aren't changing. You're not the travel police and I will be in Boston for the majority of this pregnancy, whether you like it or not." I stood, no longer in the mood to mollycoddle him. "Thank you for breakfast and a lovely evening. I need to get home and make sure Bunsen and Beaker are okay."

"And who's going to look after the cats while you're away?"

"I'll probably take them with me. Or ask Rosie."

He stood and folded his arms. "Don't think of tapping me."

"Wouldn't dream of it."

"Good, because I'm not around enough. I'm too busy gallivanting around the country *doing my job.*"

I threw up my hands. "Which is so much more important than mine, apparently!"

"Never said it was."

I walked to the door with him trailing. As I grabbed my coat, he took it from me, perhaps determined to hold it hostage. Instead, he surprised me by holding it out so I could put my arms in it.

This is why I did it. This is why I picked a fight.

All these sappy little gestures were binding me to him like he had shot a love dart into my body. In the world of gastropods, love darts were calcified barbs speared by some snails into their mates during copulation. Sounded sweetly primal, didn't it? Not so much. Research had shown that darted snails laid fewer eggs and lived for three-fourths of a typical snail life.

Malacologists were curious about this evolutionary quirk: why evolve love darts if the mother of your offspring was harmed? The current thinking was that it came down to genetic selfishness. The darts discouraged the mother from mating again. They actually curtailed her life span! Meanwhile the darter carried on their own lineage, spreading sperm willy-nilly and guaranteeing genetic superiority.

Now here was Jason Isner, shooting his dart. I needed to rip that barb out, return to the me I was before I knew him.

Still holding the back of my coat, he pressed his lips to my ear. I waited for him to speak, but all he did was emit a breathy sigh, as if he had nothing to say. Or nothing that would make me see the sense he thought I was lacking. Sense was the only thing I had going for me right now.

I fumbled with the door and pulled it open, which set the alarm off.

Danger, danger, you've been darted by a player!

"I-I'm sorry," I gasped as he input the code behind me. Then I ran, like the coward I was, the echo of the alarm ringing in my ears.

DECEMBER

CHAPTER THIRTY-THREE

Jason

I HAD no idea why I was here.

Okay, I had a scintilla of one. A smidgen. A soupçon. A ... fuck, my brain was showing off, trying to impress a woman who didn't want to know.

"So, how does this work again?" I eyed the iPhone camera setup on the tripod. Connie was adjusting it, then checking the second camera setup, all focused on the sofa and armchair combo in his parents' basement. Apparently, we were making a podcast.

This held zero interest for me, but Hatch had dragged me here after I refused his offer for drinks at the Empty Net for a fourth time. Or maybe a fifth. Basically, for the last month, I didn't feel like hanging with my teammates or my family because I was still mad about the doc's high-handedness.

Now we were on the league's mandated holiday break,

after a great start to the season—20-8—and I needed to make an effort to be sociable with my family.

"It goes like this," Conor said. "One of us reads an AITD post—"

"A what?"

"Am I the Dick?" Hatch said. "It's where the internet goes to solicit the judgment of their peers on thorny moral, ethical, and relationship issues."

"Then we discuss." Conor finished his tweaking. "I've been doing this with my Motors teammates, and the fans love it."

He took a seat and opened another phone. How many phones did the kid have?

"You okay?" Hatch asked me.

"Why wouldn't I be?"

He shared a glance with his brother. "Because of that response, right there. You've been a bear for the last month. I had kind of assumed that once you got laid, you'd be cuddly Uncle Jason again. Is there a woman problem?"

"Not everything is about women. Just because you're all loved up and you—" I pointed at Conor. "Have more fan girls than you know what to do with, does not mean that everyone's got similar problems."

"Sounds like a woman," Conor said slyly. "Tell us all about it, Uncle J. We could even record it, get the fans' opinions."

"Do not press record. There's nothing to tell. It's just a compatibility issue."

My youngest nephew nodded solemnly. "In the bedroom?"

"No, not in the bedroom!" I caught the eye of a grinning Hatchling. "The bedroom is not a problem. Far from it. We're just not on the same wavelength outside it."

We still checked in with daily texts.

How are you feeling?

Fine. Great game!

Anything you need?

Not right now. Sorry for the loss.

The small talk was killing me.

I was still annoyed, but I also recognized that she was her own person. She had always done it her way, and I'd muscled my way into her life—and uterus—and she was rebelling against that intrusion. But spending a good chunk of her pregnancy in a different city, away from her family? Away from the father of her child? Such unilateral thinking did not square with the cooperation I expected during this momentous time.

Conor narrowed his eyes. "Is this someone we know?"

"Nope." But they would soon enough. Unless …

Franky could keep her pregnancy a secret in Boston, if she wanted to. She wouldn't have to breathe a word of it to anyone. Sean was so clueless he probably wouldn't even realize she was pregnant until she went into labor.

That couldn't be her game, could it?

Even more irked than when I'd come into this stupid basement, I muttered, "Let's get this shit over with."

"HEY, IT'S JASON."

Intercom static crackled back, then a cheerfully surprised, "Oh, hi. Come on up."

I headed up the stairs, wondering if these steps were

safe for pregnant women, then dismissing it as yet another example of my patriarchal thinking. Hell, I was running arguments in my head on behalf of the doc!

After Conor's podcast, I'd come to a decision. I needed to be the bigger person here, and as it was the season of goodwill toward my fellow men—and women—this gave me the perfect opportunity to offer an olive branch.

She stood at the door to her apartment, her hair in that ballyhoo topknot, her glasses slightly crooked, wearing leggings and an oversized green knit sweater open against a white V-neck T-shirt. Her middle had thickened slightly, though maybe I only noticed because I knew.

"Merry Christmas, Francesca."

"Merry Christmas." It might have been my imagination that her voice trembled. "I didn't expect you."

"I figured I'd take a chance and surprise you. Rosie mentioned that you were heading over to her dads' place for Christmas lunch later, so I thought I'd catch you before you left." I held up a shopping bag. "Plus, I brought gifts. Ho fucking ho."

Smiling tentatively, she stood back to let me in. "Well, if there are gifts involved."

It had been a month since I'd seen her. Touched her. Smelled her hair. I had hoped that being in her orbit again would arouse general feelings of affection and friendliness. Maybe a tepid warmth at seeing her body developing with the baby we had made.

What I had *not* hoped for was a thickening of my cock and a kick of lust so savage I was having a hard time keeping my hands to myself.

The cat hissed at me the second I crossed the threshold. Little shit knew my game.

"Happy holidays to you, Bunny Boy."

She shut the door. "Can I take your coat?"

"Sure, I won't stay long. I know you're busy." I hung my coat on the hook behind the door.

"Come sit. I've been wrapping gifts for everyone and I'm way behind."

"I can help."

"That would be great. Eggnog?"

"Sure. With nutmeg?"

"Of course. We're not heathens."

I settled on the floor before assorted boxes and wrapping paper, hoping the discomfort would refocus the blood surge to my groin. While she puttered in the kitchen, I took it all in. The place was cozy and festive, Christmas tree dressed to the nines, Nat King Cole crooning about chestnuts roasting. It reminded me of how I grew up, only that was a lie. Dad had already abandoned one kid and was faking it with us. He had a girlfriend in the burbs and while Mom took him back that first time, I had already checked out.

Maybe I wasn't cut out for this family business. I tried to take my cues from Theo, the best dad I knew, but was that enough? Was I trying to force this, make a family where none existed?

Franky placed a couple of glasses of nutmeg-dusted eggnog on the coffee table and took a seat. "I'm glad you came over."

"Yeah?"

"I'm not happy with how things went the last time."

"Well, why would you be? I was a jerk. I'm not used to such strong-willed women. Well, I am. My mother. My family. Lauren. The Chase sisters."

"But not the women you impregnate?"

The sass was strong with this one.

"Or date. Not that we're dating, but I guess the dynamic isn't far off. You occupy that space in my head and I'm used to the women I date—or potentially impregnate—listening to what I have to say."

"Probably because you tend to date women who have barely graduated—"

"Uh huh."

"College," she said with a grin.

"I do like 'em educated."

"Sure, yet you don't like when they talk back. Or decide they have lives independently of you. Or make their own choices."

I leaned back against the sofa. "I'm not saying I was wrong—I should have some input here—but I did probably go about it in a less-than-subtle fashion."

"And I should take some responsibility. I blindsided you. I could have been gentler about it." She looked like she wanted to say something else but held back at the last moment.

I reached for her hand. "I'm just worried about you both."

She squeezed back. "I know, but I will be okay, and I'll see you when you come to Boston to play. Now drink your eggnog and tell me how you've been."

It was as easy as that. I filled her in on my travel, the games, Conor's stupid podcast, or "dick-cast" as I'd labeled it, which had her chuckling. She told me about the hoops she had to jump through to get her article funded, the office Christmas party from hell, and how different her body felt.

"It's almost ten weeks," she said. "I can't believe how the time has flown."

It hadn't for me. The last month had been excruciating.

"So, I have an appointment with the OB on January third. I checked your playing schedule—"

"You want me there?"

She looked shy. "Only if you'd like to be."

"No place I'd rather be."

She smiled, sniffed a little, and picked up her eggnog. "I'm kind of hormonal. And I really need to finish wrapping these presents."

"Speaking of ..." I placed the shopping bag I'd brought in front of her.

She pulled out the packages and as expected, read the gift cards for each one. "You got something for my cats." A gentle awe touched her voice.

"I doubt they got anything for me, but I didn't want to leave them out."

She opened that one first, revealing a couple of salmon-colored plushies. "It's a brain," she said.

"And a set of lungs. I thought they might like something with a science theme to it. They have strings, so they can play with them. And most importantly, learn."

Her cheeks turned pink, a watercolor bloom. "I think they're going to love them." She lay the brain in front of Bunsen on the sofa, who regarded it with suspicion. The lungs, she placed on the floor. A couple of seconds later, an orange paw emerged from under the sofa and snatched at the gift. (Narrator: It was never seen again.)

"Success. Open this one next." I handed a wrapped box to her.

"The card says 'Super Kid.' I worry you're setting our child up for too-high expectations with a nickname like that."

Our child. "That's just what I'm calling the kid while in

Hotel Utero. When he or she checks out, I'll come up with another nickname, after I've figured out their personality."

She opened the wrapping paper carefully, not like me who would always tear into my wrapped gifts. Flipping the lid of the box, her hand flew to her chest. "Jason."

"I figured you're almost at the three-month mark, so it's safe to go a little crazy."

The box was filled with cute clothes, onesies and little tees and adorable pants. The day after she told me she was pregnant, I bought them in a baby store in Roscoe Village, but I couldn't gift them to her until now. It would be tempting fate.

She held up a T-shirt, my favorite one. It had a snail and the words "Little Trailblazer." With her grave expression, I wondered if I had upset her.

"There's some Rebels gear in there," I said, filling the silence. "You know, Theo still gets a cut because he promotes them on Insta. He was the first player to do a Rebels baby gear tie-in after Hatch was born."

She fingered the fabric of a Rebels onesie, the cutest fucking thing you ever saw.

And promptly burst into tears.

CHAPTER THIRTY-FOUR

Franky

NO ONE HAD TOLD me being pregnant would be so emotional.

Scratch that, *everyone* had told me. I had plenty of women in my life who had already been through this, but I had assumed my innate lack of sentimentality and my ability to logic my way out of any problem would apply here. I wouldn't get upset because I said so.

But the last month had been tough. The holidays were my favorite time of the year. I loved having time off to decorate my apartment, see more of my family and friends, and catch up on my scientific journal article TBR. Only, I hadn't reckoned on how much I regretted my fight with Jason.

Or how much I would miss him.

All the hockey franchises had a two-day break, so I knew he would likely be spending it with his family.

Knowing he was less than a mile away and not speaking to me had been excruciating. I had picked that fight, and here *he* was apologizing. That should be me, but I didn't want to explain why I'd done it. Why I needed to push him away.

And now I was acting like he had upset me, when he hadn't. Not one bit.

He moved in quickly beside me and placed an arm around my shoulders. I sank into him like he was my weighted blanket and a cup of hot chocolate, all in one.

"Francesca, what's wrong? You're feeling okay, aren't you?"

"Y-yes, I'm fine. Physically. Everything is as it should be. It's just …"

His lips touched the top of my head, then strayed to my temple. As much as I loved having them there, I couldn't take the risk.

I drew back. "I hated that we haven't been talking properly."

His expression shifted from concern to relief. "I've hated it, too."

"And for you to come over today with these gifts. Even ones for B&B, who don't deserve it—"

"Everyone deserves a Christmas gift, even a little asshole like Bunny. Beaker, too."

I chuckled. "I suppose. It's made me realize that you will always have the moral high ground with our kid."

"And that's a bad thing?"

"No. Maybe. I think you're going to be the amazing, thoughtful, fun parent, while I'll be the logical, boring, let's-look-at-this-reasonably parent."

"Pretty sure we need both types of parenting styles. And I need to learn to look at things reasonably, too, such as your career plans in January. That situation needed a bit more logic and a lot less knee-jerk reaction. I tend to blow up, but I usually calm down pretty quickly."

His hand on my back was so soothing, so perfect. I'd missed this closeness.

I was falling for him, this man who would be my child's wonderful dad. I had to get a grip. Even if I couldn't wish it away entirely, I could minimize the damage.

"I know you like to be in control," I said. "I think we both do, so that makes for locked horns, on occasion."

"Yeah, there's that, but also ..." He hesitated.

"What?"

"It occurred to me that maybe you wanted to hide the pregnancy from people you know. People *we* know. If you're in a different city, you wouldn't have to answer questions about it or reveal who got you into this fine mess."

He really thought ... oh my God. "Jason, when the time is right, I will be happy to tell people you're my child's father. Did you really think I planned this guest lectureship with subterfuge about my pregnancy in mind?"

"Stop it with the big words, Doc. You know it turns me on."

I shook my head. "You're impossible. No one will believe it, but I won't mind them knowing. The Nerd catches the Jock—what a story! That *Hot Goss* rag will be all over it."

His lips twitched. "Pretty sure the Jock caught the Nerd. I had to beg you to let me deliver the goods."

And that had us both thinking about the night we conceived our baby, and how sexy it all was. How crazy the chemistry was between us whenever we were in the same room together. I needed to douse the flames, and the best way to do it was to recalibrate our relationship.

"Can we be friends again?"

His brow crumpled, just for a second. "Were we before?"

"I thought we were getting there. And as co-parents, friends would make it easier." A position I was determined to maintain. I couldn't have him any other way, but I needed us to be here for each other.

"And I'm assuming this is a friends without benefits kind of deal?"

I gave him a prim look, to which he answered with a naughty grin.

"I think that's why I've been pushing you to be with someone. If you were, I wouldn't feel like a placeholder in your life. The person you can screw because screwing anyone else makes you feel like a bad person."

He considered that. "You feel like a placeholder?"

"Somewhat. I'm attracted to you, Jason. Very much so. But I'm also exceptionally hormonal, so the combination of 'you're the daddy' with 'awesome orgasms' is pushing this into shaky territory. Neither of us went into this looking for a relationship, at least not with each other. A relationship with our child, yes. And I want to put the baby first. We need to do that."

He nodded. "The baby will always come first."

This was good. Both of us were children of divorce, and I knew that marriage or anything like it was not for me.

I was too weird, too insular, too out there to hold the attention of a man, let alone one as conventional and normal as Jason. He had also made his position clear: he wasn't interested in a relationship, either. At least, that was his mantra now. This man could get anyone—images of Miss Perky Texan Tits flooded my brain—so when he decided *that* was back on the table, that fatherhood wouldn't block him from a truly fulfilling life, he would do it. And I would be happy for him. Because the man was my co-parent and now, my friend.

"So, we're good?"

He blew out a breath. "We're always good. There's another gift."

Right, something for me. This was a medium-sized box, and when I opened it, I was greeted by a black and white cushion with a cat face on it, Hello Kitty style.

"A cat cushion?"

"Turn it over."

I did and found a cat ... skull? It took me a moment.

"Schrodinger's Cat? In cushion form?"

He shrugged, almost diffidently. "I saw it on Instagram and thought it was cute. For the science nerd in your life."

That was me. *Holy Superposition, Batman.*

"I went as Schrodinger's Cat at a Halloween party at Theo's. The one before last."

He grinned. "You wore a cardboard box and kept bumping into people with your sharp edges."

A metaphor for my life. I couldn't believe he'd remembered.

"I have one more gift," he said.

"Jason! Let me give you something before I faint with embarrassment."

"Alright. Better be good."

As if I could compete with all this perfection. I headed to the tree and picked up a wrapped gift.

"I'm behind with wrapping all the others, but I bought this one a while ago."

Unlike my calm approach, he ripped the paper off in seconds. He opened the lid of the box and stared at it.

"Francesca." His voice was a low, sexy rumble. Almost reverently, he touched the front of the dark green T-shirt emblazoned with "Hockey Dad." I thought it would go nicely with his eyes.

"I know we haven't announced it yet, and I'd rather see the OB first before we do that. Just to make sure everything is okay."

"In the meantime, I'll wear it around the house." He looked up at me, his eyes shiny with emotion. "It's a great gift. Thank you."

"There's one more, underneath it. I can do plural gifts, too."

Chuckling softly, he pulled the soft cotton aside. Holding up the onesie I had bought, he burst out laughing.

"Too right I did!" The onesie said, "Daddy slipped one past the goalie." "I love it."

My phone buzzed and I checked it quickly. It was a text from Violet.

I'll be there in about ten minutes.

"That's Violet, telling me she's on her way. She's giving me a ride to Dante and Cade's for Christmas lunch."

"Okay, I'd better be off." He placed the box I'd given him in the shopping bag he brought, and I followed him to the door. "Sorry I wasn't all that helpful with the gift wrapping. Just with the gift unwrapping."

"No problem." As I pulled his jacket from the coat hook, I noticed the cap of something familiar. "Is that an EpiPen in your pocket?"

"Or maybe I'm just glad to see you." He waggled his eyebrows. "I figure it doesn't hurt to carry it in case I come across someone who might have an allergic reaction."

Perhaps he knew someone else who was deathly allergic

to nuts, but I suspected that was for me. He wanted to be ready.

I could barely get the next words out. "I'm glad you came over. That we cleared the air."

"Me, too." He turned at the door and held my gaze, clear and true. "You look good, Francesca. Pregnancy suits you."

"Thanks," I whispered, and for a moment I was tempted to say, "stay. Be here so I can tell Violet you're the dad. You're the one."

But that would be absurd. Wishful. Besides, Vi knew me too well. She would see my lovelorn expression and figure out that I was in love with the father of my child.

What a disaster.

"I have one more gift." He slipped a small, wrapped box out of his jacket pocket and placed it in my hand. "Text me about the doctor's appointment."

"Okay."

For a moment, I thought he might kiss me. For all my insistence that we were friends and nothing else, I would have welcomed it. A holiday kiss under the—well, I hadn't put up mistletoe, but I could have imagined it was there.

But he was conscious of our secret, and with the reflexes that made him a star on the ice, he left before I could beg him to stay.

I unwrapped the gift, not carefully as I had done with the others, but frenzied and completely unlike me. It was a jewelry box. With shaky fingers, I opened it and found a charm embedded in velvet.

A silver snail with a black pearl for its shell.

Ten minutes later, when Vi knocked, I was still standing at the door, stunned at Jason's generosity and thoughtfulness.

And with none of my presents wrapped.

JANUARY

CHAPTER THIRTY-FIVE

Jason

"JASON, ARE YOU NERVOUS?"

On the wheeled stool, I spun back toward the exam table and ground to a halt.

"Why would I be nervous?"

Franky squinted at me. "Because you've fondled all the equipment, spun around on that chair like it's an amusement ride, and pretty much babbled nonstop since we got here."

What did she expect? This was an important appointment, the first one that gave us the all-clear for the baby.

"Just want to know everything's okay."

She grasped my hand. "We'll know soon enough."

And right after, she was leaving for Boston. I was supposed to be cool with it. I most definitely was not. But a surefire way of pushing someone away was begging them to stick around.

The door opened and an older Southeast Asian woman came in. I'd met Dr. Patel before because she had been the OB for all of Theo's kids.

"Hello, you two." Official introductions were made while the doctor washed her hands and fiddled with some of the buttons on the monitor. "How are you feeling, Franky?"

"Not bad. A little nauseous and tired, but I'm eating well"—she raised her eyebrow at me, healthy lunch provider—"and I haven't noticed anything out of the ordinary. At least, not according to the books I've read on the topic."

The doctor nodded. "Okay, feel free to raise your shirt so we can take a look."

Franky stared at me, willing me not to look.

Eyebrow raise from *moi*. You couldn't pay me to turn the other way.

She was thicker than the last time I'd seen her naked, more round, and her skin had stretched slightly to accommodate Super Kid. Color flushed her cheeks, though that might be because the gel Dr. Patel applied was cold, not embarrassment at me seeing her increasing size.

I caught her eye and mouthed, "So. Hot."

She shook her head, reddened, and did that thing where she tried to pretend that I wasn't the most annoying person in the room. Within a couple of seconds, her gaze found mine again, probably because I was irresistible.

"Beautiful," I murmured, because she was, and I needed her to know, even if she didn't take me seriously.

"And there we are," Dr. P. said after a couple of moments. "Mom and Dad, meet your baby."

Dragging my eyes away from Franky, I focused on the black-and-white screen image, which seemed to pulsate in step with my heartbeat. Then I realized that was the baby's.

My baby has a heartbeat.

"Is everything okay?" I blurted out, though a heartbeat was probably a very good sign.

"Your baby looks to be doing just fine. The head, torso, limbs—all within normal parameters."

I met Franky's wet-eyed gaze and curled my hand around hers. With a bone-crushing squeeze, she held on as we both watched that monitor, listened to that echo of life, and let it all sink in.

"Look at that, Francesca," I murmured. "She's as healthy as can be."

Dr. Patel smiled. "Well, we can't really tell the sex from this position. Baby's a little shy. Maybe the next time."

Franky swallowed. "I-I don't need to know. I think I want it to be a surprise."

I hadn't given it much thought, but the moment she said it, I knew she was right. "No rush to reveal it, Doctor P."

"What about the due date?" Franky asked. "We have an idea, but wanted to be sure."

"Let me see ..." She checked Franky's chart and ran a calculation on her phone. There was an app for everything. "I'd estimate about July eighth."

So, after the Finals. I grinned at Franky. "Perfect timing."

"Yes, I had your hockey schedule in mind." She sniffed, and I raised her hand to my lips. So we weren't a couple in the traditional sense, but this was huge. I would use any excuse to maintain this connection. To touch her. To kiss her.

"And what about the nuchal translucency test?" Franky tightened her grip on my hand.

Dr. Patel nodded. "That looks okay from what I can see here. But we'll also complete your bloodwork and get back to you in a couple of days with a final assessment on any chromosomal differences. Right now, everything appears normal. Mom and baby are doing very well. Any more questions?"

I had a million, but none she could probably answer. Mostly I wondered where did she get off calling my kid "normal" when it was clear she would be in the "super" range?

Franky and I shared a look, then turned back to the OB.

"Think we're good," I said.

She nodded. "Now I understand that you'll be spending the majority of your pregnancy in Boston, Franky."

"Yes, I've already found an OB there, but I'll be back long before the baby is born."

"Okay. Just let our assistant know where to send your files and results, so we can maintain that continuity of care. And you can pick up a photo of your baby at the front desk."

We thanked her and watched as she left the room.

I released a held breath. "You okay?"

"We just saw our baby, Jason. If it wasn't real before ..."

"I know. We've got ourselves a little plum in there, veering into kiwi territory." I'd memorized the fruit comparisons chart for fetus sizes.

She rolled in her lips. "I think you've done more research than me."

I PULLED up outside her building. The joy I'd felt at seeing my kid on that monitor was starting to fade, evicted by a growing dread.

"I'll walk you up."

"Oh, okay."

At her front door, she turned to me. My heart clattered wildly in my chest. Tomorrow, she was leaving for Boston, and while I would see her a couple of times when my playing schedule took me there, the mere fact of her absence from my everyday life felt all wrong. We had just witnessed something miraculous—the life we'd created, the heartbeat of our child—and there was no going back to before. I wanted to see her and my kid all the time and walk this journey together.

Suddenly I had no words. Me, Jason Isner, who could talk the hind legs off a herd of mules, was tongue-tied. All my nervous energy had been expended, and now a cloud of sadness had rushed in to take its place.

She placed her hands on my chest. "Thanks for coming with me. It meant a lot."

"Wouldn't have missed it for the world." I placed my hands over hers, trapping them against my pecs. "All packed?"

"Mostly." She smiled. "I'm going to miss my special lunches."

She didn't know yet, but I'd be taking care of her nutritional needs in Bean Town. The last thing I needed was for the doc to get distracted by some snails banging and not get her recommended daily calorie intake.

"I'm going to miss your snark," I said.

"Oh, I can still provide. Text. Video call."

"Telegram. Carrier pigeon."

"It's not far. And not for long." She stepped back, setting space between us. "Take care and keep winning, Jason."

I would. But it sure would be easier, knowing she was

safe. That they were both safe. Time to activate my network of spies.

But there was one more thing I needed to do. I stepped back into her space, cupped her fine-boned jaw, and inclined my head. Her gray-blue eyes turned silver as I stamped my mouth over hers, claiming what was mine.

For a split second, she made no reaction. But then she moaned, right into my mouth, and I deepened the kiss, telling her everything I couldn't say with words.

This means something, Francesca. We are bonded forever.

Then I broke away before she could.

She touched her lips. Her eyes were on fire, her cheeks flushed. "What was that for?"

"Just a little something to keep you warm in Boston."

She opened her mouth and closed it again. *Congratulations, Isner, you left your woman speechless.*

Turning heel—kind of pissy about it, too—she headed inside. I waited a moment for ... I wasn't sure what. The gods to change her mind?

This was Francesca St. James we were talking about. She was the captain of her own ship, and I was merely a deckhand.

One week later ...

"WHERE'S YOUR BUDDY, THEN?"

I looked down into suspicious green eyes as they quickly adjusted and attended to the main event: getting fed. Bunsen was kind of dainty but once that bowl of food made an appearance, he turned as savage as his ancestors.

Beaker, when he deigned to show his cute orange face, alternated between scared silly and a hurricane making landfall. When he wasn't hiding out under the sofa, he'd taken to settling behind the screen guard in the empty fireplace.

"Beakster! Food's up!"

A crashing noise, which sounded like the logs in the basket by the hearth, was followed by a cartoon-quality skitter and Beaker's appearance in the kitchen. Bunsen looked up absently and returned to his food bowl. I stepped in front of him and pointed at the other one.

"That's for you, buddy."

Rosie had said they preferred their own bowls but that sometimes Beaker forgot and went for Bunsen's. I hadn't realized how much time I would spend on this kind of food-distribution nuance when I volunteered to look after the cats while she took a weekend trip to help Franky get set up in Boston.

I was surprised Franky didn't bring them with her, but Bunsen was old—maybe twelve—while Beaker was about six, a teen in cat years. She worried that the elder statesman wouldn't like the journey so Rosie was subletting Franky's place to look after them, and I was the backup.

Also, Rosie knew I was the father of the kid. Franky had told her at Thanksgiving.

I was cool with that. It also gave me leave to tell my kin, though part of me held back. How would they feel about me essentially "giving up" as Lauren termed it, foregoing a shot at the regular nuclear unit? Most of my family were in real relationships, some with kids, some not yet on that road. They were doing it "conventionally," and here I was, grasping at the first opportunity to procreate that came my way.

What I knew for sure was that I had to tell Sean, especially given the fact he was Franky's first choice. With the cats mid-feed, I took a seat on the doc's sofa and video-called my brother.

"Hey!" he said. "Hold on a second. Let me find a quiet spot."

"Thought you'd be at home." It was a Saturday morning after all.

"Mel had a brunch thing with her girlfriends, and I tagged along. This place does an amazing bread pudding, as good as M. Henry."

"Doubt that, dude." M. Henry did the best breakfast bread pudding in Chicago, and I was damned sure it could take all comers from Bean Town.

Sean scrunched up his eyebrows. "So, that doesn't look like your place. Is everything okay?"

"Maybe I should call later. Let you get back to it."

"No way. I hardly ever talk to you these days now that you're back in Chicago." He settled somewhere, maybe the corridor to the restrooms. "Is this about Mom?"

"No, she's fine. We're all fine." I hadn't really thought this through. "So, have you run into Franky?"

"Not yet. She's been busy getting settled, and I think Rosie's visiting this weekend." He frowned. "Why?"

"Just wondered. You guys are good pals and all that." Still frowning. When he got like that, he looked like Dad. "I have news. Franky's pregnant."

He blinked. Blinked some more. "She is? That's great."

I waited.

"Jason, why are *you* telling me this?"

I inhaled quickly and blew out a harried breath. "Because I'm the father."

"No way! That's wild! How did this happen?"

How about she was desperate enough to take me up on my offer? "After she asked you, we started talking about it. The whys, the why-the-fuck-not. I want a kid and she wants a kid and—"

"So you're going to be involved in the baby's life?"

"I know it sounds strange, but we have similar viewpoints when it comes to raising children." We had similar viewpoints about a lot of things—the ick of domestic pets in costumes, cheese first always when building a taco, that *Better Call Saul* is superior to *Breaking Bad*. You know, the important stuff.

"I'm kind of stunned here, but happy for you. If this is what you want."

Of course it was what I wanted. But his words confirmed my suspicion: people thought it was a strange way to go about things. I'd thought so, too, when Franky first suggested it.

"I do. But we're keeping it under the radar for now, so not a word to Mom." The "or Dad" coda was unnecessary. "I just figured you might see Franky soon and I'd rather she didn't feel compelled to lie to one of her oldest friends."

"Yeah, that makes sense." Said as if it was the only thing about this situation that did. "I thought you guys despised each other."

"'Despised' is a bit strong. More like a 'healthy dislike,' but that's changed to a healthy respect that will center us as we co-parent our child."

Sean snorted. "You read that in a book?"

"Maybe. Look, I know it's hard to wrap your head around it, but I thought you should know. Plus, she asked you first, and I figured you might have ... feelings about that."

"Feelings?" He chuckled. "Oh, I have feelings alright. Confusion, bafflement, puzzlement."

"Pretty sure they mean the same thing," I gutted out. He was starting to piss me off.

"If you're worried I might be, oh, *jealous*, then don't be. Franky and I have never—well, there was that one time ..."

"One time what?" It came out as a bark, and was soon followed by a red mist veiling my eyes. His next words were indecipherable, lost in the background noise of the restaurant.

"Listen, I have to go," he said. "But seriously, J, I'm thrilled for you guys. And I'll be seeing Franky soon, which will be great." He spoke to someone off-camera. "Yeah, be right there." And then he clicked off.

One time what?

One. Time. What?

My brother and Franky? I knew nothing about this, and suddenly I was thrown into a cauldron of black-biled jealousy. They had a long history together, had things in common, were confidantes. Not that it mattered. Sean had found his girl, and he and Franky were just friends. If my brother had feelings for the doc, he would have jumped at her offer.

Right?

Bunsen had finished his meal and decided he needed someone to acknowledge this. He jumped up on the sofa beside me and hissed.

I knew exactly how he felt.

Now that I'd done my duty—cat feeds and the sharing of good tidings—I needed to go. I had morning skate in half an hour, and then lunch with Lauren to share the baby news. But maybe I should check in with the doc. Let her know the boys were fed and petted.

Bunsen sneered. Forget *petted*. *Fed* would have to do.

I took a photo of him and texted Franky with the caption: "I'm still hungry and this asshole thinks I'm cute."

No response. I was weighing what that might mean when a text came in from Conor—or rather a photo of a pile of baby books.

On my living room table.

Next was a video clip of Duran Duran singing "Is There Something I Should Know?"

That little shit. I stabbed the call icon.

"Hi, Uncle Jason."

"What are you doing in my house?"

"I have a couple of days before the Motors-Rebels game, so I came into town early. I wanted a little me time, so I stopped by yours. You gave me a key, remember?"

Me time? I was going to have to change my sheets, wasn't I?

"You don't text first?"

His chuckle was pure evil. "How else would I find out what the fam is up to? Care to explain?"

"Just holding them for a friend."

"Oh, you need to do better than that."

I blew out a breath. "We're keeping it on the downlow. No announcements yet."

"Like 'secret meetings at a children's birthday party' downlow? Or 'hooking up in a Detroit hotel' downlow? Or maybe 'dirty rendezvous in your niece's bedroom at Halloween' downlow?"

Fuck. All this time?

Franky had texted back.

He's such a curmudgeon! I assume
Beaker's hiding.

"This is at a delicate stage," I growled at my nephew.

"Jason Isner, did you knock up Francesca St. James?"

"Bye, Connie." I clicked off and returned to the text thread with the doc.

ME

Yeah, he came out for food, though.

I told Sean the news.

DOC

Oh, wonderful! How did he take it?

ME

Good. Surprised. To be expected.

The three dots popped up, did their merry little dance, then disappeared. My phone rang instead, and something crashed behind me because that dummy Beaker got a fright.

I answered the video call. "Hey."

"Hey there!" She looked a little flushed, which sent me into a mild panic.

"What's going on? Have you been running?"

"No, just unpacking. I did most of it last week, but I had forgotten one suitcase, and I just brought it upstairs."

For the duration of her stint in Boston, Franky had taken over a sublet in Cambridge from another professor who was currently in the original Cambridge, as in England. Apparently, professors were guest lecturing and subletting like there was no tomorrow.

"Isn't Rosie there? She should be helping with that."

"She went out for bagels." She sat down on a bed. "Tell me about Sean."

"Nothing to tell. He didn't really get it, but then not many people will, I suppose."

"I told Rosie and my family, and they got it. It's not so out there, is it?"

Now I was projecting my insecurities onto her. Just because I expected people to respond with, *that guy, a dad? And with that beautiful, intelligent woman?* didn't mean she felt the same way.

"No, not at all. It's just weird telling people this personal thing." I wasn't even going to bring up the fact Conor was currently flipping through the baby books I'd left out for all and sundry to find.

"I suppose it is. But when it comes down to it, this is between us, Jason. We made this decision, this pact, if you will. We're the ones who will be responsible for loving this child. For making sure she's never hungry or scared or unhappy. It doesn't matter what anyone else thinks."

She was right. But that didn't stop me thinking about Sean's reaction and how that wide-eyed blink would be playing on repeat with everyone I told in the coming months. And it wasn't much of a leap from that reaction to me drawing another conclusion.

She needed your sperm. That's the only reason she's even talking to you right now.

Because she certainly wouldn't be, otherwise.

CHAPTER THIRTY-SIX

To: Franky St. James
From: Marcus Bilson, Chair
Subject: Future grant funding requests

Dr. St. James,

It has come to my attention that your grant funding request to the Animal Behavior Society was not vetted by my office before submission. I understand that my predecessor gave you significant latitude to conduct your research and its ancillary activities. However, my memorandum, dated September 15, specified that all grant applications originating from this department's faculty are to be funneled through my office first. While this might seem restrictive, we must all work together in the spirit of cooperation to ensure alignment with departmental goals.

Allied to this, congratulations on being awarded the grant from the Animal Behavior Society. The department is proud of your work and how well it reflects on this institution.

Marcus Bilson, PhD
Chair, Department of Biology
Lakeshore University

Franky

"DID YOU NEED A CHAIR, Dr. St. James?"

I looked over my glasses at the graduate student who had offered and shook my head.

"Thank you, but no. Let's continue with the examination." Leaning carefully over the terrarium to ensure Super Kid's increasingly noticeable bump didn't get too close, I indicated with a pointer at the subject of my presentation during this graduate seminar. The *Deroceras cecconii*, a terrestrial pulmonate gastropod mollusk, a species of slug local to central Italy, was currently engaged in a vigorous—for it—bout of copulation with a mate.

"See how the penial glands are starting to evert over the partner to deposit a secretion."

"The secretion has such an unusual shape." June was one of the more promising grad students. "Like translucent antlers."

"Yes, exactly. You'll also note that our specimens have already undergone a reciprocal exchange of sperm. Note the off-white blobs here and here. So what is the purpose of the post-exchange secretion? Any ideas?"

June looked thoughtful. "Similar to love darts of some snail species?"

"It's possible. The secretion could be a way of marking the mate, ensuring they don't mate with someone else too soon. Or perhaps it's an additional bonding element. See the—"

"Dr. St. James?"

Looking over my shoulder at the source of the voice, I was surprised to see the assistant to Dr. Al-Hadi, head of Harvard's Department of Organismic and Evolutionary Biology.

"Yes?"

"Sorry to interrupt, Professor. Dr. Al-Hadi was wondering if you could stop by his office this morning. We tried to call, but it went straight to voice mail."

The specimens in the Harvard Malacology Lab were sensitive to sound when the terrarium lids were removed, so I usually required all cell phones to be on mute or vibrate. It looked like I'd turned mine off altogether.

"Please tell him I'll stop by after my seminar."

I turned back to the small group of students and researchers. "Okay, where were we?"

MELISSA AND SEAN had invited me over to their apartment in the Back Bay—Melissa had moved in right after the holidays—and we'd had a lovely meal of pumpkin soup, chicken pesto pasta (nut free), and garlic bread. Now that Sean knew about the pregnancy, we were having a good laugh about my original "special" request.

"I can't believe you didn't tell me!"

A blushing Sean gazed in adoration at Melissa, who was

all agog at the situation. "It was a delicate time. You and I had just reconnected, so that kind of complication might have scared you off."

"I like to think I'm made of sterner stuff." She sent a grin my way. Melissa and I had hit it off immediately, which was unusual because people had a hard time warming up to me. "Just think, I could have been having dinner with my boyfriend's baby mama. You've denied me a great cocktail party story."

Sean reached over to cover Melissa's hand. "Sorry, honey. Next time someone asks me to be a sperm donor, I'll consider the future entertainment value."

Melissa chuckled, then turned to me. "Sorry, I don't mean to make fun."

"Not at all. I did ambush him and I so wish I'd recorded it. His face was priceless."

"Oh, I bet!" She jumped up from the table. "Time for the peach cobbler. Vanilla ice cream for everyone?"

"Yes!" both Sean and I said in unison.

With Melissa in the kitchen, the mood turned a little more reserved. She was a bubbly individual, the kind of person who brightened every room she entered. I thought it interesting how well the two of them balanced each other. "My Seven lifts the spirit of his Six," Melissa had said. While I didn't completely buy into the pseudoscience around Enneagram personality types, I recognized that some people just fit together.

Sean was still digesting the reveal of my baby's father, and now that Melissa was occupied, I could tell he wanted to analyze it further.

"When Jason told me, I couldn't believe it. Still can't, to be honest."

"I know, it seems like a strange choice."

"Maybe not so strange. Jason's always wanted kids. I didn't know about your baby fever, but it's been on his radar for years."

"So, why hasn't it happened? Many men his age are already married with families." Now that Sean knew, I felt safe asking for more in-depth knowledge about his brother.

"I think he's worried he'll turn out like Dad."

"But he has so many stronger male influences in his life. You, Theo, his teammates. And he's such a family-oriented person."

"It's because he could be traded in an instant," Melissa said as she placed the peach cobbler down before me. The scent of sweet fruit and fragrant biscuit crust filled the air. "He was, what, ten years with the Cougars? He could have settled down here, but he didn't."

Sorry, but that explained nothing. "Again, plenty of pro athletes marry and start families with the risk of trade hanging over their heads." My dad did, though I'm not sure he would have married Mom if she hadn't become pregnant with Cat. As new parents, barely twenty years old, the relationship was doomed from the start.

Sean picked up his spoon. "I think he hasn't committed to anyone because he saw what Theo had and wanted the same. He wanted it to be perfect. Now that he's getting older, he's—"

"Not so fussy?" I offered.

"That's not what I meant." He sent a guilty look my way.

"It's okay. I understand what you're saying. Life is a series of compromises." Jason and I both saw an opportunity with each other that would have once seemed extremely improbable.

Sean considered that. "Are you regretting your choice?"

"Not at all. Everything I learn about Jason assures me he's going to be a great dad. I would just hate for him to regret choosing me."

"He doesn't." Sean broke up his cobbler with his spoon. "He's very invested. Calls me every day to ask after you."

"As long as the boundaries are clear," Melissa said airily.

"What boundaries?" Sean asked. I was glad he did so I didn't have to.

"Well, you're co-parents but not ..." She waved to intimate the rest.

"No, nothing like that."

Melissa dug her spoon into the cobbler while I dug my nails into my hand to suppress my burgeoning blush.

"Then you have to assume that he's going to be dating, and you will be, too, eventually. How will you feel about that?"

"Fine!" My voice sounded a touch shrill. "I've encouraged him to do it, but he feels weird about it while I'm pregnant."

"Oh, that's interesting," Melissa said. "So you told him to date and he refused?"

"Refused isn't the right word. More like, declined." Of course, I only had his word for it. Not that I needed his word or his promise. Jason was his own person.

Just not my person.

Melissa slid a look at Sean, then back to me. "And during this conversation, did he say how he felt about *you* dating?"

"It was a while ago. I told him I would, if the opportunity arose, but it was more to make a point that we both could. That the pregnancy should have no impact on our dating lives."

Sean laughed. "And let me guess, he said, 'no way!'"

"Correct. But I credited his reaction to some recessive or not-so-recessive knuckle-dragging trait inherent in the male species. Most men would be concerned about the future mother of their child having sex with another man. We see it a lot with gastropods, a marking of sorts to limit their re-mating potential. It's almost like he felt the need to react this way, from a biological perspective."

Melissa looked puzzled, though it was hard to tell if it was because of my comparison of Jason's behavior to that of gastropods, or something else. "You thought his reaction was performative?"

"I assumed it was his id talking. Primal urges, my woman, my baby, that kind of thing. There's not really anything substantive or intellectual underlying it."

My mind strayed to that kiss he laid on me before I left Chicago: a typical example of Jason Isner marking his territory. It had initially annoyed me, but now I just added it to my bank of sensual memories.

Sean was looking at me strangely. "I wouldn't be so sure. If Jason is saying he won't sleep with anyone else, and is asking that you don't either—"

"Then he's trying to tell you something," Melissa finished, at which point they turned to each other, all gooey-eyed, thrilled to be completing each other's sentences. Melissa went on. "Call it the id talking, primal urges, what have you. It boils down to feelings that neither of you are willing to acknowledge."

That was months ago. We'd had sex since and neither of us had brought it up again. Neither of us wanted to know what the other person was doing.

Or maybe we were modeling our behavior on what we *wished* for each other.

I didn't want him to be with anyone else.

He didn't want me to be with anyone else.

Because we wanted to be ... together?

I gave a mental headshake at the absurdity. Sure, I had hopes, but I was busy suppressing them along with my cravings for Spicy Sweet Chili Doritos.

I touched the knot of the silk scarf tied around my neck, the one Jason had bought in the Detroit hotel gift shop. When packing for Boston, I had found it. Such a pretty piece with its lovely dragonflies, it seemed a shame not to wear it on occasion.

"So he's not dating anyone?" Melissa asked Sean, and I wanted to hug her for speaking what my mind was too afraid to verbalize.

"Not that I know of. Not since Everly." He gestured to me. "And whatever's happening with you."

Everly was Jason's last girlfriend in Boston. They broke up a few months before he was traded to Chicago, so perhaps she didn't want to make the move. I hadn't asked about her, mostly out of a desire to not appear clingy, but perhaps I should. She might have hurt him or burned him on relationships. I wanted to assure him that he could still find the one, even if that one didn't look like me.

How depressing. Time for a subject change. "So, I had an interesting chat with the head of my host department today."

Sean made a face. "Was it about slugs?"

I caught Melissa's eye and its puckish glint. "He's always been squeamish about my work."

My old friend blurted, "You had wing-snails at the baby-making proposal!"

Melissa burst out laughing. "This story gets better and better."

I waved it off. "I'm not the most conventional of women. But apparently my strange talents have caught the attention of the powers that be at Harvard. I've been invited to apply for a faculty position." Rather surprising, considering I had only started the lectureship a couple of weeks ago. But my work was well-known in malacology circles.

"Here?" Sean asked.

"Yes. Of course, these things take a long time. The academic appointment process is slower than a slug making its way to leafy undergrowth, but it was a surprise to be asked."

Melissa raised her spoon. "Why would it be a surprise? You're here on this guest lectureship. Of course, they think you're amazing!"

Women lifting up other women. Sean had chosen well.

My friend frowned. "But what about Jason?"

"Jason and I are not a couple. We just had a whole conversation about it at this very table."

"But he wants to be involved in his kid's life. And that'll be harder if you're here and he's there."

I knew that, but I had made it clear to Jason that I was ambitious and that ambition might require a change of scenery. Now that Marcus was my department head back at Lakeshore, and insisted on micro-managing all my decisions, I questioned how much further I could rise in that environment. I hadn't even broached the idea of a sabbatical with him so I could work on my book. I saw a fight for protected research time in my future.

Moving to another city would have an added benefit: not seeing Jason so much would ensure those feelings I had caught could be thrown back into the ocean. I might miss him now, but a prolonged absence would only serve to cauterize any wound.

"Jason has always known I might move somewhere else if my career demanded it. But this is just a castles-in-the-air notion right now. I'd like to have the baby first before I even think of the next steps in my career."

But I refused to allow Jason Isner to limit me, in my professional life—or in matters of the heart.

CHAPTER THIRTY-SEVEN

Jason

"SO THIS BOOK club is about hockey players?"

Lauren raised a glass of white wine to her lips, then lowered it again. "It's about *Rebels* hockey players."

"But it's not an actual book, right?"

"It's fan fiction. So the author, or maybe authors, I don't know, uploads to a website about this fictional"—she finger-quoted that—"hockey team called the Chicago Renegades. And the stories are thinly veiled sexy adventures for your teammates. The names have been changed, ever so slightly, to protect the guilty."

Tonight, the Empty Net was filled with very real hockey players, veteran and rookie, all here to celebrate Theo's retirement. Everyone he had ever played with or against, mentored or menteed, sneezed on or bought coffee from, was here to wish him well.

Which I planned to do, right after Lauren finished

telling me how her book club regularly discussed the fictional sex lives of non-fictional professional athletes.

"Who's in it?"

"Well, there's Beau Coden, a goalkeeper who likes threesomes."

I gasped like a schoolgirl at this incredibly lazy fictionalizing of the name of my team's tender, Noah Boden. "No!"

"Oh yes." Lauren was practically giddy. "And Thatch Cockslaw, who is *very* well endowed. Summer's been getting a kick out of that one."

I tutted. "And you guys meet and dissect this junk?"

"We have a regular book club where we read bestsellers and fun romances, but then we set aside a few minutes each month for the latest adventures of the sexy Renegades."

"Sounds faintly libelous."

"It's all in good fun. And none of the stories are real—or are they?" She winked. "You're in there."

"What's my alter ego up to these days?"

"Mason Listener is quite the ladies' man. He's having an affair with the team owner, who has a side hustle as a dominatrix."

"Definitely not me then. No one would ever accuse me of being a sub."

She shuddered. "TMI."

"Speaking of gossip—"

"Uh, fictional gossip."

I rolled my eyes. "I heard a rumor that Nazarov might be trading into the Rebels." Word on the ice was that he was ready to move.

"Yeah, I heard that, too." Her eyebrows drew together. "But it might not happen. People like to spout utter nonsense."

Bit of an overreaction, especially considering Lo loved

to gossip about trades. She looked over my shoulder toward the bar entrance.

"So where's your guy?"

"He'll be here. You're not going to be weird, are you?"

"With this man you found on an experimental dating app and who you've refused to introduce to me? Nah."

She shook my shoulders. "Damn your big brother energy around people I date. I'm three months older than you!"

"Well, Lo, you've gone for some doozies. The dickhead poet—"

"He was very romantic. In iambic pentameter."

And never picked up a check. "The volleyball player. What was his deal again?"

She sighed. "He kept shouting 'spike!' when he came."

Still cracked me up to hear it. "Maybe shoot for someone a little less odd?"

She considered my excellently vague advice. "I wish. That's the thing with women, they're either trying desperately to find a guy exactly like their dad or the opposite of him. I've spent most of my dating life avoiding guys who give off Jonah Yates vibes." Lauren's ex-con dad had certainly modeled a blueprint no daughter would want to follow for a boyfriend. "It hasn't really worked, so this time, I'm going for a normal guy with a normal job who looks good in a suit."

"Like a hockey player?"

"No sportsball people! Too much conflict of interest. But someone in banking who might defraud a bunch of investors? I could do that." Her expression turned dreamy. "He's a nice guy. I think you'll like him."

We would see. It might seem odd to be protective of a woman who could crush the balls of any guy I knew, on the ice or in a boardroom, but it had been that way since she had first checked me—against the rules, mind you—on a practice ice rink over twenty years ago.

Lauren thumped my arm. "Never mind *my* love life. Have you told your family yet?"

No need to ask about what.

"I've told Sean, but not my mom or Theo. We're giving it a little time until we're completely out of the woods." Franky was at seventeen weeks and was healthy as a horse (her words), yet we were still keeping it mostly to ourselves. As soon as it was out in the wild, we would lose control of the narrative. "Also, love life isn't relevant here."

A skeptical eyebrow arch was my reward.

"Franky and I are friends. We're committed to the welfare of our kid, and neither of us wants to mess with that."

My friend's scandal antenna went on high alert. "Mess with it? Because—ooh, you've already messed with it, haven't you? You've got *super* messy and you want to get messy again!"

"It's complicated." My stock answer for everything Franky-related.

"How did you think it wouldn't be? So you might not seem like the likeliest pair—"

"As the universe keeps telling me."

"But that doesn't mean it can't work. Do you want more from this situationship?"

I thought I did. But I may have been confusing my feelings with the emotions around becoming a dad, not to mention my sex fast. The last few weeks had been busy—games, travel, party planning, a stint on Conor's dick-cast, and plenty of fun times with my right hand. The doc might have given me leave to bang any bunny I wanted, but every other woman repulsed me—and I blamed *her* for showing me that a sweet rack and a pretty smile would no longer cut it. I could barely hold a conversation with any of these women. How the hell was I supposed to enjoy a roll in the sheets with them?

Thankfully I didn't need to come up with an answer because Lauren's attention was diverted. I turned to see a guy in a suit approaching us. My heart sank because he had crypto-loving finance bro written all over him, which meant I was predisposed to hate him. As long as he wasn't a Brad or a Chad.

"Jason, this is Thad." She kissed her guy. "Thad, this is my friend, Jason."

"Rebels rule, man!"

Be nice. Be nice.

"They sure do," I said gamely.

———

FIVE MINUTES LATER, my brain had started leaking out of my ears during a conversation about financial derivatives and mortgage-backed instruments. I managed to make my escape and was chatting with Hatch when Conor walked in. More like bounded, just making me tired by looking at him. He was having a stellar debut season with Detroit and was in the running for the Calder for best rookie. I loved being a witness to his success. So talented, the kid deserved it.

On the other hand, he was also a nosey little fucker who had somehow worked out that I was about to be a daddy.

He spent a few minutes shooting the shit with Hatch and Summer, before nudging me. "I see your sworn enemy is here."

I followed his gaze. Rosie had just walked into the Empty Net.

With Franky.

Stunned, I turned to Conor, but I had nothing to add. He mouthed "okay" and dropped a knowing grin.

Don't get me wrong, I was thrilled to see her. But here? No warning, nothing. We hadn't spent any time together around other people since our new arrangement. I had no idea how I was supposed to act. Ignore her? Be civil? Spin her around so everyone knew she belonged to me?

Well, not in that sense. But our connection was something worth celebrating.

I wanted the world to know this woman had chosen *me*.

Rosie hugged Summer, then kissed Hatch and me on the cheek and launched into some nonsense about one of Summer's bras stuffed in a sofa cushion. I tuned out because all I could see was *her*. Not just the woman who would soon give birth to my child, but the doc. The sexy brainiac who haunted my dreams and fueled my fantasies.

She stared at me, gave a tiny shrug, then clamped those pearly whites on that succulent bottom lip. I tried to communicate with my eyes: *Why are you here?* She frowned, then took out her phone.

I did the same, and there it was: a text. I'd had my phone in Do Not Disturb mode because Conor had spent the entire afternoon trash talking one of the New York D-men who went hard for Hatch in last night's game. I had needed a nap before the party, so the Connie Chirpfest was put on hold. I'd forgotten to turn my phone's notifications back on.

DOC

I'm coming to Theo's party. Kind of a last-minute decision. Hope that's okay?

Like she had to ask permission. But it would have been good to get our stories straight—Holy fuckington!

Francesca St. James had just taken off her coat to gasps from the crowd, and there it was.

My baby bump.

Conor side-eyed me then turned to Hatch with a smart-assed, "Yep."

Franky pushed her glasses back up her nose. "As you can see, I'm pregnant. I was loath to steal focus from Theo's party, but Rosie insisted I come. I hope he doesn't mind."

She looked over to where my brother was holding court at the bar. I probably should clue him in before someone else did.

"I'm sure you have questions," Franky said.

This statement was greeted with a chorus of "oh, no!" and "not at all!"—liars, the lot of 'em—followed by hearty congrats. Franky eyed me and mouthed "sorry." I had never wanted to hold someone so badly and soothe that worried frown with kisses.

"I should visit the bathroom before I ingest any liquid," she said with a pointed look at me. *Understood.* But the plan was foiled when Summer and Rosie took her by the arm on either side. "We'll come, too."

As they headed off, Franky threw a nervy look over her shoulder.

Hatch turned to Conor. "Okay, spill."

"Remember that time you warned me to wrap it before I tap it because I said people were too attached to their sperm?"

Hatch's expression froze. As if the doc would have bothered with a boy like Conor Kershaw as her donor.

"Don't worry, bro, it's not me! Someone else we know decided that it was time to unwrap it and tap *his* swimmers for a very important mission." He added a chin jerk my way, just in case it wasn't clear.

We had agreed that when people knew she was pregnant, they would know the rest.

"Well, kids, let me tell you a story." I filled them in with an abbreviated version of events.

"So, turkey baster?" Conor asked. "Sounds sexy."

"I'm not going to elaborate any further, but I really need to talk to your dad before this game of telephone gets out of control."

Both of my nephews looked blank.

"Whisper network. Later."

I pulled Theo out of a conversation with former Rebels greats, Gunnar Bond and Cal Foreman. "Could I have a word?"

"Sure."

Blood was fizzing through my veins. Finally, I felt like I was in the right place at the right time with the right woman. Except she wasn't interested in me and I wasn't sure anyone else would see this the way I did.

Here goes. "Franky's pregnant and I'm the dad."

He looked like I'd walloped him with a hockey stick. "You're the dad?"

"She needed a donor. I stepped up."

"Dude, this is huge." Regrouping quickly, he gave me a hug. "When did this happen?"

"She's due in early July. We've known for a little while, but we wanted to keep it under the radar until we got through the first trimester. She's here tonight, so we thought it was time everyone knew."

He smiled. "A lot of 'we' in there. So you two ...?"

"No, it's not like that." My heart felt heavy. "But we're

going to co-parent. To be honest, I'm not sure why she agreed."

"Because she recognizes a good thing when she sees it."

"She only wanted a donor. I kind of muscled my way in." Put like that, it sounded like I'd taken advantage of her desperation for a child. *Agree to my terms or watch your dream wither on the vine.*

Theo was studying me closely. "So the co-parenting was your idea?"

"It was. I've always wanted kids; I just didn't want the hassle that goes with it."

"Like a wife or partner?"

I sighed. "I'm not like you, T."

"No, you're not. Doesn't mean you don't have it in you to settle if you find the right one. Hey, I've been there. Baby first, falling in love later."

I gave a mirthless laugh. "You knocked up Elle, but you were already falling for her long before that."

"True. But maybe you and Franky might—"

"That won't be happening." She had made it very clear, and I wasn't going to push those boundaries. This torrent of speculation about why we had agreed to this arrangement only laid bare what I couldn't have. I needed to nip it in the bud.

"The Jock and the Nerd are not a thing," I added.

If I said it enough, maybe I could make myself believe it.

CHAPTER THIRTY-EIGHT

Franky

SUMMER WAS POSITIVELY giddy at my news.

"Franky, you look amazing! That sweater is so cute and the perfect fit to accentuate that bump."

"Not really my intention but Rosie said I should wear it. Make a big splash."

I slid a look at my sister, who had called me yesterday and insisted I come to Chicago for Theo's party. For a good twelve hours, I weighed the decision and because I was leaning toward no, I hadn't included Jason in the process. But my sister was persuasive.

This way, everyone finds out at once. You rip off the Band-Aid, accept heartfelt congrats from everyone in the hockey universe, and then fly back to Boston. The perfect heist.

So I used my miles for a last-minute ticket and here I

was, four months gone, and the center of attention. I was not a fan.

"I'm so pleased for you," Summer said. "Hatch looked just as surprised, which is good because if he had known and I hadn't, we would be having words right now."

"We've shared with family only. I told my parents and brother a week ago because it would be a bit much to blindside them."

"They must be thrilled," Summer said.

"Oh, they are." I met her reflection in the mirror. "I suppose you want to know how this all happened."

Rosie chuckled. "I think we all know *how* it happened. What people want to know is the *who*, sis. But you don't have to say anything."

"It's okay. The father doesn't mind being identified, especially as we've agreed to co-parent."

Summer leaned in.

"It's Jason."

Her violet eyes widened. "Oh! Did not expect that. I thought you two weren't very friendly."

"We're not. Or weren't."

Rosie cut in. "But they got friendly enough to make the magic happen."

"And the co-parenting thing? How's that going to work?"

"We have a contract." That sounded cold and sterile, the complete opposite to how Jason and I worked together. "We want the best for our child."

Summer hugged me. "I so want to be you when I grow up, the woman who decides what she wants and goes for it." She grinned. "Not so temperamentally unsuitable after all."

I had once showed my spreadsheet to Summer with all

its damning notes and variables. That seemed like a lifetime ago.

"I've become more open as I grow older. Being too rigid about things means you might miss out on something amazing."

"Ah, the wisdom of our elders." Rosie threw an arm around my shoulder. "You ready to meet everyone as a pregnant lady?"

"No," I said morosely.

"That's the spirit."

THE FIRST PERSON we ran into was Theo, who as the guest of honor, really should be mingling with his guests.

"There she is! Congrats, Franky. I couldn't be happier for you."

"Thanks, Theo. I promise it wasn't my intention to steal your thunder."

"Are you kidding? Hearing about my future niece or nephew is the best news ever. Now how are you? I heard you flew in from Boston this afternoon. My brother really should be making better arrangements for your travel. Private jet or charter."

"I flew business class, so I was very comfortable."

Theo's smirk was that of a man who had not flown business class for a long time.

"Listen, Elle will want to be involved with the baby shower. You might think it's too soon, but everyone is very excited."

"Maybe you should throw it," a voice cut in. "Not sure why your wife should be on the hook."

My gaze met Jason's, who was smirking up a storm

himself. Beside him stood his mother. I didn't know Jenny Isner all that well, but right now she was positively buzzing with grandma-to-be energy.

"I am looking for something to do now that I'm retired," Theo mused. "Okay, I'll take care of it."

"You don't have to—" But he was already gone. I shook my head at Jason. "Is he serious?"

"Don't worry about it." He took my hand. "So, Franky, someone wants to say hi in person."

Mrs. Isner elbowed her son out of the way and threw her arms around me. "I can't believe I'm only finding out tonight! But I'm so happy for you both. Now don't worry, Jason's explained everything, so I know you two aren't together in that sense. I also know you have a lot of people in your village. I hope you don't mind one more."

Tears welled, and I marveled at how lucky I was to have so much love in my future child's life. I hugged Jason's mom back, and when I opened my eyes, I couldn't help noticing how approving her son looked. I did think it odd, though, that he had told Sean, but not his mother. Or anyone else. I had assumed he would share the news with everyone over the last few weeks once the ultrasound gave the all-clear.

"I won't mind at all, Mrs. Isner. There can never be enough love for our baby."

She gave a big grin. "Franky, it's Jenny, and please call on me for anything you need. We're all here for you." After a few more moments of excitement, she headed off to the restroom.

Jason took my hand. "Let's find a quiet spot."

Here? I didn't think it likely. But the Rebels knew this bar inside and out. We ended up in a storeroom, which had a cushion on a keg. Jason placed me there.

"You okay?"

"It's a lot of attention."

"Yeah, it is. You sure know how to make an entrance, Doc. Sorry, I had my notifications on mute. Conor, specifically."

"I texted that I was coming, and you didn't answer, so I did wonder—but you're okay with this? That everyone knows?" I wanted to ask why he had delayed sharing the news, but part of me feared the answer.

You embarrass him.

"We agreed that we wouldn't keep the details—well, the daddy details—a secret. Other details, such as sexy ones, shall remain between us."

As far as everyone was concerned, this was done by artificial insemination. No one would believe we'd gone natural.

"How did Hatch and Conor take it? They looked a bit surprised—well, now that I think of it, Conor didn't."

"He knew. Told me a couple of weeks ago that he had it all worked out. That's Connie for you—nothing gets by him." He started pacing the room.

"Jason?"

"Huh?" He stopped and faced me.

"You seem worried."

"Me? Nah. I'm just—I dunno—excited. Now that it's common knowledge, it feels different. More real. And I'll be honest, when you took off your coat, showing off your baby bump ... I felt so proud."

My pulse picked up. "Look at what you hath created."

"Yeah, that." He grasped my hands and pulled me upright. "But also, I'm proud of *you*. Sure, you're carrying my baby, but you're also making this dream of yours happen. The woman with the plan. I know I was skeptical at first. Why are you doing it this way? Why are you making your lists?"

I laughed, feeling more relaxed. "Why am I asking your brother for sperm? Why don't I just find a boyfriend?"

He moved his hand down to my bump. "Well, your unconventional way of bringing a baby into your life has been a blessing for me, too." He cradled the swell and spoke directly to it, his voice soothing. "Hey there, Baby Naval Orange." He met my surprised gaze. "That's the size about now."

That this man thought he wouldn't ever be in a significant relationship with a woman sounded crazier the longer I knew him. He would make any woman the perfect partner, assuming she was a normal girl, and not some weirdo who begged men she knew for a cup of sperm.

"I'm so glad Sean turned me down."

"Damn, Francesca, so am I." He smiled. "Hey, is that my Christmas gift?"

I touched the pendant around my neck. I had placed the snail charm he gave me on a chain.

"It's such a lovely piece. Thank you."

He touched my clavicle, slipping his finger beneath the chain and raising the charm to get a better look. My skin tingled where his fingertips skimmed.

"Best gift ever," he murmured. "Snailed it."

I started laughing—who didn't love a good pun?—and he joined in, the sound deep and resonant against the bottles and metal kegs in the storeroom. In this moment, I felt nothing but joy. Everyone out there was thrilled for us. I had the best partner in Jason, a man who wanted to travel this journey with me. I had everything I needed, the support network, the resources, the baby in my belly. Everything but one thing.

Him.

Maybe it was my pregnancy brain, but this proximity to him was driving me wild. At one time, he would have been interested, but now, with my body so changed? And it wasn't as if I would be less confused afterward. I would still be holding onto the dream of a conventional life, only I would be dragging this man into it, purely because I might not relish the idea of being a single mother after all.

His eyes dipped to my lips, and my mouth dried at the prospect. *Oh God, kiss me. Please.*

"Think that's you," he murmured.

Yes, it is. It's all me.

"Your phone."

"Oh!" I pulled it from my purse, expecting a message from Vi or Dad or my aunts. It was from Rosie.

And it wasn't good.

"What's up, Doc? And I mean that literally."

I blew out a breath. "I have no idea why, but my mother has come to the party."

CHAPTER THIRTY-NINE

Franky

I LEFT the Empty Net storeroom, feeling like I'd been up
to something naughty, but without the benefits that usually
accompanied a quickie under the radar. What if someone
had seen us? They would probably assume I'd taken advantage, hooked my love dart, and trapped him. The cougar
egghead with her dried-up ovaries, desperate to drape
herself in the sheen of vitality a hot stud like Jason
presented.

"Francesca."

I kept walking.

"Francesca."

Still walking.

"Doc!"

I turned. Jason stood behind me, his expression one of
concern. "So your mom's here. It's no big deal."

I barked out a laugh, though it emerged a touch hysterical. "This might be a lot of things, but 'no big deal' is not one of them. I don't know how she heard. Vi and Dad wouldn't have said anything." Maybe Cat? I doubted it. "She's going to have ... an opinion."

He scoffed. "Everyone has an opinion, just like everyone's got an ass—"

"Yes, I know the phrase. I just don't want anything to overshadow Theo's big night. And I already came in here and stole his glory. What was I thinking?"

He pulled me close and curled his hands around my thickening waist. "You haven't stolen anything. Everyone loves hearing baby news, and your mom is going to have to get with the program, like the rest of 'em. Come on, Doc, let's deal."

I'll say it again: some lucky woman ...

I let him hold my hand. I figured no one would assume we were a couple, just proud parents to be. I got plenty of curious looks from the Chicago Rebels WAGs I didn't know very well. For them, I was ready with my scales up, but my mother? She still had the capacity to find my soft underbelly and bury the spear of criticism.

On spotting us, Rosie rushed forward to intercept. "This is kind of weird, but I think your mom is looking for ... a husband?"

Oh, that made more sense. Cat had told me that things had rapidly deteriorated between my mother and Xavier over the last few months. A retirement party for a veteran hockey star would bring out all sorts of athletes and legends, providing a fertile hunting ground for a woman on the make.

Rosie's gaze dropped to my hand, currently grasped by Jason's, then up again to my face with a superior grin.

"I see."

"See what?"

Rosie hummed. "Doesn't matter. I already saw it."

I peered up at Jason. "Not sure this is helping."

"I think it is."

Secretly, I thought so, too, especially as I spied my mother beelining toward me. At almost sixty, Kendra St. James Cassidy Delahunt was still trying her best to defeat the ravages of time, but they were clearly nipping at her heels.

"Franky! You're not going to believe what I just heard." She grasped my arms and pulled me into a hug. "Someone said you were pregnant! I said, *my* Franky, the girl who would rather watch slimy creatures do it than carry a child —oh, hello." My mom blinked up at Jason, her mouth agape. "You're Jason Isner."

"Sure am. You must be the lovely Kendra. I've heard so much about you."

The lovely Kendra giggled and touched her chest above the leather bustier that struggled to maintain her over-tanned flesh.

"You have? Who from?" She turned wide eyes on me. "My daughter?"

Jason chose that moment to circle my waist and pull me in close.

"Who else? So I'm guessing this is a surprise to you, but I figure you're a veteran now. Grandma all over again!"

"But Franky, is this true?" She leaned in. "I thought you looked a little heavier than usual. But then I haven't seen you since, what, last Christmas?"

"Thanksgiving, two years ago, Mom. We met at Cat's place in New York after she announced her pregnancy."

Mom did not like to be reminded of further evidence of her mortality.

"Right. And now they cry so much, but so did Caitriona. So sensitive. Not like you, my tough-as-nails girl. And now, a mom!" Flabbergasted, she raised her gaze to Jason. "How did this even happen?"

She would hear about my baby caper soon enough, so there was little point in keeping it to myself. I opened my mouth, but he got there first.

"How do you think, Kendra?" He inclined his dark head and whispered. "Great sex."

"Oh, I know that's how babies are made, you devil. I'm just fascinated with—*this*." She waved between us, every word and gesture a pin-prick critique. "God, I remember Franky was wild for hockey players when she was fourteen or so. Kind of a late bloomer because I was sneaking into locker rooms when I was thirteen, but oh well! Maybe she's more like her mom than she cares to admit." She pointed at me. "Oh, look at her face. She hates hearing that! Okay, what does a girl have to do to get a drink around here? I think I spy Mike Jenner over at the bar, and I haven't seen him since he won the Cup with the Quake over ten years back. I'll catch you later, darling, for a little heart to heart."

When I would hear what I needed to do to keep my claws in a catch like Jason.

JASON CONTINUED to hold my hand.

I could have told him it was unnecessary now that my mother had moved into Husband Hunt mode. But I didn't. I wanted him to stay by my side, our hands clasped in unity as everyone congratulated us on a job well done.

Of course, most people in our inner circle understood what was going on—or thought they did. This was transactional, I was the desperate one, and Jason was doing me this huge favor. They didn't know about Jason's needs and desires, his heartfelt wish to be a dad. I didn't mind looking like the succubus. What I did mind was how my heart wanted the reality to match the fantasy.

I wanted Jason to want me as much as he wanted our baby.

A foolish wish. But I still let him rub my back as we chatted with Dex O'Malley and his lovely wife, Ashley, and I let him squeeze my waist as we accepted congratulations from my aunt Isobel and Vadim.

I expected he would be hands-off as soon as my dad approached, but Jason Isner had titanium in his spine.

"Sprite," Dad murmured as he kissed my cheek. "Your mother behaving herself?"

"Oh, you know Mom."

"Aye, I do." He turned to Jason. Although I had told him the news a week ago, he and Jason had yet to connect. "Isner."

"Dad, be nice."

My dad raised an expressive eyebrow. That was as nice as it got.

"See you on the ice." And then he left.

Jason shivered. "Chills. Should I be worried?"

"If you don't show for a session with the Three Wise Men, he'll assume you're chicken." I stepped away from his heat. "You don't have to—you know."

"I don't have to what?"

"Be so demonstrative. People might mistake us for a real couple. I know you were doing it because my mother made her little digs. I appreciate it, but it's really unnecessary."

His expression flickered, like a flame catching an unwelcome breeze.

"Sure, Doc."

The energy changed. I had allowed my mother to get into my head, but deep down I knew she was right: Jason and I were an odd pair, and everyone here could see it. Even my father, though he was far too kind to say it aloud.

I RAN into my mother while she was on her way to the restroom. She waylaid me as I was coming out and trapped me in the corridor.

"Darling!"

"Hi, Mom. Having fun?"

"Of course. But I have to say I feel a little foolish that you didn't tell me about the baby before everyone else. Always the last to know!"

"Jason told his family today, so you're not behind the eight ball."

That he had left the news until I forced his hand still niggled at me.

She gave me a sad smile. "This is a little strange, even for you."

I shouldn't have expected any support. This was Kendra we were talking about, the woman who saw motherhood as the heaviest of burdens.

Still, I would defend my decision. "It's been on my mind for a while now. I'm getting to the age where the science might take it out of my hands. I could adopt—"

"Oh, God, no. A stranger you're not even related to?"

"I wouldn't mind that. There are so many children that need a home. But I think my single status might make adoption difficult, so trying for one of my own seemed like the best option."

She made a tutting noise. "So that business with the father ..."

"Jason and I are going to co-parent." My mother wouldn't be fooled by a little handholding.

"Meaning he'll provide financial support. But basically, you'll be alone." Being alone was my mother's greatest fear.

"Not entirely. I have friends and family to help out." I was anxious to get off the topic. She would never understand an unconventional approach to parenthood. She could barely wrap her head around a conventional one.

"But darling, he's going to find someone. A wife. A girlfriend. Someone younger. Just like your father did."

Never mind that Mom and Dad were long divorced before he fell in love with Violet. But the point was taken. My mother didn't hold out much hope that I would find a partner for myself, never mind have a shot with a guy like Jason Isner.

"And I'll be happy for him."

CHAPTER FORTY

Jason Isner in Baby Daddy Shocker!

While everyone was celebrating Theo Kershaw's retirement at the Empty Net in downtown Riverbrook, the legendary defenseman's sendoff was upstaged by a surprising announcement: Theo's brother, Chicago Rebels D-man Jason Isner, will be a father soon. And the lucky lady? Only Francesca "Franky" St. James, daughter of veteran Rebels center Bren St. James! A source, who preferred to remain anonymous, told us that Franky—a professor of biology at Lakeshore University and a world-renowned expert in snails and slugs—chose Jason as her sperm donor after a rigorous selection process. But never fear, ladies! Jason, also known as the Green-Eyed Monster, is still on the market. The couple are not in a romantic relationship and have agreed to co-parent their child.

"People expected she would keep the donor anonymous," the source said, "but Jason wants to be a part of the child's life, so she had to agree to his terms or no dice." Here in the Hot

Goss bullpen, we're surprised that Jason would go this route, given his many fans and the numerous options available to him. One insider commented that Jason's generosity is well known, so that might explain his actions. Of course, he's going to help when a damsel in baby fever distress needs a prime genetic sample, and as we've witnessed with other recent relationships in the Rebels universe, they are notorious for "keeping it in the family."

From all of us here at Hot Goss, *congrats to the parents-to-be!*

- @HotGoss

Jason

ON THE JOURNEY HOME, she was quiet, and I suspected that none of the congratulations and well wishes from her friends and family could overcome the long shadow cast by her mother. I followed her inside her apartment, though she didn't ask. I wanted to make sure she was okay. The kitties wanted to know, too.

Bunsen came rushing out the moment his mama stepped inside and around her suitcase, left in the hallway before she headed to the party. No sign of Beaker but I expected he'd make an appearance sooner than later.

After a few vigorous pets, she headed into the kitchen where she picked up the kettle and filled it with water.

"Would you like tea?"

"Sure." I could have offered to make it, but she needed something to occupy her hands.

She grabbed a couple of mugs off the tree and placed teabags in them. "I have to drink herbal because I'll be up all night. You didn't have to see me home. That was kind, but I could have taken an Uber."

Rosie was spending the night with her dads, so we were alone. Franky was always alone, or at least that was how she saw it. The way her brain worked set her apart from other people, and she took that difference to heart. Nowhere was this more obvious than when she spoke to her mom.

"I wasn't going to put you in some stranger's car." A flash of orange streaked by, heading for the pantry. "There's my guy. Hey, Beakster."

The kettle boiled behind her, its increasing noise volume likely the reason for Beaker's blur through the kitchen.

"Your mom doesn't know you, Francesca."

She shrugged. "She's my mother."

"Yeah, but she doesn't know you. Like my dad doesn't know me. Some people are too narcissistic to take the time to get deep with people. Your mom? She's one of them. All she sees is surface."

With her back still turned to me, she poured the hot water into the cups. "But surface can be very revealing. What my mother sees—it might be a surface snapshot, but it's not wrong."

"What does she see?"

Another hurt shrug. "That weird little girl with her ugly glasses and strange habits. I've grown up and turned my strangeness into a profession, into a successful career. But it doesn't really change *me* at the core. I'm still the odd girl out."

My younger self, that little asshole, hadn't helped. When I met her, I thought of her as "Slug Girl," the weird daughter of one of my sporting heroes. As fascinating as I found that contrast, her friendship with Sean had bugged the shit out of me. My jealousy of their closeness, as well as her clear disinterest in a dumb kid like me, prompted my childish taunts. Now I couldn't imagine wishing her to be any different.

I moved behind her, circled her waist, and lay my chin on her shoulder.

"Why would you want to be like everyone else?"

"Because it ... hurts less." She heaved in my arms, releasing a sob that cut me to the quick.

"Turn around."

"No."

"Francesca, look at me."

She whipped around, her eyes red, tears streaming. She stared up at me, that stubborn chin set defiantly.

"I'm glad you're different from everyone else. Because if you weren't, you wouldn't have figured out the baby plan with that amazing brain of yours. You wouldn't have carved out this path to motherhood or even considered adding someone like me to your list. And I *know* you wouldn't have disguised yourself as some chick out of *Ocean's Eight* to fool a bunch of hockey players. Most of all, I'm glad you're different because I love watching you think, how you weigh it all up before pronouncing, how your nose twitches and you get this little crimp between your brows while you're working stuff out." I touched that little crimp now, smoothing it with my thumb. "You're one in a million, Francesca. And fuck anyone who doesn't appreciate that."

Her chest heaved. "I-I know you're trying to help—"

I kissed her. Not sure it would help her but it sure as

hell would help me. All night, I'd watched her in the crowd, trying her best not to be blinded by the spotlight in which her pregnancy had placed her. A spotlight not made easier by the fact a famous pro-athlete was the father.

The appearance of her mother should have been a boon. But a woman like Kendra hated that her daughter—her strange, beautiful blessing of a daughter—was the center of attention.

"Jason," she murmured against my lips. "You don't have to—"

"But I do. I've wanted to do that all night. I've wanted to touch you and hold you and kiss you and do absolutely filthy things to you."

Her eyes went dark and smoky. "What things?"

"Not sure your delicate ears could handle them."

She moved a hand between my legs and cupped my straining cock. "Tell me."

I could have viewed that as a threat—the words, her hand, that fiery look in her eyes—but instead I considered it as an opportunity. A chance to get deep and dirty with this woman after months without her touch.

"Want me to show, not tell?"

"I want you to show *and* tell."

Franky got off on the verbal, so I had no problem there. I lifted her skirt to her hips and found the border of her tights, nestled below that rounded belly. "Gonna need these off."

"D-do it."

I pulled at the elastic, then hunkered down to finish the job, or at least as far as the tops of her boots. A problem for later.

"Hold up your skirt, baby."

She did, revealing a pair of white panties. Not skimpy,

not particularly sexy. But the package? Damn, my mouth watered at the prospect.

I ran my hand up the insides of her milky-white thighs. Skin so soft against my calloused hands, and I was the rough, brute invader of the virginal maiden.

"Wonder how you taste."

"You've tasted me before."

I looked up to find her watching me avidly, her teeth clamped in that plump lower lip.

"Yeah, but that was before. Your body was different. Now it's growing a new life, and I bet everything is different about you. How you feel, how you taste, how tight that pussy will grip my cock." I rubbed a knuckle over the front of her panties.

She shuddered and swayed a little.

"You okay?"

"F-fine. Continue." Said a little imperiously, like she was trying desperately to assume power over a situation she'd lost control of hours ago. The moment she walked into that bar and told the world with her body that she was carrying my child, the game had changed.

I kissed her inner thigh, then the other, and worked my way up. Slowly. She started to shake, parted her legs as best she could, given how the tights were knee-cuffing her.

"Please," she whispered.

"Please what?"

"Make it better."

I peeled down her panties and moved my fingers to where she was wet and wanting. She gasped, a desperate, needy sound, and I let my digits wander, soaking in her desire, driving her a little crazy.

Driving myself even crazier.

Her thighs were parted but not nearly enough for what I needed.

More access. More Franky. More everything.

I stood and placed a finger over her ready-to-object lips. "Trust me." Leading her to the kitchen table, I sat her down in a chair, then knelt before her. I removed one boot. Then the other. Her tights. Her panties.

"Comfortable?" I asked.

She scooted forward a few inches and parted her thighs, pulling up the skirt of her dress as she settled.

"Yes."

I moved my hands up her thighs, placed my thumbs over soft, sensitive, wet flesh, and stroked. Her bottom lip quivered.

"Put your hands on my shoulders, Francesca. Squeeze if you need to. Use me for support. I'm here for whatever you want."

And then I bent and took what *I* wanted. That sweet tang, the delicious nectar of her pussy, while she gripped my shoulders and rolled her hips, searching and seeking the release I insisted on denying her.

Not yet.

But soon.

LATER, I lay beside her, sated but not entirely satisfied. Tomorrow, she would return to Boston, and now that everyone knew the score, I felt as though we had moved into a different phase of the pregnancy.

Of us.

She ran a finger over my collarbones. "What's on your mind?"

"Ethical porn."

She leaned up on her elbow. "Excuse me?"

I gave a low chuckle. "That's what you offered me the first time I came to your boudoir."

"I was *trying* to be a good host."

That just made me laugh harder. "Tea, coffee, porn?"

"You got there in the end, didn't you?"

"Only because I imagined you on the other side of that door. Eavesdropping."

"I was in the kitchen, letting my imagination run riot. Now look at us." She let out a little sigh. "Thanks for being here. For listening about my mom."

"You've got so many amazing people in your life, Franky. Don't let one person be a blot on it." I pulled her close and kissed her temple. "That's what you told me on Halloween when I was pissed about my dad."

"And then I pissed you off more by not letting you plunder my school uniform. Or navigate inside my tights."

"I beat those tights in the end." I watched her blue eyes sparkle in the low lamplight. "So, I have a question that's going to sound weird."

"Okay."

"Did you ever sleep with Sean?"

Her eyes went as wide as pucks. "Sean? God, no."

"He said there was one time you and he ... but I never heard the rest. Was he messing with me?"

She giggled. "Oh, that. When we were sixteen, I think? We kissed. More a 'let's try this and see if there's anything there' kind of thing. And there wasn't. No chemistry whatsoever."

Thank Christ. "Good. It's already weird enough that he was your first choice."

"Is the Green-Eyed Monster ... jealous?"

"I've every right to be."

She nodded. "Sure, sure, Mason Listener."

I laughed. "Lauren told me about that tonight. Kind of wild."

"Yes, so wild that there are all these fan fiction lovers reading about your sexy adventures with team owner Tabitha Mace in the locker room showers. Am *I* allowed to be jealous?"

Yes, you are, baby. "It's not about me. It's about someone who looks like me, living in an alternative world. Like the Multiverse." I *loved* that it bothered her, though. Turnabout was fair play. "What's with the Ferris Bueller stuff?"

She cast a glance at the shelving unit where the movie-themed diorama and Cameron Funko Pop figure were displayed.

"Just souvenirs of a great day from my childhood."

"Tell me."

She settled her head against my chest. "I was nine and Cat was eleven. We had just come to live with Dad during the playoffs, and we—me, Cat, and Violet—kidnapped him from the Rebels practice rink and spent the day in Chicago doing fun things like we were in the movie. We couldn't replicate it exactly, but Violet came up with all these amazing activities. Afternoon tea at the Drake, a visit to Sears Tower, even though Dad was terrified of heights, dinner at Harry Caray's, all in a borrowed Bentley that belonged to Dante.

"I brought a snail with me in a jar, a *Cornu Aspersum*, and I tried to feed it under the table with a sliver of lettuce from one of the tiny sandwiches they give you for the fancy tea. The waiter spotted me, and we almost got thrown out." She laughed, then turned serious. "Violet was the first adult I met who didn't judge me. Well, Dad didn't, but he was so self-absorbed at the time with drinking and hockey and atonement, I suppose. Going to live with him was the best thing that could have happened because I met Vi."

I understood all too well. That was the place Theo held for me.

She ran her hand over my chest. "I think people show up in our lives when we need them, kind of like angels."

"You believe in angels?"

"Not the Biblical kind. But I do believe that something in us—what some people might term a soul, perhaps—will cry out for help, for a friend. For a sperm donor." She lifted her head and cupped my jaw while she stared into the soul that cried out for her. "You showed up when I needed you, Jason Isner. Not just with this genetic contribution but with your generous heart and protective nature. I don't think you get how special you are. But I do. And our child is going to be so blessed because of it."

She snuggled into me, claiming the last word, as usual. And as her soft snores vibrated against my chest, I considered that I was the one who was truly blessed.

And more than a little fucked.

APRIL

To: Franky St. James
From: Marcus Bilson, Chair
Subject: Adjustment in laboratory funding

Dear Dr. St. James,

A recent audit of your laboratory's funding has uncovered a processing error which resulted in an overpayment to your staffing budget. These funds were used to hire an additional assistant in the Malacology Lab, a hiring decision that will need to be reversed at the end of the fiscal year unless you can obtain renewed funds to cover the shortfall. With the current research funding climate, I expect this will be difficult, but I am happy to discuss your lab's options when you return to Chicago. My door is always open.

Marcus Bilson, PhD
Chair, Department of Biology
Lakeshore University

Franky

"SO SHOW US," Violet said.

Standing, I positioned the phone to take in my very round, six and a half months in, belly. I patted my bump and whispered, "Let's cook for a little longer, Super Kid."

Cat went "aw," and when I took a closer look at my laptop screen, Violet's eyes were suspiciously shiny.

"If anyone should be emotional, it's me."

"This Boricua can get emotional for both of us. Your father will be annoyed he missed you."

I chuckled. "He probably won't mind missing my frequent visits to the bathroom or my whining about my back pain."

Vi grinned. "Oh, he remembers it all when I was pregnant with Rosie and Devon."

"Where's my little brother today? On a hockey rink, I suppose."

"Yes, but he's doing much better in algebra after you gave him online tutoring. Got a B+ on the last quiz."

I so wished I could be there. I hadn't realized how much I would miss my family. I longed for my own space, my cats, and time to nest before the baby was born.

Though I imagined my pregnancy hormones were contributing to my homesickness and mood swings. Also contributing, the various micro-aggressions I was suffering from my department chair, even when I was over a thousand miles away and in a different time zone. I bitched about him to Cat and Rosie, but kept mum around Violet, as she would probably slash Dr. Bilious's tires or chuck a brick through the window of the office she thought should have been mine.

Instead, we chatted about the anniversary trip my dad and Violet were taking to Scotland this summer for the first time in over twenty years.

Violet looked teary-eyed again. "Remember the two of you at Loch Ness, both of you pretending the monster didn't exist?"

When I was ten and Cat was twelve, we visited my dad's place of birth the glorious summer after he won the Cup and fell for Violet. Getting down on one knee on the muddy shore of the loch, he proposed to her while Cat and I squealed our heads off.

"It was so romantic," Cat said. "Best proposal ever."

"Agreed," I said. "But I was most definitely not 'pretending' about the Loch Ness monster. It's a myth, and I was very aware of that fact at the time."

"Sure." Violet laughed. "But you still brought those high-powered binoculars you borrowed from Dante."

"So I could look for wildlife typical of the British Isles."

"Like Nessie."

Maybe I had been a touch hopeful as I scanned the murky surface of the loch, watching every dark ripple for signs of monstrous life. The dreamer in me wanted to abandon logic and embrace the possibility of magical thinking.

"It was a special trip for all of us, the happy ending we all craved."

Violet looked wistful. "I couldn't believe how blessed I was. This man, these girls, my sisters—a life I barely allowed myself to dream of. Watching the two of you grow into such lovely young women has been my greatest privilege."

"Vi." Cat sniffed.

"*We* were the blessed ones," I said.

"And now, one of you is a mom and the other is about to become one. Cariño, I'm so happy for you and Jason. Every time I run into him, he's constantly asking if I've talked to you, if you're okay, if you're getting enough food and sleep. He's going to be such a great dad."

I didn't doubt it. Each morning, I sent him "proof of life" photos of my growing belly and whatever I was eating for breakfast. Toast and tea weren't good enough for Super Kid; I was up to my neck in fresh fruit deliveries and enough folic acid to supplement multiple growing babies.

"I'm lucky to have such a great partner in all this."

"And maybe more?" Cat said with a cunning tilt to her lips.

Before I could issue a forceful denial, Violet spoke up. "You've never told us and I haven't asked, but"—she lowered her voice—"did you and Jason conceive this child naturally?"

"Violet!" My cheeks heated.

"I saw the way he looked at you at Theo's party. That boy has the hots for you!"

That was over two months ago, and our conversations since had remained disappointingly unsexy. Understandable, given my appearance.

"He was merely being supportive because Kendra was there, absolutely *shocked* at this turn of events. He was also happy that the secret was out, so he displayed an exuberance suited to the moment."

And later he made me feel better by going down on me in my kitchen. Standard friend behavior.

My stepmom looked skeptical. "I know you went into this, thinking it was the Franky & Baby Show with everyone else as a supporting character. Literally, because we are here for you, Franks. All the way."

"She's right, sis," Cat affirmed.

"But if you and Jason—oh, please don't cry! I don't mean to upset you."

I swiped at a tear. "I don't want to feel this way about him. It's so inconvenient."

"And how exactly *do* you feel?" Cat asked. "Fond? Horny? Mad about the boy?"

Rather than answer, I made my case for not being in love with him. "We're not suited at all, you know. He likes young, pretty, perky blondes who gaze at him adoringly and tell him he's the best, the absolute best." I added a flirty fluttering of my eyelashes that likely made me look demented. "And he wants a trad wife who cooks five-course meals for him and his multiple children before she dons lacy and likely very uncomfortable lingerie that embeds in her butt crack. I don't have time for that. I have important research to do!"

They blinked at my very scientific assessment of the situation.

Violet broke the silence. "Has he said he wants this butt-cracking Wunder wife?"

"Oh, Jason Isner claims he doesn't want a relationship with *anyone*, but I don't believe that for a second. I've never met a hockey player who's happy to go solo." The man would make someone a wonderful partner, but he certainly didn't see *me* in that role. "I think it's better we stay friends and adhere to the contract. Anything else risks upsetting the careful balance I'm trying to curate here."

My stepmom sighed. "That's the thing about love, Franks. It's not really something you can curate."

Cat gave a sympathetic nod. "Franky, if you have feelings for Jason, and you'd like to be more than co-parents, then you should talk to him."

A nubbin of hope sparked into a flame in my chest. Jason and I talked all the time, and not just about the baby. I kept him abreast of my research, and he told me all the ways I could insult someone Boston-style. The night of Theo's party, as we lay in bed together, we had both admitted to feelings of jealousy—he about Sean, me about the ravenous readers of Chicago Renegades fan fiction—but that was normal, given what we meant to each other. Wasn't it?

Despite our growing closeness, the idea that it might signify more than concern for our joint enterprise felt distinctly unreal.

I had no doubt he cared about me—and that he once found me attractive—but daring to think he might want more without clear evidence defied the logic and method that had been my watchwords all my life.

THE *DEROCERAS INVADENS* was resting in the terrarium, though with slugs, it was hard to tell. I made some notations on a clipboard, then rubbed the twinge I felt in my back.

A slight cough sounded behind me, and I turned to find the department chair, Dr. Al-Hadi. While I had met him several times in his office and at a couple of faculty mixers, this was the first time he had appeared in the Malacology Lab.

"Dr. Al-Hadi, welcome."

"Dr. St. James, I hope I'm not disturbing you." He surveyed the lab with interest. The chair's research was focused on bumblebees, particularly nest behavior and thermoregulation, so our worlds, or the worlds of our subjects, rarely intersected.

"Not at all."

He came forward, smiling. I'd always found him an amiable individual, and not like the typical fuddy-duddies I usually encountered in academia.

"How are you feeling? At this point in my wife's pregnancy with our first, she was ready to punch anyone who came near her."

I chuckled. "I'm not quite there, but I can definitely empathize. It'll be good to be home in Chicago with my family."

"That's what I wanted to talk to you about. We discussed once the possibility of making Harvard your home. We still believe that your research would add a missing dimension to the department's scholarship."

"My work is rather esoteric."

"But important, nonetheless. We must remember that we can learn so much from the tiniest organisms."

My thoughts exactly. "I appreciate the offer to apply, Dr. Al-Hadi. I've loved my time here, but with the baby about to be born, I'm anxious to maintain the support network I've built. My family is in Chicago, as is my baby's father, and while I've no doubt we could thrive here, those connections are key in the early years of a child's life. Perhaps, I would reconsider when my child is older."

Cat's advice had needled its way under my skin. *If you have feelings for Jason, and you'd like to be more than co-parents, then you should talk to him.*

With each day we came closer to meeting our child, I

wondered if there might be a chance for us as a couple. Once I was back in Chicago, we could discuss the potential for a partnership beyond co-parenting. Investigate if a man like Jason Isner could love an odd duck like me.

Dr. Al-Hadi nodded. "As long as I'm chair, a place will always be open for you, Dr. St. James."

MAY

CHAPTER FORTY-TWO

Second Round of the Playoffs
Game 3
Chicago @ LA

Jason

"YOU SEEM NERVOUS, J."

I turned my head slightly to Hatch, who really should be sitting in his own row on the plane. There were plenty of seats.

"Not nervous. I've played playoff games before."

"Yeah, but one more game and we're in the conference finals."

"Again, been here before."

We were two up in the series and heading to LA for Games 3 and 4. Sure, I was excited about the prospect of being one round closer to the Finals, but I was more excited about something else.

Win the next two on the road, and I would have five days before the conference finals began. Five days to rest my body and head out to Boston to see Franky. Sure, she'd be back in Chicago in less than a month, but I didn't want to wait. I needed to see her and Super Kid.

I cast a quick glance over my shoulder to the row behind me. "Still not sure why you're on this plane, Connie."

"Because Auntie Harper adores me. Rebels Air, man. Free travel for life."

Despite Conor's best efforts, the Detroit Motors had not qualified for the playoffs. He'd played like a demon. The team? Not so much. Now, he had decided to tag along, though I was pretty sure there was some liability issue with letting him fly with us.

The kid poked his head through the seats, which I (a) appreciated so I didn't have to get a crick in my neck, but (b) wished he hadn't bothered because he was about to annoy the fuck out of me.

"So when are you going to make an honest woman out of Franky?"

Hatch shook his head. "Conor Kershaw, whose filter between brain and mouth is permanently broken."

"It's not that kind of relationship."

"Yeah, but ... why not?"

It was a valid question. Rarely a day went by without a check-in by text or video call. When I couldn't talk to her, I peppered my brother and Melissa with questions about how she was, what she was eating, and whether she had mentioned me. (Not so much that last one, but I lived in hope that he might help a brother out.) We were the perfect example of cooperative co-parents and good friends.

She was the first person I thought of when I woke up and the last person to fill my brain as I lay my head on my pillow—or took a little recreational time with my right hand. I didn't think I was cut out for marriage or a love partnership, but we had this amazing thing, didn't we? A baby on the way, mutual respect, blistering sexual attraction, and neither of us wanting to lose our independence. It might not be the perfect bond I saw with my brothers and their partners, but did it have to be?

"I don't really have time to think of anything but hockey right now, Connie."

My nephew smiled at me. "Don't think it's hockey on your mind."

LA CAME OUT HARD. They had to win one of these two games to stay in the running, though I didn't reckon with their chances if we left with at least one win and they had to recover in Chicago.

But I was determined not to even give them that shot. All I could think of was getting to Boston to see Franky. Every blocked shot kept the enemy at bay. Every scream to my teammates to scramble, defend, push, break away, just *do* this thing, was done at the top of my lungs. From some deep part of me, I found untold reserves of strength. If I could do this, I got the prize of seeing her.

We won the first game, 4-2.

The younglings couldn't believe we were 3-zip up in the series. The old guard—Nyquist and me, basically—had to put our skated boots down to ensure they limited the celebration to the hotel bar. One year, I came this close and ended up in a brawl with a Seattle fan that almost took me out of the next game. No way was I risking anything that might interfere with Game 4, the day after tomorrow.

"One round of drinks," Nyquist said, using his captain's voice, with a quick glance at me for backup. I gave a curt nod of agreement.

"Only one?" Conor said.

"You're not even on this fucking team," I snapped at him.

Hatch winked at his brother. "You can have two, bro. Some of us still have a series to win."

As NoBo got the drinks in—"beers only!"—I checked my phone, scrolling through the multiple messages of congrats and well wishes until I found the one I was looking for.

> Nice work in that first period, Daddio.
> Super Kid kicked every time you blocked a shot.

> Or maybe it was indigestion.

No way. I had no doubt my child knew exactly how hard I was fighting to come see her and her mom. I wanted to talk to Franky. Maybe throw out some feelers about how she saw things between us in the future. I wasn't even sure I wanted to stay for one round in this bar, not when the alternative was a moment celebrating with her.

"Back in a second," I murmured to whoever was standing closest, and I moved off to look for a quiet spot. Near the short side of the L-shaped bar would work, but as I moved that way, someone stepped into my path.

Everly.

"Hi, Jason."

She looked good. Really good. A touch tired, but that

was understandable. Her little boy was a couple of months old, and while I thought I would have weird feelings about that, nothing significant came to pass. I was in a better place than I was the last time I saw her, that was for sure.

"Hi." I looked over her shoulder. "Coughlan here?" He was on IR for the LA Quake, so he wasn't playing in this series.

"No, he's at home with Joey."

I smiled. "How is the little stinker?"

She returned my smile. "Amazing. Keeping us up all night, but I wouldn't have it any other way. Thanks again for the bassinet. We use it all the time."

"Sure, glad to hear it."

"And congrats on the game tonight. On the whole series."

"It's not a done deal yet."

She made a skeptical face. "I saw how you played, Jason. I don't think anyone can stop you guys this year."

I leaned on the bar and let a couple of beats of silence pass. Ball was in her court.

"You're probably wondering why I'm here," she said.

"Maybe you love celebrating when your husband's team loses? Some people get their kicks in all sorts of ways."

She chuckled. "Actually, I wanted to … apologize."

Not expecting that. "For?"

"For giving you the impression that you might not be a worthy partner. I didn't think we were compatible, but I didn't handle it well."

Okay. "You didn't see me as partner or dad potential. I get it."

"That wasn't it. I actually didn't think I wanted those things until I met Ryan. And when I did, I saw my whole future laid out before me in a way I never saw with you." She shook her head. "I'm making it worse."

I touched her arm. "No, you're not. I get it. To be honest, when we were together, I was at a point of my life where I was ready to take the next step. Marriage, kids, the whole thing. You happened to be there, so I fixated on you, even though you weren't the right person. I realize that now."

I also realized that the person you thought would never fit your life might be the most perfect person of all.

She stepped in closer. "I read that you're having a baby. I'm really happy for you, Jason."

"Thanks. It's changed my world."

"It does that. What's the mom like?"

Indescribable. But I would try. "She's everything I never knew I needed."

CHAPTER FORTY-THREE

Franky

I AWOKE to a slew of messages from family and friends, celebrating last night's Game 3 win for the boys in LA. But the only person I wanted to hear from was Jason.

They were so close to making the conference finals. I wished I'd been able to stay awake but with the time difference on the West Coast, I was out for the count before the third period had even started.

I sent him a message.

He was probably still asleep, but I expected he'd call soon to make sure I had enough blueberries and bananas in my overnight oats. I also wondered if I should tell him something more personal. That I missed him. That I couldn't wait to see him again.

That maybe we should discuss the evolution of our partnership.

Put like that, it sounded like a business merger. But falling in love wasn't unlike a merging of lives. Of hearts and souls and everything in between.

My phone buzzed. Not Jason, but my mother.

Kendra had been in contact intermittently over the last couple of months. She and Xavier had finally called it quits and were fighting over alimony, so most of her messages centered on her "rights" and "what she was owed." I felt sorry for her, but after how low she pushed me the last time I saw her, I was trying to re-establish the boundaries, for my sake and the sake of my child.

Today, she had sent a photo. It was Jason in a bar with a woman.

Here we go again.

I looked closer. Pretty, blonde, and ... familiar.

Kendra's text filled in the details.

So that was why I recognized her. Everly, the woman he dated when he lived in Boston. I didn't know much about her. Didn't want to know, to be honest, because wanting brought me closer to wanting something else. Something more.

The phone rang, and against my better judgment, I answered.

She was already talking. "I thought you should see."

"Mom, I've already told you: Jason and I are not a couple."

"Well, I *know* that. I could see it at Theo's retirement party, but I remember what I was like when I was pregnant with Cat. So emotional. So hormonal. And your father was no help." She twittered on about how much she cried during her first pregnancy, but not so much with me, probably because my aura was different. Calmer. "I know you're approaching this with bucketloads of common sense—that's my Franky to a T!—but I'm sure a little part of you thinks, 'maybe?'"

I closed my eyes against the pain every word caused. Why couldn't she be on my side? "I don't think that, Mom."

"Your head knows the score, but the hormones—and the heart!—always think they know different. Now, the ex just had a baby and she's with another player in LA, so I'm sure there's *nothing* to that photo. But the article was clear that he wanted that life with her when he was in Boston. He wanted a baby with her."

My mouth felt dryer than sand.

"I-I knew that. He was clear about what he wants from the start." Nothing had changed, had it? Except for me thinking he might want more.

He might want me.

"Well, good, then! I saw how you looked at him at that party. Of course, he's very handsome so who wouldn't want that kind of eye candy in their life? But you're a realist. Always have been, which is a blessing right now."

"Mom, I should go. I have to go to work." Work was what I needed to focus on. That, and my baby.

On hanging up, I didn't go to work, at least, not immediately. Instead, I sank into Dr. Dube's sofa and clicked the link my mother had sent from *Hot Goss*. Did I need to know anything more about Jason and Everly? No. But data and facts were my bread and butter.

Scientific method, Franky. Always the method.

The title blared like a DEFCON 1 warning.

Old flames reunite as the Chicago-LA series heats up!

The "article" described how Everly was now married to an LA Quake player and had recently had a child, a little boy. How she and Jason were the Boston Cougars super couple until she broke his heart. A few months later, she became engaged to someone else and announced a pregnancy.

At the end of August.

My heart plummeted to the floor. That was when Jason offered to be my donor.

Armed with this hypothesis, I trawled back through the *Hot Goss* archives, gathering every data point I could find. Items about their breakup, anonymous sources talking about how he pushed for kids and marriage, and she said no.

I added it up in my head, assigning each point to a mental spreadsheet, titled "All the Reasons Franky is a Fool."

The swing set.

The love for his nieces and nephews.

The desperation for a child that led him to offer me his super sperm and tie himself to my dream.

But he had once wanted this dream with Everly.

And he would want it again with someone else. A whole brood. I wouldn't be able to give it to him. I no longer doubted Jason's interest in our child—he would be there for her, through thick and thin. But he would eventually meet a woman who suited him. Who would give him the family perfection he craved.

Not a four-eyed loser like me.

It would be tough to watch. Sharing custody of a child meant our lives would be intertwined forever. I had known that, but I had assumed I would never actually fall for someone like Jason, that our differences would keep my heart safe.

Now I would have to see him with the woman who made him happy. Pick-ups, drop-offs, birthday parties, doctors' appointments. At one time, I would have said a baby was all I needed, but Jason Isner had given me hope that I might have more. That I might deserve more.

But that was a fallacy. I would always be Slug Girl, and he would always be a superstar, far and away out of my league.

Still too close, though, unless I did something about it. Return to first principles, the reason I was doing this in the first place. For me and my child. This was my baby project to start with, and I didn't need the father to be a constant in our lives.

And I had the perfect solution to mending what my foolish heart had broken.

CHAPTER FORTY-FOUR

Finally! Rebels win against LA

Chicago could have done it in four on the road, but the Quake came back in Games 4 and 5 of the second round playoffs before the Rebels were able to finish them off at home. Jason Isner has proven to be a worthy replacement for his brother, and the new pairing with Lars Nyquist is on par with the best we've seen on the D-line. At right, Hatch Kershaw was in superb form as was young Francois Gaultier in the center. On the other side of the bracket, Vancouver and Utah are tied at three apiece, with Game 7 tomorrow night. Heading into the Western conference finals, due to start in less than a week, Chicago will have a couple of extra days to rest those legs—and they'll need them.

-@RebelsInsider

CHAPTER FORTY-FIVE

Rebels are Finals-bound after shutting out Vancouver in four

The Chicago Rebels are back in the Finals for the second year running after winning four straight against Vancouver to become Western Conference champions. The hometown team played like their lives depended on it, and no one was stronger or more determined on the ice than Jason Isner, who lived up to his moniker, the Green-Eyed Monster.

He never won the Cup with Boston, but now it looks like he'll have to go through his old team to earn the hardware. Boston are up 3-1 in the series against the New York Spartans and could clinch the Eastern Conference championship in tonight's game.

-@RebelsInsider

Jason

IT WAS the last week of May, and I was ready to lay it all out there.

I knocked on the door of a nice-looking brownstone in Cambridge, praying that she hadn't left for work yet. If I had my way, she wouldn't be going into work at all, but I didn't think that opinion would go down well.

She answered the door, looking so damn beautiful my heart keened with yearning. Same messy bun, same glasses off center, same ocean-blue gaze. The video calls and check-ins were great. Necessary. But nothing beat seeing her in person. In the four months since she last visited Chicago, she had grown. At thirty-four weeks, the baby was the size of a pumpkin.

"Hi, Francesca."

Her eyes went round. "How are you here?"

"Chartered a flight from Vancouver. I have four days off, and there's nowhere I'd rather spend it."

I wondered if maybe I'd made a mistake. She might not want me here. Maybe I was interfering with her research process or her routine. But then something shifted in her expression, a softening that I took as a good sign.

She moved to pick up my duffle.

"Hey, are you crazy?" I swatted her hand away and picked it up.

"But you're tired. A warrior returning home from battle."

"Get inside, woman, before the neighbors accuse me of God knows what."

She stepped back to let me in and shut the door.

I grinned at her. "Tell me how you're feeling."

"Tired but as healthy as can be expected given where I am in the process and my age. My research is going well, too. We were able to get fascinating video footage of the

Deroceras invadens during its mating cycle. This type of slug doesn't employ selfing all that much—"

"Like self-fertilization?"

She smiled. "Right. They prefer to seek a mate and sometimes copulate with the same mate several times. It's unusual in the species."

"Maybe the mate provides something they can't get alone."

"Well, that's a valid assumption. Its goal may be a higher rate of fecundity. I think—or we think—that sticking with the same mate makes them happier and more fertile. It's so odd, because biologically, it's not necessary. But there's some imperative, driving them to seek out a mate instead of reverting to self-reliance."

My smarty pants professor was babbling a little. Was she nervous to see me? I wanted to hug her, kiss her, strip her down so I could run my hands all over her body. But if I touched her, I wouldn't be able to stop. Plus we should talk first before the hormones got a jump on us.

"Maybe the snails can teach us something." I yawned and leaned against the banister as tiredness suddenly enveloped me. "Do you mind if I sit for a while?"

"Of course! Here I am yammering on about slug sex. You must be wrecked." She led me to a sofa in the living room filled with books, mostly on geometry and calculus. There was an empty bird cage and a fireplace filled with big candles. "You should have gone home to Chicago to rest."

I sank into the soft cushions. "I can rest when I'm dead or a Cup winner."

I hadn't seen her since the last season game against Boston, and that was only a few minutes outside the locker room with Sean and Melissa there, along with my team-mates and the press, then it was full steam ahead to the playoffs. "I can help you pack. Bring you home. How's she been?"

"Kicking up a storm."

"Yeah?"

"I think she knows you powered through to the Finals."

That made me laugh. I had missed her so much. Missed this warmth between us. It had been a long, cold, lonely winter.

"Still sure we have a girl?"

"We didn't want to know, so until then, a girl she is."

In the last couple of seconds, we had inched closer, drawn by the undeniable energy between us.

"Oh!" She grasped my hand. "There she goes. Feel that?"

I had always thought that holding a hockey stick, feeling it as an extension of my arm, was where my hands were meant to be.

I was wrong. This was it. My hand on her belly, absorbing the kick of my child. I didn't just want a family. I wanted this, the whole stinking lot of it.

And I wanted it with her.

I continued to rub her stomach. Being this close to her and watching that light glitter in her eyes was the most satisfying thing in the world. Super Kid appeared to have calmed down, but I hadn't. I was like a starving man with a can of Pringles: once you pop, you can't stop. My hands couldn't leave this woman's body, but they were in a losing battle with the rest of me.

My eyelids grew heavy. "The snails are our teachers," I murmured.

"They sure are."

"They work better with a mate."

"Not work better, just are more fertile. It's all about ensuring the continuation of the species."

I smiled, feeling so, so sleepy. But happy. I was where I was meant to be.

"So not just one kid, but a whole brood of 'em. That's what the snail wants."

My eyes fluttered closed, and I fell off the cliff into sleep.

CHAPTER FORTY-SIX

Franky

FIVE HOURS LATER, I returned home to find him sitting at the breakfast bar, scrolling on his phone.

"Hello."

He smiled, a flash of white through that dark beard. My fingers itched to touch it. I'd seen it online, but the reality was truly magnificent.

"Hey, Doc. Sorry to drop in unannounced."

"That's okay. I had to go into the lab to check on my specimens. But I managed to move some things around so I could spend time with you."

He moved off the stool and closed the gap between us. My heart beat wildly. I still couldn't believe he'd come to see me right after the series ended. Part of me wondered if it was damage control, because of Everly.

But he hadn't even brought it up, probably because he

didn't think it was any of my concern. After all, several weeks had gone by.

He placed a hand on my bump. "Are you sure you're not overdoing it? You're about six weeks from lift-off, and I worry this might be too much."

I bit my lip. I needed to say something. I needed to hear his side instead of condemning him in my mind. Love should have no boundaries when it came to communication.

"You never told me that your ex-girlfriend just had a baby."

"Everly?" He looked genuinely confused. "Didn't think it was relevant."

"But ... you wanted to settle down with her and have a child? And she didn't?"

"She did, just not with me." A flush darkened his cheeks.

"After you split up with her, she met someone and got pregnant."

"Yeah, pretty quickly, too. Which tells me she wasn't for me."

"And you knew about her pregnancy before you offered to be the father of my child?"

He thought on that, probably wondering where I was going. The trap I was setting. My heart thundered while I waited for his answer.

"Well, yeah. But that wasn't why—Doc, you needed a donor and I needed—"

"A child."

He bristled. "I've never lied about that."

"No. But now it reads like you're trying to prove something to Everly. That you can find someone to have a kid with, too. That you didn't need *her*."

We were merely providing each other with the biological means to create a life that we would both share. A baby, nothing else. It made no sense that I would be upset. He had been honest from the start. He wanted to be a father.

Of course he would rather have Everly as the mother. Maybe more. The family package that once made sense until she hurt him. A proper WAG, a glamorous wife and mom, who met his needs perfectly. Young, dewy, fresh, and able to pump out more kids before the bloom was off the rose.

"I'm not trying to prove anything to anyone. I want this baby. I want this baby with you."

"And you'll have her." I smiled, though it felt wobbly around the edges. "That's what the contract says."

"The contract? I think we're beyond the contract."

My lip trembled. "How so? You said you didn't want a relationship. A marriage. A wife. Has that changed?"

He frowned, not liking my tone. All he had to say was, *yes, it's changed. You've changed everything for me.*

But he didn't. He couldn't. "We don't have to put labels on it. We're co-parents, with respect and affection. We make a great team, don't we?"

We did, but one of us had dreamed a little dream. Now she was waking up.

"There's you. There's me. There's the baby. We're not a family unit, no matter how we try to spin it. Neither of us had the other person in mind beyond what was necessary for this enterprise. Be honest, Jason. If you could have had a baby with Everly, you would have."

"Yes! That's what I wanted. Or thought I wanted." He started pacing, my hotheaded warrior. "But not now."

"It's easy to get our emotions mixed up in all of this. I'm hormonal and want the assurance that you'll be there for the baby, and I've mistaken that as wanting you to be there for *me*."

"It's the same thing."

Oh, but it wasn't. "You're excited to be a father and I'm the woman carrying your child. You're bound to feel certain things, affection and a bond with your child's mother, but if the baby wasn't in the picture, you wouldn't have looked at me twice. In fact, you would have walked to the other side of the street to avoid me."

Storm clouds skittered across his handsome face. "The baby brought us closer together and made us *both* see each other in a different light. I'm not going to deny that. Those are facts. But I don't find you sexy and attractive and god*damn* infuriating because you're pregnant with my kid. Somehow, you've managed to come up with that allure all by yourself."

I didn't believe him. He was trying to convince me that this was the case to keep me calm and centered in the lead-up to the birth.

"You're certainly not what I had in mind," I said.

"Hell, don't I know it."

"You're still not."

He looked stricken, or at least his ego did not enjoy that. I hated hurting him, but I needed time apart to get my bearings.

"And let's be honest, Jason. I'm not what you want either."

"Why, because you're going to take a job in Boston?"

I snapped my head back. "Who told you that? Sean?"

"*Sean* knows?" He grabbed an envelope off the breakfast bar. It was the interview schedule from Harvard's Department of Organismic and Evolutionary Biology.

For the job I applied for two weeks ago. Seeing that

photo of Jason and Everly had clarified my thinking. I would never be what he wanted and I needed to focus on my strengths. My career and the baby.

"I haven't been happy at Lakeshore since Dr. Bilson came on board. His actions have been curtailing my research freedom and ability to do things my way."

"God forbid anything curtails your ability to do things your way, Francesca."

All these men, looking to control my decisions. "The contract specifically said my career might take me out of Chicago. You knew that, but you still went ahead with the baby plan."

He was pacing again, hands on hips. "The contract said, the contract said. Sure, I went ahead because I wanted a kid. But I thought we'd still talk about the big decisions, the ones that affect our child. I thought we'd co-parent like mature adults. But this has always been your deal, hasn't it, Francesca? You've never seen me as a partner in this. I'm just the stud."

He sounded so wounded. Maybe he was right. Maybe I felt more ownership over this because it started with my heartfelt wish. I had the spreadsheet and the thermometer and the syringe. He merely arrived on his white charger, dick out, ready to deliver.

But the last few months had shown me the side of him I craved in a partner. In the man with whom I had fallen hopelessly in love. He might say he wanted us to move forward with respect and affection, as a family unit, but that could only take us so far. My research was important, too. I never planned to be the kind of woman who stayed in the background, supporting the man's supposedly more important job.

"Of course I see you as a partner. But our child needs

stability, and when the parents aren't a couple, then one person has to step up as primary caregiver."

His color was high. "And that's supposed to be you? The woman who would rather spend time with snails and slugs than the people who are supposed to be the most important in your life? Mothers are supposed to make sacrifices, but you seem to think you can carry on like nothing has happened. Move across the country, take a new job, leave everyone you know behind. You'll birth a baby and then it's back to what's important—your career."

As if every choice I made was for me and me alone, instead of with my child's future at the forefront.

"And I thought you'd be supportive. But what you really want is a hot WAG back home, two steps behind her man, popping out all those babies to make the perfect family your father denied you. The *who* doesn't matter."

He looked like I'd bashed him in the sternum with a hockey stick. His expression shifted from storm to ice.

"Well, it sure as hell looks like you're right. I don't mind saying it, Doc. We are *not* compatible. You've had the truth of it from the beginning. I don't know why I thought we might be more than co-parents, not when you are so damn determined to do it all by yourself and screw everyone else."

"That's your job. Off you go and find another incubator for your spawn. This one's already occupied."

He shook his head, grabbed his duffle bag, and stormed out, at which point I burst into tears because hormones, and—

Well, there could be no other reason.

It couldn't be because my heart was broken, and I had only myself and my foolish dreams to blame.

JUNE

CHAPTER FORTY-SEVEN

Jason

WHEN I WAS PISSED OFF, I ran. The lake path, the park, a track. If it gave me a good stretch of road, I ate it up. But it was kind of toasty out there and I didn't want to run into any fans or paps, so here I was on the treadmill in the Rebels gym, hopeful for some alone time to marshal my spiraling thoughts.

Franky and I had reverted to our small talk method of communication. Just enough to ensure our contractual obligations were fulfilled, but not enough to have a real conversation about why we had fought.

I didn't think I was wrong. I had told her that she was not what I originally had in mind for my baby's mother. That I wanted a family and saw a chance to get it. That my feelings had changed and I wanted to make a go of it with her. Make it real.

Those were all facts. As a woman of logic, she was supposed to *love* the facts!

I had also told her I was pissed about her trying to take my kid to live in another city. Hell, I just left Boston! And she was considering leaving everyone who loved her in Chicago and starting over solo? Put her career before my chance to be a great dad all because there weren't enough snails around the shores of Lake Michigan? That made no sense.

And that business with Everly—absolute bullshit. I wasn't going to lie and say that Everly getting married and pregnant so soon after we broke up didn't hurt. *Maybe* it had influenced my offer to father a child with Franky. But that was where Everly's influence ended. As if she could hold a candle to the doc. No other woman turned me on like Francesca did. That brain, that mouth, that body—the pregnant and the not pregnant versions. I loved her glasses and her messy hair and those full lips and the freckle on the nape of her neck. I loved talking to her about her work and hockey and how brilliant our kid was going to be.

Was that the same thing as "being in love"? I didn't know, and I didn't really care, because what we had worked. The doc was acting like we weren't compatible, and while I might have agreed in anger because she was being so damned difficult and opinionated about it all, I didn't truly think that. We were different, that was for sure. But incompatible? Not a chance.

Setting aside the career advancement opportunity at Harvard, which she had mentioned was a possibility, what was our basic problem? She had said I wanted a picture-perfect family, a woman to push out the kids and keep the home fires burning, and she didn't fit that mold.

Sure, I wanted to fill my house with laughter and joy

and cats and dogs. When I had originally imagined those things, I had conjured up some blonde cheerleader type, like Everly or that Farrah chick who bored me to tears in Dallas.

I didn't see an egghead with books on every surface and glasses off kilter while she breastfed our baby.

I didn't see a smarty pants professor with chalk-stained fingers holding an entire room rapt with her lectures on earthworms.

I certainly didn't see a femme fatale strutting across a hotel lobby in the Baby Conception Caper.

But that's what I saw now.

Only *she* couldn't see it. She could only see the reasons we didn't work.

"Hey, J."

I switched off my headphones. Theo stood before me in warm-up gear.

"Hey there." We fist bumped while I switched off the treadmill. "You here to work out?"

"Just a light skate with the vets."

"Franky calls them the Three Wise Men." Damn. Just saying her name was a stab to my heart.

Theo looked like he wanted to say more than what he eventually came up with. I hadn't told him anything but he knew me well and had a sixth sense about these things. "Want to join us?"

"I sure do. Let's skate."

THE WORKOUT WAS GOOD. As much as I enjoyed sweating while running, nothing got my juices flowing like a vigorous skate with my fellow pros.

Thirty minutes in, I grabbed my water from the bench just as Bren skated over and stopped before me. We hadn't spoken much in the last few months, and I wondered what his daughter had told him about us. Or if she had mentioned me at all. Maybe I was surplus to requirements once my donation was delivered.

Some masochistic part of me couldn't resist bringing her up.

"Have you talked to Franky?"

"Have I talked to my daughter?" With his Scottish burr, it came out as "dotter."

I swallowed, realizing too late I had not thought this through.

"We had an argument in Boston a few days ago. I just wanted to know if she's okay. I mean, I'm guessing she's fine or I would have heard about it, but …"

Theo, Remy, and Vadim had skated over as that sentence petered out.

"Everything okay here?" Theo asked, carefully, like he was expecting trouble. Maybe he knew St. James better and could tell when the guy was about to kick someone's ass.

"Is it?" Bren asked me, his eyes as cold as the ice beneath our feet. "Or have you been upsetting my daughter while she's in a precarious position health wise?"

So Franky hadn't told her dad about our falling out. Apparently, that was *my* spectacular achievement.

"I thought we were on the same page about raising the kid, how that would look, where it would happen. But it seems not."

Bren chugged down some water. Made me wait.

"Sounds like this is between the two of you."

If she hadn't told them we fought, then maybe they

didn't know the details. Telling tales out of school wasn't really my bag, but he needed to know.

"She's applying for a job at Harvard. Leaving Chicago and everyone she knows."

Leaving me.

Bren remained stoic. For Christ's sake, didn't he care that Franky might be a thousand miles away on a permanent basis?

"Do you ... like my daughter?"

"Of course I like her."

Vadim snorted. Remy grinned. Even Theo looked amused.

Bren? Not so much.

"What I think Bren's asking is if you *like*-like her," Theo said.

I turned to Bren. "Is that what you're asking?"

Silence, made only more eerie by the craggy-faced veteran standing before me.

"Yeah. Yeah, I do. But I don't think she likes me the same way."

Another snort from Vadim. How did he make it sound so Russian?

"Knew it," Theo said.

"What? That she doesn't like me the same way?"

My brother laughed. "No, that you like her. God, you kids are a mess."

We were. I didn't mind admitting it.

"I'm not what she expected and she's not what I expected. And rather than thinking that's a good thing because surprises are the fucking best, she's sticking to her guns. The rules were set in the beginning, and the ending can't be any different than what she planned."

Never mind that the middle had changed everything.

"Perhaps you should come up with a pros and cons list," Vadim said. "Franky is a woman who likes to think things through. She would like a man who comes at it logically."

Remy scoffed. "Logic? This is the heart we're talking about. Francoise needs a big gesture, maybe something on the Jumbotron during the Finals."

Franky would hate that. Me, on the other hand? I kind of liked the idea.

I turned to Bren, expecting a contribution. He raised an eyebrow, and then ... nothing. In other words, *you've done enough to upset her, asshole.*

A taut moment later, Bren skated off, followed by his cohort, while Theo raised an eyebrow and patted my arm.

We were here to skate. I needed to forget my head and my heart and think only of my hands, feet, and the blood pumping through my veins. I had a cup to win.

AFTER PRACTICE, Theo and I went to the Sunny Side Up Diner for breakfast. He had been relatively quiet during the on-ice Francesca debrief, but I expected he'd have more to say now. We put in orders—the Theo omelet for him, the French toast and pancake stack for me—and then I sat back and waited.

He stirred his coffee. "So tell me what's going on."

I inhaled a breath. "Somehow, she's gotten the impression that I might have offered my sperm donation services purely to prove Everly wrong. Like, 'look at me, I can have a baby, too.'"

Theo looked horrified. "Dude, tell me that's not what happened."

"Not ... really? Sure, seeing Everly happy and knocked

up by Coughlan got me thinking about what I was missing. Kids, the wife, the life." *Everything you have, brother.* "The chance to have a kid was right there. I didn't really care about the wife part until—"

"You did."

I sipped my coffee. "She thinks she's the pinch hitter. The stand-in because I didn't get what I wanted with Everly. But hell, Theo, neither of us went in expecting more than a bundle of joy at the end of the nine months."

"And now you're in love with your baby mama and she's not buying it."

"I'm not—that's not ..." I'd been trying my best not to put a label on it. That seemed the safest way to approach the situation. Now I felt like shit, so I guessed I'd screwed up somewhere.

I was madly in love with Francesca St. James.

"I'm not even sure what that looks like."

He waved over my face. "It looks like this."

Misery? That was about right.

"She wants to take my kid away."

He raised an eyebrow. "Explain."

"She's interviewing for a professorship at Harvard. Harvard, Theo! She did say at the start of all this that her career was important and it might involve a move out of Chicago, but that seemed like something that would happen years down the road. I just saw red. I think I could have persuaded her that we had a future, but as soon as I objected to her leaving Chicago for good, she got on her high horse and told me my opinion didn't matter. She already knew how annoyed I was about the guest lecture-ship for most of her pregnancy, but this? She's talking about leaving and the kid's not even here yet."

My brother looked at me with pity, then out of nowhere said, "Dad's a jerk."

"What the hell does that have to do with it?"

"He screwed you and Sean over, not to mention Jenny. Luckily, you had me to pick up the slack and be the perfect father figure, so I'm not sure why you're so fucked up."

"I am not fucked up!"

"Yeah, you're all little orphan Jason, and as soon as you think Franky might skip town, you're acting like she's leaving you behind. Pulling a Nick."

Well, she was, wasn't she? "Are you saying I have abandonment issues?"

"Nah. How could you?" He patted his chest. "Perfect older brother here who stepped in and acted in loco parentis. You didn't need Nick. None of us did. We had each other."

True. But it still hurt not to have him around. To find out that he had wanted to start over, to make a life without us. The second I heard Franky might be leaving, I was that thirteen-year-old kid, wondering why Dad was packing a suitcase.

"I was pretty messed-up when he left."

"I know, dude. I was there. To be honest, you've grown up to be remarkably well-adjusted, considering. Awesome brother, great uncle, cool teammate, or so I've heard." He grinned. "You're one of the best men I know, J, and you're going to make a great dad. And whether Franky's in Chicago with Baby Isner or halfway around the world, you will still be a family. Nothing's going to change that."

His lips twitched. "Unless you do something about it."

CHAPTER FORTY-EIGHT

Franky

"ANYTHING I CAN GET YOU?"

Violet eyed me over the lip of her coffee cup as she moved off a stool at the kitchen island.

"I'm fine with my oatmeal, thanks."

A few days ago, I returned to Chicago and had decided to stay with my parents while Rosie packed up her stuff at my place. She was still looking after the cats, which was probably good because I couldn't bend over to feed them.

"Tea? I have the herbal junk."

"No, I'm okay. Honestly."

Super Kid was very active today, making sure I got my kick counts in quickly. Maybe it was the oatmeal or maybe it was the fact she would be here in a few weeks, screaming her way into the world. Our Valkyrie shieldmaiden.

Violet smiled at me. "We're thrilled to have you here, Franks. We've missed you so much."

"I missed everyone, too. I loved my time at Harvard, but it's good to be back in my hometown."

Until I left again. *If* I left again. My interview at Harvard had gone well. Of course, there were a few peculiar looks about my advanced pregnancy. Federal law forbade questions about my child-rearing plans, but people clearly wanted to know about my support system and if a baby would interfere with my research. The idea of being alone in Boston with my child scared me, but being here in Jason's backyard and witnessing his life without me, scared me more.

"Just four more weeks until we meet the little one. Jason must be so excited."

I tightened my grip on the spoon. "He is."

We were still texting, the stiff, daily check-ins that were our normal during the times when we weren't getting along. *When He was Mad and I was Stubborn: The Jason and Franky Story.*

"I'm surprised he hasn't been around."

"We're in touch. That's what we agreed to."

Violet remained placid. "Agreed to?"

"In the contract. Regular check-ins, attendance at doctor's appointments, if available, but on the whole, we both do our own thing. He's his own person. I'm my own person."

"Okay."

They expected me to be like them. Anxious for a life partner, lonely without a man. If I'd made a baby with Jason, I must want something to happen with him.

I hated that they were right. That underneath it all, I was absolutely conventional, craving the white picket fence and a life of domestic banality.

"Vi, I hope you're not wishing for something to happen with Jason, other than what's already occurred—"

"Well, I—"

"Because that's not in the cards. We both went into this arrangement with clear ideas about what we wanted out of it." My voice had risen slightly there, which was not good for the baby. I fought for calm. "And it's all going according to plan."

"Good to hear it," she said cheerfully.

"And now I need to review the proofs for my article on the role of sexual selection and the courtship rituals of the *Arion Vulgaris*." I slid off the stool, carefully, and steadied myself before taking a step.

"Gotcha."

I caught her eye. "He didn't hurt me. I'll admit that I might have let my imagination stray to 'what if,' but I quickly realized that anything more than our current contractual obligations would never work. We have different requirements of a mate."

Violet let me ramble. She knew what I was like when I was nervous.

"I don't need a partner in my everyday life. I have so much love and support. So much." My voice broke on those final words.

"I know, cariño." She gave me a hug, holding on a little longer than necessary. "So I'm heading out to yoga and then a grocery store run. Anything I can get for you?"

I shook my head, my mind already straying to my article proofs and longing to bury myself in my work. Classic avoidance, but at least I recognized it.

Violet turned back and said casually, "By the way, Jenny, Elle, and Theo are throwing you a baby shower tomorrow."

"What?"

"Usually, it happens earlier but you were out of town, and everyone wants to give you gifts and welcome you home. It'll be small. Intimate."

"Let me guess. A hundred people or so?"

She winked. "At least."

I spent the next hour working on the article galleys and checking in with the snail-cams at Lakeshore U. Rusty and Billy Bob had mated over the weekend. Good for them. I was musing on how life always found a way, to paraphrase the great chaos theorist, Dr. Ian Malcolm in *Jurassic Park*, when I got a text.

DAD

Can you meet me in the kitchen?

I waddled out to find my father tying off his apron. Not just any apron, though. His uni-bow one, a combination of unicorns and rainbows. Faded and threadbare from years of washing, it was only used for one specific kitchen task.

Making apple pie.

It was a tradition in the St. James household, usually undertaken the day Dad came home from a road trip back when he played professionally. We used to make an apple pie together while Mom went out to one of her girls' lunches, because she was dying for some "me time" after days trapped with us. For a while, Cat and I had made it alone because Dad "needed his rest" (aka, was hungover), but the tradition started up again when he was in recovery.

He looked up. "Hey, sprite."

"Hi, Dad." Tears threatened, which was ludicrous. It was only pie.

"Up for peeling some apples?" He had gathered the supplies I would need, so I took a seat at the counter and picked up the apple peeler. His hands were already a yellowy-white as he combined the butter and flour.

"How was practice?"

"Good. Petrov moaned about his knee and Remy gave him shit for it as usual. Kershaw decided to join us, because Elle told him she was finally calling a contractor to finish the deck he's been building for the last three years and he needed to get out of the house instead of telling the pro everywhere he was doing it wrong."

I chuckled. "Retirement must be tough on him."

"Aye."

I started peeling, determined to keep the strip of skin intact and as long as possible. "Remember when we came up with the nanny plan to woo Violet into our clutches?"

He raised his clear blue gaze to me. "It was your idea. One, make an apple pie. Two, dazzle her with slug talk. Three, feed her pasta."

"I was quite the little manipulator."

"You just wanted a mom."

True, but mostly I wanted an adult female presence in my life who didn't recoil at the weirdness. "Violet fascinated me. She was such a maverick with her pink hair and tattoos and short skirts. She didn't care what anyone thought."

"That was all a front. She cared greatly. She wanted a place to belong, with her sisters, with us. She just didn't know it yet."

I picked up another apple. Cooking apples we called them. Too sour to eat, but perfect when stewed for a while.

I met his gaze. His beard was salted with flour, and a wave of nostalgia hit me so hard I almost keeled over. If a girl had her dad keeping her safe, what else did she need?

"Vi thinks I might be lonely as a single mom. I tried to explain to her that I have everything I need."

"What about everything you want, sprite?"

"I'm about to get it, Dad. This baby is all I've ever wanted."

He grunted. "And Isner? Do you want him?"

"Why does everyone assume I can't be happy with what I have? That I need a man as that perfect cherry on top? Most of all, why can't people see that Jason and I only have this baby in common? That's it. Sure, we became close because of our joint enterprise. Nothing else."

"Tell him that."

I snapped my head back. The dough was now in a messy ball on the counter. As a girl, I would insist on kneading it, though my small hands weren't strong enough to make much impact. Dad would stand there patiently, letting me learn about effort and pie.

"You spoke to him?"

"He was out on the ice with his brother this morning. We sparred a little."

Sparred? "You'd better have been nice to him."

"Why?"

"Because he's the father of your grandchild. I would like if you got along."

He shrugged. "Why would I make nice with the man who hurt my daughter?"

"Why do you think—did he say something?"

My father bent over to pull the rolling pin out of the drawer and gave the mound of pastry a whack, as if letting it know winter was coming.

"He mentioned the job you're applying for at Harvard."

That snitch. "I haven't made any decisions yet. I just want to keep my options open."

He nodded. "When you were a kid, you used to invent stories for your slug friends. Send them on adventures. Give them happily-ever-afters."

Bit of a non sequitur, but okay. "Until I decided to release them back into the garden and set them free. They were flesh-and-blood creatures. It wasn't fair of me to impose my wishes or desires on them. Besides, slugs and snails don't experience emotions like we do. They have nerve endings rather than brains. All instinct."

Like Jason. But he was smart, too. Much more so than he gave himself credit.

"Guess what I'm saying is that you had quite the imagination," Dad went on. "Your mind was open to possibilities then, and sure, I know you've grown up and put away childish things as the poem says."

"Bible, actually."

"Oh yeah?" We weren't religious, but I knew that much. "Anyway, what I'm trying to remind you of is that you used to have dreams and desires. Not just basic needs. Not just living inside your head. You spend a lot of time there, sprite. And it's served you well, but there's nothing wrong with wanting things for yourself."

"That's where the baby comes in, Dad. She'll make me happy."

He studied me with his usual gravity. "Your mother has never understood you, Franky. So why would you listen to her?"

"I-I don't. With Mom, it's in one ear—"

"Where it scrambles your brain for a bit, and then out the other. She never encouraged you. She had a certain idea of what a little girl should be, and you weren't it. And I worry you carry some of that weight with you. Some of that pain. Sure, you're professionally successful and you're about to have a baby you've longed for. You have people who love you to the moon and back, but you still let your mom put you in a box when it came to your lovability. She told you that you were kooky and weird, and you took that inside you and let it fester."

I set an extra-long apple peel aside. In Dutch folklore, it was said that throwing a long strip of peel over your shoulder would reveal the initial of your true love. No matter how hard I wished, this one looked more like a G.

"I don't mind being the weirdo. I accept that."

"I know you do. You're the most interesting person I know. But sometimes I think you don't want to be seen as interesting or kooky. Sometimes you just want to be seen the same as everyone else. Worthy of the things everyone else deserves. Like a boyfriend. Or a husband. Or someone who loves you for who you are instead of how it reflects off them. Your mother is a selfish woman, and she only ever cared about how good you made *her* feel. How you reflected off her."

"But ... she's not wrong, Dad. I'm not the kind of girl who gets the hot guy or the hunky athlete. Yes, I fell for Jason against my better judgment. But I never really *believed*. Something inside me knew it was utter nonsense. Jason wants to be a dad, and I happened to be on the spot to fulfill that need. Just as he happened to be available when I needed him. To make a baby. Expecting anything more is like inventing fairytales for my slugs and snails."

He looked at me with such love I wanted to melt on the spot, preferably into his strong arms.

"We all have dreams, goals, desires, needs. It's okay to want things. The way I grew up, thrown from pillar to post with my parents, half the time in Scotland, half in Canada— the minute I had a chance, I bought this house. Before I had even met Kendra, I had it because I knew it was the first building block to what I wanted. Family. A life that was more than hockey. More than alcohol. I wanted to fill the rooms with laughter and games and little girls who liked dolls and science, music and slugs. But it all started with a wish, sprite."

He winked at me. "You're never too old for that."

Jason

THE FRONT DOOR of Theo's house opened. I looked down to find Tilly dressed in a tutu and a tiara, with a star-tipped wand in her hand.

"Hey, Tillington, what's shakin'?"

"Uncle Jason!" She reached for me, and I dropped my shopping bag to pick her up.

"You're so big. How did that happen?"

"Fairy magic." She shoved her hand in my face. "I have my bracelet."

I touched my wrist to hers. "Me, too. So I heard there's a party."

I could hear the noise of party attendees, the collective *oohs* and *aahs* that accompanied gift-opening. We were two days off from Game 1 of the Finals, starting at home, thankfully. I wasn't sure throwing a baby shower in the middle of all that was such a good idea, but my mom and Elle were determined that it should happen before Super Kid was born, and not the week before, either.

No longer were baby showers considered the sole domain of the mom-to-be and her female friends. I had attended enough of them over the years to know the expectant dad and the male spouses were welcome—no, *required* —to show their faces.

"Franky has a baby in her stomach." My niece sounded both horrified and fascinated.

"Yep, she does. That's my baby. I'm going to be a daddy."

Tilly twitched her nose. "Like my daddy?"

"Yeah, just like that." I moved forward, still carrying my niece, and stood near the entrance to the great room. The place was packed with family, teammates, spouses, and boxes of every shape and size. I hadn't even realized we were registered anywhere. I had assumed I'd buy all that stuff when we needed it.

Franky was seated in a wing-back chair, one of the firmer ones that I knew was probably better for her back pain. My mom was passing her gifts, like she was the lady-in-waiting to her queen.

"Finally, he shows," Cody Jacobs said, which turned everyone's head in my direction. I heard congratulations and best wishes, but it barely registered. All I could see was her.

She lifted her hand and gave me a small wave. I waved back. So did Tilly.

This morning, Franky had texted me.

They're throwing a baby shower for us.

I'd love if you can make it.

Only if you want to.

Try to keep me away.

My mother approached me with Elle. "I was a little worried you weren't going to show!" Mom was so excited about the baby, and I suspected she secretly hoped that Franky and I were more than just co-parents. Apparently, we all did, except the baby mom herself.

I set my niece down and turned to my mom. "Franky is over eight months gone, Mom. This is tiring for her."

My mother smiled knowingly. "Oh, we're taking care of her."

"Don't worry, Jason," Elle said as she smoothed Tilly's hair. "She's doing fine. And if she wasn't, she'd say so."

Would she? Franky was outspoken and forthright with her opinions, but she also wanted to fit in.

"Excuse me." I moved toward her, stepping around diaper pails and baby baths, until I loomed over her.

She looked up, blinking large, blue pools behind those sexy glasses. "Hello."

"Hi, Doc. Need a break?"

Her eyes lit up with amusement. "I'd love one."

I called out, "Okay, folks. Let's take ten and give my baby mama a moment to pee and accept a daddio belly rub."

A few people clapped, the usual idiots who thought a man looking after the mother of his child was "cute," I supposed. I held out my hand, and she accepted, gripping hard for leverage to pull herself to a stand. Damn, she was huge, and with another month to go, I didn't see how she could grow that baby to term and still remain upright.

"Thank you," she murmured as I navigated between strewn wrapping paper and boxes and unopened gifts.

"You need the restroom?"

"No, I'm okay for now. Could we talk?"

"You bet."

I led her to Elle's office, which I knew had a nice, comfortable sofa. As I closed the door behind me, I took a breath and figured out my plan of attack.

When I turned, she was seated on the sofa. "I thought you might not come."

"Elle asked me to stop by Sweet Mandy B's for cupcakes, and the traffic was hell."

She nodded. "I worried you couldn't bear to be in the same room as me."

"We had an argument, Doc. That doesn't mean we've stopped talking, does it?"

"Generally, that's exactly what it means."

I'd had some time to think about this. To give her space. Typically, I resisted thinking things through, but I figured I'd take a leaf from the doc's big book of wisdom and wait until she came back to Chicago.

"Can we talk about what happened?"

She gestured to the sofa, and I took a seat at the other end.

I inhaled deeply. "I've never been all that interested in settling down. Relationships seemed like such hard work. I'd seen how my dad treated my mom and marriage looked like trouble. But then I started thinking more about kids and what that would look like. As I got older, panic set in, I suppose. I knew the women I dated weren't ever going to make good moms. Does that make sense?"

She nodded.

"Then I met Everly, and she fit the bill. Hot, interested in hockey, young enough that I could see a Theo Kershaw-quantity brood in my future. I'm not sure we ever had that much in common, but it was easy to gloss over the cracks when you spend as much time on the road as I do. You come back and it's great sex and let's party. You're never really talking about the deep stuff. About six months in, I brought up the topic of the future, and she made it clear she didn't see me that way. And I was pissed. Here was this chick shitting on my dream, so when I was acquired by the Rebels, it was a good time for us to break up."

"And then she met someone else."

"Pretty quickly, maybe even before we broke up. To be honest, I didn't even mind that much, until I heard she was pregnant. Turns out she wanted the same things as me, just not *with* me."

She rubbed my arm. "That had to hurt."

"It did. I'm not gonna lie. I saw this dream I had of a family, slipping out of my hands."

"And then you saw a chance to get part of it back."

"Yep." I stood, reminded of that first time I came over to her place to plead my case. I was a nervous, pimple-scored kid trying to win the approval of his teacher. "Opportunity knocked, this stroke of amazing luck just when I needed it. And I like to think it knocked for you, too. We both went into this with a baby as the only goal, Franky. But something changed along the way."

She took a steeling breath. "I let my hormones start making the decisions."

"Not just your hormones. Don't tell me your heart isn't engaged."

She glared at me. "Is this why you're here? To force a declaration out of me?"

"I'm here to tell you that I love you. It wasn't supposed to happen. I didn't come into this looking for anything more than—"

"An incubator."

"If that's how you want to look at it."

"That's how it *is*, Jason. I have no doubt you care for me, in your own way—"

"In my own way? What the hell does that mean?" Like 'my way' wasn't good enough for her? I'd suspected this all along. My kind of love wasn't what a smart, intelligent woman like Dr. St. James craved. She wanted it neat, tidy, and reasonable instead of messy and unpredictable.

"If you'd let me finish, I would tell you that we're both guilty of getting swept up in the emotion of it all."

"Are you saying you don't love me, Francesca? Even in 'your own way'?"

"I don't know how to separate it. But it doesn't matter if I can or can't. You want a big family, this idyllic life you imagined from the moment you figured out your dad was a jerk. You would do it better than him. You wouldn't make the same mistakes. You would be the perfect dad. And I still think that can happen. I know you'll love our baby, but I don't trust that you'll love *me* the way I want."

She didn't trust ... I had just told her I loved her. I didn't even tell Everly, and she was the woman I had planned to spend my life with.

Freakin' intellectuals! Why couldn't she just trust her instincts and believe what we had was right?

"Tell me how you want to be loved."

"I-I don't know."

"Oh, I think you do. I think you know exactly how you want to be loved. You've seen it in action. Big love, big gestures. Your dad and Violet, your aunts and their husbands, hell, every retired Rebel you know. But you didn't think that was in the cards for you because you're a weirdo. An egghead. A geek. Who would want Slug Girl with her dorky glasses and her very strong, but often incredibly incorrect, opinions? That girl has her books and her snails and her family, and soon she'll have a baby to fill the void in her chest. She's like one of her snails that doesn't need another snail. She can self-fertilize or self-love or whatever it's called, and get the desired result, but it's not what she really wants."

Her eyes were round with fury—and a little fear. "You don't know what I want. I can do this alone. I don't need you."

"So you keep saying, Doc. But I know something you don't. Damn, even your snails have it figured out."

"What's that?"

"That it's better with two." I sat down close and cupped her jaw. "I don't mean sex, though that's definitely better with an extra person. I don't mean parenting, though two responsible adults usually make things easier for everyone as long as they're not at loggerheads. I mean that my body is just a hollow shell when you're not around. My mind is fuzzy if I go a day without a text or message or the sight of your beautiful face. And that includes your slutty little librarian glasses. My heart doesn't beat right when I can't be with you. All of it"—I waved a hand around—"is better with two."

She peered at me, her eyes shiny with emotion. I was finally getting through to her.

"But I'm not what you had in mind." Barely a whisper.

"Nope. And I wasn't what you had in mind. Pretty sure we established that during the BFB."

"BFB?"

"Big Fight in Boston. Trademarking that."

She blinked away tears. "I didn't mean to hurt your feelings. I was trying to be logical."

I kissed her forehead. "My sweet, smarty pants, mistress of logic. So nine months ago, the idea of the two of us being parents—together—was incomprehensible. For us both, right?"

She nodded. "Snowball's chance and all that."

"But it's happened. And yet you've gone this whole time thinking everything is carved in stone. Feelings should stay the same. People should stay the same. Any deviation is wrong or disastrous to the experiment. You seem to think that people can't change, but you see evolution all the time in your work, don't you?"

She looked at me like I was an idiot. "Over thousands of years."

"So I can't evolve into a man who loves you over thousands of seconds or minutes? What's it going to take, Doc?"

A small sniff. "I interviewed for the job at Harvard."

Of course she did. "And they'd be idiots not to offer it to you." So I couldn't compete with that, with all Harvard had to offer her. But neither was I prepared to give up.

Francesca St. James was mine no matter where the hell she ended up.

There was a knock on the door.

"Yeah?" I called out.

"We have more gifts to open," my mom said. "Are you guys up to it?"

"Be right there, Mom." I turned back to Franky. "I've got a gift for you. Not baby-related, or not really. Just something to remind you of where we started."

I pressed the item into her hand. She looked down at it and gasped.

"You had it all this time? I thought I'd lost it."

It was the "I heart Detroit" key ring, the one I bought in the hotel gift shop right before we conceived our baby.

Along with that first ultrasound picture, I had carried it into every game since, except for the ones against the Motors because that would have been a fuck-you to the hockey gods.

"You said you weren't superstitious, that you didn't believe in good luck charms. But look how far we've come, Franky. If that's not the universe on our side, what is it?"

She let that settle, then touched her fingertips to the side of my head. "You have paint in your hair."

"I've been getting the baby's room ready."

"You have?"

"Yeah, the one in my house. I went with yellow. Nice and bright, and you can almost see the water from that room. Super Kid's gonna love it."

Her eyes filled again. "You're such a dick."

"I know."

Her heart wasn't enough. I planned to use every tool at my disposal to win this woman's trust. But I wouldn't press any further because she needed to keep her shit together for the rest of this day.

"Let's get through this and the Finals," I said. "Then you and I are going to have a reckoning."

CHAPTER FIFTY

Cup Finals
Series score: Chicago 3, Boston 2
Game 6
Boston @ Chicago

Franky

"OH, THIS IS SO EXCITING." Melissa looked around the owners' box in Rebels Arena and gave a small wave to Sean, who had stopped at the bar and was talking to his brother, Theo. "Now, which one is your aunt?"

"Harper, the CEO." I gestured to the knockout blonde, still vivacious at almost sixty, seated in the front row with Rebels GM, Ryder Calloway. "Well, she's my step-aunt. My stepmother Violet is her half-sister, so that's step-half-aunt, I suppose? But I've known her and my aunt Isobel all my life because Dad played his entire career with the Rebels."

Mel posed a few more queries about other people in the box—executives, spouses, former players. The place was packed. Everyone wanted a piece of the Rebels during the Finals.

I shifted in my seat, looking for a modicum of comfort from the back pain. These chairs weren't designed for women carrying the weight of a whale, but I wouldn't want to be anywhere else. In a little under three weeks, our baby would be here and I thought she should be here to see her father achieve the ultimate goal of his career. They could win the Cup tonight.

The puck dropped at 7:31pm and it wasn't long before Jason was in the fray. He blocked so many shots, it was a wonder he wasn't in goal. The man was rock solid in that back third, and by the time the first period was over, the teams were at a cagey draw. No one was getting by Jason Isner when he was on the ice. I loved seeing that—Jason's solidity, strength, and protectiveness of his players and that net.

He would be like that with our baby.

Maybe even with me.

He had said he loved me, that I was too stubborn to accept what was staring me in the face. It wasn't stubbornness. It was fear, plain and simple.

The game headed into the first break, just as Rosie sat by me.

"Think I'd better use the restroom."

Melissa touched my arm. "Need company?"

"Oh, I'm fine." A twinge in my abdomen pulled me up short. "Ooh."

"You okay?"

"It's just indigestion."

Rosie looked at me skeptically. "Indigestion? No one wants to hear that from a woman at thirty-six weeks pregnant."

"It's thirty-seven and three days, and I'm sure it's fine. I had one of those mini tacos—oh!" That didn't feel like indigestion. That felt like a baby on the move.

I levered myself upright. "I'm just going to walk around for a bit. It's probably Braxton-Hicks."

"You just said it was indigestion. I'm going to text Violet." Rosie started stabbing at her phone while I stepped outside the owners' box. Walking helped, distributing the discomfort to my extremities. It couldn't be labor—it was too early, and I had been careful, not wanting to upset Jason or interfere with his game preparation.

Another dull ache. Maybe I should head to the bathroom. Yes, that was what I should do.

Theo was at the door, just as I reached it. "You okay, Franky?"

I gripped his arm, probably because he had raised it right when I needed it. Something about his expression gave me pause.

Outside the owners' box, I saw Violet and my dad approaching. "Hey, Franks, are you okay?"

Suddenly it was very wet. "I think my water just broke."

Violet exchanged a quick look with Theo, who had possibly already predicted this when he offered his arm to me a moment ago. The man had fathered five kids, after all.

"Yep, I can see that." Violet placed a hand on my back. "Let's sit you down—Harper!"

A minute later, I was sitting in one of the roomy leather chairs in the box while Harper and Remy ushered people out.

"You-you can't make people leave," I managed above the discomfort. "It's Game 6!"

Violet scoffed. "Don't worry, all those hangers-on can find another box to watch it in. I've called for an ambulance, but the streets are pretty backed up out there."

"Stupid hockey," I murmured.

"Pays the bills," Violet said.

I barked out a laugh, but it was snatched away on a wave of pain. More than that—what I recognized now as a contraction. Had I had one before? Maybe. I needed to start timing them.

A few minutes later, Rosie sat down beside me. "How are you feeling, sis, or is that the dumbest question ever posed to a heavily pregnant woman with indigestion?"

"I'll live. I'm going to head to the hospital ..." I gripped the armchair and tried to stand only for another wave to take me down.

That was pretty close to the last one, perhaps five or six minutes?

I sank into the armchair again. "I don't know if I can make it to the hospital."

Harper's voice rang out. "The team doctor is on his way, honey."

"Don't tell Jason." I looked up at her, then at all of them. "The game is too important, and he needs to be out there."

I couldn't believe my stupidity. This morning, I applied the science—irregular, weak twinges of discomfort with no other verifiable symptoms of labor—and self-diagnosed with Braxton-Hicks. It was too early for the real thing, and it hadn't felt like it, or at least how everything I read told me how it should feel.

Books! What good were they to me now? I was in labor, stuck in a hockey arena during Game 6 of the Finals!

"My OB," I panted to Violet. "Maybe she can come here."

"I've already called her, sprite," Dad said.

"Dr. Sykes is here," Harper called out.

But the first face I saw wasn't the Rebels team doctor. It was a bearded ice warrior.

Jason.

"What are you doing here? You should be in that rink!"

He smiled. "It's still the break, Doc."

"You're playing ... great." I barely got that last word out as the pain took hold and turned me into a blithering fool. "Your blocking stats are stellar."

His grin vanished at witnessing my distress. "That's what happens when you have a baby to look forward to, but your woman won't see sense."

"You play better?"

"You play like everyone's the enemy."

Oh Jason. This was what I had done to him. Pissed him off to the extent he saw red on the ice.

"Glad I could help," I muttered.

"Jason, if you don't mind," another deep voice cut in. "Hi, Ms. St. James—"

"It's Dr. St. James," Jason cut in.

"Sure," the team doctor said indulgently. "I'm also a doctor and—"

"Have you ever delivered a baby?" Jason again.

"Let the man get a word in!" Another sharp pain walloped me.

The doctor touched my arm. "I think we might want to lie you down on the floor, Dr. St. James."

"It's Franky. I think we're about to get *very* personal."

Moments later, I was flat on my back with a cushion under my head, and my thighs splayed. Luckily most everyone had left the box and all who remained were the people who mattered: Jason, Vi, Rosie, my dad, Harper, and Dr. Sykes.

"I'd say you're approximately six to seven centimeters dilated, Franky," the team's doctor said.

That was much further along than I expected—and definitely too late for me to leave this room and expect a good outcome.

Jason's brow was as lined as a corduroy swatch. "That's almost there, right?"

"It's close," Dr. Sykes said, sounding worried.

I patted his arm. "Don't worry, I won't blame you if something goes wrong—"

Jason exploded. "Screw that! I will blame everybody in this room if this does not go the way I expect! You had better make sure my baby and my woman are okay."

"Jason." I grasped his hand. "This could take a while longer. You could play an entire period, maybe win the whole thing, and be back in time for the delivery."

"Harper," he called out without averting his burning eyes from my face. "Do I need to go back on that ice?"

My aunt responded, clear as a bell. "I've already informed Coach that you are otherwise occupied."

I groaned.

Jason leaned in and whispered, "You're not getting rid of me that easily."

CHAPTER FIFTY-ONE

Jason

I COULDN'T BELIEVE a woman as supposedly smart as Francesca St. James P-H-fucking-D had come to a hockey game while in labor.

Because that was the level of stupid we were dealing with here. You didn't *suddenly* become seven centimeters dilated without being close to having the baby. And we were here with the team doc, who I doubted was qualified to do this. Sprain an ankle or catch a blade to your forehead? Dr. Sykes was your guy. Deliver Super Kid? Nope. Not having it.

Violet recognized my concern. "Bren reached out to Dr. Patel—"

"Is she coming?"

"She's on her way. There's a good chance she'll be here before the baby is."

"Hear that, Doc? Think you can hold on?"

"Only if I close my legs. Which I probably should have done in the first place." Her face crumpled as she absorbed another wave of pain.

I hated seeing her like this. Sure, I knew it would get to this point, but I'd assumed we'd be in a hospital, surrounded my special equipment and birthing professionals and access to incredibly strong drugs. Not a bunch of well-meaning hockey fans.

"Do you want everyone here?" I whispered.

"No. Just you, only you."

My thoughts exactly. Even though her family meant the world to her, Franky was reserved and wouldn't want them to see her so vulnerable.

That was my privilege.

"Violet, do you mind if we give her some space?"

Franky's stepmom looked at me, then her. "Of course." She kissed her daughter's forehead, murmured an endearment I couldn't hear, then guided everyone else to the door. Rosie called out, "Love you, Franks!"

Franky sniffed. "I love you, too."

Bren St. James also kissed the top of his daughter's head. "I'm so proud of you, sprite. I can't wait to meet my grandchild." He turned to me. "Take care of my daughter."

I nodded, the emotion of the moment almost too much. Finally, we were alone with the doctor.

Franky reached for me. "I need to ask you something."

"Anything."

She panted a few short, shallow breaths. "Why didn't you tell anyone about the baby after the first ultrasound? I know you told Sean and Lauren, but not the rest of your family until I forced your hand at Theo's party."

This was what she wanted to know? "We can talk about it later."

"Now. Tell me now."

"I was worried they might question—"

"Why you chose me?"

"Why *you* chose *me*, Francesca."

Her eyes welled up. "But—that's obvious!"

"Is it? You had your lists and variables and plans. Basically, you could have anyone. Sure, you wanted someone healthy, with good genes, but smarts didn't seem so important to you. I imagined everyone asking themselves, 'why did she settle for that dumb jock?'"

"Oh, Jason. We've been so stuck in these boxes we built all those years ago." She winced as another contraction dug its claws in. "I'm sorry I didn't believe you. About being in love with me."

"It's okay. You're a natural skeptic."

She slid a look at Dr. Sykes who was busy trying not to be overly focused on the spot between my woman's thighs. *Damned if he do, damned if he don't.*

"I wanted to believe. To take it on faith, but—" She winced.

"You needed evidence. It's okay, baby. Let's focus on the here and now."

That contraction lasted longer than before and seemed to ratchet up her pain levels.

"I need to push."

"I know."

"But maybe I can hold on?"

I looked at Dr. Sykes. "Should she wait?"

"She should do what comes naturally."

"Hear that?" I said. "What comes naturally."

"Oh sure! For eons, women have been doing this. Pushing out a bundle the size of a bowling ball. So natural! So—agh!" That scream could probably have been heard on the ice. While my boys were birthing a victory, my lady was birthing my kid.

During the next respite, I fingered the scarf she wore, tied loosely around her neck, wondering why it looked so familiar.

"Is this—?"

"Yes," she gasped. "No harm in a little superstition, right?"

The last time I saw this beauty, it was triple knotted around my wrist, tying me to a hotel room bed while this woman sank down on my cock. I smiled. The doc had finally let a little magical thinking enter her logic-bound world. Praise be.

A noise behind me announced a new arrival.

"Hello, you two!" Dr. Patel had finally joined the party. Though we weren't out of the woods yet, it was a relief to see the woman who knew the ropes.

I saluted the Rebels team doc. "Thanks for subbing in."

"Happy to help." He filled Dr. P. in on the story so far.

Our OB went into full baby-delivering beast mode, while I knelt beside Franky, smoothing her damp hair away from her face, whispering how amazing she was, how she could do anything, how much I loved her and our baby.

Seven minutes later, on one massive push, Super Kid arrived in a slippery swoosh. A few seconds of breath-stealing quiet were interrupted by a wail that told the world the next generation of Rebels or Nobel-prize-winning scientists had burst onto the scene.

Dr. Patel wiped the baby's head and cleaned up with a bar towel. "Well, Mom and Dad, you have a beautiful, healthy, noisy baby girl."

A daughter!

Franky sat up on her elbows, her face still red and damp

with exertion, and accepted our baby into her arms while I sat behind her and supported her back, defending all that was mine.

"Jason, look at her," she said, her voice filled with awe. "She's beautiful."

"Of course she is. She's yours."

She dragged her eyes away from the baby and met my blurry-eyed gaze. "She's ours. We made her together."

I swiped at a tear and inclined my head to my daughter's. "Hi, gorgeous. Welcome to the world." Checking her over, I noted all the little things that made her perfect. Fingers, toes, eyes, nose, her cupid bow mouth. She even had a mop of dark hair, which tracked because I came from a long line of lustrous locks.

Then everything started happening fast. People came in to gawk at the baby—which was okay, they were her relatives, after all—and the paramedics arrived to take Franky to the hospital. Dr. Patel insisted everything was okay, but that mom and baby should be checked out in more sterile surroundings.

The third period had started, a fuzzy, whip-fast backdrop to the main event. I happily turned my back on that rink-facing glass. I didn't know the score, had no idea how my boys were doing without me. There would be other games. The birth of my first child would only happen once.

Sean squeezed my shoulder as the gurney carrying Franky left. I was holding my baby girl to my chest, wrapped in a fleecy Rebels blanket that had miraculously appeared, courtesy of Harper ("I get so cold in that box!").

"Congrats, brother. I'm so thrilled for you."

"Thanks, Sean-o. I'm so glad you were here."

Theo followed up with a huge hug and a kiss for my daughter. "Good job, J. Welcome to the Daddy Club."

Thank God he'd come down to the locker room to tell me Franky and our baby needed me. Now he looked over my shoulder, inside the owners' box, which had all the hallmarks of a crime scene.

"Damn, I think they're going to need to triple-steam clean that floor."

CHAPTER FIFTY-TWO

Franky

I WOKE UP TIRED, sore, and a little anxious. My first sight was Jason and our baby sitting in an armchair by the window, a faint nightlight illuminating them like something out of a Rembrandt. My body relaxed. She was safe.

And why wouldn't she be, asleep in her daddy's arms? He was awake—which was probably good because he was less likely to drop her—and was whispering to her. I listened in.

"You have the best timing, Super Kid. So we lost the game last night, but we still have a Game 7 to play. And if we win that one, or should I say, *when* we win that one, it means you were here to see your daddy lift the Cup. Pretty cool, huh? Also, Harper said you're the first baby born in the Rebels arena. You're already making history and not even twenty-four hours old."

He nuzzled his nose against her soft thatch of hair and inhaled her deeply.

"Is she okay?" I asked.

His tired gaze fixed on mine. "Hey, Mama. She's fine. Got her all checked out and even though she's a couple of weeks early, her weight's on the money. Seven pounds, three ounces."

"I knew she was going to be supersized." Calling her Super Kid had somehow manifested a giant baby.

She turned her head and opened her mouth, which I knew from my reading was called "rooting," a sign she was hungry. I had already fed her once after we arrived at the hospital, and while it took a few tries, we figured it out. Now Jason brought her to me and adjusted the bed, so I was sitting up. When he placed her in my arms, my heart burst with all the love I felt for her, and when she latched onto my nipple, the initial pinch soon gave way to warmth and comfort.

"The Rebels lost the game?" I whispered as she suckled away.

"What can I say? I'm indispensable." He smiled, his tired grin bright in the dark of his beard. "We'll get 'em next time."

After she had been fed and burped, he placed her down in the cot beside the bed, then pulled his armchair close to me.

"How are you feeling, Doc?"

"Like I played four back-to-back best-of-seven series and won the Cup. Or at least I imagine this is what that level of tiredness would feel like." I reached for his hand and squeezed. "I'm ready for that reckoning, if you are."

"Always, Francesca."

I blinked away a tear. "Everything you said at the baby shower was right. I'm the weird geek who created a shell, just like my beloved snails, an armor that would keep me safe. From bullies. From mean girls. From the boys I liked and who never liked me. From the mother who never thought I was pretty or worthy. I used my brains to scare off anyone I saw as a threat to my heart. Even though you offered to be her father, a small part of me wondered, why? I doubted your motives. And I especially doubted your attraction to me."

"For a woman with a genius-level intellect, you're kind of a dummy."

I sniffed. "I know. I'm not sure you could ever be that good an actor."

"Hey now."

I laughed at his affront. "The thing is, attraction is just that—our bodies telling us another person can make us feel good. Anything more than that requires true chemistry and an alignment of values. You called it mutual respect. Compatibility. You also said that it's better—all of it—with two."

He arched an eyebrow.

"Not just sex, Jason."

"I did say that. Sex, parenthood, love. I meant every word."

I believed him. My nipples were leaking. My vagina felt like a bomb had exploded. No doubt I looked like I'd been dragged through a hedge backwards. Yet this man was gazing at me with so much love that none of it mattered. I could make a mental spreadsheet and outline all the evidence, but for this, I think I needed to take a leap of faith.

Despite all my weirdness, or maybe because of it, this man loved me.

"If it's better with two, it might be even better with three." I cast a glance to our sleeping daughter.

"Love that combo." He applied a soft kiss to my damp forehead. "Love you."

"And I love you," I whispered. "Truly, I do."

"Sure that's not the endorphins talking?" His voice held a note of doubt, like he was suddenly the one who couldn't believe.

"If it is, they've been chatting away for months. Since I spied that EpiPen in your pocket. Since I turned over that cat cushion and saw a cat skull. Since you brought me home the night of Theo's party and loved my hurt away. Those endorphins might even have been whispering in my ear when I saw you give a little girl a handmade bracelet for her birthday and wore the one you made for yourself." So, making a list of reasons didn't hurt. "The real question is: how could I not love you, Jason? You're cocky and hotheaded and arrogant and bossy. But you're also kind and generous and funny and I'm happy to be darted by you any day of the week."

He narrowed his eyes. "Darted?"

"It's a snail thing."

"Of course it is." He lifted my hand and softly kissed my thundering pulse. "Those Boston fuckers have no idea what's coming their way in Game 7."

"What's that then?"

"Utter annihilation. I'm a new dad, a man in love, and a player who's hungry for that Cup. Besides, we need it to baptize Cammi."

I blinked. "Cammi?"

"After Cammi Granato, the first woman player in the Hockey Hall of Fame. Just an idea. We can wait, see if it suits her. We just need to decide before my day with the hardware."

Which he hadn't won yet. That, and the fact that neither of us was religious didn't seem to matter. If Jason Isner wanted his daughter baptized in a silver-and-nickel alloy bowl while the Cup made its victory tour this summer, I had no doubt he would find a way—and a priest—to make that happen.

Gloriously in sync, we turned to our daughter and gazed at her with naked adoration. Cammi did have a nice ring to it.

"Will you stay?" I asked, feeling worn out, both mentally and physically. Birthing a baby and finally giving into the love you deserved took a lot out of a woman.

"I'm going nowhere, Doc."

EPILOGUE

One month later ...

Jason

"MOMMY, I want to go on the swing."

"Just a second, sweetie." My sister-in-law Elle nudged me as her very strong almost-six-year-old pulled hard on her hand. "You sure that thing's safe?"

"I had a guy come in to ensure it was anchored properly and add that shock-absorbing rubber surface beneath. Just make sure she's supervised."

She looked amused. "You're giving *me* parental advice now?"

"Like it's hard?" I waggled my eyebrows. "Ask me anything."

"Just like Theo. A month in, and he knew everything, too."

What could I say? The men in this family were a very confident bunch.

I looked around my backyard, packed with friends, family, teammates, and at the center of it all, the Cup. It was my day with it, and what a thing of beauty it was, glinting in the late July sunlight. A couple of hours ago, it had looked stunning with Cammi sitting in it while everyone did their best impressions of paparazzi.

Now in my arms, my daughter expelled the cutest snore as she snuggled in closer. This baby wrap carrier made me feel like a kangaroo, but there was no place I'd rather be with my little joey. I touched my lips to the top of her head, ensuring it was completely dry after her baptism earlier. I wasn't religious, but after the events of the last year, I'd be a fool not to believe in a higher power.

"Can Cammi go on the swings?"

I looked down at my niece. "She's too small, Tillington. Maybe next year."

She frowned, not liking that. "Can I kiss her?"

I looked at Elle who smiled and lifted her daughter up to baby head level. Tilly applied a gentle kiss to Cammi's forehead and whispered, like it was a secret, "We'll play next year, Cammi. You, me, and Mabel."

Finally relenting to Tilly's urging, Elle headed off to examine the swing set's sturdiness. I wandered over to a just-vacated Adirondack and took a seat beside the mother of my child and the woman who had somehow fallen for me, despite her better judgment.

"How is she?"

"Still out like a light. How are you, Doc?"

She smiled, a little tired, but so beautiful that my heart squeezed. "Happy."

I'd only meant her health, but to hear her express that sentiment without me trying to pry it out of her lifted my spirits to the blue sky above our heads.

"Really?"

I had reason to be doubtful. Yesterday, she had withdrawn her name from consideration for the Harvard faculty appointment. She had also told Dr. Bilious at Lakeshore University that she would be taking a sabbatical following her maternity leave—and whether he approved it or not made no odds. While she wrote her book on the mating rituals of snails, she planned to look for another job in Chicago.

Any of this city's big universities would be thrilled to have her, but in the meantime, she would be keeping the home fires burning. I hoped she would be content. That life with me and Cammi would be enough for her, at least for a while.

She reached over and stroked a finger along my newly shaven jaw. She missed the beard but I think she liked what was underneath, too.

"The room on the southeast side would make a good office."

My breath hitched. "You're moving in."

"As soon as I've cleared it with Bunsen. Once he's on board, Beaker will capitulate. He's a follower at heart."

She was moving in. Technically, she already had. After a couple of days in the hospital, I had taken her here the day before I flew out to Boston for Game 7. The paint smell was gone from the nursery, but she and Cammi slept in my room all the same. Rosie and Violet stayed with her, and when I returned, Franky was still here with my daughter. Where they both belonged.

"I'd better get to work on Bunny Boy. What do you think will sway him? Cat treats? More toys? His own room?"

"Just knowing he has someone else to hiss at semi-regularly will probably suffice." She adjusted her sexy glasses. "Are you ready to have your space overwhelmed with books and toys and an academic who spaces out in the middle of conversations?"

"I've been ready forever." Taking her hand, I kissed her wrist. "I just needed to meet the right malacologist."

She smiled. "Love it when you use those big words."

"And I love you, Francesca." Big words or not. Everything about this woman filled my heart to overflowing.

She blinked, wiped at a tear. "I love you, too. So much."

On cue, Cammi opened her eyes and stared up at me.

"Hey, baby girl. Decided to join the love fest, huh?"

Still staring, not even blinking, which boded well for my daughter's future as a hockey player. My little face-off princess.

"I think she might be hungry," Franky said. "I'll take her inside."

Watching them go, I reveled in this feeling of contentment. A Cup winner, a new dad, a man who had found a woman I didn't deserve, but who I sure as hell planned to hold onto forever.

"God, could you *be* any smugger?" Lauren plopped down in the chair beside me.

"I probably could be. But I'll try to keep it in check around green-gilled haters such as yourself." I grinned at her. "Where's your boy?"

"*My boy* is over at that cooler, talking to his favorite Rebels player."

"What?" I looked over and sure enough, Finance Bro Thaddeus was chatting with Boden. "A goalie? Who picks a goalie as their favorite player?"

"Well, if you were nicer to him, maybe he'd pick you."

I frowned. "Been a little busy to be bromancing your boyfriend, Lo. But if it's serious, I'll make more of an effort."

"Oh, it's serious." She leaned in. "He's going to propose."

"Did you tell him I'm taken?"

She stared at me.

"Shit, this is for real? Lo, that's—wow!" Not sure I approved of the planned proposal, which was kind of light on the romance. When the time came for me, I'd do something really special. But if Thaddio made Lauren happy ... "Is this what you want?"

She inhaled a quick breath. "I see everyone moving on with their lives, having babies and falling in love, and I want that for myself."

Not really an answer, so I pressed further. "But you and Thadly? This is the real deal?"

She blinked at me. "Of course! But there's a tiny problem that has to be resolved before I can marry him."

"How tiny?"

My innuendo surely merited an affectionate eye roll. Instead, I was rewarded with a nervy smile and a statement that would have knocked me flat if I wasn't already sitting down.

"I need to divorce my first husband."

The next book in the *Chicago Players* series is:

SECRET HUSBAND

BONUS EPILOGUE
FOURTEEN MONTHS LATER

Franky

I WOKE up anxious and alone.

At one time, that would have been a tricky prospect for a woman of my temperament and advanced age, but not anymore. Today I could trace my nerves to a number of sources. (Look at the data, Franky.)

One, I was starting a new job.

Two, my book on the mating habits of snails was three weeks out from publication, and while I knew its audience was likely smaller than the *Angustopila psammion*—the tiniest snail in the world—I still wanted it to be a success.

Three ... well, I would know soon enough if my concerns *there* were warranted.

The one thing I wasn't worried about was my empty bed. The spot beside me was still warm, which meant Jason had left our cozy cocoon mere moments ago. I knew exactly where he was, too, and after a quick visit to the bathroom, I sought him out.

I hovered outside the room next door, listening in as Jason chatted with our daughter.

"Now Cammi, I know you're a little attention hog and normally I'd be just fine with that, but today, I need you to be nice to your mama."

"Mama?"

"That's right, sweetheart. She's starting her new job and I think she's a little worried the other kids won't like her."

Cammi made an incredulous snort worthy of her father.

"I know, hard to believe. But even smarty pants professors want the world to think they're great. Good thing she's absolutely ace, but try telling her that. All I know is that those eggheads at Northwestern University won't know what hit 'em."

My nerves calmed a touch. Nothing beat having a D-man like Jason defending you to the world.

"Dada!" That meant Cammi wanted her daddy to hold her, so I left them to a little more father-daughter bonding time while I took a shower.

Five minutes later, I had just applied conditioner when the glass door creaked open and the space became considerably smaller.

"Need help getting to all those nooks and crannies, Doc?"

I leaned back against his strong chest and let myself enjoy his support.

"Managed to pull yourself away from your best girl, I see."

He touched his lips to my shoulder, the stubble delicious against my damp skin. "Don't be jealous, now. I've got more than enough love for *all* my girls."

I turned in his arms and cupped his strong jaw. "Such a big heart."

He gentled me against the shower wall. "Not just my heart, Francesca. Oh, I see that eye roll, but damn, I know you love when I throw in a splash"—he clamped his palm to my butt—"of"—curled a strong hand beneath my thigh—"innuendo." And raised my leg so he could position his hard body just so.

"Is it still innuendo when your penis is already nudging —ohhh!" I moaned because he did more than nudge. God, that felt good. "Jason," I gasped.

"I know, baby. I've got you."

He meant it to be supportive but I took it for something else: he had me, completely and utterly. Every part of me belonged to him. With each thrust into my body, we fused, our souls becoming one. A connection I felt whether he was inside me or out.

We worked so well together. Who would have thought it?

Afterward, as he dried me gently, he ran his hands over my curves, my tender breasts, the stomach that wasn't flat before Cammi and was even less so now.

"When are you going to pull the trigger?" he asked.

"What's that?"

He raised an eyebrow. "I know your body pretty well, Doc. I think we're having another baby."

Of course he knew, Mr. Expert in Female Anatomy. "I need to take a test. Several, because I can't trust one or even two. Last time, I took six different branded ones." I gazed up at him as my babble petered out. "But I feel pregnant."

"Uh huh, but you need to test that hypothesis. My woman's all about the method."

I was trying to be more instinctual, but I did like my

evidence to be solid. "I was going to wait until I got the first day at the job over with. I can stop at the pharmacy on the way home—"

"Or, you can figure it out now while I get started on breakfast for Cammi." He opened a drawer and extracted one, two ... *five* boxes. Then the drawer below, from which he took out two more.

Pregnancy tests.

"You're that sure?"

"I am. And I'm thrilled. But if I'm wrong, that'll be okay, too." He applied a gentle kiss to my lips. "We're a family whether there's three, five, or ten of us."

"Ten?"

"Can't leave out my boys." Meaning Bunsen and Beaker, who adored their new overlord. We were also in negotiations to get a dog, which was all part of the Jason Isner family fantasy.

Ten minutes later, I was dressed and heading for the kitchen, again ready to listen in as Jason showed Cammi how the coffee maker worked. Our little girl was so curious that I questioned if that was such a good idea—she'd be climbing onto a kitchen stool and making lattes within twenty-four hours.

Watching them had me thinking of all the milestones she had hit over the last fifteen months. Her first crawl—which resulted in a full-on assault on Beaker. Her first steps —toward her daddy, of course. Her first word—"Cobbie" because Conor spent two months coaxing it out of her. (After which Jason banned him from the house for ten days until she finally said "Dada.")

He turned and gifted me that cocky grin. I so wanted him to be wrong one of these days ...

"Bingo, you've hit the bullseye again, Isner."

"Hell, yeah! You hear that, Cam, you're going to have a brother or sister soon."

"Hell, yeah!" Cammi shouted, though she had no idea what that meant. Either way, it frightened Beaker. Something about her pitch always sent him scurrying the opposite direction.

Jason wrapped his arm around me while Cammi patted my hair. "Wet, Mama."

"Yes, it is, darling." I blinked at Jason. "I don't think she's said that word before. A new one for her growing vocabulary."

"Yeah, I spilled water on Bunsen the other day and I repeated it a couple of times. And here she is, filing it away like the very smart cookie she is."

He placed her in her high chair, gave her a sippy cup of juice, then gathered me close.

"How are we feelin' about this, Doc?"

"We said we'd try again, so bravo for results."

As I approached the big 4-o, we were both conscious of the tick-tick-tick of my chances to conceive again. The last year had been amazing: working on my manuscript, spending quality time with Cammi, and falling even deeper in love with Jason. Going back to work, releasing a book, and finding out I was pregnant felt like the bubble bursting and reality intruding.

He leaned his forehead against mine. "This time, I'll be with you every night I'm not on the road. I'll be taking care of all your needs: nutrition, foot rubs, nut watch, and S-E-X."

"She doesn't know that word yet."

He scoffed. "But she's smart enough to learn it. If I have my way, she'll *never* know it."

"She's so lucky to have you for her daddy. And I'm

lucky to have you as my partner. I don't need you to take care of all my needs but I love that you do."

"Mama! Bunny!" Cammi pointed her sippy cup at Bunsen who was trying to eat his food in peace.

"I know, darling. God, she's so smart."

"Don't worry. I'm thinking a few more months and I'll get her on the ice. Balance the smart with the sporty."

"Before she's two?"

"She needs to learn to fall down, Doc, and know that I'll be there to pick her up. Anyway, you'll be too preggo to be of any use in skating lessons." He nuzzled my nose. "I can't believe we're going to be blessed again. Damn, I love you."

"And I love you *and* your very powerful swimmers."

"Dada! Ohs!"

That meant oatmeal, which meant Daddy was falling down on the job as breakfast provider. The doorbell rang, which was likely Maisey, our part-time nanny and was my cue to dry my hair and get organized.

Within thirty minutes, I'd said my goodbyes to Cammi with tears in my eyes because I wouldn't see her for at least eight hours, a positive age after the closeness of the last year. Jason had morning skate in an hour, so he would leave later. He walked me out and in the foyer, handed me a lunchbox.

A snail-themed lunchbox.

"Oh, that's so cute." I swiped at a tear.

"Make sure you eat it all. Don't be slacking because you got distracted by some slugs doing it."

"Thank you. I'm going to miss"—*sniff*—"you"—*sniff*—"all."

"We'll be right here when you get home, Doc." His tight hug, affirming his love for me, was the fuel to send me out the door.

Once I had rounded the corner of our street, I pulled

over to compose myself because the tears streaming down my face were making driving dangerous.

I slapped at the steering wheel. "Pull yourself together, woman! Mothers have been leaving their babies at home forever. You will get through this."

Aiming for calm, I took a sneak peek at my lunch. A ham and cheese sandwich, a small side salad with Jason's homemade dressing in a separate container, a peach yogurt, and a chocolate chip cookie. There was also a note.

I opened it.

Dear Francesca,

I know this will be a tough day because it's the first one away from our precious. But you're so strong, a woman without equal, and you will get through this. Have I told you how proud I am of you? Here you are, off to earn a living and keep us off the streets while wowing the world of malacology. But in case you think I'm only in this for your amazing brain, I'm here to disabuse you of that notion. I happen to think you're a total fox as well. Some days, I can't decide if I'd rather bang you or discuss gender politics in academia, so it's a good thing I'm enough of a multitasker to be able to do both. Which is my way of saying I love everything about you, and am so excited about our future together.

I'm betting at this point, I've taken your mind off that little sad you've got going on, at least for a short while. Just know that we'll be here for you when you come back from making a difference.

A million kisses,
Jason, Cammi, Bunsen, and Beaker

I pressed my hand to my chest, against the heart at risk of making a break for it, and took a deep breath.

Then I closed the lunch box, checked the traffic, and rejoined the world.

ACKNOWLEDGMENTS

Thank you to my editor, Kristi Yanta. Thanks also to proofreader Julia Griffis for your perfect attention to detail.

To the team at Qamber Designs, my gratitude knows no bounds for the beautiful illustrated covers you've created for this series.

All my thanks goes to Miranda for helping me stay on top of communication with my readers.

And thank you, Jimmie, for all your support these last few years as we adjusted to a nomadic life. Onward to the next adventure!

ABOUT THE AUTHOR

Originally from Ireland, *USA Today* bestselling author Kate Meader cut her romance reader teeth on Maeve Binchy and Jilly Cooper novels, with some Harlequins thrown in for variety. Give her tales about brooding mill owners, over-sexed equestrians, and men who can rock an apron, a fire hose, or a hockey stick, and she's there. Now traveling the world with her soulmate, she writes sexy contemporary, sports, and LGBTQ+ romance featuring strong heroes and amazing women and men who can match their guys quip for quip.

HOOKED ON YOU
WRAPPED UP IN YOU

Hot in Chicago Rookies
COMING IN HOT
UP IN SMOKE
DOWN IN FLAMES
HOT TO THE TOUCH

Hot in Chicago
REKINDLE THE FLAME
FLIRTING WITH FIRE
MELTING POINT
PLAYING WITH FIRE
SPARKING THE FIRE
FOREVER IN FIRE

Laws of Attraction
DOWN WITH LOVE
ILLEGALLY YOURS
THEN CAME YOU

Hot in the Kitchen
FEEL THE HEAT
ALL FIRED UP
HOT AND BOTHERED

For updates, giveaways, and new release information,
sign up for Kate's newsletter at katemeader.com.

www.ingramcontent.com/pod-product-compliance
Lightning Source LLC
Chambersburg PA
CBHW061210190726
48288CB00001B/124